Searching For A Way Out

Kurios, Volume 1

John Moon Forker

Published by John Forker, 2024.

This is a work of fiction. Similarities to real people, places, or events are entirely coincidental.

SEARCHING FOR A WAY OUT

First edition. November 14, 2024.

Copyright © 2024 John Moon Forker.

ISBN: 979-8227278456

Written by John Moon Forker.

1

She communicates with the dead. But they do all the talking. She just listens. They speak through the things they've left behind: the utensils, the art, the weapons, the inscriptions on clay tablets.

When she studies an artifact, an arrowhead, some pottery, anything, she experiences a sense of connection to the people who used it, who handled it daily. It's as if she inhabits their lives and becomes them.

She sees connections between an artifact the archeological team might find and a pattern of behavior, a clue as to where they walked, where they hunted, where they spent the night. They tell her of their brief moments of glory, the birth of a child, a battle won, a home defended. They tell her of the daily hunt for food, the injuries, diseases, and the deaths they all suffered, and they tell her of their fear and wonder at what lies beyond their time in this world.

But that feeling of being connected to them is what matters because she doesn't feel all that connected to the living in this world. The dead are always there for her and they will never trouble her, bother her, demand of her, or ridicule her. They invite her to become a part of their own distant lives. Even if just for a moment, this connection lessens her sense of being alone.

Some people say what she has is a gift, but that's not how she sees it. For her, the connection lets her escape from the world where she is a prisoner of her own personality, of her own shortcomings, of her own futile quest to change herself and break out of this prison. A prison she made for herself and cannot unmake because there are three dead who do not speak to her, who will never speak, who would be alive today if she hadn't been so foolish twenty-two years ago when she was eleven years old. Her mother, father and younger brother.

JOHN MOON FORKER

Jane Ozzimo—most everyone calls her Oz—rides in the back seat of Mervin's gas-guzzling Chevy. One of the last few thousands of petroleum-powered cars on the streets of Los Angeles. Most every other vehicle these days is electric. Trying to reduce carbon emissions and slow down global warming, but the horse is already out of the barn.

So she is kind of embarrassed riding in this polluting pig of a car. But Mervin stubbornly holds on to this piece of junk—he likes the sound of the engine—and will probably do so right up to the deadline next year when the city is forcing all gas-using cars off the road. Tough to buy gas anyway.

Mervin Chimney and Melissa Canovoot, her roommates and fellow archeology grad students at the University of Southern California, sit in the front. Roommates being a financial necessity for her.

Many of the students in the department have been called to an excavation site downtown. A city inspector found something on the grounds of an abandoned building about to be demolished and the city called the school to evaluate what was found.

Maybe she'll see something interesting on this site. Not likely, but the city is very jumpy about preserving what they think of as historical artifacts and is halting construction projects every time something pops up out of the ground. So this is probably nothing.

She hopes to graduate with her PhD in December. Less than two months away now. But she's worried that she'll never find the acceptable evidence that will convince Dr. Eisenfield. Worried that maybe it was a mistake to have changed her thesis topic.

What she had was safe. Very safe. But safe was so boring. Her taking a stab at deciphering the two mysterious Minoan languages, Linear A and the hieroglyphic language seen on the Phaistos disk.

SEARCHING FOR A WAY OUT

What realistic hope did she have of unraveling these languages? No one else has. But just the attempt would have gotten her the degree.

However, after the experience in the cave on Crete last summer, there was no way she could continue with that. A transformative experience that let her escape the prison of herself even if it lasted only for maybe two minutes.

And with the change of topic, she's gotten a lot of resistance from others in the department. Sure, Professor Vasquez, the head of her dissertation committee, believes in her. Go for it, she said. But Dr. Eisenfield, the graduate adviser, doesn't like it, doesn't want it, and has warned her to drop it. Threatens to reject it. He has that power.

And if he does, she doesn't graduate. No degree, then no job in archeology. And in this miserable economy, then what? Back in the gutter. Go full time at the kennel shoveling dog shit? Become homeless again. No hope, no future. No way out. No thanks.

Oz looks out the window. Worries. It's only through archeology that she will ever find anything like what she found in that cave up on Mt. Ida on Crete. That one moment stripped away all the garbage in her life, filled her with real joy, gave her a powerful sense of vitality, and freed her from herself.

What she saw on the floor of that cave, those drawings, and that experience, that powerful experience by the pool of water, showed her that the Minoans of thirty-five hundred years ago were exploring the workings of the mind and had progressed pretty far, so far that their technology—if that's what you want to call it—gave her the best moment of her life ever since the day that her parents and brother died. Deaths that never should have happened. Wouldn't have if she hadn't been so insistent on going down into that canyon. She should have died too.

But once that Minoan cave collapsed in the avalanche, the door to freedom and most of her evidence disappeared in the dust.

Before that, she had run down the mountain in sheer excitement at what she had discovered and brought Dr. Eisenfield back up. He was right there in the cave. Saw the drawings. But him stupidly swinging that flashlight beam everywhere somehow turned off the technology happening in the pool of water and he never experienced what she experienced. If only he had, then he would have believed.

But she hallucinated nothing. She knows what she saw. She knows what she experienced and more evidence has to be out there somewhere. That technology couldn't have all been in just that one sanctuary cave. The Minoans must have had it in other locations. She just has to find it. Must find it.

Just ahead, on the side of the Santa Monica tollway, she sees one of those King Zee Whitehead billboards. This guy seems to be everywhere lately. Here he's standing up, arm upraised, gazing out into the infinite as if he sees a vision, beckoning all to follow him to God. Of course, it's animated and 3D, like they all are, imparting a strong sense of motion which, with that weird 3D sense of depth, gives it a sort of unreal feeling like it's not grounded to anything but just hanging untethered up there in the air.

"He's getting more popular," Oz says.

"Who?" Mervin says.

"This billboard we're about to pass. This King Zee Whitehead."

Melissa says, "Yeah, I have a friend—you remember Nancy." She nudges Mervin. "And she did one of those ceremonies, private one I think, not one of those public extravaganzas that he puts on, and she, well, I think she liked it but thought it was pretty intense. Not that she spoke to God or anything, like he claims you can, but still."

"I wonder what God would say if you could?" Oz says, gazing out the window.

"Fucking scam," Mervin says, shaking his head.

SEARCHING FOR A WAY OUT

Melissa uses her thumb and forefinger to pinch his cheek, a big smile on her face. Mervin smiles too and uses his right hand to scoot his fingers up her leg to where the seams on her pants meet in a big Y.

"Oh." Melissa's forehead arcs in surprise beneath the bangs of her hair. These bangs tend to puff out a little, like a tent on a windy day. Kind of matches her puffy cheeks.

Mervin is a little squat, a little heavy, long dark-blonde hair dipping across his shoulders, and a face that often looks quizzical even when he's not.

Since they share the same first and last initials in their names, they have taken to calling themselves the M.C.s. They laugh uproariously almost every time they say it. Oz found it funny the first time she heard it.

She feels a brief ache of longing watching Mervin and Melissa. A long-ago memory. But she stomps it down. Stupid foolish feeling. Her former boyfriend. Sam Delgatto. She must have been delusional. Must have thought she was in love. But the love part she doubts. That's not really what she was looking for, but maybe she thought it was at the time.

She realized he was just another trap. A substitution for a family she did not have.

And she let this feeling of being trapped grow and grow until the rainy January morning when she whispered to him she had to leave, and he grew more and more furious, as she could not explain to him why she was doing this.

Within minutes she was gone. Out on the street. Out in the rain. Nowhere to go.

She planned that really well, didn't she?

2

As they pull up to the site, Oz can already see about a dozen people, mostly undergraduates, milling around. Summoned by Dr. Eisenfield. Probably thinks he's lucky to have this opportunity so close by where he can teach archeological field techniques to the undergrads with no expense to the school.

The blistering October sun bakes the barren and torn-up ground. The entire area around where the building stands has no vegetation except for a thick, ten-foot hedge that must have once enclosed the property but now only surrounds about three-quarters of it.

Something about this place seems familiar.

Pockets and piles of debris scatter across the lot, maybe some of it from inside the building, but more likely just trash that someone else has dumped.

Recently installed cyclone fencing surrounds the site, but she sees a few gaps. With garbage being so expensive to dispose of, the illegal dumping of it is common. Abandoned sites invite it.

She hates waste. Why can't people see the connection between excessive waste and resource depletion? When you don't have much, you can't afford to throw anything away, as she well knows from growing up with Aunt Della. They had to use whatever they had until whatever they had fell apart. Like her bicycle tires that were never replaced, but just kept getting patched over and over. Or the empty egg carton that Aunt Della kept a collection of buttons in which she used to repair shirts.

But it's more than that for her. It's mental. Waste breeds dull perceptions and a sloppy way of thinking that creeps in like some virus eating up your attention until the ability to focus scatters in the wind.

She's never going to let that happen to her.

SEARCHING FOR A WAY OUT

A huge unmanned crane with a forged steel wrecking ball hanging from a chain sits to one side of the building. Waiting.

Three men in uniforms one by one saunter around the property. Three that she can see, anyway. They must be from the city. The LASS. Los Angeles Security Services.

Mervin parks in a gravel lot across the street. Not much traffic around here, especially since many of the nearby small businesses have closed.

They are on Santa Fe Avenue, a block or two south of 1st Street, just east of downtown, fronting what would be the Los Angeles River if it had any water in it, and close to all of those railroad tracks emanating out of the nearby Union Station.

When Oz and the MCs cross the street and arrive on the site, Dr. Eisenfield calls all the archeology students together around to the back of the department's truck.

She has an eerie feeling that she's been here before. But when?

Gathered around Dr. Eisenfield are Mervin, Melissa, Sid Juvelics, Gina Woolander, and all the undergraduates.

She needs to speak to him, but alone. He is the obstacle to her having her thesis approved. She needs to persuade him to change his mind.

She gives herself a little pep talk.

Okay, this time she will keep her temper. She needs to be calm, be reasonable. Yes, he will listen to reason. He's a scientist after all.

Dr. Eisenfield introduces an inspector with the city's Department of Resource Reclamation and Environmental Stability and tells the students that this department covers the preservation of historical artifacts.

The inspector nods quickly as if in a hurry. With short gray hair and large bags under his eyes, he holds up a clear plastic envelope that contains a rusty horseshoe.

JOHN MOON FORKER

"This is what we found here earlier today. We believe it's from the nineteenth century and may have come from a stable or a blacksmith working then. At the far end," here he points, "we see some parts of something larger—it might be a carriage—sticking up out of the ground."

Oz figured this little expedition wouldn't turn up much, and she was right. A horseshoe?

"Can you tell us a little about the land?" Dr. Eisenfield asks.

"As you all can see, the Signal building here is just a four-story structure, but it has much more land around it than a building like this would ordinarily have. It's almost all cleared away now—except for those hedges—but this place was a veritable jungle of plants, vines, fruit trees, you name it."

Now she remembers. The Signal building. She's been here. Just a couple of months after Aunt Della brought her out to southern California to live, she had gone on some school field trip here. But it looked so different then. Lush. Full of plants of all sizes—grasses to tall bamboo—densely packed together, covering the whole block. Like a little paradise right in the middle of the city.

She had wandered away from the group enchanted by the clean air, the nature sounds, the connected feeling. Walking off the path, she had plunged into the foliage. Numerous birds chirped above her, insects and bees flew all around her.

She came upon a small pond and a thin ribbon of water feeding it. In the water, she could see a toad, eyes just above the waterline. And in the air two silent insects that somehow didn't entirely look like insects.

She felt she had entered a magical environment and wanted so badly to stay. Soon, someone found her and took her away. She promised herself she would come back. But she never did. Could never get a ride and by the time she was old enough to take public transportation, she had forgotten.

SEARCHING FOR A WAY OUT

But the whole time she wandered the grounds, she had an eerie feeling she was being watched.

"Who were the tenants?" Oz asks the inspector. She notices that Dr. Eisenfield getting a sour look on his face. Doesn't like her butting in. Yeah, maybe she shouldn't have opened her mouth, especially since she needs him to be in a good mood. Or as close to one as he can get.

"As far as we can tell, it was just a bunch of artists. Created some beautiful work. You know the obelisks up in Pershing Square? They did those. But somewhere along the line, they just left. Abandoned the building. And now some enormous cathedral is going in here next. That Whitehead fellow is building it."

Whitehead, huh? Wonder if he is on to something with this God thing. That surrender experience that people go through. What could that be like?

"And I understand," Eisenfield says, "that we don't have much time here."

"No, unfortunately," the inspector says. "The powers-that-be have given you a week."

"Thanks inspector," Dr. Eisenfield says quickly before he can continue talking. "I guess we'd better get to work and see if we can find anything." He waves his hand in a "let's go" gesture.

As the inspector walks off, Dr. Eisenfield briefly scans the student's faces and goes on, "Before beginning a project like this, we normally work up a research design, know which procedures we're going to employ, our methodology, how much we'll dig, what methods we'll use and the equipment needed. Here, we only kind of know that. We're basically coming in with a sledgehammer approach."

"This doesn't sound good," Sid Juvelics says, using his forefinger to push gold-rimmed glasses back up his nose.

Oz's mouth is dry, and she is only half-listening, waiting for her chance but looking around trying to remember this place when she saw it as an 11-year-old.

"We have little choice," Eisenfield says. "The owner—this Whitehead fellow—of the land doesn't want us here and wants no delay. As you heard, the city has given us very little time." He looks around at all their faces again. "Okay, let's get going."

As soon as everyone scatters across the lot, Oz walks over to Dr. Eisenfield, whispering to herself.

Stay calm. Don't blow up, no matter what. That will only make things worse. But he has to see reason. I will find the evidence. I already practically spend all day—unless I'm working at the kennel—researching every tiny bit of existing evidence while constantly monitoring the archeology nodes for anything new, seeing it the minute it comes up. There is plenty of other material to make the thesis work, like the drawing of the priestess before a pool of water that was found in Knossos. A drawing just like part of the one I saw in the cave. And I have the translation of that Linear B text, which talks about looking at one's reflection in the water and seeing beyond thinking into the real and the imagined. Seeing beyond thinking. Doesn't he wonder about that?

He has to forget about what happened in the cave, about me losing my temper because of him and his flashlight, which when he eventually turned it off and it was all dark and warm in there and he had some kind of spasm of lust or something, touching me, trying to get closer. Okay, so I acted badly, but I felt shocked and scared and angry that the experience—that wonderful experience—the images, the altered mind, or whatever it was, had stopped and me losing that feeling of pure freedom.

"Could I have a word?"

Dr. Eisenfield looks at her over the rim of the cup of water that he is drinking from. His face is getting jowly and the dimple on

SEARCHING FOR A WAY OUT

his chin seems to be getting deeper. Massive sideburns streaked with gray.

"Go on."

"Listen, Dr. Eisenfield, about my thesis, if you would just give it a chance—"

"Jane, I am keeping an open mind. I do think you're making a mistake. There is still a lot of work to be done to find a way to translate Linear A, and your original thesis would have added to that body of knowledge."

Clouds of frustration creep in. Been down this path too many times already. "But I've found something much more important . . . even Professor Vasquez believes I have."

"And I am seriously considering Dr. Vasquez's recommendations on this matter."

Oz can see that he is doing no such thing, feeling only a small torch of anger igniting in her head.

"Besides what's being discovered every day on Crete . . . what Alexandros himself has turned up just last—"

"Papadakis? That old fraud. That was another mistake you made, listening to him and all his wild theories about the symbols on the Phaistos disk referring to higher dimensions of existence. What hooey."

Anger rising, Oz's voice ticks up in volume. "But what about what we have learned from the legend dug up eight years ago? That's proof right there that the Minoans were much farther advanced than anyone had previously thought."

Eisenfield points a finger at her. "That legend you hold so high was nothing more than a fragment of Linear B referring to some earlier and now lost Linear A text that does what? Mentions—at least we think it mentions, although even this is not at all clear—of the Minoans sending one of its people to the other side of the earth with their most prized technology so that the barbarians wouldn't get their hands on it. And what is this wonderful technology? Who knows? They seem to call it Life with a capital L. What the hell does that mean? Everyone and their brother have an opinion, interpreting it as a forever potion, immortality drug, or the key to Atlantis or some kind of mind control."

Eisenfield throws up his hands in a dramatic display of exasperation.

Oz turns inward. Old armor engages. Mind bound tight. Backed into a corner. No way out. He won't listen. He's got to listen.

"You felt something in that cave, didn't you?" Oz's now raspy voice comes down in volume but up in intensity.

"Don't be ridiculous."

"And you would have felt it even more if you hadn't started waving that flashlight around."

"It was dark."

"Dark for a reason. That's what allowed the mechanism to work."

"You're way off base. You should watch your tongue."

She knows he's right, but it's too late for that now. The impulse rolls downhill, gathering steam, just like those rocks raining down from above that crushed the cave after they were out, an avalanche started by two of the local mountain goats, the Kri Kri, butting heads and kicking down those stones from so far above. Poof. Evidence gone.

"What happened to you in there? Putting your hands on me. What did you think was going—"

"Okay Jane, that's enough. Bring me actual evidence and then we can talk. This conversation is at an end." Dr. Eisenfield turns, walks around the truck and off into the hot, dusty lot.

Oz clamps her teeth together, scrunches her eyes closed and shakes her head. Why can't she just keep her big mouth shut?

So much anger inside her. And it just keeps leaking out. Or should she say pouring?

3

This interview is going nowhere Lamont Nickell thinks as he sits in a booth across the table from Neil Gutlog, Special Assistant to the mayor for the City of Los Angeles, in this whirlwind of noise at The Grub Spot, a downtown lunchtime diner just a few blocks from city hall and currently overflowing with mostly government workers blowing off mid-day steam all seemingly at the top of their collective voices.

Nickell wants the Special Assistant to say something politically revealing about the city's inability to repair the solid waste treatment plants while somehow believing that constructing huge, open vats to pile the ever-accumulating human waste into is a good idea.

But getting Gutlog to actually say something politically revealing is not what his news organization—The Data Transfer—wants. No, their focus is on celebrities and celebrity scandal. And the only way he managed to schedule this interview in the first place was to promise that it would focus on the mayor's upcoming HOPE event, where more than a few celebrities would grace the stage.

Today is his birthday. Turns thirty-five. And it scares him. If he wants to work for a top-notch news organization, he needs to do it soon. Lately, he's felt anxious, hurrying through things like brushing his teeth or locking the door to his apartment and then forgetting that he has done those things. Or maybe he didn't do those things. He can't remember. That's the problem. He's not paying attention.

So getting nuggets of inside info from people like Gutlog would be very useful in climbing the ladder to a better job.

A job, for instance, with the L.A. Beacon. Now there's a hard-hitting online media channel. Of course, all news organizations these days exist only online. Publishing an actual physical newspaper is out of the question.

JOHN MOON FORKER

"Don't even bother asking for water. They won't serve it." The chubby Neil Gutlog says as he lifts his oversized spoon piled high with a vegetable paste the color of burned squash he's ordered because real whole vegetables cost a fortune, are sometimes a little scarce, and this cheap paste from Vietnam does the job. "Unless you're willing to pay for it." Delivered with a smile so tight it looks more like a grimace.

Nickell doesn't smile.

He and Gutlog try to eat in the baking heat of another scorching October day inside this long, but narrow, eighty-year-old restaurant without the expected relief of air conditioning, which the restaurant likely has but just cannot afford to run anymore.

Nickell puts a finger on his collar and pulls it open a bit, hoping for a little air, but to no avail. This heat pretty much kills any interest he might have had in his own food.

With the heating of the environment really kicking in these last few years, the weather just stays hot. And here in southern California, it stopped raining three winters ago. At all. Everything has just dried up. Fires up in the hills regularly. Some homes burned, others evacuated. Trees turned to ash. And city infrastructure has broken down with this whole human waste thing, waste of all kinds, and it all just keeps stacking up.

"Now Lamont, look, the HOPE Event in four days is the mayor's way of trying to bring . . . to lift the spirits of all the citizens of this city. We've been down for so long that it's time for a change. Time for us to regain that American can-do attitude."

Nickell wishes he wouldn't call him Lamont. Hates that name. But he listens while glancing at his commD—short for communication device—to make sure he points it directly at Gutlog's face. The device sits on top of a short tripod in the center of the nicked table sending a live feed back to The Data Transfer headquarters in India where this video is being cut and reassembled

SEARCHING FOR A WAY OUT

as it's happening and which will broadcast in less than two minutes after he's done.

For all that Nickell can see, the HOPE Event is nothing more than a city-sponsored pep rally being held at the L.A. Coliseum. Boost everyone's spirits. Paper over the problems just long enough for the mayor to get re-elected next week.

The city is using the acronym HOPE in its marketing campaign to stand for both: Help Our People Excel or Hurdle Over Problems Everywhere, but many are calling it Hopeless Our Putrid Excrement, which kind of turns the intent of this whole thing upside down.

Another con job, he thinks, and he so wants to puncture Gutlog's facade and get a statement he can use.

Nickell leans forward to cut through the restaurant's din and says, "So what is the city doing to fix the solid waste plants? I mean, you can't expect to keep dumping human waste into those vats. I'm told it attracts a lot of flies, among other things. This is sure to spread disease. In fact, we've already seen the beginning of this up in Sun Valley."

Gutlog's face tightens in a here-we-go-again formation.

"As far as this fly infestation goes, the city," Gutlog says, in a voice laced with bored exasperation, "is working with the top entomologists from UCLA and USC to find a solution to this problem. And as soon as they come up with a solution, we will implement it."

Nickell's head throbs with dead-end frustration. "But there are people sick now, kids with severe diarrhea, people dehydrated, Pacifica hospital up there is already beginning to turn the sick away because they have no more room."

Gutlog holds the empty spoon in the air, halfway down from having just dumped its content into his mouth on its way back to the plate. Jowls clamp down. "We are doing the best we can with the tools available to us."

Nickell lets out a small amount of air because he knows he won't get Gutlog to cough up that meaty tidbit he's looking for, but he has to press ahead anyway. It's a momentum thing.

"Yeah, but what about the disease? Isn't this mostly because of the waste, the human waste, the flies landing on it? Spreading it?"

"The waste issue is an entirely different matter." Gutlog waves his free hand through the air as if discarding an entire version of reality.

"Oh, really?" Nickell's eyebrows zoom up. "As I understand it, flies eat by vomiting digestive juices and enzymes onto their food to turn it into liquid, which they then suck up. If this food contains disease-causing viruses and bacteria—and human waste contains plenty of those—then when those flies later come into your home or to restaurants or wherever and vomit and eat again . . . well, this is how the disease will spread. It's no mystery. So, if all that human waste wasn't lying around, the flies would not be sucking up and spreading those germs. Why isn't the city doing something about the waste?"

"We in the administration are working day and night to rectify this situation." He wipes his mouth with the small paper napkin. "As you know, the city's infrastructure is ancient and all previous administrations have completely ignored these problems and now, when it all starts falling apart, somehow we're to blame for it."

Out of the corner of his eye, Nickell notices a message streaming across his commD screen. From his editor, Ramesh Shastri, in India. "What the hell are you doing?"

Nickell nearly groans. He can't even try to bring something a little more substantial to this organization without Ramesh breathing down his neck every moment. He'd quit this job in a nanosecond if he thought he could get another one. But in this economy, good luck brother. The only way he can leave here is to move up, and the only way he can move up is to show that he can play hardball.

SEARCHING FOR A WAY OUT

He never planned to be a journalist. Used to be an athlete. Spent a few years as a minor league baseball player. Not good enough to make the majors, but eventually professional baseball folded anyway, and the league shut down when the economy went south. Not enough people could afford tickets, owners couldn't pay the players, people gave up.

"Look," Gutlog says, with such exasperation that has him spitting out some of the vegetable paste as tiny flecks of yellow and green. "It would be different if we had the resources, if the economy was sharp, but we don't and we have to work with what we have. What we can do," he continues, "are things like the HOPE event. The turnaround for all our problems starts with the belief by people that a turnaround is possible."

"How exactly will this event at the coliseum change minds?" He might as well try this route.

"Well, for instance, we're having many speakers. More than thirty. From all walks of life in the city. Speakers who can inspire. In fact, we've just added another speaker who is well known for his ability to lead and to give people hope—King Zee Whitehead."

Nickell almost knocks his coffee-energy drink off the table.

King Zee Whitehead! The holier-than-thou, self-help guru turned religious zealot.

A man that Nickell hopes to nail shortly in a story about a sex scandal he has gotten himself into. All he needs now is for the woman to confirm the story, to tell of how Whitehead used his power and that phony surrender ceremony to seduce her. Fucking your parishioners when you are Mr. Holy can hurt your bottom line.

The Data Transfer might not be an investigative stalwart, but when it comes to scandal, they eat it up and this Whitehead story is just the kind of thing they live for. But he has to get that woman to go on camera.

17

JOHN MOON FORKER

"Yes, that's quite the addition to your line-up." He hopes Gutlog doesn't notice the sarcasm.

He presses his fingers into the table as if to center himself and observes Gutlog's continuing assault on the food, eating with such ferocity that his forehead bears a line of tiny droplets of sweat.

Maybe Gutlog believes calories equal freedom.

Nickell sits back. He looks up into the air. The ceiling, the air ducts, the discolored paint. He rubs the back of his neck with one hand and his mouth crunches up into a small grimace.

He hears the blurry din of voices choking the small space. Workers talking between mouthfuls all over the restaurant. Ding and clang of metal utensils. The crack of ceramic plates on tables. The whoosh of air trailing every hurrying waitress. And here he sits. Him stuck here while the world keeps on spinning around him.

Gutlog flashes his eyes down to his own commD on the table. This is text, no audio, no image.

He reads for almost fifteen seconds. "I'm sorry," saying this in a heavy, thudding, official voice. "Seems I have been called to a meeting. As always Lamont, a pleasure."

With that, he squeezes out of the booth, heaves himself to his feet and walks up the aisle and out of the restaurant.

Without paying.

Hopefully, Nickell thinks, The Data Transfer will reimburse him.

His own food, a cucumber split down the middle and laden with grated radish, has degraded somewhat. Looks a little brown around the edges.

Perhaps he should have stayed in Seattle. But then the baseball thing ended and the opportunity to write for that sports node out of L.A. came along and jobs were already hard to find. He just took what was easy. Didn't even really look around, did he? And then The Data Transfer gig opened up. More money. Closer to real journalism

SEARCHING FOR A WAY OUT

or so he thought. Just took it without thinking. And so here he is still with The Data Transfer and it doesn't have that much to do with journalism. He's coming unwound.

His life feels like one failure after another, the baseball, this job, this interview, his entire childhood, a childhood during which his father was never reluctant to point out Nickell's shortcomings.

He hates it when he gets down on himself like this.

He wonders if he'll ever be married again. The second time has to be better, right? What a mistake that first one was. He only realized that afterward, when it was too late. Great. Story of his life.

This is when he receives a disturbing transmission on his own commD.

4

Hours pass, the sun's heat builds, the digging continues. Oz stands in a three-foot deep hole about fifty feet from the original one out of which the horseshoe had come.

Nearby, workers dug a deeper and wider hole and uncovered an old mid-nineteenth century carriage. An example of a time that has been called the carriage age. This one looks as though it transported goods. Maybe building materials, stone, metal, wood. Which explains the horseshoes.

Her hands are hurting from all the shoveling.

Still pissed about Eisenfield. Mostly at herself for blowing up when that's exactly what she had warned herself not to do.

But she needs more evidence. But maybe with him, it's not about the evidence. Maybe he and Dr. Vasquez don't get along and he's using her to get at Vasquez. Some degrading academic rivalry thing.

What if she goes over his head to Professor Schailbe, the department chair? Or, better yet, what if she could get Professor Vasquez to talk to Dr. Schailbe? But with him looking to retire and Eisenfield angling to succeed him, he might not want this fight.

She wipes sweat off her face with a blue and white bandanna.

But if she could find that technology from the cave, then everything else falls into place. He couldn't ignore that.

The knowledge the Minoans must have developed is what she's really after.

Imagining this gives her hope. Hope in a world with little of it. And sometimes she thinks that having tasted this and wanting it so much but not being able to have it is worse than if she had never known it existed. Her own private Pandora's Box.

For better or worse, she's committed.

SEARCHING FOR A WAY OUT

She really needs to go back to Crete. That's where she's going to find the evidence. But how is she going to do that? Don't have that kind of money. And this has to happen soon. Real soon. Well then, she just has to get Alexandros to help her. He's already over there. He discovers things all the time. She just needs to plant the seed in his head as to what to look for. If he'll do it.

A tiny spark of light draws her eyes toward the Signal building. Up on the third floor? Not the sun. Wrong angle. On then off. What could that be?

She looks around to see if anyone is watching. They have been told to stay out of the building, but curiosity pulls her, so stealth is in order.

She walks in a roundabout way toward the squat four-story office building that looks as ordinary as a thousand other office buildings in L.A.

She checks out a few rooms on the first two floors but they're empty, nothing but dust and old, cracked linoleum.

But then, on the third floor, she comes to a room that is a hurricane of desks, metal file cabinets, and copious amounts of paper.

There's no sense of symmetry here. The desks and file cabinets appear to have been placed haphazardly. And there are so many of them there's hardly space to move around.

The desktops loaded with papers. In-boxes, out-boxes, all filled to overflowing. The antithesis of how everything has gone digital in the last twenty or thirty years. This could be a snapshot of how an office might have looked way back in the twentieth century.

She can't start rooting around in all this. It's just too overwhelming. She has an impulse to turn right around and leave, but decides to look in the closet first.

Pulling open the door, she sees a statue of a bull that nearly fills the entire space of the closet. Long sharp horns. Rearing up, almost standing on its hind two legs. And Oz gapes at it in wonder. "What the..."

She touches it just to make sure it's real. Whatever this material is, it feels extremely smooth. Hard like metal, but it doesn't have metal's inflexibility. Almost like skin.

This is exquisite, so why hide it in a closet? It couldn't be a decoration in here. No one would ever see it.

Bulls were an important symbol for the Minoans. She has seen a lot of bulls in Minoan art. Makes her wonder.

She runs a hand up and down the statue, even stretching up on her toes so that she can feel the horns. Just as she touches the tip of the right horn, she hears a click. The pedestal upon which the statue stands rotates counter-clockwise.

Startled, she steps back so quickly she slams into the doorframe, then scampers back even further into the cluttered office until she can see that it will not fall on her.

She rubs her elbow to ease the pain and, while she's rubbing, the right wall of the closet slides away and the now half-turned pedestal slides into the open space. Once the bull is fully inside, the panel closes and all Oz sees now is an empty closet.

Why go to all this trouble? This is very weird.

For a moment she thinks this is like one of those physical animations you see in high-end restaurants, but then comes another click. Now the rear wall of the closet swings back to open on what appears to be a completely dark space. No, wait. There is a faint bluish light. Getting stronger now. And as it strengthens, it turns white.

A secret room.

Her anticipation skyrockets. What could this be? Something valuable, something hidden away.

She peers intently into the room beyond, but it looks completely barren.

SEARCHING FOR A WAY OUT

If there is nothing in here, it would be a huge let-down, but it would make sense that these people took whatever was in here when they moved out.

She cautiously steps inside the room but closely examines around the opening to see if it's safe, to see if it won't suddenly snap close and trap her in here. Wouldn't want that.

Nothing here. Slick white walls, no windows. Even the floor is white. And the white light is increasing in luminosity, making everything clearer and clearer. Extreme contrast. It's so bright in here. But she's not squinting. In fact, her vision has never been sharper.

Even her thoughts seem clearer, more precise.

This is the opposite of the other room. That's all chaos and this is all order. Order by absence. Simplicity.

What could be the reason it's here? Where is that light coming from?

Then an old woman appears. Walking straight across the room, right in front of her, right there in sharp detail.

Oz takes another step back, but not so forcefully as last time. But where did she come from? Another entrance does not exist. Is this a ghost? Is she hallucinating?

She touches the wall for a reality check.

Ancient-looking woman. Ninety? One hundred? Moving—almost gliding—her back straight as an iron rod.

The woman's hair is white and silver, lustrous, all pulled back and tied at her neck with a black ribbon. Every hair appears distinct and aligned with all the others. The skin on her face is clear. Her warm, chocolate-brown eyes sparkle with a hidden smile.

She doesn't appear to be aware that Oz is in the room and Oz doesn't know what to do but feels frantic, like she should do something. So she says, "Hello."

No response. But the woman is passing right in front of her now, so Oz reaches out to touch her and her fingers glide through empty space.

What? Shocked, Oz steps back again. But she looks so real.

Her eyes dart around the room. What is real? Spooky in here. Can't make sense of it. So much less in here than in the next room, but the sense of overwhelm is so much greater.

She needs to sit down.

The woman must be some kind of holographic image. And this holographic image keeps walking and passes through the wall and out the other side.

What is this all about?

Oz wants out. She pivots left, and this is when she notices a folded document lying in the corner. Darts over, picks it up, and dashes out of the room, through the closet, into the office beyond, not wanting to stay a second longer in the white room.

In the desk-and-paper-cluttered room, she looks at the document. Lines and writing. Looks like . . . no, it can't be. Looks like ancient Minoan script. Both Linear A and Linear B. Look again. This must be a mistake.

She tries to hold the paper steady, but her hands tremble. First the bull and now this. A definite connection to the Minoan culture. Was someone in this building studying this?

Needs to clamp down on her excitement. The possibility of finding an answer, of finding evidence, looms large. This could be something.

If this is what she thinks it is, then she will have the Linear B translated. Someone successfully cracked that code in 1953. But the Linear A has never been.

Then she notices the lines. Like a diagram. And she immediately identifies it as a map of the ancient palace of Knossos on Crete,

SEARCHING FOR A WAY OUT

the intricate network of rooms, the intricate structure where it was rumored that once you entered, escape was impossible.

Yes, it looks like that palace, but now she sees differences. There are more curves, more switchbacks, more of a maze-like quality to this image.

So maybe not Knossos, but then what? What is this doing here? This is both exciting and mystifying. But it could be something. Her heart must be pumping a thousand times a minute.

Her eyes relentlessly search the map, looking at the lines and boxes that probably signify rooms, and then her eyes end up on the bottom corner and there, in English, is the word Atlantis.

She stops breathing.

Did she just find this by coincidence?

If not, who? The holographic woman?

Her hands twitch, her nervous system feels numb, then cold.

5

Nickell sits in a soft chair in his living room. Three journalism buddies sit around him joking, laughing, and wishing him a happy birthday.

He smiles but with no juice to it.

The message he received back at the restaurant was from Zukor Blandmoretop, his colleague at The Data Transfer, who lounges on the couch, right now pulling on a pipe with the latest herbal concoction, Uzbekistan Mint.

Zukor texted him that the woman who claimed that King Zee Whitehead had sexually assaulted her had recanted. A message that killed the story he's been working on about Whitehead. A story that would have laid Whitehead open to charges of high hypocrisy. But it all just fell apart. The woman said it never happened. Said she made it all up.

He paddles in the swamp of his own perceived failure, flooding his body with a numbed, washed-out feeling.

At least he's home.

Home is an apartment in Echo Park in a house that was never designed to be divided into apartments. But this house has three and his is on the second floor.

Odd arrangement of rooms. The front door is in the kitchen. People have to walk through that to get to what might be called a living room, but it's small and much more rectangular than square and the windows are on the narrow ends of the room so it is easy for someone sitting in it to feel squashed.

Zukor, having passed the pipe on, says "Hey, yeah, tough break about that Whitehead thing. Thought you had him this time."

"I thought so too."

SEARCHING FOR A WAY OUT

Nickell had done two previous stories about Whitehead, back in the summer, one of which focused on disaffected One Faith members, and the other a scientific analysis of Whitehead's so-called Surrender Ceremony, which is the supposed mechanism by which One Faith members can speak to God.

Both stories were unflattering.

And even though Nickell must be on an enemies list within the One Faith organization, he didn't think those stories went far enough, and they certainly didn't get the support from The Data Transfer editors that would have brought it to more people's attention.

He supposed they weren't scandalous enough for The Data Transfer.

But this story would have been. He had sat with the woman. Coaxed the story out of her. Told her how much she would help others in the same predicament and she had finally agreed. He could see the pressure on her face, the lines, the paleness, the worry on her lips. But he chose to ignore that.

The guys are supplementing the herb with some home-brewed beers which is kind of a hobby of Zukor's. He tends to brew them a little heavy on the alcohol content side of things.

As Zukor brings a glass up to his lips, he says, "He must have gotten to her somehow. Paid her off, threatened her, whatever."

"I guess," Nickell says, knowing in one part of his brain something like this makes sense yet still finding room to criticize himself. He hates to fail. Makes him feel small.

But fail again, he has. He clamps his teeth down and shakes his head ever so slightly. This is just the latest in a long string.

Back in high school, he worked on the school newspaper with Dana Mostonlinni, a girl he joked around with, felt comfortable with, almost asked out except he was afraid to, and eventually might have except for what happened.

Abraham Tolliver, the high school football star, raped and beat her. But that's not what she was told to say.

What really happened and who did what wasn't that clear to her at first. Her memory of the event was fragmentary.

After the parents took her to the hospital, the police arrived, and she gave a confused story, leading to the arrest of Tolliver and his friend, Solly Hemus.

She came back to school pretty much right away, putting on a brave face, wanting to regain her life. She told Nickell about it but was very confused.

But then the pressure started. With football being tremendously important to the school, losing Tolliver was just not acceptable. So the principal and Tolliver's father cooked up a scheme to blame Solly Hemus. Make it appear Tolliver, while being physically present, actually tried to discourage Hemus.

When Nickell heard about the switch—by this time Dana was no longer coming to school, so he didn't talk to her—he became suspicious when the principal seemed to be the leading advocate for this other boy's guilt. So Nickell went to his tech-geek friend Tad, who had one of those Interceptors. An illegal device that could intercept mobile phone transmissions.

Nickell bicycled over to the principal's house in the middle of the night and crawled underneath the house and placed the device. He could monitor it from anywhere with the receiver that was about the size of a pack of cigarettes.

What he heard stunned him. Yes, the principal and Conrad Tolliver were framing Solly.

He recalls hearing Tolliver telling the principal that they needed to keep the girl under control—meaning Dana—and the principal saying that he should have kept his son under control in the first place. Nickell knew then for sure who did it.

SEARCHING FOR A WAY OUT

For this to work, they had to get Dana to name Hemus specifically. The principal talked to Dana's father. He asked after Dana. He asked if she was any clearer about what happened. If she could identify Hemus as the one. That Abraham was really a fine boy and it couldn't have been him. And would the father let him come over and speak with Dana?

This visit apparently took place and somehow the principal got Dana to positively identify Solly Hemus as the attacker.

But to the police, this seemed shaky and it might have stayed that way except, strangely enough, shortly after this, someone found Dana's underwear in Solly Hemus's car.

A day later, Nickell walked over to Dana's house—she hadn't responded to any of the messages he had sent her.

She lived in a corner house and he saw her wandering around in her backyard. He called to her and she looked over. What a haunted face. Vacant eyes. Didn't recognize him at first but then came over, walking in a funny way, not directly toward him but sort of back and forth as if she wasn't sure where she was going.

He told her what he had found out and she started crying. Pleaded with him to help her. She had made a mistake. A mistake she didn't think she could live with. She had remembered something else. Remembered Solly's voice. He pleaded with Tollilver to not do this. Yes. Those exact words, "Do not do this." And so she realized it was all Tolliver, but when she told her father, told the principal, they wouldn't listen. Said she was confused.

Nickell said he would help her. He would put the recording of the principal's phone calls out on the Internet.

Yet, he felt scared. If it ever got back to him he had released that information, then the principal, the Tollivers and the police would have come after him. So he needed to release the information anonymously, but to make sure that happened, he needed to get over to the principal's house and pull that device back out because they sure as hell would look for something like that right off the bat.

The fear paralyzed him. What if he didn't do this right? What if he screwed up?

He spent the day trying to gather enough courage and force himself to act.

But he wasted a day. Thought he had the time.

He didn't. Dana committed suicide. Her father's gun. He had made an irreversible mistake. He was a coward. He had failed.

Nearly twenty years of beating himself up over this.

He needs to find another way.

6

"Man, you're really worked up over this," Zukor says. "What have you got against Whitehead?"

Nickell leans forward, takes a sip of his beer.

"My younger sister Bonnie. Who used to be a physical fitness trainer. Who used to love life until she got into Whitehead's One Faith organization. Until she started going up those levels doing more and more intense surrender ceremonies, until she flipped out, became very dreamy, was a no-show for appointments, said that God was talking to her and that she had some kind of higher purpose which I could never get her to tell me what it was. Finally, she stopped taking care of herself, not bathing, not cleaning, not preparing meals, just eating jar after jar of peanut butter and laying on the couch."

"Sorry, man. I didn't mean to . . ."

"I just think he's lying to people and that when he falls from grace, it will be a good thing for everyone. Plus, it will make a terrific news story."

"Like how he got his start?" Zukor sits motionless inside the cloud of herbal smoke drifting up through the sunbeams.

Nickell rubs his face and lets out a breath. "You mean the story that he went out alone to the desert, out past Twenty-Nine Palms, into the Cleghorn Lakes Wilderness area to get away from the distractions in the city? To be alone with God? That beginning?"

"Right, and that he was out there for forty days and forty nights eating insects and snakes and cutting open cacti to drink the juice." Zukor laughs.

Yes, Nickell thinks Zukor can laugh about it, but it is this story that has given Whitehead a large following. More so every day. People want to believe. He has seen it. He saw his sister believe it.

No, he can't laugh about it. This story is like some disease spreading and spreading infecting all who lie in its path.

Infected him too. But not to believe, but to hate. Hate this hypocrite. Hate what he's doing to people. To Bonnie.

He'd like to find out what really happened out there.

The story, as Whitehead tells it, is on the fortieth night he saw an extremely bright shooting star, flames trailing out behind it, falling to earth where it burned a sixty-foot cross into the ground just a few feet from where he sat.

It infused him with tremendous energy, staying awake all night, gradually falling into a deep silence, not only him but the world around him, until sunrise, when the heavens resounded with booming thunder and he had his vision. A vision of God and God told him that having so many religions and them fighting with each other was wrong and that he, Whitehead, needed to unite all people, throw away these tired old religions, and bring everyone under one big tent and create a way that He could speak to all of His children, and do so in direct communication with each and every one of them.

"Makes you wonder how people could believe Whitehead did this. But there were no witnesses. No way to prove otherwise."

"Drink up," Zukor says.

Nickell feels stymied and blunted with the frustration of running into all these dead ends. But he won't quit. Not this time.

7

On his hands and knees, King Zee Whitehead feels a drop of sweat roll down his forehead, hesitates at his eyebrow, and then launches off toward the bed below.

Just twenty minutes ago he had been in the spacious living room in front of eighteen people, mostly couples, women sitting on the chairs and couches, the men standing or perching on the arms of the furniture.

He told them how their hopes and the hopes of the country could be re-kindled by One Faith, by a direct connection to God. That in these dark times, only the guidance that God can provide would see them through this ordeal.

And they nodded their assent when he explained again that organized religion was a barrier to this connection, not a gate. That you didn't need priests or ministers or rabbis or imams to act as a go-between for you and God. Because if one of these age-old religions actually worked, they would have been providing this direct access to God from the get-go.

They just got in the way.

There was only the one God, anyway. Having all these different religions and sects only muddied the issue. Which, of course, he told them, is why he named his organization One Faith.

They applauded. They chattered. They wanted to believe. Hope is what they wanted and the connection to God that he promised he could give them with the Surrender Ceremony.

And they had money. His planned Palace of God that he is building near downtown would need plenty of that.

At times like these, he feels more like a filthy, begging salesman and although he would bow to no one, and didn't here, asking for anything did not adhere to his purpose. He'd spent years sacrificing and experimenting to bring himself closer to God because this is how he would find the one true path. A path uncluttered by distraction and temptation. A path leading to a pure life.

And he had acquired a taste for command. It just felt right. Commanding in God's name.

So he needed to wash the salesman feeling out of his mind after these fine people had left. Left just him and Ruthie Shallcross alone in Ruthie's house in the affluent Hancock Park neighborhood. Where shade and quiet predominated. Where money grew on trees.

Now Ruthie lay quivering on the bed. Naked as the day she was born. Her dark hair arrayed on the pillow, her square jaw locked into place by the tension, yet trying to smile, causing her mouth to look more like rippling asphalt during an earthquake.

Is she quivering with fear? With excitement? With anticipation? Whitehead didn't care. This isn't about her. It's about testing himself.

On all fours, he is also naked. Tumescent. Hovering just inches above her, another drop of sweat splashing down onto her stomach.

His desire is sharp, a razor of intensity that so wants to take him over and bathe in this consuming pleasure.

But he makes certain that no part of him touches her. No contact whatsoever. No small patch of skin accidentally touching hers. He is so close though that he can easily feel the heat of her rising. Inviting him into her arms, into her body, into this moment. Yes, he is strong, but actual skin-to-skin co-mingling would be too much for him right now. Maybe that's an experiment he can try later. But no, this is excellent. He has accomplished what he set out to do. And it's always good to leave them wanting more.

He backs down the bed, gets to his feet, and says to Ruthie, "I've got to go."

Denying himself this indulgence is the path to self-mastery. Not giving in to the beast of pleasure. And this self-denial he believes

SEARCHING FOR A WAY OUT

will make him shine in God's eyes. Bring him closer. Give him the guidance he needs.

Nothing is more important.

8

Throwing herself into the backseat of Mervin's gas-guzzling Chevy, Oz tries to make sense of what she saw: the woman or, more accurately, the holograph of the woman, the Minoan map, the bull, and a room so filled with light that it made even the air distinct.

Trying to get a handle on this, she feels as though her mind is spinning like an industrial-strength dryer, slinging her numerous wild and chaotic thoughts and bouncing them off the walls of her brain at an increasing velocity.

Why would a document written in ancient and long-dead Minoan appear in an abandoned building in Los Angeles? Who was that old woman? And what does Atlantis have to do with it?

Someone in that building might have been a collector of Minoan artifacts, but no paper artifacts exist from three or four thousand years ago. If there had been any, they would have disintegrated long ago. So that means that the map is more recent and, sure, since Linear B can be translated, maybe someone wrote in that script and knew what they were saying, but Linear A? Impossible. If someone had broken the code, she would know it. That person would shout about their achievement from the mountaintop.

She bends forward and rubs her fingers hard against her forehead.

Mervin and Melissa lower themselves into the front seat, all three of them dusty and beat-tired, having labored for hours digging and troweling and sifting and hauling. Now with dusk and the oncoming darkness, there is the cauterized hope for cooler air.

"I'm like so hungry," Melissa says. "After that fly landed in my soup, I had to throw it out. Didn't get one taste."

"Good thing too," Mervin says. "Hear they're carrying disease."

SEARCHING FOR A WAY OUT

"All those vats of human shit they got all over the county is what's causing it."

Oz taps her fingers on her eyebrows. But even stranger was that holograph. She's no expert in that kind of thing, but she doesn't remember ever seeing a holograph that real. Okay, so maybe the technology has reached that stage and she's just not aware of it, but why show up there? On the third floor of a building slated to be demolished and, as far as she knows, whose power had been cut off.

Most likely, she guesses, is that someone who used to occupy the building worked with holographs and this must have been left over. But where was the equipment? Where was it projecting from? She had seen nothing obvious, but then she was freaked out in there. She really needs to go back and look at that much more closely.

But then, who was the old woman? Just some random manifestation that the inventor cooked up? Maybe so. Something running on an endless loop. But she looked extremely real. Like I could touch her.

But maybe the most mysterious thing of all is reading the word Atlantis on that map.

Oz has got to think. What does she already know about Atlantis? What did she learn this summer when she was over on Crete?

Well, that's the thing. None of the archeologists on the island showed much interest at all in Atlantis. She didn't. The subject hardly ever came up. It's largely regarded as make-believe, just as is the legend of King Minos and the Minotaur.

Naturally, the mythology portrays it as a blissful paradise. Plentiful beauty and food and intellectual achievement. Just the kind of thing that people today—so desperate for hope—would want to get their hands on.

Got to get more info. Oz flips on her commD to the "Look What I Found" node where archeologists from all over the world share what they've been working on and what they've been digging up.

Within this node are many sub-nodes. She goes directly to the one for Crete and quickly scans. Since she checks this node almost every day, she is very familiar with the various ongoing discussions. So she begins by looking for anything about Atlantis.

Nothing so far. Goes to the sub-node of the sub-node, this one being Santorini. Santorini and its neighboring islands lie about sixty miles north of Crete. But they used to be one larger island called Thera before the most powerful volcanic explosion in all of recorded history blew it apart.

And then she spots him. Alexandros Papadakis. He's in this sub-node right now. Perfect.

She knows him from the summer in Crete. Met him in the local tavern where many of the students on the dig hung out. Alexandros headed the Greek team. In his fifties, maybe even sixty. Deeply tanned with all that time in the sun and has more than a few white hairs.

She had overheard him speaking in English about the ancient Sumerians and their development of irrigation, which allowed cities to form, with a couple of members of a British archeological team.

She normally would never approach a total stranger. Just a border she couldn't cross. But she had been drinking the local spirit, Raki, made from the leftovers during wine production, a strong drink to which she was advised never to take on an empty stomach so she was nibbling on feta cheese and olives but feeling the effects of the alcohol anyway and maybe a little reckless.

"You study ancient civilizations?" Oz asked.

Alexandros Papadakis turned forty-five degrees, looked down his long nose at her, then broke out in a beaming smile. A smile that Oz warmed up to immediately.

SEARCHING FOR A WAY OUT

Oz found they had a common interest. The search for ancient civilizations and the knowledge they possessed.

She messages him, using the sub-vocal feature on the commD. Don't want Mervin and Melissa asking any questions.

"Ah, Jane, what a delight to hear from you." Text only. Visuals don't work so well going sub-vocal. Has something to do with hearing words coming from a face upon which the mouth and lips don't move. A psychological dissonance.

As she silently speaks, the words form the text and shoot over to him.

He's never gotten around to calling her Oz. Says a name is a name and you don't take shortcuts.

"It's good to see you're still kicking around too." She hesitates for a moment. The car practically stops on the tollway, jammed in, no air coming in through the open windows, the heat strangling. "You're still doing... still interested in Atlantis, right?"

"Of course, and it's funny that you should mention that now."

"You're still on Crete?"

"No, no, not there. In Greece. I've been digging... well, me and the lads from the Greek Archeological Institute have been doing a little more work on the site of Plato's Academy."

Oz smiles. "Oh yes, Plato, who ignited the legend of Atlantis in his transcript called Critias."

"Very good, my child."

She can almost hear him laughing. A deep, resonant laugh that put her at ease last summer.

"But hasn't Plato's Academy been thoroughly dug up many, many years ago? What could be left to find?"

Founded in 387 BCE, the academy had been in a sacred olive grove dedicated to Athena, the goddess of wisdom. Which seems fitting to Oz.

"You know, Jane, you can always dig deeper, and when you do, you usually keep finding things. And find things we have."

"And what would that be?" Oz says, eager to hear it.

"Only some writings that might be by Plato himself. Or maybe just the notes made by one of his students."

"That's fantastic. Tell me."

"That's why I say it's funny that you should contact me now and ask about Atlantis. As you know, in Critias, Plato puts Atlantis out in the Atlantic Ocean beyond the straits of Gibraltar, but here, he reverses himself and indicates that it was in the eastern Mediterranean. Seems that the original material, the story that Plato got from Critias, who got it from his grandfather Solon, only said it was west of Egypt."

"This is confirmation then? Really great news. Been rumored for years but now... puts it much closer to Crete."

"Exactly. And he seems to better identify what brought about its end, and it sounds suspiciously like the volcanic eruption on Thera."

She's thinking hard now. Imagining. Speculating. If this is true, then maybe that word on the map really could lead to a discovery. Oz taps her lips with the two fingers of her left hand. "So Plato is... is he speculating that Crete or Thera was Atlantis?"

"He doesn't really get that specific, but he implies it. One or the other. But let me ask you why you have this sudden interest in Atlantis?"

She tells him about her experience in the Signal building, the finding of the map, and the word Atlantis written in English, the bull, the woman, the light.

Papadakis is silent.

"Alexandros, you still there?"

"Yes, yes... but I'm a little stunned. You say this was all found at some office building in downtown Los Angeles? Incredible. I'm wondering if—"

SEARCHING FOR A WAY OUT

"What could this all have to do with the Minoans?" In her excitement, she finishes the thought for him.

"Of course. But this is so out of time. The Minoans basically ceased to exist in 1500 BCE." He pauses again, then says, "Jane, could you scan the map and send it?"

"Yeah, give me a sec."

She unfolds the document, careful not to make too much noise and have Mervin and Melissa ask questions about where she got it, but they are still talking about open vats of human waste.

She scans the map with her commD and shoots it off to Alexandros.

As he waits, he tells Oz, "This might connect to the legend. If what we've found here makes it more likely that Atlantis—if there really was an Atlantis—was a part of the Minoan civilization and if the legend is true—"

"Two big ifs."

"Yes, indeed. But if it is true, and the Minoans sent someone to the other side of the earth to protect their technology from the barbarians, then that technology might have come from Atlantis."

Just hearing this makes Oz all the more excited. She sub-vocally blurts out, "If this technology, whatever it might have been, was created in Atlantis and if it could be found, it would be the discovery of the century, no, the millennium."

She grips her knee hard. Would like to jump up and down but don't want to have Mervin and Melissa see her all excited and then have to explain.

"Okay," Alexandros says. "I see the map. I see its resemblance to the palace at Knossos and the differences. Since they seem related, I think you should carefully look at the land around that building. There is a good chance that this map is showing us something real and would likely be near there. Possibly something underground."

"I'll do that first chance I get. Tomorrow. If Dr. Eisenfield isn't watching me too closely."

"That clown."

"Yeah, he loves you too."

"I wish I could fly to L.A. but I'm really tied up here."

"Look, I'll keep you informed. If I find anything, I'll let you know." Oz sits back in her seat, just now aware of how much tension she's been holding and how her back hurts.

"Good. I'll take a closer look at the map. Stay in touch."

Oz switches off the line, feels her breath. Irregular. She can barely sit still. Need to get out of this car and move.

Traffic has come to a dead stop. Mervin taps the steering wheel with his finger. An arrhythmic tapping. More like twitching.

Melissa has her head cranked around to the right, looking out the window at the smoke from some fire up in the hills.

She has to go back inside the Signal building and search it. Study the land. Look for maybe an underground entrance. Lots to do.

Get on it first thing in . . . oh no, she almost forgot. She has to work at the kennel tomorrow morning.

9

His friends have left. He sits at his kitchen table. A table positioned near the front door of the poorly laid-out apartment.

Nickell's right foot furiously taps the floor. He focuses on the three-inch commD screen.

He should try to find Sandy Utterback and re-convince her to press charges against Whitehead for his sexual assault. At least find out exactly why she changed her mind. Never mind. He just needs to track her down.

Instead, he's coming at Whitehead from a different angle. This enormous church or cathedral he's building downtown. This Signal building. Look at a little history here. See how this started.

He's not finding much.

What is missing and should be here is how much Whitehead paid for it. All it says is "pending" as if someone in the assessor's office had just not gotten around to entering that data. But this happened about three months ago.

Well, since this is a bust, he could try finding out more about the Signal building itself.

He takes this step by step. Doesn't want to miss anything. Doesn't want to make a mistake. So go slow. Take care.

With there being several documents associated with this transaction, he uses the commD to take each one and project it out into 3D space around the table, at about eye level, so that all he has to do is look from one to the other. Get them off that small screen so that he doesn't have to squint.

Built in 1951. Purchased by someone named Aurora Pointe. Still listed as the owner. Holy smokes, that would make her really old.

Maybe a hundred. Even if she bought it as a teenager. This info must be out-of-date. She can't still be around.

Bought it from a movie studio. They had the entire city block. Couple of warehouses or maybe they were sound stages. But she tore them all down and built just the one building. A lot of extra land there.

No information about tenants or leases or anything like that. So what did they do? Pay cash? A handshake?

The building is in what used to be called the artist's district. Could these people, these tenants, have been artists?

Nickell tries to put the pieces together in his brain, like some kind of puzzle fitting them together this way and that way.

He next searches the woman herself, leaving all the other documents floating up in the air for quick reference.

He starts with the common public databases but can only find a reference to her as the owner of the building. Okay, if that's not working, he'll just move on to the private databases that The Data Transfer has purchased access to.

Again, same deal. Aurora Pointe, the Signal building, nothing more.

How can this be? Everyone in the country has practically his or her whole life exposed and cataloged in one database or another. You can't avoid it. So where is this woman?

Can't find a damn thing.

Okay, if her only connection is through the building, then let's check out the building.

Nickell stops for a moment until he can regain that feeling of being methodical. That's the way he gets things done, makes him feel centered, lets him know he is on track. He is most likely to get it all right doing it this way. One logical step after another.

He searches for sixteen minutes. Not much. Then he sees the small news report. One of the many flying news bots has a

SEARCHING FOR A WAY OUT

ten-second video of the torn-up site and the story is that the city has halted demolition on the Signal building because a historical artifact has been found on the property and the city has called on the University of Southern California's archeology school to send a team over and assess the situation and see what else might be unearthed.

Which is when he hears the footsteps coming up the stairwell.

His next-door neighbor, right across the small landing, is Gina Woolander, who just so happens to be a student in the archeology department at USC.

So who he's hearing is either her or her roommate, Brenda.

He wipes the documents out of the air, stands up and opens the front door.

"Gina. Hi."

Her head tilts up as she continues to climb. "Oh, Nickell. What's up?" Her voice dragging, her steps heavy.

Nickell thinks she looks tired. But she also looks very attractive in those shorts, with those long legs that are streaked with dirt. And her being around five-eleven means she's showing a lot of leg. He tries to forget she's about fifteen years younger than him.

When she reaches the landing, she takes a deep breath.

"Long day?" Nickell says.

"Oh, my God."

"You're not part of that team that is working at the Signal building, are you?" He's not expecting much from her because how much could she or any of the students know?

"Sure am. Who told you?" Now that she's had a few moments to rest, a tiny smile curls at the far end of her lips.

"News bot. You finding anything over there?"

"Some old carriage. Must be a hundred years old. And a stable, or what's left of it. And Horseshoes. Plenty of horseshoes. Scattered all over that site. Almost like they were planted there. Pretty pathetic."

"But the building must—"

"Just an ordinary office building. Lot of land though. Whole city block."

"Do you know what they used it for?"

"Why are you asking me all these questions?" She's looking past him and into his apartment. "Hey, you've been partying? Look at all those beer bottles." She's openly grinning now.

"Oh, that. A couple of the guys were over. Today's my birthday."

She bends forward, lays her hand on his chest, and kisses him on the cheek. "Well, happy birthday Nickell."

She smells of the earth, of her own sweat, and she must be emitting a boatload of pheromones because he's practically spinning here and for an instant, he feels an almost overwhelming desire to pull her close and just hold her.

But she's already backing away and turning toward her apartment door. With her hand on the door, she looks back. "Why are you interested in that old building anyway?"

"I found out King Zee Whitehead is building himself a cathedral there."

"Oh yeah, we heard something about that. Well, good for him."

"What? You know he's dangerous, don't you?" Panic and anger and self-righteousness all mix together in him like some toxic milkshake. It's like he can't help himself.

"Dangerous?" Gina unlocks and opens the door to her apartment. "If he can bring hope to people, then I think he's doing some good." She steps inside and shuts the door.

He raises his hand, then drops it. The air gone from his sails.

Then it suddenly occurs to Nickell that he sees a long-shot idea here, although he doesn't like himself for thinking this. But then, he's used to not liking himself.

10

The instant that Mervin stops the car and cuts the engine, Oz springs out of her seat. Finally free to move, she hurries across the street and up to the apartment, slamming through the door and knowing she's not done with the night despite the dust and dirt and how tired her body must be, except she can't feel it much and so doesn't want the day to end, wants to stay up and think and work out just how she's going to pass all these hours until she can get back to the Signal building.

As she walks into her room, her commD signals an incoming message. Her friend Midori Nakagawa.

"Oz, you at home?"

"Just got here."

"We missed you at the meeting."

Midori is Oz's closest friend, really her only friend. Six years older than Oz, she's almost like a sister.

She met Midori eight years ago when they both worked at a non-profit dedicated to the elimination of solid waste called Reduction Applications. There they discovered a shared affinity for the zero waste movement.

Midori formed an organization focused on making the city—the entire state of California—operate, producing no waste.

Which is the meeting that Oz missed.

They try to get together at least several times a month. Sometimes Oz travels out to Midori's house in the hills of Malibu. If her car, the Electron, is working that day.

She values spending time with Midori, out in her garden, walking the nearby trails, immersing herself in the tranquility of Midori's simple life. Grows most of her own food, off the grid using solar and wind and even runs her car on compressed air.

"Yeah, sorry, but we started a new dig today. Downtown. Been there all day."

"So you might be hungry?"

"I... listen I'm really glad you called. I've got so much to tell you. Some really exciting things. Strange things."

"Can't wait to hear it. Let's meet at Sprout Now. Forty-five minutes?"

"See ya then."

Oz figures she'll take a quick shower and then walk the six or seven blocks to the restaurant. She can't drive her car until it charges up and she can't even afford to charge it until after 11:00 when the rates go down. She's got to make every penny stretch. Her scholarships pay for her schooling, but daily-existence-on-this-planet money she has to work for. That's what having a job at the kennel is all about. But the best part about that is the dogs. She loves the dogs.

When she walks down the hall to her bathroom and turns on the tap, only a thin trickle of water comes out.

Then she realizes Melissa has already taken her shower in the master bedroom's bathroom and has used so much water that the sensor that monitors water usage has been tripped. They have reached the legal limit and have been cut off. Their entire water allotment for the day. That means no significant amount of water will be available until early tomorrow morning. Only this little trickle.

Well, it's not like this has never happened before. She's prepared. She has a small plastic tub and a sponge under the sink, which she now hauls out and sticks under the thin stream of water, waiting minute after minute for enough water to accumulate for her to even begin to use the sponge, not even hoping to get any hot water, not even any warm water, but just water of any temperature.

As she looks into the water, she sees her image.

SEARCHING FOR A WAY OUT

    Then the electrical power in the apartment fails. In the first instant, Oz thinks, "What? Again?" But her eyes keep the afterimage of the light, casting a glow to the air, especially across the chrome-plated faucet and maybe it's the dimness of the light or the angle of reflection or the sudden shock of darkness, but this moment, seeing herself this way in the water and holding her body in this position, jolts her memory of the water and the image of her in the sanctuary cave on Crete.

11

They had been digging at the base of Mt. Ida for weeks with the two other archeological teams from England and Greece. Dr. Eisenfield, the head of their team, had decided that almost everyone should have a day off. Rest. Stay in the shade. Conserve their strength.

But Oz couldn't sit still. Couldn't just rest. No days off for her. Too driven for that.

After her parents died, she lost any sense of her place in the world, how she fit in, or if she fit in at all.

She believes that ancient cultures—far more than modern religions—are far more likely to pursue the meaning of life and their purpose here on the planet in a meaningful way. And her being here on Crete has infused her with a powerful energy to explore, to seek the ancient Minoan culture and the knowledge that they once possessed.

And talking to Alexandros Papadakis, who filled her head with tales of his work at Gobkli Tepe in southeastern Turkey, had only fueled this desire. A collection of 12,000-year-old stone temples that were intentionally buried under twenty feet of sand two thousand years later to hide them from invaders. Stone temples shaped in perfect circles, populated by ten-to-sixty ton-pillars that displayed expert stone cutting work decorated with three-dimensional relief carvings of many kinds of animals.

Oz had listened fascinated, sitting on a stool by the window of a tiny local tavern, as he leaned forward from the other side of the long, narrow table, and described to her the close similarities between this unknown ancient culture at Gobkli Tepe and the Minoans some eight to nine thousand years later. Cultures so similar that he believed the Minoans came from this area of Turkey, this exact location.

SEARCHING FOR A WAY OUT

So, she thought at the time, the Minoans had a head start on the development of their civilization. No wonder they were so advanced.

That this line of development stretched back twelve thousand years sharpened her desire to probe even more deeply into the earth to discover what knowledge they might have possessed. What sense they made of the world and what use she could make of it to find her own place.

Alexandros urged her to go out exploring. To climb Mt. Ida and see the cave in which Zeus was speculated to have been born. He pointed a finger at her and says, "You won't find anything sitting here on your ass."

So she does. And while climbing up the mountain, she notices a Green Whip snake whipping rapidly between the rocks. A non-venomous snake common to Crete, this one seemed especially colorful with the luminescence of its lime-green color.

She follows it twenty feet to an anomaly in the rocks. Looking more closely, she discovers an extremely narrow opening through which she crawls on her stomach a good fifteen feet to the mouth of a cave.

Inside, she creeps through the inky blackness. She feels as though every muscle in her arms and legs is stretched as tight as one of those spray-on Halloween masks after it has dried and hardened, and this tension seems to permeate the thick air.

Hesitant to go any farther. Swirls of dark air whip around her. The absence of sound cottons her ears. She wants to turn around and get out. She doesn't like this closed-in feeling at all. Trapped.

But she makes herself go on. With short steps, she walks forward, putting her hands on the wall to guide her, circling counter-clockwise, getting no sense that this is anything other than just an ordinary cave, never visited, never used by anyone.

After about twenty feet, the wall stops at an opening to another chamber. She follows the wall around to the inside of this new space and here no light penetrates. A perfect darkness.

Thoughts of being trapped in here intensify. A sharp anxiety threatening to turn into panic.

Calm yourself.

She is about to turn back, thinking this is all pointless. Even if there is something in here, she won't be able to see it. In that moment, her eyes register the faintest light. And this bluish illumination grows slowly in tiny increments. It's almost as if she's tripped a sensor and signaled the light to come up.

Being hyper-vigilant, she can see well enough to walk out into the middle of the space. Completely flat. A stone surface that appears to extend out about ten feet in all directions. And as she looks, she can see that this entire circular stone floor is covered in one huge painting. People and buildings and streets and vegetation and animals. An entire town. People working, playing, walking, talking, even copulating.

"Wow," she whispers. "This is magnificent." She darts back and forth, trying to take it all in at once like some kid at a three-ring circus with all the rings going like mad.

She guesses it must have been at least thirty-five hundred years ago. At the height of the Minoan civilization.

She looks across the floor. That's odd, she thinks. Shouldn't there be a lot of dust on this floor? It's clean, but it doesn't look used and it's not airtight in here.

This is getting kind of spooky. Maybe she just can't see it.

She gets on her hands and knees, then crawls around looking at the complete town in the painting until she comes back around to the center. She now notices a section of the drawing showing a large open building with a man and a woman inside it, both sitting, facing each other. Looking relaxed.

SEARCHING FOR A WAY OUT

Their posture straight, they are looking directly into each other's eyes.

She's in her element. Yes, there is her professional archeological training, which allows her to realize the vast significance of what she's seeing, but she hopes to find the wisdom in some ancient culture that will give her the tools to change herself, to escape the prison of her past and to allow her to be free, that sparks her now.

Anticipation rises in her chest. So much to see. Almost too stimulating. Wants to go in three directions at once.

On the floor, right in front of her, the artist has drawn a sort of huge balloon over each of their heads as if this is the content of their thoughts, their minds. At least picturing the thinking process, as Oz sees it.

She continues to crawl around, looking at all the images in the drawing. Above the woman's head is another image of the same woman. Oz figures it must be her because the woman in the image above is wearing the same golden bracelet with the bull on it as the woman sitting below. And the same images as the woman below surround the woman above, except they are smaller, in proportion to the smaller rendering of her.

But right above this smaller image of the woman is a still yet smaller woman with the same golden bracelet surrounded by the same images of the town as the two below her. And this pattern continues rising above, becoming smaller and smaller. Glancing over, she sees it exactly duplicates this pattern in the balloon above the man's head. She's sure she would find even smaller and smaller representations if there was more light and she could see better.

But she sees enough. This is unlike any other Minoan painting or drawing she's ever seen. A little thrill of electricity sizzles across her brain. She needs to get someone else up here to see this. Dr. Eisenfield.

But not just yet.

What she sees in these balloons coming out of their heads, these images, has to be a representation of the content of their minds, the workings of the mind. That's got to be it.

Oz figures this woman is going deeper and deeper within herself, drilling into her mind, exploring it, seeing how it works, seeing what it is doing to her.

The images of the mind twist around in layers, almost like a labyrinth.

Oz stops. Like a labyrinth? Like the one underneath the palace at Knossos? The fabled one of the myth where the Minotaur awaits at the center to devour humans?

Is that what this is about?

So what the artist is showing us is this man and woman traveling deeper into their own minds—the labyrinth—and examining the workings of it, probing through layer after layer until . . . until what? Until they reach the core? The core of the mind? Which would be like getting to the center of the labyrinth where you face your own personal Minotaur.

That the Minoans could even conceive of this, much less do it, stuns her. Then what is the technology they are using to travel to the labyrinth's center?

Oz is already on her elbows to get close enough to see the most detail and now she just holds still, looks up into the darker reaches of the cave. Her body vibrates. Thrilled. This is the greatest find she's ever made.

Okay, look at the bigger picture. It appears that the Minoans weren't just culturally and technologically advanced in their time, they were pioneers in the workings of the mind. And this was when? About a thousand years before the Buddha? Imagine what they could have done had their civilization survived.

SEARCHING FOR A WAY OUT

She realizes she's going to have to change her thesis. This is so much more important than cracking the code of Linear A. This is what she's looking for.

She glances up and looks around the room. Ahead, toward the back, is a stone cistern. She stands up and walks over. It is filled with water.

She looks back at the floor. Wasn't there . . . yes, painted just below and in front of the man and woman is a cistern of water. Pretty much identical to the one she is standing in front of.

The stone walls of the basin rise about three feet and form a rim around a circular depression, maybe another four feet across.

Oz lays her hand on the rim and crouches down closer. Leaning over the edge, she sees her reflection in the smooth, still water. A ghostly reflection cast in the bluish tinge.

Then the image swirls, picking up speed, and within seven seconds Oz no longer has any sense of being in the cave.

She sees herself in a large hotel ballroom filled with people dressed in the most formal way she could ever imagine.

And look at her. An ivory-colored dress that flows almost down to her ankles, arms bare below the elbows, a neckline that exposes her upper chest.

In a dress. She can hardly remember the last time. But look at her hair. It's all swept up and back and held in place with two burgundy barrettes.

Violins sound a lush music that has many in the room dancing. Formal dance. Is this a waltz?

This is just about the most alien thing she could ever imagine herself doing.

Her viewpoint changes to being inside her body. No longer looking at herself from an exterior point of view, she is now inside, looking out through her own eyes.

She's a little winded and realizes she just finished a dance. A couple glides by and they both nod and smile at Oz. She realizes she is smiling, has been smiling, continues to smile.

She's enjoying herself.

And this strikes her as an even more alien feeling than being here.

A man with a dark brown mustache approaches, bows, asks her to dance, and she is swept up in the music's flow and in the arms of this man, and she is dancing superbly, completely coordinated, knowing what to do without thinking about it, and being an integrated part of this mass of humanity.

But she can't dance!

She's—and she can't describe this any other way—she's actually chatting with the man. The words just flow and the communication is like a balm.

Everything is as it should be. Her concentration is sharp, she feels engaged, feels connected, her presence total. This is a glimpse of a life she's never had put into an environment she's never experienced.

Then it comes to her she's seeing this because it is so alien to her. That she cannot only fit in here, but she can thrive. She can be this person in this ballroom acting this way and enjoying it. She could do this anywhere, at any time.

All of her loneliness, her anger, her inability to trust, her failures with relationships are now all gone. She feels free.

In this version of her life, her parents didn't die. Or their death didn't twist her into what she became.

The instant she thinks this, it all stops cold.

She looks up from the water, looks back, hoping to restart the process, but no, it does not happen.

She screams, "No." The image does not come back. But she has felt what this technology—she believes it is a technology—can do. And what she can do with her own mind. She must grab hold of this. But the harder she tries to hold on, the more it just slips away.

SEARCHING FOR A WAY OUT

She leaves the cave, runs down the mountain and excitedly tells Dr. Eisenfield about her find—what a mistake that was—and they come back to the cave and he blunders around with that flashlight and she can't re-gain the state no matter how much she stares into the pool of water and then the avalanche obliterates the cave.

• • • •

ELECTRICITY RETURNS with a flash to the apartment. Oz squints. Back in her bathroom.

What she saw at the Signal building today has triggered all of this, hasn't it?

But now she wonders. The coincidences are piling up. Was that flashing light on the third floor intended to draw her up there? Was that a random Green Whip snake that just happened to lead her to the cave entrance? And were those Kri-Kri, who started the avalanche, just right there, right then, butting heads by accident?

She now remembers that the floor of the cave had no dust, even though it appeared to have been unused for a few thousand years.

Are there still some Minoans alive and are they sending her messages?

But why her?

She feels a little unsteady and sits on the toilet seat.

Just suppose that there are real, living Minoans? And suppose they are trying to send her some kind of message, trying to get her to find something? What could it be?

Better yet, where could she find it?

There can be only one place. The Signal building.

12

Jane Ozzimo and Midori Nakagawa grab a table inside Sprout Now, pointing their commDs down at the screen in the table's center to order their food.

Bursting to tell Midori the exciting things that happened to her today at the Signal building she launches into a recitation of events the second they meet in front of the restaurant, her arms flying through the air, hands rigid and fingers tight against each other as the words pour out to her only friend, the only person she trusts.

Oz says, "But it's killing me to have to wait until tomorrow, especially since I have to work at the kennel first."

"And this map . . . you say it shows some kind of labyrinth? And that's important because . . . because why?"

"Ok. You know about King Minos and the Minotaur, right?"

"Oh yeah, isn't he the guy who, whatever he touched turned into gold?"

"No. That was King Midas. Whole different guy," Oz says as she and Midori inch ahead in the line to order their food. "Minos was the son of Zeus and he became king of Crete and all the area around the Aegean Sea. His palace was in the city of Knossos, an area I spent some time in this past summer."

"I remember you saying it was hot and dusty."

"Yeah, really hot." Oz stops her hands in mid-air, waggles her fingers and begins again. "Minos had a bull that the god Poseidon told him to sacrifice. But Minos didn't want to sacrifice the bull. This pisses off Poseidon, and so he puts some kind of spell on Pasiphae—Minos's wife—to make her fall in love with the bull. She gives birth to the Minotaur, a creature that is half-man, half-bull."

"Oh, so the bull and her . . ."

SEARCHING FOR A WAY OUT

"Apparently. Anyway, the creature is a man-eating monster." Oz interlaces her fingers, breaks them apart, re-interlaces them.

"Where do you keep a Minotaur?" Midori continuing to scan the ever-revolving menu screen.

"Well, what Minos did was he hired Daedalus, an Athenian architect, who built the labyrinth in which the Minotaur was imprisoned. This labyrinth was so skillfully designed that no one who entered could escape. And, of course, eventually anyone caught in it would run into the Minotaur and be eaten."

"But who goes into this labyrinth to be eaten?"

"I'm coming to that. Minos had a son and a daughter. The son, Androgeus, was very athletic. He represented Crete in the games in Athens and won several events, sending the King of Athens into a rage of jealousy. So he kills him. Minos, when he hears this, flies into his own rage and sends the mighty Cretan fleet."

"This is quite some adventure," Midori says. "How do you remember it all?"

"While I was there in Crete, I heard this story about a million times from the locals." In the streetlight, Oz's open, creaseless face looks all sharp angles. "Anyway, Minos conquers Greece and starts importing virgins to feed to the Minotaur."

"Gruesome." Midori twists her lips in a scrunch of bitter distaste.

"Eventually, Theseus, the Athenian King's son, volunteers to go, planning to kill the Minotaur and end this humiliation for Athens."

"Sounds like a plan." Midori laughs. "Or not."

"Theseus arrives in Crete and meets Ariadne, King Minos's daughter. She falls for him. Doesn't want to lose him to the Minotaur. Well, it just so happens that Daedalus had previously told Ariadne the secret of the labyrinth after he had finished constructing it. So what she does is give Theseus a ball of thread—an extremely long ball of thread—which he unwinds as he walks deeper into the labyrinth. This is so he can find his way out after he kills the Minotaur."

Oz stops abruptly, as if someone suddenly interrupted her, and tilts her head back as though attempting to see something in the tree line, even though she's not actually focused on anything in this physical universe. She's seeing the image of Theseus, of the string, of the labyrinth. A moment of illumination. She grasps to make a connection.

She repeats herself, out loud, as if examining the words, nearly whispering, "Find his way back out. Back out. He marked his trail. The labyrinth . . ."

Her brain on fire.

Midori leans forward. "What about the labyrinth?"

"The labyrinth!" Oz feels the edge of discovery and leaps ahead.

She grabs both of Midori's hands and now her words come out much quicker. "Okay, okay . . . the labyrinth is traditionally thought to be a metaphor for the unconscious—or for life—like a person's journey through life. During the journey, you hit dead ends, double-backs, diversions, you get lost, must face the unknown, must face mysteries, but ultimately you head for the center, which here in this version, with the Minotaur, the monster, means you go to face your inner beast, the inner animal, and since the Minotaur is half-human, you must confront and get past the beast to get to your human self."

Oz clenches her hand into a fist as if trying to grab the next thought. "The process, the labyrinth, is always described as a going in. And Ariadne's thread has been seen as a lifeline that you unravel as you go deeper—you know, getting older, more of your life is revealed. But if this thread also leads you back out? What is that saying?"

Oz paces two steps out, two steps back. "By trailing out the thread behind him, Theseus created a map. A map of his journey.

SEARCHING FOR A WAY OUT

Both in and out. His own true path. If he doesn't have the map he is lost."

"I'm not quite following you," Midori says.

"We—all of us—are already stuck in the labyrinth. We got in just fine without a map. But we need a map to find our true path and to get out. To get past the Minotaur. After we defeat it, of course, which is a whole other thing."

Oz swings her head back and forth as if to make it clear to herself. She feels as though she's been trapped in the labyrinth since she was eleven. And now, maybe this map she found is how to get out. But this idea is so tenuous, so thin, nearly invisible.

Midori peers into Oz's eyes. "What does this have to do with what you saw today?"

"That map I found. Something about . . . I think it might be a map of the way out."

"Out of what?"

"Good question." Oz pivots left then right, then back like a desperate animal caught in a pen. "We're trapped or lost in this life, but . . . but does this mean we first need to get to the center or just get out altogether?" She pauses for just an instant. "No . . . yes, it must mean we need to go to the center first, deal with whatever is there, and then back out." Oz puts her hands over her eyes as if to see better inside. "No, that can't be right. That's too easy."

She stops, stands completely still. Not a twitch. Eight seconds, ten seconds go by. Then she says with a slow deliberate voice, choosing her words with precision, "The important thing here is not the labyrinth, not the going in or finding the way out, it's the marking of the trail, it's the map. It's finding your true path in this life. With the map, you have the key. Not a physical labyrinth, but a mental one."

Midori twists her lips. "But this map you found is a real map."

JOHN MOON FORKER

Oz's voice comes out a little raspy. "Yes, it is. A real map of a real place. So then, what is it really a map of? I mean, why would I need a map to somewhere that I don't even know where it is?"

"So that you don't get eaten by the Minotaur?" Midori says.

"I need a favor." Oz puts her hand on Midori's shoulder. "Tomorrow morning, call the kennel, speak to Mrs. Ascot. Tell her you're my Aunt Della and there's this emergency. Tell her I have to leave right away."

Oz dislikes the lie, but the urgency has trampled everything in the way.

"I'll do it first thing."

"No, wait. Give me about an hour. I want to see the dogs. Especially Circuit."

A robot, carrying their food orders on the top of its flat head, rolls over to them.

13

King Zee Whitehead sits cross-legged on the hardwood floor in a small room at the back of a three-story building that his One Faith organization owns.

Located on Hollywood Boulevard, the office building and the church in front of it had previously belonged to the Methodists, until they gave up on it and handed it over to the Episcopalians. Originally built in 1912, the church underwent multiple renovations and expansions before it was eventually abandoned.

Then the office building got built. Then it got abandoned.

In that room up on the third floor, Whitehead holds an acoustic guitar across his lap, his fingers not touching any of the strings, mouth slightly open, his breathing shallow.

Jason Buggleman stands ten feet in front of the seated King Zee Whitehead. He stands out of respect. He stands because there is nothing to sit on except the hard wooden floor. But then he hasn't been invited to sit.

Years with Mr. Whitehead and he still becomes nervous. Words pile up on his tongue and trip out of his mouth.

Mr. Whitehead lives back here. About the only other thing that Buggleman can see in the room is a rolled-up futon in the corner. He respects Mr. Whitehead's desire that his life be simple. That he wants no distractions. Distractions that material possessions would inevitably bring.

"We have to get those archeologists out of there and resume construction." Whitehead says this in a low, raspy, strung-out voice, a late-night voice, a different voice than he uses when addressing the enormous crowds. "We can't let them hold this up."

"The city—"

"Yes, yes, I know the city gets all excited when any little piece of history turns up. But what have they found? I hear it's a horseshoe and some old carriage. And they're going to stop construction on God's Palace for that?"

Jason has recently noticed that Mr. Whitehead seems to look even thinner than he usually does, older than his forty-eight years. Deep lines of experience crease his face. Or maybe just lines of worry, of stress. No smile to bring out the youth, just those dark, penetrating, and now bloodshot eyes.

He's concerned and knows Mr. Whitehead has been experimenting again with the inputs to the Surrender Ceremony—the ceremony that makes it possible for people to speak directly to God.

Pushing himself maybe too far. They don't really know the limits here, and it is very difficult to calculate the impact of the varying influences of the herbs, the hybrid MRI, the pulse and frequency of the Audio-Visual system plus all the different dosages for each one. All of this makes up the Direct to God device. The DTG.

The technicians help with the machines, but Mr. Whitehead deals with the herbs himself. Brought up from South America, from some tribe he once spent time with years ago. Long before Bug met him in the desert. But he didn't have the machines then, didn't physically have the herbs, just the vision from God. The compelling vision that opened the door to speak to God directly, to receive his advice, advice Bug needed to hear, to give his life some direction because it sure as heck didn't seem to be going anywhere before that.

He worked with a geologic team just outside of the military base at Twenty-Nine Palms. Their contract with the military to map out suitable locations for an additional airfield and Bug was basically their gopher.

That's where he met Mr. Whitehead. Or more accurately, that's where he found him.

SEARCHING FOR A WAY OUT

He only wishes that Mr. Whitehead would let him fully join in these experiments. Yes, he says it's too risky, but why can't he share in the risk? He too wants to improve the technology, to deepen the experience. He too wants to strengthen and expand the direct channel to God. He too wants to do this for Mr. Whitehead, for himself, and for the thousands of others who have rejected the interfering rules and corruption of organized religion and want to gain the security that only their own personal communication with God can provide. Where God is your advisor, always steering you in the right direction. All you have to do is ask. Pray, then listen.

"I think the city gave them a week," Jason says.

"What if they find something else? Are they given another week? A month? This could go on forever." Whitehead closes his eyes for two seconds.

"I'll stay on top of it."

"Which reminds me, Bug. Congratulations on getting that Utterback woman to change her story. Could have been a problem."

"Thank you." Jason beams at the praise. "That journalist, Nickell, was all set to broadcast the story. I told her we would make it up to her. To help her through her difficult times."

"We might have to do something about this Nickell person. He's been on our tail before." Whitehead looks at Bug in a way that Bug thinks he's talking about Jerry Groot, One Faith's large bodyguard, bouncer, enforcer, and how sending Jerry over to have a word with Nickell might bring him to his senses. Although Bug doesn't think this would be a good decision, it's not his decision to make.

"We might not be so lucky next time." Bug says, thinking of all the other, even more damaged, Surrender Ceremony participants who Nickell or anyone else in the media don't know about. All of which he's either witnessed first hand or has seen the video.

Hard to get some of those images out of his head. Like that young man—Luke, just about the same age as Bug—who did the ceremony, came out of it fine, was overjoyed at having established a connection to God. Then two days later he went mad. Running into a shopping center up on Fairfax and Sunset and slashed about eight people with a long, sharp knife, killing one woman, chopping her face into bits, all the while raving that God told him to do it.

"We will make our own luck if we keep improving the Surrender Ceremony. Make it work every time for everyone. That will stop the defections. And Bug, we need to stop them. Those people talk, they spew their evil all over the commD nodes and it hurts our cause."

When Jason hears Mr. Whitehead speak like this, his own sense of certainty rises. He feels more sure of himself and what he's doing. He can see the world more in black and white and less in the troubling grays.

A single glass of water sits on the floor beside Mr. Whitehead and five candles burn on the window ledge a few feet behind. He almost appears ghostly in this light.

Whitehead says in a low, even-toned voice. "We will move ahead Bug. I have a vision given to me by God to unite everyone under one roof, to eliminate all the middlemen, and bring each individual directly to God."

Whitehead rubs the back of his neck with his hand.

"You must be tired." Buggleman shifts on his feet, a pain in his legs from standing in one spot too long. He had always hated being called Bug all through school until Mr. Whitehead had called him that too. Now he loves the intimacy of it.

"You've been experimenting again. Taking unnecessary risks. Those herbs could be dangerous."

"It's God's work." Whitehead seems to slump slightly, looks away, and Jason takes that as a signal for him to leave. He's tired too, almost midnight. Been a long day.

But when he turns to go, Whitehead stops him. "I've noticed that you've become close to one of the other staff members. Tammy

SEARCHING FOR A WAY OUT

Box. Be careful, Bug. We don't have the time for such trivialities. Our work cannot get done when we stray. You need to remember that." Whitehead looking full at him now, no tiredness, eyes boring a hole into Jason's head. "Pray as hard as you can."

"Yes, Mr. Whitehead. I will remember." Bug turns quickly and leaves the room, softly closing the door behind him.

• • • •

WITH NO ONE TO WITNESS it, King Zee Whitehead cracks a slight, crooked smile, but it's gone in a moment.

Standing, he sets the guitar down on the floor and moves over to the windows, looking out at the night, here at the rear of the building. But there's not much to see, a small parking lot, the alley, the apartment buildings on the next street over. One light post offers a dim illumination. A rat skirts the edge of the light's circle and moves single-mindedly to wherever it's going, back into darkness.

He believed he had a firm grasp on his own mind. Purging all the material desires. Clearing a direct path to God.

But maybe not. His nerves twitch and feel jangly. Maybe he took too much of the herb this time. Juiced the AVS machine too high. Miscalculated the timing with the hMRI. Did too much of something.

But these self-imposed trials are necessary to fix the Surrender Ceremony. It just needs a little tweaking. Sure, some people—but really not that many—are coming out of the Surrender Ceremony, experiencing anxiety, depression, hallucinations, compulsive behavior. But he takes care of them. In fact, some of them even recover in a short amount of time, so hardly anyone is permanently injured. Yet, he can't let these failures grow. It will hurt One Faith, his business, his work.

Thinking about his experiment with that woman, Ruthie, in Hancock Park. He should continue that experiment. Yes, sexual desire is like a virus, and if not vigilantly watched, it will come crawling back, slithering into his system, entwining itself around every nerve stalk.

But that just makes the test more interesting. And when he resists the desire, it only makes him more powerful.

14

Nickell has to park seven blocks away from the site of the explosion. Damned Beverly Hills and their parking restrictions.

He doesn't normally mind walking, but he didn't sleep all that well last night and his body sags with tiredness.

The fragmentary sleep happened because his brain was cooking up ways for him to get deep inside One Faith and get a closer look at the inner workings, at the Surrender Ceremony, at Whitehead's corruption.

But his idea as to how to do this is dangerous.

Since Gina seems to admire Whitehead for whatever she believes he is doing for the good of the people—which is complete bullshit—then why not try to bring them together. He figures Whitehead would lust after Gina. Most guys did. And if Whitehead did make a sexual move, Nickell could step in and expose him as the fraud he is. His holier-than-thou purity.

Of course, if she were to get involved with him, she wouldn't likely to be all that forthcoming with information about those inner workings of One Faith even if she stumbled across any. At least not to him. The enemy of One Faith.

And maybe he feels a little guilty about using Gina as bait, but the second anything got wonky, he'd be right there. He wouldn't let anything happen to her.

He can work it so that even if she won't tell him anything, he'll find out anyway. Maybe use one of those Third Ear Nanosensors. Stick one on her body somewhere and then he would hear everything she hears. Up to a point anyway. Not if she unknowingly washes it off by taking a shower. And not if it doesn't transmit like these things have a habit of not doing. Something about them being just too thin and having their transmissions fouled up by the skin's electrical conductivity.

Barely daylight as he walks quickly up the quiet street. Lots of leafy trees here, but they look distressed. Dry, brown leaves on many of them. Even here in Beverly Hills, they prohibit watering.

He's still about three blocks away, but now he can see the plume of dark smoke rising like a crooked finger in the sky.

Initial reports say that a flower shop about half a block up from Wilshire Blvd on North Canon Drive had blown up. Volatile sewer gas had somehow ignited.

He takes out his commD and begins recording. He stops when he sees a manhole cover embedded sideways into the roof of a parked car, like some crippled flying saucer that was forced to crash land. This could be worse than he thought.

A few early morning gawkers on the sidewalks moving toward the scene, some looking up, nearly everyone with their own commDs out.

At first, he sees the damaged street, cratered, collapsed inward. And then he comes into full view of the remains of the flower shop, a black hole in the ground, barricades already set up by the Beverly Hills police holding everyone back. But Nickell uses his press pass to be allowed to come a little closer and stand in a small designated area with about half a dozen other journalists all busy waving their commDs around to take in every aspect of the scene.

Already seven or eight news bots hovering in the air.

Nickell sees flower petals strewn over the remains of the sidewalk and the street.

Worse is the smell.

Rising out of the trench that used to be a street is a lava-like miasma. Raw sewage. Human waste.

Nickell pulls his shirt up and covers his mouth and nose. Little help. He could vomit. Make things worse. He forces it down.

SEARCHING FOR A WAY OUT

Seeing destruction like this only increases his own personal sense of despair, never mind the general abundance of it in the country. Things just can't keep going this way. Nickell is both worried and angry. We have to turn things around.

With the live stream of images he's sending back to The Data Transfer's headquarters in India, he knew it wouldn't be long before Ramesh contacted him.

"Mr. Nickell, this is excellent, this is so gratifying to see and that filthy hole in the ground is stupendous."

"What are you talking about, Ramesh? This is a disaster."

"You are in Beverly Hills, are you not? This is wonderful. The richest spot in the richest nation—the formerly richest nation—and even here the destruction happens, the human shit flows. The rest of the world will eat this up if you will pardon my pun."

Ramesh gloating. Ramesh likes to kick those who are down. Nickell presses his lips together to keep from saying something he would regret.

He so desperately wants to leave The Data Transfer and not just because of Ramesh, but if the city continues to disintegrate like this, it might be too late to catch on with another news organization. More destruction like this will only hurt an already poor economy and dry up all the few remaining employment opportunities.

"Hey, Ramesh, I gotta go." He cuts the connection.

Beverly Hills waking up. Motorists and some few pedestrians arrive for the day, but the day has already been broken. Street closed, flowers dead, routines diverted.

He's got to make things happen.

How is he going to bring Gina to Whitehead's attention? Well, isn't it likely that Whitehead is perturbed by the halt in the construction of his cathedral? And might it be possible that he would be interested in knowing someone who was actually working on the site? Part of the archeological team?

He'll suggest to Gina that they attend one of those public Surrender Ceremonies. They have them all the time.

Then he just positions Gina in a location where Whitehead is sure to see her. Then let his degenerate nature take its course.

Yes, he realizes he would put Gina in danger. And yes, it feels a little like he's betraying himself because it reminds him of his actions with Dana Mostolinni, but Whitehead is the danger. He must be stopped.

15

At the far end of the north wing of the kennel, Oz is on her knees in the last cage. She's running her hands down the dog's back.

Circuit sits, looking at Oz, her nose pulsating a mile a minute.

Circuit is a copper-colored female, weighing forty-nine pounds, of a breed unfamiliar to Oz. She gave Circuit her name because the dog relentlessly paces around and around in her cage.

She's grown very close to this dog in the three weeks that she has been here. Never a good idea because they are gone all too soon. Some adopted, but most just terminated. Luckily, Circuit here has been adopted and they should pick her up in a few days.

So Oz wants to spend a little time with her even though she's aching to get to the Signal building. But with Midori's call likely to come any minute to spring her loose, she wants to give Circuit as much attention as she can.

She allows herself to express love only here because feeling love also brings on the loneliness. Not only will Circuit be gone soon, but her showing love for anything only reminds her of the love that has been cauterized. And today it is worse because today is the twenty-second anniversary of the day that she and her parents and her brother walked down into what is called the Little Grand Canyon in the Shawnee National Forest in Southern Illinois.

They were on a camping trip. They had been hiking, and so when they had arrived at the Little Grand Canyon they were tired and her father said they ought to turn back, that they could always return tomorrow, but Oz wouldn't hear of it. She wanted to explore the enticing canyon below, the twisty path, the looming rock formations, the cathedral of trees. It appeared magical.

So, at her insistence, they gave in and walked down. But then the rains came, heavy rains, and they thought they could wait it out under a ledge, but the canyon acted as a natural funnel and soon the volume of water rushing down flooded the floor of the canyon and they were all swept away. She hardly remembers that part, just remembers the terror, being unable to breathe, trapped.

It was a miracle that she survived. The others didn't.

But she's been through this anniversary twenty-one times before, so she knows that however dreadful this day will be, she'll get through it.

She pulls Circuit closer, rubs her belly, Circuit licking her face.

Her mind drifts in the past while she mostly yet unsuccessfully tries to reel it in. She's got to get up and do some work here. Shovel out the cages. Scoop up the overnight biosolids.

But she happens to look down at her hand rubbing Circuit's belly and notices the edge of some mark there. She looks a little closer and what she sees surprises her. Looks like a labrys, the Minoan double-axe. She blinks, shakes her head. Looks again. Okay, maybe she's just reading into this. Yeah, it kind of looks like that, but not perfectly exactly totally certain. But so close. She rubs it with her finger. Still can't quite believe it. Must have this whole Minoan thing on the brain after yesterday and now she's seeing it where it has no business being. But wow, that sure looks like . . . and she recalls that labrys and labyrinth come from the same root and that map she found appears to be of a labyrinth.

Sitting back, she says to Circuit, "That's some birthmark you've got there. If that's what it is."

That's when she hears her name broadcast over the kennel intercom system. Summoning her to the office.

Midori must have called. Good. Time to get out of here.

She kisses Circuit on the forehead and says, "I will see you before you leave here for your new home."

Leaving the north wing, Oz walks toward the hub of the kennel, to the office.

SEARCHING FOR A WAY OUT

The Canine Connection is constructed like a wheel, the administration building in the center with four spokes coming out, each being a wing of the kennel where the dogs are housed. In between the spokes are mostly outdoor pens.

She walks into the office and spots Mrs. Ascot standing behind her cluttered desk holding her commD up to nearly eye level, as if searching for a secret passage. It's the posture of an older person, like Mrs. Ascot, dealing with a new technology, like the commD—although it's a technology that's been around for about ten years in its present form—and appearing completely flustered by it. She must be looking for the keypad to type in something with her fingers, but those old-fashioned keypads went out a long time ago. Doesn't she yet know that all she has to do is to speak into it?

"Jane, your Aunt Della called, says there's a family emergency and needs you to come over to her house right now." Mrs. Ascot puts her hand to her face. She makes a noise with her lips. "I don't know why she didn't just call you directly."

"She's a little old-fashioned that way," Oz says, feeling guilty to be lying to Mrs. Ascot this way, but she needs to get back to the site.

"Well then—"

A couple walk in interrupting Mrs. Ascot. Look to be in their early fifties. The balding man says, "We need to house our dog for a couple of weeks as we will be away."

Mrs. Ascot smiles, "Of course, of course, let me show you the facilities." She turns her head back to Oz. "So Jane, I hope this emergency isn't too serious." And as Mrs. Ascot escorts the couple out of the office, she quickly glances back at her desk with a worried look, but immediately turns and leaves.

Oz has taken two steps toward the door herself when she notices Mrs. Ascot's furtive look. She stops for a second. Should she? Cannot resist her curiosity. Just take a quick look.

She sees a small sheath of papers with a thin red border along the top.

From some company called Protein Providers. It looks like a purchase order. A purchase order? What would the Canine Connection be selling to some other company that required them to issue a purchase order?

In the column under description is just an item number: X34-D99. What is that supposed to mean?

She runs her eyes down toward the bottom of the purchase order and in a small box sees: 7 dogs >50 lbs. + 5 dogs between 25-50 lbs. + 10 dogs less than 25 lbs.

Hand-written by Mrs. Ascot is a list of the dogs. Oz immediately sees that Circuit is one of them.

But what about Circuit's adoption? Did that fall through?

She pulls out her commD and speaks, "Profile of company, Protein Providers."

What she sees leaves shocks her. The result of the search shows an Asian company that specializes in turning dogs into meat for human consumption.

A hollow feeling like some malevolent embolism descends on her. Mrs. Ascot is selling these dogs for meat.

How could she do this? It can't really be for the money, because how much could you get for a few dogs? But then a few dogs here and there over time, add up. Maybe it is for the money. But wait, she remembers something about the City of Los Angeles rewarding kennel owners who have a high adoption rate by giving them more business, more dogs.

Then the adoption of Circuit and all these dogs is phony. There was no adoption. Ascot is just making it look like there was.

Her anger boils. Find that old bat and slap her. But no, she must restrain herself. Wouldn't do any good and she can't trust herself to

SEARCHING FOR A WAY OUT

be calm. Look at her encounter with Dr. Eisenfield. That didn't go well.

But she has to leave, although she really wants to run back into the north wing and snatch Circuit out. Can't do that. Where would she go? Can't bring her home. Dogs are not allowed, so her roommates would freak out. But she's got to get to the Signal building. Got to check that out.

She looks back down at the documents and sees that the dogs won't be picked up until Friday, three days away.

She'll figure this out. Stop this from happening. She has to.

16

Oz is three feet down in the hole with a shovel in her hands next to five other students also digging.

She looks up at the Signal building. She so wants to break away and get inside. But Dr. Eisenfield is right here. Can't get away yet.

Frustrated, yes. Combine that with the chaos inside her head about Circuit and this twenty-second anniversary of her parent's death. Why today? Why all of this today?

Before she even arrived, the team here had uncovered an enormous mass of fungi and while digging around it, they had struck some kind of wall or structure and most of them, including her, were now working to see exactly what it is.

Dr. Eisenfield wanders off to the far side of the site to check on some others who keep finding more and more horseshoes. Mostly because the digging has gone beyond the carriage and into what must have been the stables. This is turning into an Easter egg hunt.

She sees a chance now to go over to the building, but then looks up and sees a city services truck out on the street waiting for the security guard to let them in.

"What are they doing here?" Oz says to Sid Juvelics, who has been leaning on his shovel for the last five minutes, not doing much of anything except whispering to Gina Woolander who is on the other side of him, not working her shovel much either.

"I heard that they've come to clear out all the remaining junk in that building. Something about recycling. Lots of paper. Some city ordinance."

Now she can't go, can't search for anything else. Hemmed in on all sides. Almost by rote, she turns back to shoveling while trying to push everything else out of her thoughts. Just dig.

SEARCHING FOR A WAY OUT

After another hour of digging, the archeology team uncovered much more of the slab of concrete that might be a wall and the fungi surrounding it.

Oz wonders if this might be some kind of underground room. They have uncovered a corner where two slabs meet, and this seems to indicate the possibility of it being a room.

Maybe the map will help. Oz looks around to see where Dr. Eisenfield is. Not in sight. Don't want him seeing this map or any of the other students for that matter. So she hops out of the hole and walks over to the department van to get some water, and positioning herself out of view of most everyone, pulls the map from her pocket and takes a look.

If this is a diagram of this property—which she has to assume it is if it's to do her any good—then maybe this underground wall or room is on it.

She tries to calculate where she is standing in relation to the lines on the map. So, if she is here, and that's where the building is, then this line here might be what is reaching out to that possible underground room. Then does the line show a connection between the room and the building? Is this a tunnel?

The only way to find out is to go inside and look for some kind of door or entrance.

She folds the map and puts it back in her pocket. Then, while watching for Dr. Eisenfield, hurries to the Signal building.

Inside, she goes behind what must have been the reception area to the side of the building closest to where she had been digging, and in an empty office she surprises Sid and Gina, who have beat her in here and have entwined against the wall kissing like there is no tomorrow.

Oz clears her throat.

The couple disengages. Sid smiling like some ten-year-old kid caught on one of the porn nodes and Gina looking off to the side as if trying to become invisible.

It's been a very long time since Oz has seen two people kissing in real life. Part of her is embarrassed for them, but she also feels a small magnetic pull as if she'd like to do that too—but absolutely not with Sid—and this she immediately cuts off. No, that's not for her. Not what she is about.

"Don't mind me." With that Oz turns toward the far wall, which is two large sliding closet doors. Another closet. Another bull? She hesitates, then rips forward and slides the left door to the right.

Empty. But not barren.

Sid and Gina have completely disengaged and have followed Oz across the room.

"What are you doing?" Sid asks.

Without turning her head around to face him, Oz says, "You saw that wall out there. I think it might be an underground room and the entrance might be here somewhere."

On the back wall of the closet, she sees four symbols. Definitely Minoan. The double-headed axe, a snake or serpent, the sun, and a tree.

She touches the snake, and a door, which had been invisible, opens inward down to what looks to be a dark tunnel.

"How did you know which one?" Gina says.

"Something I ran into on Crete."

Oz walks right down the tunnel, her left hand on the wall for support in this darkness, Gina and Sid trailing behind a bit more slowly.

Then Oz sees the blue glow. Just like the cave. Her heart practically skips a couple of beats. Could it be? Could she find here what she found on Crete?

SEARCHING FOR A WAY OUT

Her excitement draws her forward. Here, she can see that the massive fungi that the team has discovered topside are all over the ceiling and the upper walls, and it is this that gives off the glow.

In a short time, she descends to the bottom and finds a room. It's small, maybe ten feet by ten feet. And all across the floor is a cluster of vases. All intricately decorated with exactly the kinds of images found on many other Minoan vases dug up on Crete in the last century and a half.

Oz stoops to examine one. An image of four priestesses gathered around burning logs.

"Are these Minoan?" Gina says.

"Looks like it. Oz feels thrilled just to hear herself say it. She looks around for anything that might suggest evidence of what she experienced in that cave. Something she can absorb herself into. Get back to that place in her head where she feels that tremendous sense of freedom.

Sid says, "Oh boy, Dr. Eisenfield has got to see this. I'll go get him." He turns and runs back up the tunnel.

"Where did all this come from?" Gina asks.

"It either came from Crete, or it was made here."

"Are you thinking this might have something to do with the legend?"

"Maybe. That's what we need to find out." Oz is on her hands and knees crawling carefully around the vases. Don't want to knock one over.

Then, in the corner, she sees something leaning against the wall on the floor. Touching it, she thinks it feels like some kind of oilcloth, and when she lifts that off she finds what she assumes is a clay tablet. It has a drawing of a staff. A staff covered in symbols. It's a little too dark in here to see all of them, but she can tell it's Minoan. The bull is a dead giveaway.

Her hand shakes. This is it. This must be what she's looking for. The evidence, the key.

Gina stoops next to her. "Is that a clay tablet?"

"Ah, maybe, but it feels too heavy. This might be metal."

"Look, there's writing."

"Yeah," Oz says, "hard to see."

"Covered in dirt. All that grime. What is it?"

"We will have to clean it off, but at the bottom. Looks like it says *operating instructions*."

"I'll bet this is important. Wait until Dr. Eisenfield sees this. He'll crap."

Oz stands, glances around the room. Once he arrives, it will be a madhouse in here.

While Gina crouches down to get a closer look at the tablet, Oz slides over to the opposite corner, being careful not to accidentally kick one of the vases, hoping to uncover something else, slaps her hand on the wall and leans over to look down into this corner.

She can hear several pairs of feet slapping down the tunnel and seeing nothing in this corner is about to look away when she catches a brief gleam of low light emanating from the vase below her. Reaching down into the vase, she feels a stone. Pulling it up, it too, just like the staff, is covered in symbols.

The feet behind her are close.

She shoves the stone into her pocket and turns around.

17

Oz catches Gina looking away. Did she see her put the stone in her pocket? Oz doesn't know but just then Dr. Eisenfield and Sid and Mervin and three undergraduates all clump into the small room or try to but are mostly blocked by all the vases.

With Mervin and two of the undergraduates swinging their flashlights around, it looks like a Hollywood opening.

Gina says, "Look, here in the corner. Oz found a clay . . . or maybe metal tablet."

Eisenfield wedges himself in between the end of the vases and the wall. Picks up the tablet. "Mervin, shine that light here."

Eisenfield scans it up and down. "Is that writing? What do *operating instructions* mean? Huh, both English and what is that? Linear A?"

"Looks like it," Mervin says.

Few words visible but probably more under the crude. Oz sees the phrase *eternal life*.

Eisenfield reads out loud, "*The final mystery. Must be something.*"

Why is he saying this in such a dry, abstract way, Oz wonders? Why isn't he enthusiastic about this? Even if it is just a collection of long-held artifacts, he should be jumping up and down. The vases alone might be close to four thousand years old.

Oz finds herself virtually trapped back here in the corner. Too tight. She needs to get out.

"Well, we can't translate the Linear A," Mervin says.

Eisenfield rubs his chin with two fingers while staring at the tablet.

"Look," Gina says, "there's a couple more words, *the tool*."

"And there," Mervin says, "*Atlantis*."

Oz's thoughts jump from one phrase to another. What tool? Atlantis? Does this mean that some Minoans came here a couple of thousand years ago? How would that be possible? She can hardly get her head around it. Here! Well, maybe here. What if all this in the room is just some collection that came from somewhere else?

They mention Atlantis. Does that mean it is near here? Or they thought it was near here. But even if it is not, them mentioning it makes it more real. Definitely exciting. What if she could find it? What would it be like? The possibilities do somersaults in her brain. What if, what if...

She thinks about the stone in her pocket. The stone she should show to Dr. Eisenfield, but knows she won't. Wrong to keep it, but she has to see. Has to find out.

Dr. Eisenfield leads everyone back up the tunnel and out of the building with instructions for Mervin to get a team and cart all the vases out to the van. He warns them all not to tell anyone about this. That he will contact the city and try to buy them more time at the site.

Looking up into the sky at the increasing number of news bots, he tells Oz and Gina to get the tablet out of sight, to take it back to the archeology lab on campus and try to clean it up as that might allow them to see more.

Oz was hoping to speak to Dr. Eisenfield, to point out to him how what they've found today could be important to her thesis, how it might be the evidence he needs to approve it, except that she is more hoping than believing and what they have so far isn't really enough, but if there is more on the tablet that can be translated maybe something will turn up so she is eager to get to the lab and find out.

Outside in the sunshine and the hundred-degree-plus heat, there are already four news bots hovering overhead. The finding of the

SEARCHING FOR A WAY OUT

huge fungi and the uncovering of the underground wall have generated some interest.

But as soon as the news bots spot Oz and Gina hurrying away with something in Oz's arms two of them follow.

Sid tells some of the other students what they found and soon some of these students get on their commDs and the news spreads quickly so that even more news bots begin showing up.

And when Mervin and some others haul out the vases, even covered by tarps, the secret is out.

Thirty minutes later, long after Oz and Gina have driven away, each in her own car, Dr. Renford Eisenfield stands at the open gate leading onto the Signal building site.

He is smiling. A smile of endurance, not joy.

Arrayed in front of him are four journalists and hovering just above them are eleven news bots. Behind the journalists and across the street are forty-two interested onlookers. More arriving every minute. All of them prevented from getting any closer by a half-dozen members of the city's security force.

Dr. Eisenfield conducts a hastily arranged news conference. Arranged by him.

"What is the significance of the tablet?" A reporter from the Gotcha Channel asks.

"It was my great good fortune to find this artifact. It most likely shows that ancient civilizations could reach much farther than we had previously thought."

"What does it say?"

"We haven't fully translated it yet."

"We've heard that it mentions Atlantis. Do you think—"

Eisenfield cuts him off. "It's too early to speculate on that."

"Isn't it true that it was one of your graduate students who actually found this item?" A woman reporter with somewhat frizzy hair asks.

"Everyone here works under my direction. I am responsible for all the operations here."

Twenty feet away, Sid Juvelics says to Melissa Canovoot, "Did you hear that? He's taking all the credit for what Oz found. Oh, my God." He slaps his forehead.

"Look at all these people. Like something they've been waiting for." Melissa twiddles a strand of hair between two fingers.

18

"Come on, Sandy, open the door."

"Go away," the voice muffled by the thick black-painted door.

Nickell spins on his heels on the concrete walkway trying to think of what he can say that will convince Sandy Utterback to open the door to her apartment to let him in and then be able to talk her out of not pressing charges against Whitehead for the sexual assault that she originally accused him of but then backed away from under pressure from Whitehead, no doubt.

He drove all the way to Van Nuys, where he swears it must be twenty degrees hotter than in the basin, here on Buffalo Ave, maybe half a block south of Oxnard Street, where his shirt is already showing large patches of sweat.

And her goddamn apartment building is like some kind of fortress, what with security gates and locked doors all over the place which, for him to get in, he had to wait until someone was leaving and then catch the door before it closed. Had to do that three times to get up here. Took forever and garnered him several dirty looks from people who thought he was doing something shady but who, thankfully, were in too much of a hurry to stop and question him.

"We had him, Sandy. We were this close, and you could still make it happen."

"I've got nothing to say to you."

She's on the third floor and you'd think there would be a breeze up here. But no. He looks over the railing down into the courtyard, where there used to be a small grassy lawn and a pool. Grass dead, pool empty.

He makes a mistake touching the metal railing, which has been basking in direct sunlight for who knows how long, and he yanks his burned fingers up and sticks them in his mouth.

"So, Sandy, what are you going to do now? What are you going to do with the rest of your life?"

"That's none of your business."

A next-door neighbor opens his Venetian blinds and glares out at Nickell, clearly displeased with all the shouting.

His commD signals him. Incoming message.

He can see that it's Ramesh. Now what?

He allows Ramesh's image to appear on the screen. But before he can even greet the man, Ramesh says, "Have you seen it yet?"

"Seen what?" He's a little pissed off at Ramesh's tone.

"Holy Christ, man, what are you, blind and deaf?"

"Shouldn't you be sleeping about now?"

A comment Ramesh ignores. "The big find they are making at that archeological digging. Right there in your own city. You must be practically sitting right at the top of it."

"What are you talking about?" But even as he asks this question, he has split the commD screen and is searching the local news nodes.

He can see that video is being shot from one of those airborne bots and they are above a mostly barren lot with an empty four-story building at one end. Down below are young people running around, a couple of trucks and a backhoe.

But the bots zoom in and he sees flashes of a few things that make little sense.

"I'm seeing something now on a screen, but I don't know what it's showing me," Nickell says.

"How would you be knowing anything with your head up your rear end?" Ramesh is practically foaming at the mouth, but Nickell is watching the other screen, averting being sucked into Ramesh's rantings.

SEARCHING FOR A WAY OUT

"Found something looks like," Nickell says.

"Well, let me tell you, Mr. Nickell. They have found a huge underground fungus that they can't yet measure it's so big. And most important of all, they have found an ancient clay tablet that speaks of Atlantis. Can you imagine how our viewers will eat this up?"

"Is this the Signal building?"

"Now you're beginning to catch on. Yes. And you need to go be there right this very second."

Maybe he can find Gina there, Nickell thinks. Ask her to go to a Surrender Ceremony.

"And those celebrity interviews?" Nickell asks. "Do you still want—"

"Yes, yes, yes and do those also with no delay."

"But—"

"No buts Mr. Nickell."

19

Two of the flying news bots track Oz and Gina all the way to campus, hovering over her Electron and Gina's car as well, and right along with them to the doors of the building containing the archeology lab.

Hounded by these machines, Oz walks so quickly she's almost running. With her long legs, Gina has no problem keeping up.

But once inside the lab, Oz feels relief. Many hours spent here studying artifacts, being absorbed in her work, shutting out the rest of the world.

This part of the lab is one long room with seven-foot-high wooden shelves, stained a dark, rust color, running alongside the walls on either side for twenty feet and all crammed with artifacts collected over the years. All of it pretty much junk at least as far as having monetary value, but no matter whether pieces of thousand-year-old pottery, a coppery arrowhead, a silver-gray spear, or papyrus with written records of the financial transactions of trading items like cedar wood or incense in Egypt, they all allow her to contact that ancient world. That is their real value to her.

They walk through the long room to a much smaller one at the back. On a table sits a modified Nd:YAG laser. Oz has worked with this one many times.

A type of laser originally used in tattoo removal. Then dermatologists adapted it for working with various skin conditions and then museums tweaked it a little more and started using it to restore old artworks. After that, archeologists modified it still further to work with ancient artifacts. The addition of nanotechnology has made it a precise tool. It scans the artifact, determines what is inherent to the object, what is extraneous, and then uses the laser to separate the two.

SEARCHING FOR A WAY OUT

And this object appears to have a good amount of the extraneous.

Oz sets the tablet into the cradle as carefully as she can because she is trembling with excitement. Gina hovers right behind her.

Powering up the laser, they both watch as it scans the surface, deciding what it's going to vaporize.

Four minutes later, it begins its work with a low hum.

Oz cannot see the laser burning away the encrustations accumulated on the surface of the tablet over the assumed years of its existence. But the process ought to make the writing clearer. She hopes so. She wants to read more.

"Who do you suppose put this thing in that room?" Gina asks.

"No idea."

"Could it have anything to do with the legend?"

Oz doesn't know what to say to Gina. She doesn't have answers. Gina is popular, maybe a dozen years younger than her, gets along with everyone. Was very popular on Crete this past summer. Flocks of men.

"You do recognize the writing here as partially in Linear A?" Oz says.

"Of course."

"But you're not really interested in all this." Oz nods to the outer room. "Archeology. Digging up artifacts. Doing the work."

"My grandfather. He's rich, he wanted me to do this. He got me in."

"So you aren't at all interested in what we might find here?"

"Oh, sure. If it's important. If it leads to some kind of treasure. That would be cool."

It's easy to forget most people are not as driven as her. But Oz is who she is and can't help that now.

After sixteen minutes, the laser stops. Sixteen minutes to think about Circuit and what she might do. Thinking about that black stone she has in her pocket. Thinking about the evidence this tablet might give, hoping that it might give.

But finally it's done and Oz removes the tablet from the cradle and sets it on the table. It's definitely metal. And near the bottom are those two words in English. That's strange. So maybe this isn't that old.

Operating Instructions. Instructions to what? This wooden staff drawn on the surface here? But a staff doesn't need operating instructions.

That's not important.

But there's more to see now. More words in English. Which likely means this object is not that old. Certainly not thousands of years old.

Gina reads, "*Unlock the power of the instrument.* What instrument?"

"Maybe they mean this staff, which doesn't make much sense."

Oz picks up the object and, bringing it a little closer, reads, "*Eternal life.*"

Are they talking about immortality here?

"Something else," Gina says, "*The final mystery.* What on earth could that be?"

An idea clicks. Oz says, "The Minoans were very much investigating the workings of the mind. They found something. Some way to push ahead, to transcend thinking or the mind or something along those lines."

"Really? You see all that. I don't see that."

"There's more to the story. Crete. Last summer."

"But... "

"They weren't just investigating, they were discovering how the mind works and then, most likely . . . most likely what? Sounds as if they were moving on, progressing to . . . to somewhere. Where would that somewhere be? Is that Atlantis?"

SEARCHING FOR A WAY OUT

"Atlantis here? Where would that be? Catalina Island? Right."

Oz didn't realize Gina was capable of being sarcastic.

The lab door bangs open.

Stomping all the way to the back, Dr. Eisenfield says, "Those damn news bots are everywhere. They're swarming out there like we've found the Holy Grail."

"We've found something," Gina says. "More words."

Dr. Eisenfield walks around the end of the table and comes close to Oz, who is still holding the object.

Oz watches him closely. What's here has got to help her case.

Eisenfield nods slightly. "This is good. Fine. Doesn't tell us much, but we'll see how it goes. But what are these operating instructions about? Was that added later?"

"Isn't this a confirmation that the Minoans were investigating the mind, that they were even pushing ahead? This is the evidence."

For a moment, Dr. Eisenfield says nothing. Then he turns toward Oz and says, "Jane, this says nothing of the sort. You're reading into it. I can understand how you would think this, but you're very biased."

In the first moment, Oz wonders if she *is* too close to this. Maybe her judgment is bad. But no, that's not it. His immediate rejection of this new information just came too quickly. She now suspects there is something else going on. Does he just have some personal dislike of her? Did that incident in the Minoan cave poison him to her?

• • • •

SHE TURNS HER HEAD and glances down at the side of the object. What is that? Peering closer, she sees what looks like a port, like on some electronic device.

But something more. Her thumb is on the upper right corner of the object and it feels loose. Like a flap. One that shouldn't be there.

She pulls at it and the whole front face of the object comes off in her hand.

"What are you doing?" Eisenfield blurts out.

"It just came apart."

Inside is an empty rectangular space with just traces of wires and etchings dug into the metal surface left behind. Makes Oz think this thing was once loaded with electronic parts. But they have been ripped out.

"What . . ." Gina stops in mid-air.

"This is . . ." begins Eisenfield, but right then is a knock on the lab door. Then a voice from the other end of the long room. "Hello, hello, is anybody here?"

Gina rushes out to see who it is and the next thing Oz hears is Gina saying, "Nickell, what in the world are you doing here?"

"Well, hi, Gina."

Dr. Eisenfield frowns and then walks into the other room as well. Oz follows right behind, wanting to see.

"What is this? What do you want?" Dr. Eisenfield says with both impatience and condescension.

Nickell looks over at Oz and says, "Hello, would you be Jane Ozzimo?"

Oz has a kind of recognition. No, she's never met him before, but she knows him or knows a part of him. It's in the combination of assertiveness and hesitancy. They don't work all that well together in him. One drags the other down. Yes, there is a weight in him like he's been damaged and is now cautious. Been doing it for so long it's become instinctual.

Oz sees he's holding his commD out as though he's about to record if he hasn't begun already.

But before Oz can say anything to him, Dr. Eisenfield says to Gina, "You know this person?"

"He's my next-door neighbor."

SEARCHING FOR A WAY OUT

"I'm Nickell, with The Data Transfer. I hear you've made an important discovery over at the old Signal building."

"Which would be none of your business. You had better be going."

"And you would be the head of the archeology department here?" Nickell says, stepping into the room.

"I . . . you . . . now listen, you have to leave. You are not allowed in here."

"Could I just have five minutes with you or with Jane here? Could be outside if you'd like. Just letting the world know about your brilliant discovery."

Oz can see the gears grinding in Dr. Eisenfield's head.

He opens his mouth and hesitates, then says, "We have nothing to say at this time. Perhaps later, but not right now. Please leave."

"But if you've found something important, shouldn't the public be informed?"

"If we do find something important, I'll be the first one to let the public know. Now please." Eisenfield sweeps his arm toward the door as if to transport the intruder out on a magic carpet.

Nickell moves another step into the room. "And you, Ms. Ozzimo, what do you think the public should know?"

Oz smiles but only shakes her head. She can see that he doesn't enjoy doing this. Doesn't like it at all. And that business about the public. A trick to get Dr. Eisenfield talking. The public will find out with or without our help. It will leak out of every commD node in minutes if it hasn't already.

Eisenfield moves forward. "Okay, okay, thank you for your valuable input. Time to go now."

"Okay, but remember, Nickell, The Data Transfer."

"And if you don't need me, I'll go too," Gina says.

Dr. Eisenfield just waves his hand and looks down and to the left. And then he walks over and locks the door to the lab and then turns to Oz.

"You don't say a word about this." He points at what she thought to be a tablet and is now considered a destroyed electronic device.

"I won't, but don't you think that all this applies to my thesis?"

"Listen Jane, I've spoken with Dr. Vasquez and we've gone over your ideas for your thesis and while Dr. Vasquez thinks your ideas merit attention, she agrees with me you simply do not have enough evidence to demonstrate that the Minoans were not only exploring the mind but developing some sort of technology to improve or change it. I'm sorry, but your thesis, as it stands, is not acceptable."

"But doesn't this," and here she too points at the object, "exactly shows what I have been saying?"

"No. Just drop it. You should go back to your original thesis. That has traction."

The inside of her chest feels as if it has a large brick in it. Then two bricks, then three, then more. Packed in there tight, not letting her lungs expand and breathe, not letting her heart pump blood throughout her veins.

She's looking down at the floor. Cannot meet his eyes. Cannot say anything. The room rings in silence. All that she has worked for now flushed down the toilet.

• • • •

FIFTY FEET BEYOND THE archeology building's entrance, in the shade of a tall gum tree, Nickell and Gina talk.

"I'm sorry about what I said the other day about One Faith. I really know nothing about it," Nickell says, watching her oval face.

"That's okay, don't worry about it." She gives a small smile but is looking out over the campus and the steady stream of students walking to and from class.

SEARCHING FOR A WAY OUT

"There could be something to it. Why don't you and I go see what's going on over there? See a public Surrender Ceremony or go to one of the talks."

"Yeah, that would be good. Let's do that."

20

Oz staggers toward the parking garage.

Her world is now officially turned upside down. She is screwed. No December graduation. No archeology job. No future. Bleak, bleak, bleak.

To stay in school she would have to revert to her previous boring thesis, take another six months at least, and where's the money going to come from for that? Scholarships and grants all run out at the end of the year. Nothing in the pipeline.

She sees only smears of light. No focus. Where is her car? Memory wiped clean. Her brain simply does not work. Can't think. Throat constricting.

So caught up in her thoughts of doom, she doesn't see Nickell until he steps toward her and says, "Got a minute?"

Shock to the nervous system. "What . . . "

"Sorry, didn't mean to scare you." He looks at her. "Are you okay?"

"No, I mean . . ." She can't be a mess like this. Not in front of him. Not in front of anybody. But this is so . . . so much pressure . . . so much . . . all coming down on her at once.

Oz lurches forward, stumbles and puts out both hands, slapping them up against a cement post to keep from falling.

"What happened to you?" Nickell says this with surprise in his voice.

"Nothing. Never mind." Feeling dizzy, short of breath, she continues to hold on to the concrete stanchion. Wouldn't do to fall down. How will she . . . what does she do now?

She looks at him. Who is this person? Can she trust him? A voice in her head says "Run."

SEARCHING FOR A WAY OUT

"Hey, can I . . ." Nickell looks around. "Nowhere to sit around here. Is your car close?"

"No idea where my car is. No idea." She shakes her head as if she could empty it of all thought and maybe get a fresh start, but the black anvil of her now ruined future isn't budging.

Oz pushes away from the post and walks slowly away from Nickell and toward where she hopes her car will magically materialize since her internal GPS is malfunctioning. Got to be on this level, right? Or is it one-up?

Maybe she should look at him, really look at him. She turns.

Nickell catches up. "What does finding this clay tablet mean?"

"So you know what it is."

"Sure. The resolution on those cameras the news bots have is pretty good. And we know it was you who found it, not your friend back there, Eisenfield, who took credit for it. Your fellow students made sure of that."

"Why do you care about some obscure clay tablet?" Standing still now. Asking him questions brings her out of herself, a small distance away from the pain. A short inch of relief except looking at the future and seeing there is no future, not long-term, not short-term. She doesn't even know what she will do tomorrow and looking down a long stretch of time only makes her feel worse. Maybe after she sleeps. She's so tired.

"I don't really. Got assigned to do this by my editor. But he thinks it's not so obscure. Thinks that it might be associated with that legend you archeologists dug up years ago. That the paradise of Atlantis is within reach and that all of this hopelessness and despair eating the world can all be turned around." He shrugs. "Thinks the viewers won't be able to get enough of it."

"Paradise?" Hearing this is too much. She turns and turns again. The world spins and she doesn't know whether it's better to stop it or just to let it go faster and faster. Now the tears do come and she turns again and without knowing how it happened, her head is on his chest, his arms are around her and she's crying a flood.

She has leaped before she looked.

After a minute, she turns her head, reaches up with her fingers and touches his face.

He bends in an awkward and confused way, as if her touching him is a signal to kiss her, but a signal he's not completely sure of.

She backs her head up and says, "No."

But her fingers stay where they are.

21

Even in this heat, King Zee Whitehead doesn't wear short-sleeve shirts. The less skin exposed, the better. Less skin, less temptation. Less thinking about it.

But then he isn't in this heat, is he? No, he stands by the window in the air-conditioned, ninth floor, city hall office of Neil Gutlog, special assistant to the mayor of Los Angeles.

He wants Gutlog to do him a favor. A favor he deserves.

"Neil, we have to shut down this archeology nonsense. I need to move on this project. I've got expensive equipment just sitting there sucking up money."

Gutlog sits in his burnished, silver desk chair across the room, double-chin giving his face a sweaty look, leans back and says, "I know, I know. But at this point, there's little we can do."

Whitehead continues to stare out the window, keeping his head steady, being careful not to shift it too quickly to avoid another instant flash headache. The quicker he moves his head, the more intense the pain.

Ever since he's been amping up the herbal mixture and the electrical juice flowing through the DTG device, he's been feeling these headaches. So far, it's only when he jerks his head. Even a fraction of an inch. If he just keeps still, everything is alright.

"Nothing you can do? Neil, you owe me."

"Yes, of course, the mayor appreciates your support in his re-election campaign, but please don't forget how he helped you acquire this abandoned piece of property."

"What? The Signal building would have just been another city-owned vacant lot had I not graciously taken it off your hands."

"Okay yeah, but we can't do anything about it now. When it was just horseshoes being dug up, and maybe that old carriage, well, then yes, we could have shut it down. But now, with this underground room, those ancient vases, and the clay tablet, with the promise of finding Atlantis and all that bullshit." Gutlog lifts his hands in a gesture of it's-out-of-my-control. "Now it's a whole other story. Have you seen the number of people congregating down there?"

"And there's nothing you will do to help?"

"If we closed that down now, the media would cook us alive and all of those poor, hopeless people would probably go into full-scale riot mode if we took it away from them."

"Poor, hopeless people," Whitehead repeats Gutlog's words with a touch of disgust from the safe distance between what his life is now compared to what it was eight or ten years ago. When Jasmine left. When he was just a third-rate musician and self-help teacher who couldn't even help himself.

But thanks to God, those days are gone.

As Whitehead looks out the window, he shifts his head in extreme slow motion. Out there, too far away to see from here, is the turmoil down below on the streets of Los Angeles. Here, miles east of One Faith, where the degradation and filth are much more prevalent. Aimless, dirty people wandering the streets looking to entertain themselves, to occupy their minds with the most trivial of things, the baubles of an impure society. Why is it they can't see how pointless and self-defeating all of that is?

Well, he supposes he knows why.

They haven't found God. Not just that they haven't found Him, they aren't even looking. And to make it more difficult for these lost souls, it's not as if God has laid out some plan for them and then all they need to do is paint by the numbers. No, it's more like God wants them to do the heavy lifting, to find their own destiny.

But they're not doing any work, much less the hard kind. But then that's his job, isn't it? He makes a better life available to them

SEARCHING FOR A WAY OUT

by creating a way for them to speak to God. And more and more of them have done so.

As One Faith grows, so grows his visibility and importance and so grows his and One Faith's need for the appropriate symbol of God's majesty. And that would be the palace he intends to build on the Signal building site. The last place he ever saw Jasmine. Out there in the gardens. In the late dusk, almost like a vision, and that strange feeling he had at that moment, as if he had been transported to another world. A world that was identical to this one, but here he felt completely different. He heard that voice. God's voice. It was singing, "This land is your land," which he couldn't identify at first, but then later he looked it up. Woody Guthrie's 1940 song. But to him, it was a sign. A commitment to this land.

And he knew he couldn't just let Jasmine walk away from him. Couldn't let her do that. She was his.

Took her out to Cleghorn, to . . . let her rest, let her go back to God.

But he always had a feeling about the land on which the Signal building stands. Part of his past. His now. Full circle. In control.

A few people he's dealt with through One Faith have told him stories of having been down near the Signal building late at night—back when they were wandering lost souls—the building and grounds all shut down and locked up tight, but there being these flashes of light and these deep resonating sounds. Nothing long-lasting, just these brief emissions so vaporous that these people weren't at all sure they hadn't been hallucinating.

Now, if something really important has been found at the site, if this clay tablet they've discovered leads to this so-called Atlantis, and all of its supposed treasures—like this immortality potion—then it belongs to him. It belongs to God.

At that moment, Gutlog's assistant, Trina, walks into the room and speaks to the advisor to the mayor.

Whitehead doesn't listen to the words. Instead, he observes her form. The short hair, cut to a sharp edge, that falls forward when she angles down, the bare, vulnerable neck bowed with invitation. He would like to help her find a way to God.

He reminds himself that this is not about sex or pleasure or anything distracting like that. This is individual tutoring. Yes, tutoring. A good way to describe it. Individual instruction is the best. You can focus the student's attention so much better. You can make them see the error of their ways. Intimate instruction makes the most lasting impression, produces the greatest effect, brings the student closer to purity that much quicker.

His mind rambles. He's tired of this game with Gutlog. Ignore Gutlog. Wasted trip. Will have to get inside that archeological dig himself. Find out what's really down there. Then shut it down. Build the palace. But search those grounds inch by inch. If there is anything to find, if there is a path to Atlantis, he needs to be the one who discovers it. To possess it. To control it. It's his.

He accidentally moves his head, and the headache pierces him with pain. His vision blurs for a second.

22

Dusty, dirty, beat, broken, Oz shuts her bedroom door, throws her satchel on the floor and flops face down on the bed. Didn't even say a word to Mervin and Melissa, who had apparently already been here for a while and were standing in the kitchen boiling something on the stove.

Why bother? She doesn't care anymore. What's the point? Her mind seethes with anger, sadness, despair. All tiny thoughts banging around in her head like some near-light speed particle accelerator, them crashing together, breaking apart, re-forming into something far worse.

The far worse part is her imagining what she's going to do with the rest of her pathetic life. Except there is no imagining, there is only blankness.

If she weren't so tired, she would pound her fists against her head, hoping that she could beat the appropriate idea out of it. But she is and so doesn't.

For seventeen minutes she lies perfectly still on the bed, letting her mind wander. Wander back to her encounter with Nickell.

Touching his face was impulsive. Why did she do that? Can she not trust herself? Is she so out of whack that she'll gravitate to doing things that will hurt her later?

He says, "What are you doing?"

Oz snaps back her fingers, turned her head, "I just . . . it's nothing, It just helps me to know, to get a sense of . . ."

"Listen, can you tell me anything about the archeology—"

"You don't really want to be a journalist, do you?"

"Of course I do." He paused, closed his mouth, opened it, creating lines of wrinkles on his forehead. "I just want to work for a better organization."

"You have this hesitancy. That final step. You are afraid to take it. What is it? Failure? Perfectionism? Something else?"

He appeared as if he were about to get angry. He shook his head, turned on his heels, and walked away.

But she felt something. Some little ray of hope. Hope for what she couldn't quite say. Because there is so little hope otherwise.

She sits up, sits on the edge of the bed, her feet on the floor. Then there's the metal tablet. That plus the vases, plus the white room, the old woman, the bull statue, the map. All telling her that the Minoans came to what became Los Angeles some thirty-five hundred years ago, somehow assimilated into the local culture, yet remained distinctly different, eventually built and occupied the Signal building and have since disappeared.

But that can't be right. The metal tablet has English written on it. Maybe they sent one or two people way back then, but even that seems ludicrous. It's much more likely that they came no earlier than the mid-nineteenth century. She knows she's only guessing.

Even so, what the hell have they been doing?

If what she experienced in that cave on Crete was where the level of their technology was then, what is it now?

Hard to imagine. And what does Atlantis—whatever that is—have to do with any of this?

And, of course, that's not all. She reaches into her pocket and pulls out that black stone she found in one of the vases.

It's flat, around four inches in diameter, looks like granite, no, maybe a combination of granite and quartz, but it's wrapped in symbols on both sides just like the Phaistos disk.

She once saw it in a museum on Crete. That six-inch, clay-fired, symbol-covered object discovered in 1906 that has never been translated.

Symbols all over this too. She sees the priestess, a tree with hanging fruit, a bull, which she knows is common to Minoan art,

SEARCHING FOR A WAY OUT

the sun, the double-headed ax called the labrys, an island, and the butterfly goddess representing the cycle of birth and death.

She rolls it around in her hands, glides her fingers across the smooth surface. Each one of these symbols must have been carefully etched into the stone. It doesn't look to be thirty-five hundred years old. Probably not. Probably something far more modern.

Her thumb comes to rest on the symbol of the priestess.

She looks at the dark night through her window, but with the way the lamplight shines, she also sees her reflection in the glass.

That's when it begins.

A vapor-like shroud seems to emanate and surround her, transforming the reflection to something more like a dream, a rich, sensory dream, and in this landscape she is outside of herself as if she is some other person who can view the Jane Ozzimo who exists right now.

She sees this other Jane who is wallowing in self-pity, feeling so sorry for herself and how the world has mistreated her. But sees herself from a completely emotionally neutral distance.

For an instant, this strikes her as an odd way to look at her life, but this lasts only a few seconds before she is sucked into the Jane before her where her thoughts just funnel from one self-destructive image to the next. From the rejection of her thesis to the impending termination of Circuit, to a lifetime of loneliness to that day twenty-two years ago.

• • • •

SHE'S IN FRONT HURRYING down the winding trail into the canyon, her mother calling out behind her to slow down, her little brother crying that he's tired, but she just plows on ahead thrilled to be seeing the rock formations, the twists and turns of the Little Grand Canyon here in the Shawnee National Forest.

So green. The rocks slippery with moss, the many trees deepening the gloom already cast by the heavy cloud layer. She even remembers now thinking it could rain any second but discarding that thought because it was far more important that she go down to the bottom and see what was there.

And as the four of them reach the canyon floor, the rain starts to fall. They duck under a ledge to stay dry and her parents talk about where they would set up camp that night or even, that if the rain continued, how they might just get a motel room.

Then it rains harder, which makes them want to stay under the ledge. After a while, her parents give each other looks and then saying that they all should get out of this canyon whether they get wet or not. They could all dry off in the motel.

And Oz is a little disappointed.

But soon they hear the roar of water and the first fingers of flood washing down the canyon slopes. So they retreat, looking for higher ground and shelter. Very little of that, however.

A large tree branch comes shooting down this new raging river and one of its smaller branches hooks her brother's clothes and carries him off. Her father dives in the water after him, her brother screaming, then sucked under.

Less than a minute later a wall of water sweeps down the canyon and sends both Oz and her mother into the foaming river. At first, her mother holds tight to Oz's hand, but she can't keep that grip.

When she lets go, the water slams her mother into a rock and Oz can only get a glimpse as she is swept past and down farther into the canyon where the force of the water pushes her to the bottom and becomes tangled in a cluster of tree branches and she fights to free herself, running out of air, her mind screaming in terror.

· · · ·

SEARCHING FOR A WAY OUT

OZ DROPS THE BLACK stone and comes out of the mirror. She's trembling. She slumps back onto the bed, looking up at the ceiling and feels panic. All of her pumped-up senses, her attention, her confidence that she could at last clear this incident from her past, all this power now works against her.

Her heart beats so fast and so hard she thinks it will burst out of her chest, her fingers numb. She might throw up. Her head spins a million miles an hour. Panic and fear and regret and guilt fill her mind. She should never have insisted that they go there. She cannot live with this.

Feels like there is no tomorrow.

But in a tiny corner of her mind she thinks of that one strange moment where she was completely outside of herself looking in, emotionally separate, free of the bonds of herself just for one fleeting instant.

Could she get back there and do that again?

23

Not yet dawn, but Oz drives her fully charged Electron to Better Living Through Chemistry on Venice Boulevard to give her brain function a boost.

Her brain, like everything else in her life, isn't working. Got to fix that right now. If only she was better at planning. Maybe then... but too late now, right? But after last night she's got to do something. After that experience with the black stone, she felt like curling up and dying. Sleep would have been an acceptable substitute, but even that was hard to come by.

She parks on the street. Walks past the hydroponics store with its enormous windows, letting in as much light as possible to fully exploit photosynthesis and feed the soil-less bushy plants.

Inside B.L.T.C. she orders the Brain Spark blend, a molecularly altered and enhanced coffee created to increase the stimulation effect.

Carrying the mini-thermos to a far back corner, she grabs a chair and faces the wall. Fewer distractions.

She sips the hot liquid, still too hot, and sets it down.

Got to think. Technically, she's still in school, so there remains a chance she can go on. Will have to talk to Dr. Vasquez and see if she agrees with Dr. Eisenfield, then decide.

But exploring the Signal building property is foremost. If there is anything of value still there, she needs to find it. And, of course, she's going to use that black stone again no matter how... But wait, there's Circuit. Two days until her termination.

She lets her head drop. Tough one. No, not so tough. Somehow, someway, she's going to get that dog out of there. She'll figure out what to do with her then. Great. Her exquisite planning skills again. But wait an idea.

SEARCHING FOR A WAY OUT

She pulls out her commD. Signals Midori.

"Oz, what's up?"

"I've got a favor to ask of you."

"Good. And I've got one to ask of you too."

"Oh. What..."

"That you show up at the HOPE event on Friday. I need your moral support. You don't have to dress up and all, but you know what the group has planned."

"Ah, yeah." Oz can't think that far ahead right now. "Okay. I'll be there."

"And what can I do for you?"

"I'm going to spring a dog out of the kennel. She's scheduled for termination on Friday. I need a place to keep her. Just for a while. Just until I figure something out."

"Must be a special dog."

"She is."

"That would be fine. But temporary. See you later."

This gives Oz some relief, some space in her head. Now she can deal with that crap from yesterday. The twenty-second anniversary of the accident, which shouldn't have been all that big a deal except for what happened when she held that black stone in her hand and had that... that... what should she even call it? That experience, that hallucination. She doesn't know.

Real panic, real fear. Wants to stay as far away as possible, but then she really can't, can she?

That experience was prime evidence of advanced Minoan technology. Yes, she'll say it. That was Minoan and it wasn't four thousand years old. Far more recent. She has to find out more, has to use it again. But with caution next time, not like her grabbing a million-volt electrical wire. Can't do it that way. But she can't not let it go. If this really is some kind of device, built on the technology she experienced in that cave on Crete—which was ancient—then this is the product of several thousand years of continuing development. And if she can figure it out, it will mean a whole hell of a lot more than just her getting her thesis approved. Way more.

And maybe some of that "way more" is still on that property. So she now pulls out and unfolds the map, looking at all those lines again. Looks at that word Atlantis down in the corner. Looks back at those lines and just tries to imagine. Tries to see how they might fit here.

Then the idea of Atlantis worms its way into this train of thinking. Atlantis, the Legend, the promise of paradise. Then if these lines on this map plot out . . . but wait a second. If they've already found one underground room, why not another? And another? So these lines . . . stop . . . rewind. If this map is of the Signal building land, then these lines could very well represent something underground.

But how to get down there? The one room she found had no doors. It was self-contained. But there must be a way if this map is true. But is it?

Her mind bangs back and forth, calculating the possibilities. She's worried, she's tired. Needs sleep. Turned inward since last night.

She sips her drink and lets the chatter of voices and the hissing of the brew machines into her aural awareness.

The smell of the molecularly re-arranged coffee invades her. The air is rich with its scent. Tangential thoughts intrude.

Oz locks her eyes on the map. Stares at it. Force her now slippery attention to stay right there.

But the sounds all around her now seem inviting. They strip off shards of her attention. The door clacking open and close, the cash register drawer shutting, new orders shouted from one employee to the next, the voices all around her of people talking to each other or on their commDs.

SEARCHING FOR A WAY OUT

One distinct voice comes from the next table over where two men and two women sit. One man speaks to the others in the cadence of a sales pitch or as though he's instructing.

He has medium-length, dark hair that comes to a peak in front where it flops down. Sharp nose. Gesturing with tense hands in short-arced movements. He wears a long-sleeve black shirt with a high collar that accentuates the blackness of his hair.

Oz cocks an ear almost against her will.

"The surrender process is simple. You don't need to bring anything or do anything special. We hook you up to the DTG device and then all you really need to do is just relax. Let it come to you." He looks from one to the other, waiting for their agreement.

They nod. One woman smiles a lot of teeth.

Oz figures this guy must work for that King Zee Whitehead. Him and his pathway to God. She wonders what the surrender experience might be like.

She doesn't believe that you can actually speak to God—she kind of believes that God doesn't exist when she even thinks about it at all—but what if she's wrong? What if it is possible and what if these people have found a way to do it?

"Are you ready for tonight?" The man asks.

The two women say "Yes" and the man says "I'll be there."

"Good then. I'll see you at the One Faith building at 7:00 PM."

The two women and the man push back their chairs, stand up, say their goodbyes and leave, but the man who had been speaking remains seated, drinking his tea.

Oz is curious, but she hesitates to reach out. Always hesitates to reach out to another human being. But her interest this time overrides the block.

"Do you mind if . . . I couldn't help overhearing what you were saying. Could you tell me a little more about this process, this DTG machine, and what happens?" Oz rests her elbows on her knees. "And what does DTG stand for anyway?"

"It means Direct to God." He smiles, showing no teeth. "And yes, I would be happy to tell you about it. First, let me introduce myself. My name is Jason Buggleman. I am the senior assistant to King Zee Whitehead in the One Faith organization. And you are?"

"Jane Ozzimo." She watches his face and sees certainty. "Just how does this DTG machine work?"

"It's how we facilitate the connection to God. A joyful experience. It stimulates that part of the brain, the centro cuneus, that Mr. Whitehead discovered functions as both a transmitter and receiver so that we can talk to God. But over the centuries, this brain part has atrophied, been squashed down by organized religion. A lost ability that needs rehabilitation. That's what the DTG machine does. It helps to restore that ability. Well, really more than that. It acts as an amplifier, making the connection more viable, stronger and clearer."

Oz thinks this sounds very rehearsed.

"Really? People talk to God? And this works for everyone?" Oz knows she should stop asking questions because she doesn't have time for this. Gotta get to the dig.

"Some people simply aren't ready for this experience. It's not called surrender for nothing. For others, it doesn't always happen the first time. Or for the second or third attempt. If this part of your brain has not been used in a long time, then it could take a while for it to work again. But even if the session does not restore your ability to speak with God, it still is a very worthwhile experience."

Hearing all this, Oz wonders if this process might put a person in some kind of altered state, which might not be such a bad thing. Maybe it would even produce a feeling similar to what she felt in the cave on Crete. That would be worthwhile all by itself, but if a person could speak to God . . . what would that be like?

SEARCHING FOR A WAY OUT

"Tell me, Jason, you've used the device—"

"Many times," He cuts in speaking with a steady, confident voice.

"You've talked to God?"

Oz can see in his eyes that this is the question he always waits for, the question he expects and is ready to answer, the question that once he answers, the person hearing it will always be persuaded and he will have succeeded.

"It would be more accurate to say that God has talked to me. I mostly listen."

"And what is that like? I mean, how do you know it's God?"

A plate clatters to the floor behind the counter. The morning is expanding and Better Living Through Chemistry is filling up.

"You just know." He leans back, then forward then rubs his hands twice up and down his legs. "I think it's different for everyone. That's what I've picked up from talking to so many people who have had the experience. Some hear a voice, some have visions. For me, it's more like a memory. An instant memory that comes into my head sometimes with images, but a memory that is not mine to begin with. Once this memory plants in my brain, it then becomes my own. It's always full of advice. Concerning things I've been thinking about or worried about. And the advice is always so logical, so obvious when He says it, but which wasn't so obvious beforehand."

"Then you would say it's made a difference in your life," Oz warming to this. Maybe there is something here.

"Oh, yes. Oh, my yes. I feel infused with the spirit. I feel complete, like nothing is missing." His eyes sparkle. "You should try it. Maybe nothing would happen for you—at first anyway—but then again, maybe something would and you would be extremely glad you did it."

"Maybe," Oz says.

She has this feeling that he's a little lost. The way he holds his head, moves his hands.

She is about to stand and thank him for the information when he asks, "I couldn't help noticing how intently you were studying something when I came in."

"Yeah, school stuff." She leans forward and pushes her feet into the floor.

"Really? What school? What are you studying?"

"Archeology at USC," Oz says. "Hey, I've got to—"

"You're not part of that team that is working down at the old Signal building, are you?"

"As a matter of fact, I am, and I really need to head that way now." She pauses because he's staring straight at her.

"That must be fascinating. I've heard that some pretty strange things have been found there."

"Horseshoes, mostly."

"Wait a minute, I know where I've seen you. You were the one who found that underground room with all of those . . . what were they? Vases and that writing, that tablet thing."

"I helped." Oz feels a little uncomfortable that she has been identified. Feels exposed. Vulnerable.

"You know, you should come down to One Faith tonight. Participate in the ceremony. Just get there a little early. We'll hook you up."

"I . . . I think I'm just too busy."

"This is an experience unlike anything you had before."

Oz thinks, if he only knew. She straightens her back. "I appreciate the offer and someday—"

"The time is right. You just might let a whole new world open up for you."

And having a whole new world open up for her is exactly what she wants. She hesitates. She's got to get out of here. But maybe, just maybe. "Listen, if I get a chance, I'll try to make it."

SEARCHING FOR A WAY OUT

"Seven o'clock at the One Faith building in Hollywood. You won't regret it."

Oz stands, her thoughts roaring in layers of hope and skepticism and the cement of duties and the lack of time and the lack of money and the mystery of that map and there are just too many loose ends. "I'll try."

She gathers her things and walks out of Better Living Through Chemistry and now her mind is all clogged up again and she's splintering off in sixteen different directions.

• • • •

JASON BUGGLEMAN SITS back in his chair and watches her until she disappears from sight. Mr. Whitehead will be pleased about this. Someone on the inside of this Signal building mess. Pray then listen.

24

King Zee Whitehead would like to spit but won't because it would probably freak out Tammy Box, his loyal staff member, who he needs to be competent to operate the machines because Bug is off somewhere and not here doing his job.

Aggravates the hell out of him. Box will have to do. But still, better not to glob one and have her go all to pieces.

And he can't wait for Bug to get back. His head aches, the tremor in his hand seems worse. He's on edge, annoyed and irritated by just about everything. Need a breakthrough right now. Needs the self-control that God will bring him.

Whitehead and Box are in a small room in the basement of the One Faith building. A room Whitehead had especially built for him to use in his experiments with the Direct to God equipment. A basement room that given a different climate would be dank and teeming with mildew but here, in dry, drought-ridden, southern California, no moisture exists.

Adjustable ceiling lights turned down low, casting rough, silver shadows in the corners like some castle dungeon. Soundproofing acoustical panels line the off-white walls and ceiling, making the space feel like a padded envelope that gives shape to the hum and clicking of the machines.

The hMRI machine is off to one side, its thick black cables running across the floor to the very comfortable chair in the middle of the room. Next to it, on a metal cart, sits the auditory-visual stimulation device or AVS, the sound and light machine that will alter Whitehead's brainwave frequency. On a small table is a Mason jar, tightly capped, with a greenish-brown liquid filling about three-quarters of it.

SEARCHING FOR A WAY OUT

"What I need you to do is follow the procedure." Whitehead puts two fingers on his forehead for a second and closes his eyes. Has to be careful not to move his head. "Then just monitor the machines."

"Yes, sir." As she bends over to tuck away some of the excess cables behind a speaker, Tammy Box's rich orange Rayon shirt glides up her torso, briefly exposing the edge of a tattoo he doesn't quite see.

Whitehead circles the chair. Considers it his throne from where he commands the experiments to push the technology.

He steps from machine to machine, checking the indicators and the multiple cables that all connect to the helmet sitting on a stool just behind the chair.

This is a far more elaborate setup of the DTG equipment than anyone in the public has access to. It's more flexible. It allows changes more easily. The experimenter's toolbox.

He turns around just in front of the chair and then lowers himself into it. Tammy Box quickly moves behind and lifts the helmet, helping Whitehead fit it on to his head.

She checks the AVS device, keeping it to a low level of power. Then she unscrews the top of the Mason jar and hands it to him.

He grimaces as he drinks it all down. Has a real nasty taste, bitter and metallic and gritty. But he has hopes for this recipe of twelve different herbs. He has increased the thujone component of the herbal mixture, hoping to increase stimulation to the brain to better clear and open the channel to God. At least that's what this experiment should do.

He looks at the screen displaying the tracking information from the hMRI. This will show when the herbal mixture has energized the synapses so that the power to the AVS device needs to be increased. The timing is crucial. He needs the right amount of stimulation at when the synapses are firing the highest number of neurotransmitters across the gap to hit the receptors in order to achieve the maximum effect. The increase in thujone, he speculates, will stimulate a corresponding increase of neurotransmitters firing and being received at the other end. This will allow the power and effect of the AVS device to amplify the signal to the centro cuneus area of the brain even more, waking it up, and giving him his audience with God.

Whitehead knows the herbs will kick in at any moment. Swirling down the rabbit hole. A journey that once started cannot be reversed.

He lowers the AVS goggles over his eyes and remembers how it used to be.

He had been a run-of-the-mill, self-help teacher who barely scraped along in a sea of many others in the promise-them-everything industry, all preying upon the inherent human weaknesses of their followers that had only expanded with the continued economic and political slide of America.

One part of him believed he was helping others. Another part enjoyed directing other's lives.

But he was having a hard time directing his own life. He simplified. Stopped trying to entertain himself with alcohol, with video, with nightlife, with the thousands upon thousands of commD nodes.

He ate less, selected fewer kinds of foods, sought self-control. But the women, the flesh. The temptation of it.

He needed more self-control.

But then he saw a way where possibly he could both attain that self-control and boost his self-help business.

Years ago, scientists, in their continuing study of the brain, had discovered a tiny node parked right in between the cuneus and the pre-cuneus that seemed to have a different function than either of the other two. Because of its location, it was named the centro cuneus.

SEARCHING FOR A WAY OUT

While the scientists who discovered this couldn't quite pin down exactly its function, they could tell that it had something to do with communication. Not just communication internally in the brain, but also to some outside source as well. But they did not know what that outside source was.

Then one afternoon, in his dingy apartment in North Hollywood, while he was fucking a young, but educated woman from Guatemala, she began sobbing. Called out to Jesus.

Whitehead, startled, asked her what was the matter?

She said she was sorry. So sorry. But she felt she shouldn't be doing this. It was wrong, and she was asking for guidance from Jesus. That he would help her.

And what Whitehead took away from this encounter was not so much that she believed she could be helped, but the depth of her emotion in believing in Jesus. It consumed her.

And now that he was alert to this, he began seeing more and more of the deep belief in God from an increasing number of the people who attended his workshops and seminars. Yes, they came to him for techniques and advice, but many of them considered what he did to be little more than Band-Aids. They were really trying to ease their suffering by appealing to God and, of course, they tried to do this through organized religion—in their churches, temples and mosques.

But if that worked, why were they still coming to him?

Because they couldn't reach God.

So then he asks himself, "How could he bring God into his self-help teachings?"

What if people could speak to God directly? No middleman, no imagining that you did, no unanswered prayers, but a real direct conversation with God. Then you would know exactly what to do. God would tell you.

He began laughing at himself and then he looked again at his commD and the article about the centro cuneus he had been reading when he had last used the device. And then it struck him.

Active 2: If you could talk to God, there would need to be some kind of channel opened to Him. And if we all were God's children, we should have a built-in means by which we could communicate with our Father.

And, of course, he could say that the centuries of corruption and greed had clogged that channel and no one could, any longer, speak to God.

But what if Whitehead could show them how to unclog it?

What if this discovery of the centro cuneus was the very channel to make this communication happen?

And if he was the one who showed the way, people would flock to him. He would have the power.

Then he drove out to the Cleghorn Wilderness Area on his little errand. Got lost. No water, no food. Sun-baked. Then the vision. That all-consuming vision. When God revealed his power. When God told him what to do. When God gave him his self-control.

"Electrical activity is increasing," Tammy Box says, looking at the hMRI screen.

Yes, the strobing lights inside the goggles are grooving his brain into a rhythm.

This time it's going to happen. This time.

"Lower the frequency to alpha," Whitehead says.

Tammy Box adjusts the AVS device to bring Whitehead's brainwave frequency into the alpha range, about eight to twelve cycles per second, beginning the entrainment generated by the sound and light pulses.

Whitehead sits back deeper into the cushioned chair, feeling his body relax a little more. He is sinking. The buzz in his head, the molasses of thoughts, the enfoldment of the space around him like an old friend.

"Increase signal strength," he says.

Tammy Box turns up the amplification a notch on the AVS device.

He feels as if he's flying through clouds, streaming wisps of moisture and a touch of cold. The anticipation of sunshine ahead. Go faster. Faster.

Neurotransmitters cross the synaptic cleft in greater numbers and at a greater speed. They are deluging the postsynaptic membrane and filling the receptors.

Tammy ratchets down the AVS device to the theta range, which puts Whitehead into a vivid, waking dream.

The added thujone seems to have an effect. A fist full of colors rush and twists and streams through his brain as he descends into a pure tactile space. A sharp, concentrated point of himself.

But he feels a sensation in his gut, a sensation that soon becomes pain. Like a sprouting seed, the pain grows. It devours his attention. He can't let this happen and he tries to back his attention out, but that only diffuses it all the more. Then his stomach just lurches. He tries to control it but can't, doubling over and vomiting some of the foul-smelling herbal liquid onto the floor, some on his shoes.

He doesn't see this because of the helmet and the goggles, but he doesn't want to take them off and interrupt the consuming feeling in his brain.

Tammy Box screams.

"Shut up," Whitehead shouts. "We're not stopping."

He feels better already. Whatever that poison was is gone now. Hope he didn't eject all the thujone. But no . . . good . . . he's sinking back into it. He just hopes that Box can keep her shit together and not fuck this up.

Tammy Box adjusts the AVS machine so that the brainwave frequency entrainment sends him down into delta range.

Whitehead sinks deeper into the experience. He believes this is the deepest he has ever gone. The purging must have helped.

At first, he is excited about going deeper, but then he thinks he has plateaued. That his progress has stopped. And he has not gone far enough. Not by any measure.

He pushes the goggles up and opens his eyes. The room is small, equipment blinking, that child of a woman hovering there looking scared.

He looks at the screen above the hMRI and sees the multiple flashing colors that show the electrical activity in his brain. He needs more power, more juice.

Whitehead bends to the side so that he can reach the power dial on the AVS machine himself, Tammy bending simultaneously trying to help him and, as she does so, fully exposes the tattoo.

Looks like two intertwined snakes. He blinks. Unable to understand what he is seeing.

Instead, he twists hard on the dial, amplifying the power beyond anything selected in previous sessions.

But when he sits back, lowers the goggles over his eyes, and sinks back down into the entrainment, now bathed in a fury of electronic signals, the image comes back to him.

Snakes. Entwined. Can't get distracted. He pushes it away and the entrainment into delta and the continued influence of the thujone and the rest of the herbal concoction envelopes him.

He's humming along now.

Even at this deep and slower level of one to four cycles per second in delta, the increased electrical power and the herbal influences have ignited his mind into an accelerated turmoil. He is calm, yet he is rushing. He feels the power, yet he's completely out of control.

SEARCHING FOR A WAY OUT

Breaking through the clouds, he is now in a room so vast he cannot find where it ends.

On the edge of his vision, he now sees writhing bodies, naked, the slide of oiled flesh against oiled flesh.

Ahead are rows of empty folding metal chairs, corners perfectly aligned, stripes taped to the concrete floor, all at right angles. Everything square and orderly.

He senses some movement out there. A shape. Enormous. What is that? It's Him, isn't it? It's got to be Him. Whitehead tries to propel himself forward but his legs will barely move, just spasmodically kicking out, knocking down several of the perfectly aligned folding metal chairs.

What an awful sound they make when they clatter to the floor.

But through force of will, Whitehead surges forward. The shape ahead is still visible, but the fog is thick. He pushes harder. He's got to get there, got to meet God. And it must be Him. This must be working. The connection has been made and now it's just these final few steps. If only he could go faster.

He's slipping on the slick, oily floor, not getting enough traction, and then it's as if his peripheral vision is his main vision and all he can see are the naked bodies to either side, bodies sliding and squirming in the amber oil beginning to stain the floor, running under the legs of the perfectly aligned metal folding chairs.

And he can no longer see the shape. Gone.

A consuming sadness shrouds him. For a moment he feels a void, such a complete emptiness that he feels as if he no longer owns his own body, that the thing that makes him who he is has gone missing. But the void does not hold and seeping into it is an old, familiar feeling, now intensified. His desire, this wanting contact with flesh, the will to control, to dominate.

She must have done something wrong. Not followed the procedure. It's Box's fault.

JOHN MOON FORKER

A searing anger floods his brain.

His skin is hot.

The sexual urge is much more powerful than before.

He remembers he is supposed to fight this urge, to deny it, to suppress it, but the denial of this urge feels childish and irrelevant now.

He lifts the goggles off his head and stares at Tammy Box.

Entwined.

25

After about six hours at the dig, where nobody was finding anything except more horseshoes, a couple of saddles and some broken telegraph equipment, she had come back to campus to talk to Professor Vasquez about her thesis. But with Professor Vasquez unable to help her and now going off to her dig in Mexico, Oz feels even more alone. Something she should by now be plenty used to, she tells herself, because she's been doing a lot of it these last twenty-two years.

Oz walks across campus toward the parking structure. She'll go home, see if she can figure out how the stone is supposed to work, and then go to One Faith later on.

Even though it's late afternoon, many students are still going to and from classes, but for her they all exist as if they are on a different planet. She drags along, jammed by so many circular, dead-end thoughts.

She walks up five flights of concrete stairs arriving on the roof. Unfortunately, when she drove into the structure, no spaces lower down were available, so she had to park up here under the blazing sun where her car has been cooking for a good long while.

Argghh. She'll have to open up the car and let it air out for a few minutes.

With the doors wide open, and the heated air shimmering out, she paces around behind the Electron. Pulls out the black stone and looks at all the symbols. Touches one after the other.

She brings her eyes up for a moment, the sun glints sharply off the chrome insignia on the trunk and her eyes scoot up the rear window where she catches a glimpse of herself for a moment, her eyes torquing out from the chrome's burning glare.

She smells tacos.

Must be from a restaurant, but the only one she knows about is across the street in University Village and that's pretty far away. Then she smells the sizzling asphalt here on the parking structure roof and the out-gassing of a thousand tires and maybe even a little transmission fluid that has leaked.

That's when she notices the voices. Two young men walking up the ramp, one level down, speaking in normal conversational tones, way too far away for her to hear, but hear them she does.

"I took a drive up Mulholland with Jenny. You know, way out there."

"Isn't that where those—"

"I was about to tell you—"

"Get her alone."

"That was the idea but—"

"But then—"

"We get out there and the smell is horrible. One of those huge, I mean really huge, vats filled with human shit."

"Gross."

Oz never even saw them, but she could hear every word. And now she hears all the birds flitting from tree to building to tree and when she looks out over the campus, she can see each individual bird, sees them distinctly, with full attention on each one.

She shuts her eyes. Slightly dizzy. Must block some of this out. Walks forward a few steps and sits in the car. All of her senses are so alive. She's buzzing. Thrilling yes, but she feels as if she'll go into some sort of convulsive overload if this keeps up. Needs to sort it all out. But then realizes that all the sights, sounds and smells are sorted out already. Each piece, each sense, each object in her environment has an individual clarity far greater than she has rarely ever experienced before.

SEARCHING FOR A WAY OUT

That flash of light off the chrome must have triggered the stone, or maybe it was that brief glimpse she had of herself in the rear window.

Yes, like yesterday. The reflection must be how you turn it on. Good. Maybe she's getting it.

Right in front of her is the car's rearview mirror. Does she chance it? Does she try to work with the device right here?

She looks down at the stone. The trouble she had last night was when she had her finger on the symbol of the priestess. What if she tried something else? Like maybe the labrys, the Minoan double-axe.

Slowly, she brings her eyes up to the rearview mirror, both eager and fearful of what might happen. For one moment she sees her eyes in the mirror, then she's transported to her childhood backyard.

Wisconsin summer. Warm breeze. Green plants all around.

Sees this scene through her adult eyes, not the eyes of her maybe ten-year-old self as she was then.

Sees her mother outside, folding sheets over the clothesline, having just been washed and now hanging out to dry.

But this seems to be in a kind of slow motion, or maybe a better way to say it is that these moments are so full of things to notice that they only seem to be in slow motion. She can smell her mother, the humanness of her, hear her humming to herself, can hear the snapping of the sheets in the wind, can feel her presence so much that it feels real right now.

Which all makes Oz long for her mother, miss her so much, so much has been lost. Then she becomes aware of her own evolution from then into the closed-down, armor-laden adult she has grown to be. The selfish adult, she now thinks. The selfish adult who only thinks of herself and her pain. What about everyone else? She's been playing the victim crying, "Look what was done to me."

She feels trapped in this aspect of herself, this dominating aspect, and she hates feeling trapped. Like when she was underwater and couldn't break free. A feeling that has been sealed into her. She can't get it out. This identity that has become her.

Panic rising. Then she just pops out. Sees herself from outside herself. Some degree of relief. Some emotional distance. Watching the woman who is experiencing this but not inside of it.

But still. It hurts. She drops the stone on the car seat. Her head pretty much clears. But there is a residue to this that won't let her go.

No, she isn't figuring out how the stone works. It's far more powerful than she could have imagined. But she needs help. Help with herself.

Now she really is looking forward to tonight. The Surrender Ceremony. Maybe some kind of door will open that she can step through and come out a different person.

26

Nickell and Gina Woolander walk along Sunset Boulevard toward the One Faith building. He can see hundreds of others converging here also, some talking excitedly, the chatter of voices filling the night air, others just moving along as part of a herd.

"Find anything new at your archeological dig today?"

"Hmmm. No. All the excitement was yesterday. That underground room is all cleaned out now," Gina says, looking around as if expecting to see someone she knows.

"What about that clay tablet with all the writing on it?"

"Oh, this is part of your journalism thing, isn't it?" She glances at him.

"I've been assigned to do it." He'd like to see for himself, but with all the security at the Signal building, that won't be easy.

"Well, I suppose it wouldn't hurt to tell you," Gina leans in close and mockingly says, "I can trust you, can't I?"

"Oh, absolutely." Nickell raises his right hand as if giving an oath in court.

"Well, I don't know exactly, but something's got Dr. Eisenfield all bent out of shape."

"Any ideas?"

"No . . . yeah . . . could be this Atlantis thing. Something about the technology that was supposed to be—according to the legend anyway—this immortality potion or some mind thing or something to do with energy." Her hands flutter in the air as if she has no responsibility for these divergent choices.

Nickell looks down at Gina's legs. The bait. Her highly exposed long legs in those skimpy white shorts that she's wearing on another sultry night. Exposed long legs that should lure Whitehead if he can only get Gina into position to be seen.

He's tired. Did three celebrity interviews today connected to the HOPE event. But he had to drive from Malibu to Palos Verdes Estates to Pasadena. What was that about a thousand miles? Felt like it.

And he hopes Ramesh likes what he sees because he thinks it was just a gigantic waste of time. The only contribution these three intend to bring to the HOPE event is that by using this stage for their own self-promotion they will sell their products, their image, their celebrity.

Of course, the videos have already been posted on The Data Transfer node to be lapped up by loyal followers.

Congratulating himself on his work, he remembers how irritated he still is by what Oz said. That he didn't want to be a journalist. How would she know?

What else would he do? Just even asking himself that question brings up a big fog bank in his mind. No, she's wrong. He just needs to work for a better organization than The Data Transfer, is all.

But, of course, now that he has Oz in his brain, she's not leaving so easily. He feels again how she touched him. He hasn't been touched in a long, long time. Had forgotten how it even feels. That spark of connection between two people. And she was so upset, the crying, the vulnerability. And then she says that thing about him. Like some purely intuitive thing.

He doesn't like this memory. What she said was bullshit. Mumbo-jumbo. But still. She got under his skin and not totally in a bad way.

A part of him got switched on, a part he just doesn't have the time for, a part he has no feel for anymore.

As all the people heading for the One Faith event clump together on the narrow walk leading up to the building, everyone has to slow down.

SEARCHING FOR A WAY OUT

Here is where Nickell intends to make his move. He pulls the small piece of wax paper out of his pocket as secretly as possible. Can't let Gina see him doing this.

Unfolding it, he pulls out the tiny, thin, transparent nanosensor and lays it across his right index finger. And now that they are shuffling along in this close crowd of people, Nickell puts his hand on Gina's back, just at the base of her neck, as though to guide her in the right direction, and then he lowers the index finger to just behind her ear and attaches the nanosensor there.

Now it's just a matter of bringing Gina and Whitehead together. He might get nothing but, on the other hand, he might just catch this phony in a bear trap.

27

"Wow, look at all the lights," Gina says the second that she and Nickell have taken their seats in the One Faith auditorium, after having pushed and pulled with the thousand or so others to get in.

And now this crowd buzzes its feverish energy, looking up at the ceiling raining down thousands of paper flowers, a ceiling strung with red, green and blue lights that sweep across the stage and floor in an infinite combination of more colors, immersed in a cacophony of deep sounds coming out of enormous speakers, not music, not speech, but deep tones that reverberates up and down everyone's spine, shivering with the power that announces that you are in the presence of the Lord.

Nickell relieved that no One Faith staff member recognized him and barred his entrance. But now that he's in, he's got to figure out how to get Gina in front of Whitehead. But with this surging crowd clogging up the aisles, navigation won't be so easy. He can't even see Whitehead anywhere anyway, and if he appears, he'll likely be down near the front, far from the seats that he and Gina occupy.

So he's just going to have to stay calm and wait it out. Whitehead is bound to show up at some point soon and these Surrender Ceremonies can take over an hour so he'll find a way to maneuver Gina down front. But he's got to admit Whitehead really puts on a show. No wonder so many people fall for this. It's probably the most stimulation any of them have had in months.

Nickell looks toward the stage trying to pick out Whitehead among the more than one hundred participants in the ceremony who are just standing around with little to do as an almost equal number of One Faith staff members are preparing the DTG

SEARCHING FOR A WAY OUT

machines, the chairs, the large table with the jars of brown liquid shimmering in anticipation.

But then his jaw drops. He thinks he sees Oz up there. Yes, it is her. What the ...

Something hard flips over in the pit of his stomach. His brain feels a little frantic. No, she shouldn't be doing this. Immediately, he flashes on his now vegetable-like sister and the pump of anxiety twists his brain up even higher. He imagines Oz damaged like that and his visual field just sort of short-circuits. He wants to stand up and shout, "stop" but he instantly pushes that impulse back down. Wouldn't help, but he's got to do something.

He elbow-nudges Gina and points, "Oz."

"Oh . . . how did she . . . I wanna be up there too. This is so exciting."

Gina is practically bouncing up and down in her seat. Nickell draws in a sharp breath.

"Gina, listen . . ."

"Look, there's King Zee Whitehead. What a leader he must be. All these people."

• • • •

KING ZEE WHITEHEAD crooks a finger at Darsha, one of the Nordic twins who normally works at the reception desk, to come over. He bends close to her ear so that he can be heard over the thunderous noise of chattering voices and deep sonic tones blasting out of those speakers.

"Seat that woman," he points at Oz, "at the very back, behind everyone else."

"Yes, Mr. Whitehead.

He has plans for Oz. Will attend to her himself. Must extract the information about this damned archeology project the city has rained down on him. It's his land. He owns it. He needs them off of it right now so that he can continue to build God's house and put himself on the throne. So to speak. A house that befits One Faith's increased membership or should he say flock?

But these archeologists must be hiding something. The media can't get in there and doesn't know everything they've found, but this Oz will and he will get it out of her. Especially this clay tablet thing. Likely to be much more there. Secrets. What if it's about this technology mentioned in that old legend, this immortality potion, or this path to Atlantis or whatever it is? He needs to get his hands on it. This is a brilliant opportunity to increase his reach, solidify his gains, and put him on an upward path to even greater influence and power. With God, the sky's the limit.

But first he needs to deal with her, open her up, get her to talk, and he believes he knows just how to do that.

Everyone else on this stage tonight will use the DTG device at its lowest level, the alpha level. Anything more potent for the uninitiated would ask for trouble. But with her he is going to jack it up to the last of the seven levels, the zeta level, which means higher volumes with the light and sound component, greater electrical charge and a far more potent dose of the South American herbal mixture. That's why he's putting her at the back. If things get out of control, he can always pull her backstage and out of sight.

Then, after that, who knows, he might just take her upstairs. She'd be very compliant in that state.

His urges are becoming stronger. He needs to control it. There is a time and place for that, but only of his own choosing. He'll decide when and where, not this urge, no matter how tempting it might be.

Satisfied with himself, he looks out over his domain.

• • • •

OZ STANDS MOTIONLESS, close to the heavy curtain near the side of the stage among the one hundred and three other Surrender

SEARCHING FOR A WAY OUT

Ceremony worshipers, most of whom are swaying or gesturing or even pacing. But not her, not now.

Oz just thinks that maybe, just maybe, she will be given some answers to what she should do or how she should proceed and then she hopes that this weight will be lifted off of her and maybe she would even speak to God. Not that she thinks this is likely but, who knows, maybe Whitehead is right about that part of the brain acting as a channel and maybe his technique here will allow that to happen.

But her mind skitters to the other side of expectations where the thoughts and images are not so rosy, where she perceives she is in the midst of some deluded cult and that the best she can hope for is not to become a member and what is most likely to happen is nothing. Absolutely nothing. And then she will be right back to butting up against the dead-end that she's been up against all along but now with just less hope, less promise of change, which all hammers the energy and the drive right out of her only making things worse.

She shakes her hands three or four times to throw off the itchy energy in them, the nervous overload in her body that makes her want to bolt out of here.

Let's just get on with it.

Finally, the tall Nordic blond comes over, smiles, and seats her in pretty much the last chair on the stage, way at the back. Good, she wants to be here, wants to hide, wants to be invisible because she just feels too exposed, and back here she won't be surrounded by all the others and feeling trapped by all those bodies.

• • • •

THE NEARLY ONE HUNDRED staff members scurry about the stage, seating everyone, plugging everyone into the helmet of wires, wrapping the headphones across ears and lowering the goggles, blacking everything out.

Oz was okay until that. Now, she feels so cut off, down some black hole with no destination and when someone hands her the paper cup and tells her to drink, she at least feels grateful for something to touch. Until she tastes whatever it is, she's been asked to drink.

Whew, this is bitter.

When she pauses, the voice says to drink it all down with the word "down" lilted up as though Oz is a kindergartner being told it is nap time and this is good for you.

All the electronics simmer expectantly, the internal wave of sound and light works on every Surrender Ceremony participant.

And so they can barely hear when Whitehead stands at the front edge of the stage, microphone in hand, facing the eager audience.

"You are witnessing a journey that these people," he gestures behind him, "are taking to grab hold of their birthright. Yes, birthright. You are entitled to speak to your maker. You are entitled to speak to the Lord and to have him guide you in this life. He wants to talk to you. And this ceremony is the way to wake up that part of your brain that connects you to God. It's your own special commD to Him."

The enthusiasm of the audience is high and contagious. Some leap up to yell and applaud, then everyone stands and yells and applauds.

Whitehead says, "This is a process. You have to climb the ladder to the top just as these people up here have begun. They are all at the bottom level, the alpha level. With each new level from beta to gamma and on up through delta, epsilon, and digamma, the strength of your signal grows more powerful. And with each level, your chance of meeting God increases. But when you reach zeta, the seventh level, you *will* know God. The channel *will* be open."

SEARCHING FOR A WAY OUT

At least a dozen of the ceremony participants sway back and forth. The process doesn't take long to kick in once the herbal mixture has been swallowed.

A frizzy-haired woman, forty pounds this side of fat, calls out, "Oh, God."

Once she breaks the ice, others follow, but it's unlikely that any of the others have heard her, them being wrapped up tight in their own light and sound shows fueled by the bitter liquid.

A short man with red hair falls out of his chair and is immediately helped back into it by a staff member.

Whitehead has stopped speaking, knowing that he shouldn't compete with the spectacle unfolding here on the stage. Let that do all the talking.

The audience is oohing and aahing with each outburst from those on the journey to God and the outbursts only grow in frequency and wildness. A short woman with short arms slides off the front of her chair, ripping off the helmet and the wires, her blinking on the floor but quickly helped back into the experience by two staff members. A large black man roars, "I'm coming, Lord!"

Oz feels herself sinking deeper into some pit of her mind where she's never been. Where the walls are solid and closing in. Going down, feeling old, feeling like a delicate porcelain teacup, as if her skin is fragile. Spinning. Unable to hold on to anything, that hypnotic flashing light and those sounds washing over her, weakening her.

Now she can hear a voice, but it is too far away. Cannot make out the words over the pulsing sounds. Could this be what the process is all about? Is this God?

Now the voice moves closer, becomes clearer.

・・・・

JOHN MOON FORKER

WHITEHEAD CROUCHES down in front of Oz. Here, way at the back of the stage, behind the one hundred and three jabbering adherents and the multitude of staff members attending to them, he is almost totally obscured from the view of the audience.

He clicks on the wireless transmitter that allows him to enter the headphones of any or all of the Surrender Ceremony participants.

But here he is only interested in just one.

• • • •

THE VOICE FILLS OZ'S head. "You deserve to be with God, for Him to guide you through the perils of this life. But God needs you to talk to Him, for you to show Him you want His guidance."

The words feel hypnotic to Oz. She nods her head. Just flow along. Just go with it. It all makes so much sense.

"Then you become a part of our large family, one of us, no longer out there alone."

Hearing this, Oz senses a comforting warmth in her body. Yes, belong. Be a part of something. She's been out there too long on her own. She needs to come home.

"Home," she whispers ever so softly.

"All of us in the family share everything," the voice says. "We hide nothing from each other. We are open and free and this is how we support each other."

Oz sees a long table with a white tablecloth, brilliant, gleaming silverware laid to each side of plates lined in straight rows, people . . . family sitting in the chairs and her right in the middle of it, passing food to each other, everyone talking, smiling, laughing and her right along with them. Feels so very connected. Wants this so much.

"And because we share everything," the voice continues, "we would like you to tell us about your work. What you do in archeology. Especially what you've found at the Signal building. Yes, tell us about that."

SEARCHING FOR A WAY OUT

It seems to Oz that she has to reach deep into her mind to retrieve any memory of this. Seems so far away. And when she lifts it out, she can barely speak. Just fragments come out of her mouth.

"The stone, this technology, don't know, still finding out. Could be, looks like, maybe connected to Atlantis and some promise. The legend. Maybe immortality, some technology, so much to know. Maybe the black stone will tell me. Maybe I will figure it out."

But when she stops, the voice says, "Tell us more."

"It's a tool of some sort . . . but not controlled yet." But when Oz loses the image of the long table, she stops talking.

She feels a pressure on her leg. Like a hand?

"What is this black stone? What does it do? Where is it?"

• • • •

JASON BUGGLEMAN'S VIEW of Mr. Whitehead is unobstructed, unlike most of the audience, since he's standing at the far end of the stage but in line with the rear of the chairs. He can see Mr. Whitehead crouching down in front of Oz, sees him speaking to her, sees him touching her.

What is he doing? Shouldn't be touching her. Makes him think of Tammy. Haven't seen her all day, haven't been able to reach her on her commD.

When he asked around, he was told that earlier she had been with Mr. Whitehead in the basement, helping him with his experiments. But nobody had seen her since. And when he asked Mr. Whitehead about it, he just seemed vague. Said she just took off.

Not like her.

• • • •

"GIVE US THE INFORMATION," the voice says, filling every synapse of Oz's brain. Nothing more to say to the voice, nothing more she knows. She just wants to slip down into unconsciousness.

But her brain jolts as that hand slides up her leg. All the way to the top, fingers probing, her leg twitching as though experiencing electric shocks.

"God wants to know."

The Direct-To-God machinery and the drug continues to drag her down into its embrace, her sinking into a cocoon of strait-jacketed, frantic thoughts creating an intensifying pressure that builds and builds like a pressure cooker. Some kind of chemical twist, which wraps her up, imprisoning her. Makes her feel like giving up. Defeat. The life being squeezed out of her.

"You must tell us. You do not want to anger God. You do not want to be cut off from God. He will cast you out into the wilderness and you will be alone forever."

No, she does not want to be cut off. Not anymore. Twenty-two years and counting.

The words being rammed into her mind seem to come from everywhere. Can't escape them. Can't turn them off.

The drug, the never-ending tonal sounds and flashing lights pound her, but she's not thinking about God even though that's what this whole deal is about, isn't it? God has no meaning for her.

Two hands on her now, snaking around her middle, invading, controlling, her feeling paralyzed by the machines, the drugs, feeling that there is no way out.

Trapped.

Trapped is a familiar feeling, one she knows how to deal with.

Despite the racket in her brain, she is alert to other sounds, yet attuned to the silence outside of what she's being forced to hear. She knows the power in that silence. Being inside that silence is how she examines and merges with the ancient artifacts she touches and that's how she can listen to those long-dead people.

The voice comes back. "Tell me where the black stone is."

She can hear the anger in the voice, can smell his sweat, his fear.

SEARCHING FOR A WAY OUT

Her personality is in segments. That's how she sees it now. And one piece is stuck to that chair, unable to act. But another piece is coming alive.

At first, when Aunt Della came to Illinois to help bury her parents and brother and then took her back to California, Oz mired in shock. Her anchor to this world had been severed.

But Aunt Della had wanted to give her some sense of normalcy and so enrolled her in elementary school right away.

But she couldn't fit in. Not then, not in her condition. Maybe if she'd had more time. Instead, she was the strange loner, the new kid in school, who her classmates taunted. In response, she mentally rolled herself up into a little ball and covered this ball with thicker and thicker plates of armor.

No one would get to her. Watertight and distant. Safe. But very alone.

And she is in that place now, but with a difference. Instead of being frozen, cut off, she is now—or a part of her is—extremely alert.

Her body wants to move. A powerful restlessness grows.

She can see that this whole Surrender Ceremony is designed to weaken, to dominate, to strip your power from you. And the more she sees that, the more an ember of fierceness deep within her burns hotter and hotter.

But the hypnotic prison of the sound and light machine plus the herbal drug works to keep her down.

A part of her wants to give in, give up.

Oz knows that her mind isn't working all that well. That awareness is key. She asks herself this one question, *Do I want to live or do I want to die?*

One part would just like to go to sleep forever, but that part is weak and weak is not what Oz is all about. She's never been weak, all through school, all through her gymnastics training, through her destructive relationship with Sam, through it all.

No.

She explodes.

She rips the goggles, the headphones, the helmet off her head, swings her arm hard, her elbow striking Whitehead in the nose and him reeling backwards, landing on the floor, a fountain of blood spurting out of that nose before his hands cover it.

Oz is gliding. Every motion smooth, choreographed, as if she's in the ballet. Her body responds with a precise coordination.

Her senses are so alive.

She stands up.

• • • •

NICKELL HEARS A SCREAM above the tonal din and sees Oz arise from behind all the seated people hooked up to those machines.

Something is going on, but it's not all that clear what. He glances at Gina to see if she knows anything, but she's looking up to the stage as well. A sense of urgency streaks through his brain.

Chatter in the audience grows exponentially, people craning their necks to see what's happening and asking if anybody knows anything. One Faith staff members flock to the rear of the stage. Oz looks wobbly, but none of them seem to pay attention to her. There's something on the floor they've all gathered around.

He needs to move, but hesitates.

He can see that Oz needs help. Should go, but can't. Last night, he just walked away from her. She was in his head. Reading him that easily. Telling him he didn't want to be a journalist. That thought has been with him all day.

And more than that, she's in his head right now differently. He doesn't think he even likes her, but he thinks he might be lying. Shit.

What can he do for her? He can fail, is what. And he can't leave Gina here. He's got to maneuver her close to Whitehead. That's the plan. And if he leaves now, he can't do that. Because he's got to bring

SEARCHING FOR A WAY OUT

Whitehead down and, of course, receive the recognition and praise for doing so. His stupid career.

Gina turns to him. "You have to do something." She points up at the stage and now he sees that two One Faith staff members have gone over to Oz and are jabbing fingers in her face and shouting at her.

Oz appears dazed and they look threatening and then Nickell sees that big guy who is always around Whitehead—his bodyguard or driver or something—trying to make his way through the thick, standing crowd on the side aisle.

It's gotta be now.

He jumps up and runs down the center aisle, dodging the few people who have spilled out there, then hops up onto the stage and grabs Oz by the arm, putting himself between her and her two accusers.

She looks at him as if she only partially knows who he is.

"Oz, are you okay?"

"Yeah, I think so. Drugs . . . can't think straight."

"We have to get you out of here." Sure, she is saying she's okay, but Nickell thinks she still looks out of it. Get her outside, get her some air. But where is the damned exit?

And this is when he sees the gap in the group of One Faith people and sees Whitehead on the ground, up on one elbow, his face contorted with rage. Blood pours out of his nose, down across his lips, on to his chin, to his shirt. One staff member with a handkerchief trying to help him but he is just yelling.

He's guessing that whatever happened to Whitehead must have been done by Oz, so he needs to get her out of here right this second.

He pulls her deeper into the wings of the stage, looking desperately for the way out.

Then Whitehead's assistant, Jason Buggleman, rushes up.

"Need some help?"

Nickell wonders why this guy isn't trying to punch him out. "We need to find the exit."

Buggleman says, "Oz, how are you doing?"

He knows her? Nickell thinks this is becoming stranger by the second.

"I'm doing kind of okay, but I really want out."

"Follow me."

Buggleman leads them past a series of heavy curtains dropping from the ceiling and down a long hallway to an old scratched and dented door.

He pushes it open. Air flows in.

Nickell says, "You know who I am?"

"Oh, yes, Mr. Nickell, the sworn enemy of One Faith."

Nickell thinks he sees Buggleman almost smiling.

"Why are you helping us?"

"Seems like the right thing to do."

"Look," Nickell says, "if you ever want to talk, let me know."

He holds out his commD, Buggleman pulls out his, and they bump sensor ports exchanging contact information.

"I'll keep it in mind."

Oz says, "Thanks, Jason."

Then Buggleman closes the door behind them and they are out in the night.

28

In the alley back behind One Faith, Oz stomps in a tight circle, going round and round as though to forcibly eject any remnants of the Surrender Ceremony from her system.

She can plainly hear the electric cars whizzing by on Sunset Boulevard out around the other side of the building, can hear one bird chirping high on a tree, can hear her own heart beating at a furious pace.

The flames of anger in her are so enormous she doesn't have the capacity to feel disappointed, what with her thinking earlier that this ceremony was her last hope and then it turns out to be a complete disaster. She'd like to kill that asshole.

"What were you doing up on that stage?" Nickell says.

"Not trying to find God, if that's what you think." Oz keeps moving, feels the hot night air on her skin. "And what are you doing here? I thought you hated this guy."

"Ah . . . well, Gina, I brought . . . she wanted—"

"Gina Woolander? Archeology Gina? So she's alone in there right now?" Oz points at the backside of the One Faith building. Says this like it's an accusation.

"With about two thousand other people." Nickell cracks a small smile at this attempt at humor.

Oz lifts three fingers to her lips. "It's dangerous." She doesn't say this directly to Nickell, just sort of out in mid-air. And she feels those hands on her all over again and shudders. She did not know at the time what was going on, but now that she can piece it together, it's even worse. A part of her can't even look at it. A part of her wants to hide. Make it all go away.

"What happened in there? You were way at the back. I couldn't see."

She stops walking. "Yes, now I get it. They put me at the back so he... so that nobody could see..."

"Then Whitehead was doing what?"

Oz walks away as if moving through a molasses dream. "It was weird. I heard a voice inside my head. At first, I thought maybe he was right, maybe you could talk to God, but it must have been Whitehead."

"He was talking directly to you?"

"Had to be. The things he was saying. Asking me about..." Oz checks herself. Not going to be telling Nickell about the stone. "He was asking me about the archeology dig so he couldn't have been talking to everyone... he must have plugged into my system somehow. The apparatus."

"Why would he be asking about... no, wait a minute, he must think there is something of value there, that you guys, you archeologists, have found something or will find something. What did you tell him?"

What did she tell him? Oz remembers something about Atlantis, the black stone. What would he do with this information?

Thinking about the black stone gives her an idea. This thing she's been experiencing, this seeing herself from a distance, which allows her to not get sucked down into whatever mess she always gets sucked down into. If she could bring this viewpoint, this distance, into the next session with the black stone, then she might be able to go farther. Go into it with some specific purpose. And she definitely knows just where to start.

She turns abruptly. "Listen, I've got to go."

"Hey, if he's after something and he thinks you know about it, you'd better protect yourself."

A shift inside her. Unfamiliar emotions. Some loss, some hope, some confusion.

SEARCHING FOR A WAY OUT

She rushes over to Nickell and hugs him tight and before he can even react and hug her back, she is gone.

29

King Zee Whitehead stands backstage, well out of view of the audience, holding a blood-streaked, no-longer-white-colored towel to his nose while yelling at Jerry Groot, "Find her, find her!"

Jerry, with a baffled look on his face because he doesn't even know who "she" is, stands there like a tree stump in the Petrified Forest. Whitehead wants to kick the bloody fool. He's surrounded by idiots. He'd scream if it wasn't for that audience out there.

Five other staff members mill around wanting to be helpful but not knowing what to do until Whitehead yells at them too, "Get back to work."

Then Buggleman walks up with a tall, thin, blond beside him and Whitehead says "What? And who is this?" Says this with disgust and tiredness and dismissal, looking to sit down and prop his arm up on something while he has to keep holding the towel to his face.

Bug turns sideways. "Let me introduce you to Gina Woolander. Gina wandered up on stage to be with her colleague Oz. Gina is also an archeologist and works on the project at the Signal building."

This catches Whitehead's attention. How fortunate. He looks at her closely. Attractive too. This could work out quite nicely. He can use her to find out what's really going on over there and to keep an eye on Jane Ozzimo. Because he'd like to get his hands on that black stone she mentioned. See what that's all about. Might be some kind of key to finding Atlantis or this lost technology. And from what he could decipher, listening to her, none of this has yet been found. But he calculates he needs to move fast.

So meeting Gina here is a two for one. Info on the dig and a conduit to Ozzimo. No, make that three for one. Once he takes her upstairs.

30

Oz cracks open her bedroom door. The apartment is silent. Her roommates are sound asleep.

She tip-toes down the hallway to her bathroom. She sets the black stone down on the sink counter and stares at herself in the mirror for a long minute, finding a weary face, rubbery eyes, ragged hair. This is someone who should be asleep.

But she has to figure out how to rescue Circuit from becoming dog meat. With planning how to do anything never being one of her strengths, she struggles.

She has to get this right.

That part of her that doesn't want to think things through, that doesn't want to go back in and take the chance that the stone will open up old wounds is yapping at her, kind of like someone about to jump into a pool of cold water and dreading that cold and so stalls, stalls, stalls.

But do it she must.

With her two previous experiences using the stone, she was thrust into representations of the past so real she felt as if she were there. But in both, she was passive. Just watching. Just letting things unfold any which way they wanted to. But what if she decided which reality she would occupy? What if she directed the events? Events that hadn't even happened?

The symbols she had so far pressed when using the stone had taken her into the past but, with all the different symbols to choose from, she thinks that this technology might be a little more flexible. Given that everything she has learned about the Minoans in the last few days points toward them being inventive and relentlessly moving forward it stands to reason, she believes, that she could use this technology to help her figure out a way to rescue Circuit without her getting caught doing it.

So this time she will press the bull symbol.

Looking straight into the bathroom mirror, she picks up the stone and touches the symbol.

The mirror fogs immediately and then resolves into a deeply forested hiking trail she's been on off Latigo Canyon Road in Malibu.

Oz is fully immersed, not standing in her bathroom looking at herself but inside the experience.

Circuit runs ahead, stops, looks back, runs to her, jumps up and licks her face, grateful that Oz has freed her.

Oz feels the love. Her own face is one broad smile. Her whole body is electric and vibrant.

But she lets her mind drift just for a second.

And then she feels Whitehead's hand on her leg, crawling ever upward, and her being trapped in the light and sound of that pulsing machine, her brain swimming in that murky herbal concoction so that she could not think, could not move, feeling open and exposed, a boundary violated. A pool of toxic liquid that is spreading and spreading as she feels the hand sliding up her leg.

Then the image of Nickell intrudes into her mind. She does not want the toxic liquid to pollute her idea of him. She must keep the two separate because with Nickell she sees some little corner of trust. A rare thing for her.

She doesn't even know if she can trust her feelings about trust, but Nickell has helped her, has looked out for her. More than that, though. A kind of magnetism, a female-male magnetism, a natural feeling she has practically forgotten, completely outside of any recent experience. But something not to be destroyed.

SEARCHING FOR A WAY OUT

And she fights to overlay the image of Nickell across that hand reaching ever higher on her leg, to smother the toxic liquid spreading . . .

Stop!

She squeezes close her eyes. Shakes her head. Dispel the images.

Stay on track! She yells at herself inside.

The monkey mind. A phrase she picked up during her failed attempt at meditation. She was what, twenty-four, twenty-five? Up in the mountains north of San Francisco. One-month retreat. Fix herself. She only lasted six days. Unbelievable knee pain from her gymnastics injury, but worse were her thoughts. Just so many and none of them made any sense. Just jabber talk. Overwhelming.

Like right now.

She's got to do better than this. Get clear here. You are formulating a plan to free Circuit. Got that?

Oz stares into the bathroom mirror, finger touching the stone. She purposefully focuses on the kennel.

This thought causes the scene in the mirror to shift and she sees the old water tank behind the kennel and how it is flush up against the fence at the end of the north wing. Of course, she can just climb the fence and then easily get to the roof of the kennel.

She realizes from here she can walk across the roof and when she thinks this, it happens in the mirror, can feel the night air, can hear the dogs below begin to stir. Walking forward a few steps, she hears three or four dogs begin barking furiously. She freezes, then remembers this isn't real. But if it were real, this barking would make it impossible for her to get in and get out without attracting someone's attention.

What if she didn't walk across the roof?

The scene resets, and she stands in front of the water tank again. She climbs it, steps over the fence, and then just stands at the very edge of the roof, walking along a few feet until she's at the side of the roof over the inner courtyard. From there she grips the edge and lowers herself down, hanging for a second, then lets go and falls a few feet.

One dog barks, then stops. She stands still. No more barking.

Now she's in the dirt courtyard, outside the cages. She'll have to get inside the building to unlock the cage door and get Circuit out. So she walks across the yard and the barking begins all over again.

Okay, let's try that again. She's back at the far end of this wing of the kennel and she knows she just can't start walking across the courtyard. How does she get in there? What are the access points?

When she asks this question, her point of view rises about twenty feet off the ground and she sees all the access pathways because they are lit up like some GPS data points on a commD screen.

Looking at this sort of map, she realizes she had forgotten about one door on the other side of the wing.

Tremendous.

So she starts again from inside the fence. She squeezes between the end wall of this wing of the kennel and the cyclone fence, and then right around the corner is a door. It is locked.

How can I get through this door? She looks at the knob, at the keyhole, and nothing comes up. No light, no ideas. Maybe I'm asking the wrong question, she thinks.

How can I get inside?

She turns her head, looks behind her to the office, which is the hub of the spokes from which all the wings radiate, and she sees the open window. The window that is right above the desk she sometimes uses.

Mrs. Ascot must have left it open, which she does when the air conditioning stops working and it had, Oz remembers. Not that having a window open all day would have helped much with this heat, but that's what Mrs. Ascot does.

SEARCHING FOR A WAY OUT

Slipping through the open window, she lands her feet on the desk and then walks through and out of the office and into the north wing. She whispers to the dogs, letting them know it's only her so that they don't have to bark.

She walks right over to Circuit's cage.

Yes.

This thing is a planning tool. With practice, she could likely think anything through that she wanted to do. There might be no end to what she could accomplish with this. Which makes her wonder what the Minoans have accomplished that she doesn't have a clue about.

And as she turns her head away from the mirror, thinking that she's getting the hang of this, she doesn't pay attention to the blinking light in the upper right corner of the scene that she, being immersed in this, thinks of as real, but what is, in fact, some kind of interface created by the stone and this light had just come on when she decided she knew just what to do.

It's now early Thursday morning, well before sunrise. At least twenty-four hours before she believes the pickup at the kennel is due to happen, but why wait? Do it now.

She races out of the bathroom, gets dressed and is out the door and running to her car in two minutes.

31

Nickell paces across his kitchen floor because he can't sit still. The kitchen is where the front door is and the front door is where he can be closest to the landing and best be able to hear Gina's footsteps when she climbs the stairs to come home, which she hasn't yet done. And now that it's what? Maybe five in the morning and so it doesn't look much like she's going to come home, but if only Nickell can make himself believe she will then he doesn't have to admit that he really screwed this up and his whole plan to bring her to Whitehead's attention so that he could get the inside dope on One Faith and Whitehead while still being close enough for him to yank Gina out at the first sign of trouble was just so incredibly stupid.

Now Whitehead's got her and he can't do a thing about it.

Shit.

He tried to get some sleep earlier and might have gotten an hour or two, but he's not sure. Feels like he didn't sleep for one second, but the clock kept spinning forward, so maybe he did.

After being unable to locate Gina at One Faith, he came back to the apartment in Echo Park and tried to connect to the nanosensor he had placed behind her ear, but the damned thing only sporadically worked. This technology has a long way to go. Bet the military doesn't have this problem. Of course, he purchased the cheap model, and he's getting the cheap results. What did he expect?

He has picked up bits and pieces. Heard Whitehead say, "I want you to be my eyes and ears at the Signal building." And Nickell immediately thought of Oz and how this wouldn't be good for her but he didn't know how it wouldn't be good for her except that Whitehead might be pissed that she cracked him in the nose and so come after her, but he thinks Whitehead has got bigger plans.

SEARCHING FOR A WAY OUT

But he's heard other things and none of them are good. Like when Whitehead says to Gina, "You are a beautiful young woman." Followed by him saying, "This is the room where I experiment. Why don't you just sit in that chair."

He nearly choked on his own spit, imagining that the chair was likely hooked up to a DTG machine and then he would really have Gina all locked up.

He's to blame. His fault. Such a failure.

At one point he heard Gina say, "I should be getting home," and he clung to that hoping that she would come home and away from Whitehead, that he could then talk to her and tell her about his sister and how Whitehead and his phony Surrender Ceremony ruined her life and how he doesn't want Gina to ruin hers.

But come home she has not.

He should have known, should not have held onto the desperate belief that he could come out of this massive screw-up without blame when he heard Whitehead say to Gina, "When you surrender to me, you are surrendering to God."

And then the nanosensor cut out for about twenty minutes and when it came back, it only came back for a minute or two and what he heard then was pretty much moaning.

Nickell finally sits at the kitchen table, the fake wood kitchen table—because real wood is just too expensive—his elbows planted on it, his head in his hands, his eyes feeling like they are full of sand and he wishes he could go back in time, do it a different way. Get another chance.

Tomorrow . . . no, guess it's already tomorrow, so it would be more like later today, he'll go down to the Signal building. See if he can talk to Gina. After the celebrity interview, he's got to do for Ramesh.

32

Oz parks her Electron a block away from the Canine Connection in this industrial area of Culver City between the bone-dry aqueduct and the Metro Rail.

Oz checks her commD. 4:58 a.m.

Go in, grab Circuit, bring her home, keep her hidden until her roommates leave for the dig in a couple of hours, then tonight she will take her out to Midori's. The only tricky part will be bringing her to the Signal building. If either Mervin or Melissa see her, then she will have to explain why she has a dog. Could say she's watching the dog for a friend. Could say it's Nickell's. Yeah, that's it.

She runs up the block, staying close to the buildings so that she can duck into a doorway or behind one of the scraggly bushes if the odd car drives by.

Far away she can hear the whoosh of traffic on the Santa Monica tollway, but otherwise the night is predawn silent.

Just before reaching the kennel, she turns down a narrow walk that runs alongside the red brick J.A. Cotton Paint Company, all the way to the back of their lot, which is littered with empty and dented silver paint cans, some of them reflecting the moonlight so that they look like huge stationary fireflies. Can smell the old paint. Chemicals in her nose. Unpleasant.

Here she climbs through a hole in their fence that she's known about for a long time, which opens to the rear of the kennel property.

Way at the back here are the kennel discards, an old doggie jungle gym, a collapsing wooden doghouse, and a large, rusty old metal container where the Canine Connection used to dump all the dog waste before the city stopped letting them do that.

She feels goosebumps on her arms. In this T-shirt, she can actually feel a slight chill. Even if the temperature climbs to over a

SEARCHING FOR A WAY OUT

hundred during the day, with no moisture in the air, at five in the morning that heat dissipates and she can feel almost chilly. Or maybe she's just nervous. Scared. Breaking and entering is not something she does every day.

She stands at the rear of the north wing, behind the cyclone fence, just like she experienced during the sensory visualization with the black stone. Duplicating what she saw and experienced during that visualization, she rapidly climbs up the water tank, steps over the fence, walks along the edge of the roof, and lowers herself into the courtyard.

Slipping around the end of this wing and the fence, she sees the open office window. Climbs right in, walks down the hallway, then over to the north wing, and is standing in front of Circuit's cage. With the light coming in the small windows near the top of the wall from outside, she can just see that a few dogs are awake, most asleep. Circuit sits upright, looking at her.

She's so glad that she did this. Loves this dog. Feels her heart pouring out.

Just as Oz reaches for the latch, she hears a bang and a squeal coming from the office area. Sounds like the front door being unlocked and thrown open. The exact sound that Mrs. Ascot makes when she opens up the kennel in the morning.

It couldn't be Mrs. Ascot, could it? At 5:00 a.m.?

Oz hurries to the north wing entrance and looks through the small, clear plastic door window toward the office. The light is on. She catches a quick glance of Mrs. Ascot moving around the office. Two men are following her. She's pointing this way. Oz pulls her head back out of view.

Could they already be picking up the dogs? A day early?

She didn't anticipate this. Didn't see this happening during her session with the stone. Now she recalls that blinking light on the stone's interface that she ignored. Some kind of warning?

Well, she can't take Circuit out through the front like she had planned.

Until she can figure this out, she'd better get out of sight. She flies out of the north wing door and runs down the central hallway to one of the storage closets, just getting the door shut behind her as she hears the three of them emerging from the office and coming down the hall.

"We'll start here in the . . . yes, right here, this wing," Mrs. Ascot says. "I'll leave you to it. The cages are tagged, spread out over the four wings. I'll be in the office if you need me."

Oz hears Mrs. Ascot clip-clomp away, then the north wing door swinging open. No, not the north wing. They'll be taking Circuit right away.

She flips on the interior storage closet light, desperate to stop this, looking wildly around for something, for anything.

She makes herself be still. Okay, take a breath, look around, see what you can use. Concentrate. For a nanosecond, she thinks that this level of attention is like the diamond core of attention she feels when using the black stone.

There's the metal rack with plastic gloves, dog treats, some kibble. Most of the kibble is stacked on the floor against the wall in fifty-pound bags. But there, on the back of the door, hangs several of the Canine Connection tan work shirts.

Maybe, just maybe.

She grabs one and puts it on over the T-shirt she's wearing. One size too big. It will have to do.

Then she pulls out her commD and sends an anonymous text message.

One minute later, she strides into the north wing, holding a clipboard under her arm. "Gentlemen, could I have your attention for a second?"

SEARCHING FOR A WAY OUT

They look up from the golden laborer retriever that they had just taken out of its cage and who is growling and scrunching its neck, resisting the spiked collar they are attempting to put on him.

"Mrs. Ascot thinks it would be better if you started in the west wing with the smaller dogs. Get those nervous, yippy-type dogs out first so we don't have to hear so much barking."

"Who are you?" says the man with the dark, three-day-old beard, his round shoulders and round forearms rolled forward, his eyes pooching at the bottom of their sockets as if he has some long-term illness that has disfigured him.

Well, here it is, Oz thinks. *They're either going to believe me or not. And if not, I'm cooked.*

"I'm Mrs. Ascot's assistant." She says with as much exasperated why-are-you-asking-the-obvious attitude as she can generate, flattening her lips, half-closing eyes, while holding open the swinging door to show them the way. "If you please."

They hesitate. Thinking about it, weighing their options. Oz remains holding the door open and pretends that she is impatient with their lack of response, drawing down her features into a scowl, all the while holding her breath. If Mrs. Ascot were to come in now or if one of them were to go speak to her, not only would she be unable to rescue Circuit, she might likely wind up in jail.

The two men look at each other. They straighten up from trying to collar the retriever.

"What the hell. Which one is the west wing?" says the beefy one with his own attitude of impatience.

"Right over there," Oz says, pointing her finger that she works hard to keep from shaking.

The instant they leave, Oz sprints down to Circuit's cage, opens the door, and pulls her out. Circuit wags her tail and looks up at Oz as if to say, "What's next?"

Oz remembers the door she saw during the sensory visualization that was locked from the outside and she couldn't get through it. But from the inside, it's no problem.

They slip out that door and back between the fence and the building. She only wishes she could lift Circuit on to the roof and over the fence, but that isn't going to happen, so they'll have to run all the way around the interior perimeter to an exterior gate on the other side.

The two of them running at full tilt agitates some dogs still inside and a chorus of barking and howling begins. And once a few start, all the others join in. Just for the sheer camaraderie of it, Oz thinks. This sound can probably be heard three blocks away. Good.

But as they streak past the open window into which Oz had climbed in, she sees Mrs. Ascot standing there looking directly at her. Their eyes lock.

Oz keeps running, but she knows now that she can never come back here again. Lost job, lost income.

They reach the side gate, Oz flips it open, and they are out, sprinting down the block, Circuit running close to her right leg.

She glances at the truck out front of the Canine Connection, almost expecting to see the name—Protein Providers—on the side, but naturally they're not going to advertise it.

At the car she opens the door, helps Circuit inside, and jumps into the driver's seat. Taps the identification pad. Nothing. Tries again. Nothing.

Oh, no, not now. She pounds the steering wheel. Grits her teeth.

Ahead, she sees the lights of a vehicle approaching. She ducks down, bringing Circuit with her. Circuit actively smells Oz's face, her black nose twitching.

The other car whooshes by and Oz raises her head up just enough to see that it is indeed the city security services. So, they got her

SEARCHING FOR A WAY OUT

message. Mrs. Ascot will have to explain why she's selling dogs for meat.

But she has to get out of here.

She jumps out of the car, pops the hood, and slaps the back end of the control panel hard twice. When she races back inside the car and presses the identification pad this time, there is ignition.

She kisses Circuit on the top of her head, Circuit sneezes, and as they drive down the deserted predawn street, Oz now realizes what she's gotten herself into. Now she's responsible for this dog. And she already can barely take care of herself, which will only be harder now that she's unemployed.

But she'll just have to deal with it.

33

Jason Buggleman turns over on the hot, sweaty sheets and opens his eyes. Daylight floods his small single-room Hollywood apartment, the sunshine overwhelming the flimsy, translucent blinds.

The first thing he looks at, as always, is his commD, right next to the bed on the floor. There might be a message from Mr. Whitehead.

But this one is not from him. It's from Tammy.

"Jason, I know you've been trying to reach me but . . . I've just not, no . . . I guess you don't know what happened yesterday. When you were out, he took me down into the basement and I was supposed to be helping him use the DTG machine, just assisting you know, but then he went crazy and attacked me. What the hell am I saying? He raped me, Jason. He forced himself on me. He's an animal and the best thing you could do would be to leave One Faith and him far behind and to do it right this second. Or even better. Bring him down. You could do it. Sorry. I don't . . . I can't ask that of you. I don't know. I don't know. I'm leaving. Moving away. I can't stay here anymore. I wish you well."

Bug immediately tells his commD to connect to her, but she's not receiving.

His brain is in some kind of shock. Like it's seizing up. Strangling his thoughts into chaos and incoherency.

Tammy?

Gone?

He climbs up from the mattress and starts walking around the small room, trying to clear his head. He has to make sense of all this.

Sure, he's observed Mr. Whitehead's—what should he say?—his fondness for women. But for him to do, to attack, to rape . . . this is—and here he wants to think it is not like him. But it is. It really is.

SEARCHING FOR A WAY OUT

Observing him last night, on the stage, stooping close to that woman from the archeology school, Jane Ozzimo, putting his hands all over her. And then later that other woman, another one working on that archeology project, Gina. What he witnessed then.

He had been sitting on a hard plastic chair in the security office video control room.

It was almost midnight. Hardly anyone moving around in the One Faith building. But on the monitor, he watched Mr. Whitehead and Gina in the kitchen.

She was eating a slice of a lustrous chocolate cake.

Mr. Whitehead had his hand on her lower back. Very low.

Then Mr. Whitehead took a handful of the cake, smeared it on Gina's face and then licked it off. Her head snapped away, but he just guided her head back with his hand.

Whitehead pulled Gina even closer and licked the icing off her nose. She giggled.

Then they went up to his private apartment, where there were no cameras.

But then Bug didn't need to see what they were doing because he already knew.

One after the other, Tammy to Oz to Gina. And on and on and on.

He sees now what he didn't see or didn't want to see. But Tammy was not just asking him to leave, she was asking him to bring Mr. Whitehead down.

Impossible. How could he do that? After all these years. His commitment, his loyalty.

But now this seed of destruction has taken root.

His mind is a swamp of betrayal. Thoughts, like poisonous mosquitoes, bite him again and again. He feels doomed. He knows the right thing to do would be to keep Mr. Whitehead from ever doing anything like this ever again, but it's killing him to think it.

JOHN MOON FORKER

What would happen to One Faith if Mr. Whitehead was gone? Could it continue? Who would be in charge? It wouldn't be him. He's too young. But then who? Somebody would rise to the occasion, wouldn't they? Too much good work to just throw it all away.

He stands in the middle of the room. If he walked seven or eight feet in any direction, he would hit the wall. This is a shabby place. His life is shabby. He should find Tammy and talk to her.

He should talk to God. Pray, then listen.

34

Adrenaline still floods through her veins and she feels wired as she sits on the edge of her bed rubbing Circuit's neck.

"You and me."

She feels closer to this animal than she does to most humans. A dog will not hurt her and there is no social awkwardness, no calculating how to behave. You just are who you are and the dog doesn't care.

Once she hears Mervin and Melissa leaving for the dig—Mervin firing up the gas-guzzler—she then goes into the kitchen and steals a piece of chicken and a few eggs out of the refrigerator.

Circuit swallows it all in seconds. Barely even chews.

Oz sits on the bed and watches her eat. Guess that Mrs. Ascot didn't feed her lately, knowing that the dog would be gone. Saves money that way. Nice touch.

Which reminds her. She speaks a message into her commD and transmits it to Midori, telling her she will bring the dog out later today.

Take Circuit out for a short walk, then to the dig. Has a leash and doggie bags in the car. A benefit of working at a kennel. Correct that. Used to work at a kennel. That's something else she needs to deal with. But not right now.

She walks Circuit up the block where there are some actual real houses, not just clumps of apartment buildings. Of course, the houses don't have green-grass yards anymore, not with all the water restrictions, but at least there's more room.

Since she's discovered that she can use the black stone to lay out the exact pathway to accomplish some particular objective, she could try to change Dr. Eisenfield's mind and accept the premise of her thesis.

But even if she could manage that, she would still need more evidence to make her case. And she still wants to know exactly what she experienced in that cave on Crete and experience it again. Can the stone give that to her? Unknown. If it can, she has to figure out how to make that happen. If not, then she needs to find what will.

Her thoughts turn to the Minoans themselves, setting up some kind of outpost here, setting it up thirty-five hundred years ago. What did they accomplish in all that time? The black stone is one thing, but there must be more of their technology here. Then where is it?

As Circuit pees on someone's front yard, Oz sees a rat scurrying in the gutter and then disappearing down a sewer grate. Down into all of those sewer tunnels.

Yesterday morning, when she was looking at the map in the coffee shop, she thought maybe those lines were representations of possible underground tunnels beneath the Signal building. In all that has happened since she had almost forgotten about that.

But yes, this is where she should focus next. And she has to do it quickly. Running out of time. The pressure coming from all sides. Her experiences with the black stone are bringing out all kinds of wayward thoughts and powerful emotions from within herself that she just feels overwhelmed by. She needs to buckle down her almost lifelong armor.

The resurrection of all those old feelings about her parents and the accident is bad enough, but now her opening up to Nickell, which is scary, and now her love for Circuit. Feels good but also makes her feel vulnerable, like she's going to get whacked any minute, and soaking into all this was that slimy experience with Whitehead that makes her feel polluted, unclean, violated.

So then, how best to find an underground tunnel? She knows exactly how this might work. Run by the archeology storeroom on campus, pick up the ground-penetrating radar unit, and haul it to the

SEARCHING FOR A WAY OUT

site. She doesn't know how to operate it, but Sid Juvelics does. She'll just need to keep him on task. Not let him wander.

If there is anything else down there, she will find it.

35

Sleep. He needs it. So bad. Wasted the entire night waiting for Gina and she never showed. Nerve endings trembling with exhaustion like an unhappy overdose of caffeine.

Now he actually has to go to work. Interviewing yet another celebrity who will participate in tomorrow's HOPE event. A celebrity he's never heard of. One Mitch Yellowjacket, although his real name, he discovered, is Slobotnov.

He peers at the street signs as he drives down Los Feliz Boulevard. There. He turns south on Commonwealth, one block to Avocado Street and then east one block.

The entire north side of the street is lined with two-story, stucco apartment buildings. Every one except Yellowjacket's is narrow and long, stretching far back into the property. But Yellowjacket's building, while narrow, is stubby, leaving a space for a backyard where Nickell can just see the nose of a car that looks as though it's been parked there for a few years.

Across the street is a wall of bushes and vines, which normally would obscure the back end of the houses over on the next street. But with all the water shortages, the wall of green shows many gaps. Neighbors exposed.

His legs feel like lead weights as he struggles to get out of the car. And his head is pretty much spinning. He'll have to sleep soon, otherwise he'll just nod out. Just get this interview over with.

He knocks on the door. Can just hear faint voices coming from inside.

The door opens and there stands Mitch Yellowjacket, all five feet five inches of him, speaking into his commD, waving at Nickell to come in, saying "I need it by tomorrow. Tomorrow morning. Yes, yes, yes it's important. No. Gotta go."

SEARCHING FOR A WAY OUT

Yellowjacket turns his head toward Nickell and smiles a big grand smile that Nickell instantly knows he's being sold something.

"Mr. Nickell, I presume?" Yellowjacket says in his high-pitched voice while bending and setting down his commD, touching it once as if to make sure it's real or won't fall off the table and then straightening back up. "Sit down, sit down, sit down," he rapidly shoots out and scurries around to pull out a chair that's already been pulled out.

Nickell doesn't know how much he could take of this guy on a good day, but now, feeling this tired, he might have a nervous breakdown. Talk about hyper-kinetic.

But sit he does and glad of it.

Yellowjacket hovers for a couple of seconds, darts back around to the other side of the table. Sits. Then can't sit and stands. But can't stand still so paces around the room.

Nickell found out that Mitch here is sixty-eight years old, but looks fifty-five, and acts like he's twelve.

"What are you going to be doing at the HOPE event?" Nickell is tempted to make this a one-question interview, with this being the one question.

"Bring my comedy reach-for-the-stars, human potential message to these poor downtrodden souls who need a hand to lift them up." Now Yellowjacket stands in one place, but his foot furiously taps the thin carpet.

"Your commD show?"

"Of course, of course, of course. What else? I'll be injecting a barrage of positive affirmations into everybody's subconscious where they can work their magic. I'm going to sting them all into happiness."

Yellowjacket here pretends he's a bumblebee, arms outstretched as if they are wings, and buzzes around the room.

Yes, now Nickell remembers, he's heard that "sting into happiness" before. He wonders if he is so sleep deprived that he's actually hallucinating.

He's recording all this on his own commD and one small thing he's grateful for is that it won't be him editing this tape. Let the boys in India handle this.

"Will you be on stage before or after King Zee Whitehead?"

This makes Yellowjacket stop in mid-flight. He lowers his arms. "Oh, that guy."

"How well do you know him?"

"Did that Surrender Ceremony thing of his a year back. Nearly drove me out of my mind." He winks at Nickell and Nickell is being let in on the joke that Yellowjacket doesn't really have any mind that he could be driven out of.

"So you don't buy into that vision thing of his, the direct connection to God, the—"

"Vision?" Now, Yellowjacket is motoring around the room again, holding out his left hand and jerking it up and down in the male masturbation gesture. "That desert vision he had, that forty days and forty nights bullshit. You know what he had? Yeah, sure, he went out there, but it was with a fully stocked van. Had all kinds of food and booze and women and that South American drug he's passing off as some kind of spiritual herb. Vision? Ha! What he had was an orgy."

"But why do that?" Nickell has not heard this version before. Could be worth checking out.

"It was a stunt. Doing just the self-help thing wasn't paying the bills. He needed to upgrade. Upgrade." And here Yellowjacket turns this second utterance of the word *upgrade* into a three-syllable word. "So he cut God into the deal. Now he's mister high-and-mighty, mister I-have-the-answer-to-everything. What a load of horse manure that is."

SEARCHING FOR A WAY OUT

Now Nickell feels a small surge of energy. Here's something he can use. That is if this Yellowjacket is telling the truth, which seems doubtful. But the real value here is that Ramesh back in India is seeing all this and so it might prod him to give the Whitehead story a green light.

"No love lost between the two of you."

Yellowjacket snorts, "You could put it that way."

"You've met Whitehead, right? What's he like?"

"Met him, yes, know him? Not much." Yellowjacket attempts to sit across the table from Nickell again but lasts only about ten seconds before he's up and then bending over his commD looking at it as though he expects it to do something, then touches it, straightening it, although to Nickell it looked pretty straight to begin with.

Nickell feels even more tired just watching this guy.

"Funny thing, though. This place in the news. Downtown. This archeological dig. That—what was it called—the Signal building?" Yellowjacket looks at Nickell as though he's dropped enough clues and Nickell should fill in the rest of the blanks.

"What about the Signal building?" Nickell glances down at his commD. Normally, he just sets the thing down and points it at the person he's interviewing, and that's it. But with Yellowjacket roaming all over the room, he had to initiate the tracking function so that the lens could follow. And watching it continually rotate its position to keep Yellowjacket in view is almost hypnotic, which is not helpful given his current state.

"You know he was a musician before he became a self-help teacher?" Yellowjacket says.

"Yeah, I read something about that."

"Un-huh. Well, he was in this duo with a woman—what was her name—Jasmine something-or-other and they kicked around in the south not really catching on, then decided to come out here. Not long after that, she left him high and dry and what I heard was she told him she was splitting up with him right there on the grounds of that building."

"The Signal building?"

"You betcha."

Nickell straightens his slumping body up. What if he could find this Jasmine? What could she tell him?

36

Where is he?
Oz stands near the rusty, battered gate through which all the archeologists file onto the Signal building site every day.

She smells the concrete dust of the sidewalk, the sweet, candied piece of gum flattened in the walk's crevice, the sour fumes rising from the sewer out on the street, the sharp detergent neuro-toxins on the clothes of her classmates as they go by. Her hyper-sharp sense of smell pulls her attention all over the landscape.

She holds the handle of the ground-penetrating radar equipment, which she has just picked up from the school storeroom. Beside that, sniffing the air, is Circuit.

As long as Dr. Eisenfield is not on site, having Circuit here shouldn't be a problem. And she found out from Soquel in the department office that he's over at UCLA today for some conference or something.

But where is Sid Juvelics?

She scans the site. Must be over twenty students here today, a couple of heavy machine operators, and a few members of the city security force, who pretty much stay in their security vehicles, out on the street, blasting their air conditioning. Because, as usual, it's fry-an-egg-on-asphalt hot. She can already feel the drops of sweat rolling down her face, her back, her arms.

Even so, there must be eighty or ninety onlookers out there broiling, hoping to witness another exciting and rumor-stimulating discovery.

Well, standing around here will not find him. Her concentration zeroes in, distractions fall away.

She lugs the GPR across the site by its single wheel toward the cluster of holes up ahead. Each one a little project with the digger probing for artifacts.

Then she spots him. "Hey, Sid."

Sid leans against one edge of the dusty, crumbly hole he is five feet down in, his gold-rimmed glasses off, wiping his face with a small red and white checkered towel.

"Who's your friend?"

"Her name is Circuit."

"Here to sniff out some important artifacts, no doubt."

"No, that's what we have you for."

"They don't call me the nose for nothing," Juvelics says.

Oz looks down at the GPR unit. "I mean this."

To Oz, the data gathered by a GPR unit would look primarily like lines and shadows on the screen. But Sid had been trained and he could tell her what those lines and shadows actually were.

"Oh." He peers at the GPR. "This is not the one owned by the department, is it?"

"Yes. Is that a problem?" Oz standing above him casts a gray shadow over his face, blurring the edges.

"Only if you actually want to find something."

Oz makes a clicking, impatient sound with her mouth. "Come on, get out of the hole and come with me. I think there's something buried here and I need your help."

She doesn't want to spend the day trying to motivate Sid. She grabs the handle of the GPR and starts wheeling it away toward the far end of the property, Circuit right beside her.

"What's buried?" Juvelics says.

"Come find out." Her voice trailing off.

"Okay, then." He climbs out of the hole and follows.

SEARCHING FOR A WAY OUT

She walks all the way over to the far eastern end of the site, on the other side of the Signal building. No students here. No one thought it worth digging in this section.

"Let's start right here," she says.

"Wait a minute. What are we doing?"

Oz puts a hand on her hip and looks at him for a second before saying, "Sid, you know how to read this thing and I need your help."

"Okay, okay, just asking." Holding his hands up in surrender.

"Good."

As he readies the machine, he asks, "How deep are we looking?"

"I think fairly deep. We might set it for twenty to thirty feet and see what we come up with." Oz is guessing here, but that was about the depth of the underground room.

The GPR is a metal box, packed full of sensors, about a foot and a half square, with a large wheel attached so that it can be moved over the ground surface.

Sid rolls the GPR slowly across the soil, letting the box contact the ground.

Oz knows the GPR operates by pulsing high-frequency radio waves into the subsurface and those waves bounce off different substances in different ways and return that data to the receiver. These fluctuations then appear as wavy lines on the screen, which mean little to Oz, but that's Sid's job.

Because of the limitations of GPR—or instance, it's not so great in clay or rocky soils—the more modern versions of it have an added acoustical sensor array that sends sound waves down to bring up more data to help increase the reach of the signal and sharpen the resolution.

Juvelics wheels the GPR up and down an imaginary twenty by twenty box, spacing out each pass so that he ends up crossing back and forth about fifteen times.

Reading the screen, he says, "Looks like a few scattered objects, nothing really of note. Just what are we looking for again?"

"Something like the underground room we found yesterday."

Circuit sits thirty feet away in the shade of the Signal building, watching her.

Next, they search closer to the building where Sid imagines another twenty by twenty grid. As he walks with the device, he sees something.

"This looks like an opening." Juvelics draws his finger across the screen. "Might be a tunnel."

Oz pauses for a moment, studying the screen. "It looks like it's running straight to the building. Am I seeing that right?"

"Yeah. And see over here. At the far end. It looks like it connects to something out there toward the street."

"How do we get down there?" Oz says more to herself than to Sid, but he raises his hands and presses his lips together, thinking.

She feels a ragged electric charge almost, skin tingle, on the edge of discovery.

"Okay, if there is no obvious way into this space—and there isn't—maybe there is an entrance inside the building. Let's check it out."

Gaining access to the building presents no problem since the doors have been ripped out. They find the stairwell going down and the three of them descend into an increasingly dark environment.

Both Oz and Sid pull out their commDs and switch on the illumination function, just enough light to see where they're going.

At the bottom of the stairs, the absence of natural light is total. Oz thinks the temperature must be forty degrees less than out in the sun above. Not much to see down here, just darkness and emptiness.

"Now what?" Juvelics says.

"Let's go over to the eastern wall, where you saw the tunnel."

Circuit's nails click on the cement floor.

SEARCHING FOR A WAY OUT

At the eastern wall, they stop and Oz hastens thirty or forty feet along the wall but there is nothing but more smooth, blank concrete. She is calm. Her search is methodical. This is what she does best.

"I'm cold," Juvelics says and rubs his arms.

If Sid is right and he did see a tunnel, then there has to be a way in. But it's not obvious. But then, why would it be? So if there is a way in, she just has to find it.

What is that smell? Is that water? Does she smell water? But water is odorless. Must be whatever is in the water. Metals? She can't even identify half the smells she perceives.

"What are you looking for?" he says.

"An opening, an entrance."

"Yeah, I know, but . . ." Juvelics throws his hands up in the air and spreads his arms wide. "Is there anything here besides a big, fat concrete wall?"

"You want to give up?" Oz looks at him like maybe he's four years old.

"Well, no, but I don't see . . . you know, it's cold down here."

"Should be a relief after being in that oven up there."

"Yeah, sorry . . . well, never mind. Do you see anything that looks like an opening?"

Oz slides her hand, palm down, against the wall, walking ahead about twenty feet. "Wait, hold on a second." Her fingers find an indentation in the wall. She studies a series of black lines that don't appear to be random. Looks like an eye. An eye with long, flowing tentacles. She presses her thumb right in the middle of it.

Immediately, a panel lifts out from the wall in a deep rumbling sound, causing all three of them to jump back. Circuit barks and starts whipping around in a circle.

The panel is the size of an ordinary door. It lifts all the way out and slides to the side of the newly exposed opening.

Oz is startled but buzzing inside. Yes, we found something. Something big. All of her explorer instincts kick in, eyes wide, nostrils flaring, hands pressed hard against her chest to hold down the rising anticipation.

Oz and Sid look at each other.

Sid says, "I guess this must be the tunnel entrance."

This is when Circuit stops her frantic circling and shoots through the opening like a bullet and is swallowed up in the darkness.

Oz screams, "Circuit!"

37

Oz steps into the darkness of what appears to be a tunnel, Sid Juvelics right behind her, both their commD illumination apps casting a diffuse light quickly swallowed by the inky black.

The dirt walls feel smooth to her touch. Unnaturally smooth. Just the kind of thing the Minoans would do. Make it aesthetically pleasing. Another piece clicks into place for her. Just a little more certain now that the Minoans lived on.

About fifty feet in her eyes adjust and she becomes aware of another source of light. She stops and switches off the illumination app.

"What?" Juvelics says, caught short and has to stop abruptly right behind her.

"Turn off your light."

"Are you nuts?"

"Could you just do it?" Oz says with a tiny amount of impatience.

When he does, a blue glow emanates from the earth all around them. The light is more like an atmosphere than a defined source. Overhead, Oz sees thin tendrils embedded in the soil. Must be the fungi. She knows that some kinds of fungi glow, and this must be one of them. Only this one's on steroids. The entire tunnel seems to be illuminated. She thinks the Minoans must have seeded the fungi to do just this. Increases her eagerness. Push on.

Juvelics has his head back, mouth open, looking up. "What the hell?"

"Fungi," Oz says, continuing forward. She remembers telling Midori about the ancient labyrinth on Crete and wonders now if she is in another Minoan labyrinth because why would these modern Minoans—whoever they are—build all this unless it was a labyrinth?

And if it is a labyrinth, is there a Minotaur roaming around down here?

She smiles to herself at this child-like fear. A fear of the dark, a fear of monsters, a fear of the boogeyman.

And somewhere off in the distance, she hears a roaring sound. Like machinery or water, but too far away to tell what it is.

As they go on, the tunnel takes a sharp right turn and widens by inches.

"Do you think we're still on the property?" Sid asks.

"Not likely. Not anymore."

"How far could this go?"

"What do you make of that noise?" She asks.

"What noise? It's like a graveyard down here."

Graveyard? Shakes her head. Doesn't need that image in her brain.

She pats her pocket, feeling the stone inside, and thinks that once she finds Circuit and explores these tunnels, she'll give it another crack. Driven now to find out more and, she believes, there is plenty more to find. Search out the Minoans.

They come to a T-junction.

Left or right? She thinks that roaring noise is coming from the right. The sound bothers her. Don't know why. But that's probably where she needs to be. Move toward what she finds difficult. Face it. Time for her to stop burying her emotions, her damage deep inside, especially now since her experience with the stone has opened up old wounds that she now sees are not even close to being healed.

But as she turns right, Sid says, "Do you think we should get some help? Call Dr. Eisenfield? He's going to want to see this."

"He will. But we need to find the dog first." No backtracking now.

SEARCHING FOR A WAY OUT

Sid nods and blinks but doesn't move. With the blue atmospheric light, Oz sees the boy in him. Maybe he just needs the reassurance of having someone else around. Maybe she does too.

"Come on, Sid." She waves her arm and moves forward. Sid follows.

She doesn't walk twenty-five feet before she hears Circuit howling.

38

Oz sprints ahead, zigs left, zags right, hits a dead end, pushes her elbows out in front just before her face would have clobbered the wall. She stops, flips around. Which way? There is a pattern to all this, but her brain right now cannot access patterns. This is blind, brute force. Just move, move, move.

Zero sense of knowing where she is, along with a growing feeling of being trapped, like two dark claws racing after her, snapping at her, casting a shroud of fear that threatens to wrap around and smother her, this only driving her to sprint faster, to be more reckless.

Circuit has got to be here somewhere, this tunnel, that turn. Where?

The eerie blue light provides just enough illumination so that she's not banging into the walls full on, just glancing blows with her arms and shoulders.

She smells the richness of the soil—earthworms?—and fresh hydrogen as if from water, as well as hearing a faint buzzing noise like tiny wings beating extremely rapidly.

She stops to listen, trying to focus and locate Circuit. The tunnel has spilled out into a small open area, which splits into three more tunnels ahead.

Listens intently.

Circuit not howling now. Which way?

And that roar seems louder. Like rushing water. Exactly like the sound of that water in the canyon twenty-two years ago. That oncoming unstoppable sound and now here in the dark, far underground, where she could so easily be trapped. Trapped again. The panic digs in. The eleven-year-old girl panic.

Circuit howls. Closer too. She has to find that dog and get out of here.

SEARCHING FOR A WAY OUT

She hears the pounding footfalls behind her and shouts before the onrushing Sid can slam into her.

"What?" he says, breathing hard, stopping himself with the wall just a little ahead of her.

"You heard the dog howling?"

"Yeah, but I don't know from where."

"One of these three tunnels."

She shifts her gaze from one tunnel opening to the next, each one looking identical to the others giving no clue, the pounding sound of the water driving into her brain screaming urgency, screaming pressure, screaming for her to run now.

Out of the corner of her vision, she catches a glint of light. A tiny sparkle, a hum of wings, and she thinks she just saw one of those flying insect robots she saw topside a couple of days ago.

Did she see it? But whatever she saw flies off into the far right tunnel and she races after it, first immediately falling to the ground, tripping over a root or maybe a rock, but scampers right back up and rushes ahead.

Sid walks ahead several steps, bends over and picks up a circular black object off the ground, right where Oz fell.

39

Circuit barking much closer, Oz running full bore. Behind her, she hears Sid, but he's way back.

Suddenly, the narrow tunnel passage opens up into an enormous cavern.

Spread before her is a vast arched dome stretching twenty-five feet into the air. It is so wide she cannot see the far edge of it, visibility tapering off first into a misty gray, then turning to impenetrable charcoal.

To her left is a path twisting off among the rocks, but right in front of her is a rapid-flowing river, twinkling with the turbulent, white choppy foam, blasting a roar amplified by the high domed ceiling bouncing the sound off the walls. Echo upon echo.

Now she gets it. This is why the tunnels are so long. To arrive here. And here is unbelievable. All this water. Where does it come from and where is it going?

The blue luminescence continues to glow, but it is fighting a losing battle in this large space. Stalagmites rise from the visible floor of the cavern, worn smooth but still jutting up maybe five feet. Stalagmite is probably the wrong word, as limestone would have to be present and she doesn't think she's seen any limestone here.

Circuit stands at the water's edge, looking at her. Then comes toward her, tail wagging, then moves away as if to draw Oz forward.

And Oz moves forward. She is so glad to see her. What a relief. She kneels and hugs her. Circuit licks the tip of her nose.

It's almost as if the dog is talking to her or has brought her here on purpose.

But then Oz hears Sid plodding up behind her.

"Where'd all this come from?" He says.

"That is the question, isn't it?"

SEARCHING FOR A WAY OUT

Yes, that is the question. This is a lot of water to be hiding away down here, especially since it hasn't rained for three years and didn't rain much at all before that. So it's got nothing to do with rain or lack of it. This must be located directly under the long-dry aqueduct above. So that would make this the real Los Angeles River.

And the Minoans wanted access to this water. This raging river. Then whatever they were doing must be close.

Circuit barks, runs forward a couple of steps, then back toward the river. Oz walks forward to see what Circuit is all excited about and as she looks ahead, she sees three small rowboats tied up to a large round post stuck into the ground at the water's edge.

Ordinary boats. Boats to take you somewhere out there. That's where she'll find the answers. The Minoans have something on the other side of this river and she is desperate to see it.

But if there is a boat, then there must be people. She turns in a full circle but doesn't see anyone. No people. Not now. But these boats look to be in good shape, like they get used and taken care of.

She feels a powerful urge to get in one and row across the river.

Goosebumps on her arms from a chill in the air, which is dank and penetrating. All this water brings the temperature down. A relief from all the heat above ground.

Go, she tells herself.

Circuit runs toward the boat, then runs back toward her, barking along the way.

"What's wrong with the dog?" Juvelics asks.

"Looks like she wants us to go for a ride." Oz walks to the water's edge.

"Hey," Sid says. "You dropped something back there."

Without even turning, her hand goes to her pocket and feels the empty space where the stone used to be. When she looks at Sid, he's holding it up in the air as if he's showing her a badge.

Oz quickly walks toward him, her hand out. "Please give that back to me."

As she approaches, he holds it up higher, out of her reach. "Mind telling me what it is first?"

Should she make something up or tell him the truth? "I found it in the underground room."

"Looks an awful lot like the Phaistos disk."

"Just give it back." She's got to get it. This is how she's going to find the experience that will free her, that will give her what she's lost.

"You didn't tell Dr. Eisenfield about this, did you?"

Oz looks above his head off into the cavern, the roar of the river a steady, churning background. "I was going to . . . but it . . . I was studying it. I wanted to find out . . ."

"Right, and if you gave it to him, he'd take all the credit and never let you see it again."

Oz thinks maybe Sid is on her side. That maybe she can get the stone back without telling him anything. "Yes, that would be just like him."

"If you've been studying this, what have you found out?"

She doesn't know Sid all that well. Sure, he has the reputation of trying to seduce every female in the department. He's something like five or six years younger than her. He even asked her out once—which she declined—during the one class they had together. Paleoethnobotany. Which for her was a way to look at how ancient cultures dealt with waste, but for him, the class connected to his interests in Native Americans and how they lived.

When she was on Crete, this past summer, he was up the coast, near Morro Bay, on a dig there looking at sites of California tribes.

"Why don't you just give it back?" She hears the pleading in her voice and doesn't much like what she's hearing.

"Why don't you just tell me? I could give this to Dr. Eisenfield, you know. I'm sure he'd appreciate it. But I'd rather you tell me what's

SEARCHING FOR A WAY OUT

going on. I'm interested in all this, too." He spreads his arms wide as though to encompass the entire archeological site.

"It's a device. I believe it to be Minoan. Not ancient Minoan, but something far more modern." It both hurts her and feels liberating to say it to someone else. Too bad it's only Sid.

"What?" The way Sid's voice climbs, she can tell he doesn't believe.

"One thing I know, you can figure out a way to get anything using that stone. It projects you into a reality where you try out ways to get what you want, see the shortcomings of your plan, the consequences of your actions, and then you can change them before you actually do anything so that when you do take action in the real world you succeed."

Sid gets a big, sloppy grin on his face. "Then let me try this wonderful thing."

"More to it than that. You have to discipline your thoughts, otherwise things can go pretty wrong." She sees where this is going and doesn't like it. She's way underground and this guy is a loose cannon.

"I want to try it." He grips the stone tighter.

"Sid, you should—"

"Let me try it," he practically shouts.

Oz shakes her head. "We need a mirror, some kind of reflective surface."

Sid steps back and forth and then walks closer to the riverbank. Most of the water is rushing by, but a few small pools of water accumulate to the side just calm enough so that he can see himself in the water.

"Here, this will work, won't it?"

"Sid, why don't we wait until we're out of here?"

He's already bending over the water, holding the stone, looking at himself in the reflection and Oz is about to tell him to press the

189

tree symbol because that's probably the safest but before she can even suggest that he falls to his knees, his eyes glued in their downward gaze, he utters the word "No," gives a short laugh—the kind you give off when something isn't funny but you just don't know how to handle it—then his whole body shakes like he has just jumped into the Arctic ocean.

Oz rushes forward and tries to yank the stone from his clenched fingers to stop whatever he's going through, but she can't get it out of his hand for three full seconds. But in those three seconds, when both of their hands touch the stone at the same time, Oz feels something like electricity and senses a feeling of herself merging—as strange to her as anything she's ever experienced—that she's entering Sid's mind.

It's not a visual thing, but it feels as though it is.

Swimming through a life of data—that since it's been created in his mind, she can't really translate it, but she senses some meaning. Something about a woman, a pregnancy, a child, an emptiness, an abandonment, a self-loathing.

Oz instantly knows in her gut what she had known only in her head, that everyone else has their own demons, that she is no different and that Sid here has his own set of armor, which he uses to deal with the world and go on and be his Sid-self and all of his flirtations and attempted seductions are behaviors by him because he just wants to bury his own past and to be liked.

But she finally gets the stone out of his hand and he slumps over into the puddle.

Oz drags him out of the water and lets him lie on the riverbank.

She might be breathing harder than him. She has just seen another world, and she is stunned. But she's got to deal with what's in front of her.

"Sid. Sid. Can you hear me?"

"I . . . I . . ."

SEARCHING FOR A WAY OUT

"You're okay. It's over. Come back."

He blinks about six or seven times, looks at Oz for a second as if he has no idea who she is, then recognizes her, and says, "What happened?"

"You let your thoughts take control. You wandered off into dangerous grounds."

"Dangerous... yes."

"Let's get out of here."

40

She's not at all sure she wants to do this, but sees no way around it.

Standing in the baking sun, near the gate, Circuit right next to her, Oz thinks about what she's going to say to Dr. Eisenfield. Even though she's convinced that Minoan descendants built the tunnel system, there's no way to persuade him that is true unless she delivers the black stone to him, which she's not about to do. But what *will* convince him must be down there. And with Sid's meltdown, she didn't get a chance to search for it.

But if there is anything down there as advanced as the stone, she'd like to examine it first, before Dr. Eisenfield could take it away.

So she wants him to see the tunnels and the river and what defining artifacts she suspects they will find—which will prove the Minoan connection—yet not stop her from finding the truly advanced technology that she believes is there. She's going to have to move extremely quickly.

In any case, she has to report right now. She can already see Sid off in the distance, excitedly talking to the other students. News of the river and the tunnel system will spread like wildfire in seconds, if it hasn't already.

She pulls out her commD to make the call.

At first she gets that "do not interrupt" symbol. But she signals the message is urgent, and the screen dissolves into the frowning, why-are-you-bothering-me face of archeology professor Dr. Eisenfield.

Oz just says, "We found something."

"And what might that be?" Dr. Eisenfield says with annoyance running all through his voice with the lethargy of assumed superiority.

SEARCHING FOR A WAY OUT

Oz would like to slap him. "That would be a vast tunnel system underground that leads to a large and rapidly flowing river."

She can see Eisenfield was not expecting this. His mouth hangs open for a second. A little tiny mouth on a little tiny screen. "A what?"

"An underground river."

"Okay, okay. Who discovered. . . who saw all this? Just you?"

"Me and Sid."

"Then I want the two of you to keep quiet about this. Tell no one."

"Too late for that. Sid is . . . well, he's pretty much telling everyone here."

"That stupid . . ." Dr. Eisenfield grinds the word between his teeth, stops talking, and in the several seconds of silence that follows Oz can practically hear the machinery in his head working to spit out the next command. "Okay, this is what we're going to do. Nobody, I mean nobody, is to go down there until I arrive. Got that?"

"Yeah, got it." She's got it all right. Him wanting to contain the damage already done and then to lead a team down there so that he can claim he discovered the tunnels. A behavior she knows only too well.

Conversation over.

Overhead, several more news bots race to the site to join the two already here but the security bots keep them from crossing directly on to the property, but with their high-resolution cameras the news bots don't really need to cross that boundary.

The crowd on the other side of the street stirs, knowing something is up, but not yet what. The members of the city security service step out of their air-conditioned cars.

She feels the rising pressure. A concatenation of small signs, small actions, rushing headlong into a kind of explosion that she can only watch happen but can do nothing to stop.

JOHN MOON FORKER

She glances around at the barren landscape of the old Signal building, at all the mounds of dug-up earth, the litter of debris, and feels an odd, but powerful sense that her life is about to change in a sudden and enormous way.

Circuit nuzzles her leg.

But first she has to figure out what to do with Circuit. Dr. Eisenfield will have a coronary if he sees her here with a dog.

41

Gina Woolander stands at the bottom of the hole, her head still above ground where she can see across the property. Can see, in fact, Sid Juvelics roaming around, stopping everyone, waving his arms, his jaws pistoning up and down, getting whoever he's talking to all animated about something.

She never feels much like digging, but especially today, not in this heat, not after last night.

Sweat drips off her tilted oval face, her white-blond hair stringy with the dirt and sweat.

King Zee Whitehead. The man is electric. A real mover. Makes things happen. She is so excited. This could really be something. She thinks he likes her. She knows this because he's giving her the responsibility of reporting to him about anything that we find here. After all, it is his property and he should at least know what's going on. And he asked her to do it. So he trusts her.

He's such an important person. If she is with him, then some of that rubs off on her, doesn't it? She then becomes important, too.

What if she no longer had to think about things archeological? She might fly off with Mr. Whitehead to who knows where. At the very least, she won't be stuck in some hole with a shovel and practically boiling to death.

This is when she spots Sid heading straight for her. Not that she wants to see Sid right now, but it gives her a reason to climb out of this hole for a while.

"Hey, do you know what me and Oz just found?" Sid says this to her before he has even stopped walking.

Gina just gives a tiny shake of her head. She notices Sid is a couple of inches taller than her, while she's maybe three or four inches taller than Mr. Whitehead. Which is a little awkward, but she thinks she'll get past that.

Sid puts a hand on her shoulder. "Don't you want to know?"

Such little boy eagerness. "Yeah, sure." Uncomfortable with that hand on her.

Sid points with his free hand. "Right over there. We found an underground tunnel system, and there's an enormous river down there. Huge."

"What?" She lifts her head to look in that direction. This might be just the kind of thing that Mr. Whitehead asked her to look out for.

"Yeah, long, long tunnels. And there's a boat. Three boats. I wanted to get in it and see what was on the other side, but Oz chickened out saying we needed to get Dr. Eisenfield's permission first, so we came back up here."

"A tunnel? A boat? Where does it all go?"

"We don't know yet." Sid appears to be encouraged by her interest and so he pours it on. "And guess what Oz told me? A couple of days ago, she found this black stone thing right here on the property. In that underground room we were all in. Like the Phaistos disk in Crete. Says it is some kind of device. Does things."

"What kind of things?" Gina doesn't remember Oz finding anything except for that clay tablet.

Sid smiles. "Well, she told me it's some kind of fantastic tool that anything you want to do, you can make happen just by using it."

"Using it? Using it how?"

"Ah, don't really know, but it's some kind of Minoan artifact that gives you a lot of power. Something too about leading to Atlantis. Like a map maybe, or knowing where it is, sort of."

"Wow, Atlantis." Gina Woolander looks at him for the first time. "What does Dr. Eisenfield say about this?"

"That's the weird part. She never told him."

SEARCHING FOR A WAY OUT

Sid moves in a little closer, slipping the hand that is on her shoulder deeper around her back. And then she sees him bending his head toward her, his eyes closing, his lips thrusting toward her, and she freaks, not wanting him to touch her, not wanting him to kiss her. She jerks back in an almost involuntary spasm, her foot catches on a discarded piece of concrete, and she falls to the ground, hitting her head hard enough so that a certain non-working sensor pasted behind her ear now comes back to life.

"Gina, Gina, are you okay?" Sid says, bending down but Gina, holding both her arms straight out, blocking him from getting any closer. "What the fuck is wrong with you?"

"Are you—"

"Just get away!" Gina scoots back, then stands up, dusts herself off, feels the back of her head for dirt and damage.

At that moment, Dr. Eisenfield arrives at the other end of the site and Sid sees him. "Hey, there he is now. Guess I'll head back."

"Yeah, you do that."

42

Nickell needs to retreat, to shut out the present, to remember when times were good.

That's why he is sitting in his car in the empty parking lot in a state park just north of Chinatown. A park that used to be called The Cornfields—until the corn got all cut down—and then called the State Historic Park until that name was switched to what it is now, the Los Angeles River Park. A name that over reaches what it really is, which is only a small part of a much larger river restoration project started many years ago to restore the Los Angeles River to its natural state, or as near natural as the city and the long-suffering citizen groups could get it. Which included ripping up the concrete massively laid out by the Army Corp of Engineers about a century ago and slapping parks and other greenbelt zones alongside the river itself to beautify it and therefore attract city residents, which then—it was hoped—would act as a lure for commercial enterprises to establish themselves down near the newly refurbished river and so generate and boost desperately needed revenue for the city.

Only one problem. No rain, no water, no river.

The Los Angeles River is bone dry from head to foot. It's ugly, it's trash strewn, it's abandoned. Nobody comes here anymore, which is why Nickell has parked himself in this location. To be alone, to be absent from his life.

He's watching old videos of himself on his commD from back when he pitched in the minor leagues, calling out the names of hitters he faced, who later went up to the bigs and who he even sometimes got out.

This is pretty much the last time he remembers actually enjoying what he did for a living. Although it wasn't much of a living.

SEARCHING FOR A WAY OUT

Better than celebrity interviews. Which brings his thoughts back to Mitch Yellowjacket and his tip about Whitehead's old girlfriend or singing partner or whatever she was, Jasmine Too.

Yes, after his meeting with Yellowjacket, he had tracked her through the Internet, saw she had some kind of relationship with Whitehead, split with him and then sang at local nightclubs until one night she drove her car to a nightclub on Cahuenga in Hollywood but then apparently never made it from the parking lot to the club. Disappeared. Gone. Never heard from again. Couple of years ago.

And then he tracked down the guy she left Whitehead for, an Ezekiel None, a small-time actor in commD soaps, a stage name, his real name Nickell didn't find out. None wasn't real happy to be getting a communication from a journalist and had to be sweet-talked into telling him about Jasmine, but who started gushing out volumes when Whitehead's name came up, blaming Whitehead for her disappearance and her probable murder.

But since no body had been ever found, no crime was considered to have been committed. And he was pissed about that too.

What Nickell came away with is the odd coincidence of Jasmine Too's disappearance with the supposed dates of Whitehead's transformative experience out in the desert. Could be his trip to the desert had another purpose altogether.

But what's he going to do? Grab a shovel and drive out to the Cleghorn Wilderness area and randomly start digging around? Not likely.

So if Whitehead did kill her, then it would seem she was more his girlfriend than a business partner, but maybe both, and her leaving him ignited an angry fuse. He blew up. Love gone bad.

All this carries his brain into thoughts about girlfriends and relationships and love and then Oz. How does he really feel about her?

Sure, he likes her, misses her sort of, but is he moving toward love? And what are her feelings for him? That hug she gave him last night. Was that a you're-a-really-great-guy-and-I-want-to-spend-more-time-with-you hug, or was it a thanks-for-the-help-don't-call-me-I'll-call-you kind of hug?

His commD sounds an alert.

Nickell is plugged into a network that constantly monitors breaking news, and if a journalist has set up his commD to receive these alerts—which almost all of them do—then they will know when something local is happening.

This one has originated from a single news bot flying over the Signal building site. It just hovers there and watches. Hour after hour, day after day. And its tiny digital brain has an advanced algorithm that tells it when what it is watching is newsworthy or not.

This lonely news bot watched as Sid Juvelics went from person to person blabbing all about the tunnels and the river. And the excited and blooming reactions from the other archeology students triggered this algorithm to decide that it was indeed witnessing a newsworthy event and the signal was sent.

Nickell realizes he is not all that far away. Yes, there will probably be a lot of traffic between here and there—he'll have to go through downtown after all—but he might be able to beat most of the other journalists to the site.

He starts the car and roars away from the parched river.

As he drives, he zeros in on the video feed from the site. Already there is a second news bot, and it is also transmitting video.

Driving and watching a video simultaneously is a balancing act. Hopes he doesn't crash into anything.

As he slows in the snarl of traffic, he can see that the energetic movements of the archeological students have slowed. Could be it's not news after all.

SEARCHING FOR A WAY OUT

He relaxes, easing his chest back away from the steering wheel. No real rush, but he'll head over there anyway because Ramesh keeps bugging him about it and then he can make some kind of report.

A few minutes later, driving south on Alameda Street, his commD gives him a much different signal.

That nanosensor he stuck behind Gina's ear has started transmitting again.

At first he's just glad that she's safe, but then hears her placing a call on her commD. And when the other person answers, he recognizes King Zee Whitehead.

This is not good. She doesn't know what she's getting into.

"Hello, Mr. Whitehead."

"Hi, Gina. Are you at the Signal building?."

"Yes, and I just heard something. One of the grad students found some device, a stone, a black stone, and from what I'm hearing . . . you see, she told this other grad student that it is some kind of magical device that you can use to make things happen that wouldn't normally happen and there's something also about Atlantis."

"What about Atlantis?"

"I don't know really. Something about this is a key to Atlantis, or it's a clue to finding Atlantis. That part wasn't real clear."

"Who has this device?"

"Her name is Jane Ozzimo."

"And she's there right now?"

"Well, kinda. They also found a tunnel system underground here, and a lot of them are about to go down there right now."

"A tunnel system?"

"Yeah, and they said there's a river down there, too. A big river. I mean with water. Lots of water."

"Gina, I need for you to go down into this tunnel too. Keep your eyes and ears open and let me know the second you find out anything else, okay?"

"I'll do that Mr. Whitehead."

Nickell instinctively stomps down on the accelerator.

Man-o-man, there really is news. A big story. And he needs to get over there pronto.

No longer looking at the video feed, he concentrates solely on zipping around other traffic, searching for shortcuts and keeping an eye out for any random city security forces that might want to impede him on his journalistic mission.

If Oz has discovered something that Whitehead wants, then well ... what Whitehead wants Whitehead takes. Oz is in danger, which can work to his advantage because if he can help her, then she could be a great inside source for whatever is found down in those tunnels. But it's more than that, isn't it? He does care, does want to help her, does even feel a little protective. Shit, what is *he* getting himself into?

He grabs up his commD and calls Oz, voice only, don't want to be distracted by visuals when he's driving this fast.

"Nickell," she responds.

"Listen, I'm on my way to the Signal building. Should be there in a couple of minutes. Whitehead knows about this device you found. You'd better watch out."

All Nickell hears on the other end of the line is stunned silence.

"You still there?"

"How do *you* know about that?"

"I'll tell you when I get there."

"Okay, okay, meet me across the street, in the parking lot."

"Be right there," Nickell says as he slams the accelerator.

Just before she cuts the communication, Oz says, "You'd better like dogs."

43

King Zee Whitehead sits forward on the cushioned chair, his hands folded one into the other so that the tremor will not be noticeable.

He speaks to the sixteen wealthy potential donors in the Beverly Hills home of Mr. and Mrs. Abruzzi, all members of One Faith, all having done at least the first level of the Surrender Ceremony. And most say they now have a direct relationship with God.

Few of the wealthier class in One Faith. Mostly it's the poor, the ones who need the most help, the ones who play the lottery, the ones who are looking for a magic ticket out of their current lives.

But these people in this room have a strong connection to their faith, and they want that connection to God. They want to polish their spiritual lives, which, in its own way, is their magic ticket.

He's telling them the story of his time in the desert. The most dramatic manifestation of God he can give them. The one most designed to reach inside them and free their generosity.

"On the fortieth day, when I was dehydrated and hungry and didn't know how much longer I could survive, I crawled into the shade of some large boulders there in the Cleghorn Lakes Wilderness area. And by the way, there are no lakes in Cleghorn, at least not for the last hundred thousand years, anyway."

A few chuckles roam around the room.

Bug stands way off to the side, leaning on the doorjamb. Whitehead smiles at him, bringing him into the aura of this intimate tale. A tale that Bug knows better than anyone else.

"I wanted to give up. I wanted to go home. But I didn't really know where I was. I didn't know which way would lead me out and back to civilization. No GPS. And even if I had known the best way out, I also knew that it would be a long and dangerous journey. I dozed and sweated. I waited for the night.

"The stars came out, and I marveled at their magnificence. The Lord's work, I said to myself. And while in the glorious state of wonder, the sky changed. A tremendous light burst overhead and I heard a voice come right out of that light, a voice that was both in the sky and in my head. And it said to me, *You have shown your loyalty, your willingness to sacrifice and I know you want to do good work. There is much to be done. You are my messenger in this world. Spread the word. Bring the people to me. Let them find my guidance. Go forth.*"

Whitehead looks around the room, making sure everyone catches his eye. A sensuous snake of a woman lounges just off dead center, sleeveless shirt, moist lips. What was her name? But he can't linger there. This is not the time.

"Now I am asking you to help me continue this work, God's work. The cathedral we're building near downtown will be magnificent. It will be a center for those who truly want the direct connection to God. We will serve so many more people there than we can at our current overflowing location. But, of course, to build this palace for God, we need funds."

He pauses. He's made his pitch.

A man near the end on the left asks, "What about this archeological work being done there? Hasn't it stopped all progress on the building?"

"It's just a temporary halt to the demolition of the existing building. They've found some old horseshoes, and the city is trying to preserve the historical record of the city's beginnings."

Every time he tells the story of his desert experience, he almost believes it. He did have a vision of sorts. When he found that tiny pool of water, back under the rocks, and he was so thirsty. He looked at the water, wondered how contaminated it was, what microorganisms might be in there. It looked clear, but who knew? He could drink, then be heaving his guts out twenty minutes later.

But he had to have water. So he drank it. Drank a lot of it and it saved him. Wasn't that God's work?

He's careful now not to move his head too quickly. The headache is not as bad today, but any sudden movement of his head gives him a sharp jab.

He wonders if he's done something to himself that's irreversible. He isn't getting any better. Give it time. Lay off the herb. But running out of time.

Feeling pressure. Defections in the flock, revenues lacking, a sense of not making progress, of losing the head of steam that has carried them this far. Getting the cathedral built will go a long way to solving these problems. But he is on a grand mission and he will not be stopped.

His nose is still tender. That bitch really walloped him. She'll get hers in due time. But first he needs to clear up this archeology mess. Get them the hell out. Stop these questions from his donors, remove their hesitancy to contribute.

With the talk over, Mrs. Abruzzi brings out the finger foods, with the help of two of the other women, the genetically modified celery and carrots, the nano-coated, long-lasting hummus that won't spoil no matter how long you leave it out.

Some of the men stand, a couple come over and talk to Whitehead. He pretends to be interested. Waits for their commDs to come out and make the funds transfer.

But then his own commD signals him. He has all the filters in place, the automatic responses engaged, so no call can disturb him at a time like this—when he is extracting money from the donors. But he sees this one is from Gina Woolander. Could it be that she has something already?

JOHN MOON FORKER

She tells him about the tunnels and the river and more information about that black stone, so that three minutes later he is in a terrific mood. Exultant even. Hearing this news from Gina is just the kind of thing he's been hoping for.

With this river—hard to believe there is actual water—and the tunnel system, which hasn't been explored at all yet, all this suggests there is a purpose and something to be found. He might very well be on the trail to discovering the technology spoken of in the legend, this immortality potion, or even a key to finding Atlantis.

But what he must do and do without delay is get this stone thing she mentioned from that Ozzimo bitch. Here's his chance to kill two birds with one stone, ha, ha, ha.

He walks, no glides, across the room, stopping to touch a shoulder here, say a word there, but he is feeling very much back in the game. His problems are insignificant, not even worth thinking about.

He reaches Bug. "Contact Jerry. Tell him to meet us at One Faith in half an hour. I've got an assignment for him."

A second call comes in on his commD. He sees that it's from Neil Gutlog. Finally. Must be bringing him good news about tossing those archeologists out. Getting his land back.

Whitehead steps into the hallway restroom for a little privacy.

"Yes, Neil."

"Hello King. Sorry to have to tell you this, but the state of California and the federal government have decided to do a thorough exploration of your property at the Signal building and you won't have access to it for a few more weeks."

"What? They already know about the river and the tunnels?"

"What river? What tunnels?"

"I'll have to get back to you." Whitehead cuts the connection. Shit, shit, shit. Once the government finds out what's down there below the Signal building, they'll never give the land back.

SEARCHING FOR A WAY OUT

The anger inside builds. He's going to explode. The headache is fierce. He wants to kill.

44

Oz stands in the dusty, unpaved lot across the street from the Signal building that the archeologists have been using to park their cars. She stands next to her Electron, Circuit right by her knee. She scans the horizon in a minor panic.

How does Nickell know about the Minoan stone? Could it be Sid? That's the only one who knows. At least, she thinks he's the only one. Could someone else have seen it?

Oz notices the additional news bots flying over the site, along with quite a few news vans rolling in as well, a forest of transmitting antennas sprouting up out of their roofs.

She vividly smells the dust in this parking lot. The dry powder, its fine particles drifting invisibly in the air with the odors of old paint, minerals and ants.

She also notices Dr. Eisenfield now gathering the graduate students to take down into the tunnels, him looking around, probably for any stragglers of which she is one.

Come on, hurry up, she thinks, mentally urging Nickell to arrive. She realizes she is beginning to trust him, that if he wasn't coming here, she wouldn't know what to do with Circuit, that there was no one else she could rely on. A funny feeling this. Funny as in strange.

• • • •

AS HE COMES WITHIN range of the Signal building, he acutely sees that he is far from the first here. Damn it.

He pounds the steering wheel.

Look at all those news bots flying in. And the . . . no, even the City News Bureau is already here. Crap.

SEARCHING FOR A WAY OUT

Word must have leaked out. Maybe some of those students have been busy on their commDs spreading the word. No doubt. Now the entire world knows, and he's late to the party.

But none of these journalists have the sources that he has, knowing both Oz and Gina.

He spots the dirt parking lot to the left, the area where no one is except the one figure, well two, counting that dog.

• • • •

"FINALLY," OZ MUTTERS as she sees Nickell drive up.

She glances over at the site, the circle of city security forces blocking access to all journalists and onlookers at the gate. Of course, the news bots are zooming in as far as they can before being blocked by the security bots, but all they're seeing is the archeology students working or gathering around Dr. Eisenfield.

She's got to get over there now.

The second Nickell emerges from his car, she runs forward. "Look, I need a favor from you. I've got to go with the team over there, but I can't take the dog. Please take care of her for me."

"I can't take any dog. I don't know . . . I mean, I've never had a dog. I—"

"It's simple. Just watch her. Give her water." She hands him the leash.

"But—"

"She won't be any trouble, just see that she is safe. That's all I'm asking."

Mervin calls from across the street. "Oz, we're going. Come on." She can hear every syllable in exquisite distinctness despite the noise of the security forces shouting orders, the journalists pleading for access, and the mounting hum of converging vehicle traffic.

This is leftover from the stone. Somehow boosting her senses. But why? Must lead to something. Preparing her. Something she's going to hear? To smell? To see? That she wouldn't have otherwise?

Maybe amplified by her excitement at going back down there to explore. It really matters here. Maybe find some answers about the Minoans, what they did thirty-five hundred years ago and what they've been doing since.

"I'll make a deal with you," Nickell says. "I'll take care of your dog if you tell me what's going on down there." He points to the earth. "And I mean everything, what you see, what you find, and anything about that river."

"Who told you about the stone?" Oz holds Circuit's collar in one hand.

"It was . . . look, I'll tell you when you come back up."

Oz just shakes her head. "Yeah, sure. You have a deal."

"Take this." Nickell hands her a small, mostly round object. "It's a bot, like those," he nods up to the sky. "When you get to some large space, just throw it straight up into the air and it will do the rest."

Mervin is much closer now, at the site entrance, calling to her.

She stoops, strokes Circuit's head, tells her to stay with Nickell, then sprints across the street, melts through the security perimeter and joins Dr. Eisenfield and the others walking across the lot to the tunnel entrance.

45

Dr. Eisenfield turns away from the river and steps back toward the scattered group of eight graduate and four undergraduate students.

"We're going to search as much as we can today." His voice echoes faintly off the cavernous walls, doubling and doubling again. "But if you find anything, tell me first before you disturb it."

Oz can barely keep still, wants to get started, to find out what lies ahead. Rubs her arms against the cool air.

Finally, they move out, taking the path that branches away from the river, twisting around the jagged rocks thrusting up out of the ground. But once in the tunnel corridor, Oz notices it has the same smooth, packed walls, same ambient light.

What were the Minoans up to? Can understand them having a tunnel to the water but where is this one going? Must be something here. All those years they occupied the Signal building above, not calling attention to themselves, not doing anything that anybody thought was out of the ordinary, but most likely what was important to them was going on down here out of everyone's sight.

Oz falls in with Mervin to bring up the rear, them walking a little more slowly, letting the gap between them and the others widen. Oz taking more time to pick up clues and study what's around her.

"Did you and Sid get this far?" Mervin asks.

"No, we just got to the water. Then he wanted to come back." Don't want to explain to Mervin about the stone. But if Sid has blabbed it all over, the secret won't last long. But he must not have, otherwise everyone, including Dr. Eisenfield, would have been all over her. So who did he tell?

"What do you think this place is? I mean, why build all these tunnels?" Mervin says.

"Look at what we found yesterday, those Minoan vases, that clay tablet." She has to be real careful what she says here. It's all right to run these ideas past Mervin because he's not likely to say anything to anyone, not like Sid, but still she needs to protect herself. "I'm starting to believe that the people who used to occupy the building right over our heads are descendants of the Minoans."

"You've got to be kidding," Mervin says, continuing to tramp forward along the narrow dirt tunnel. "You believe in this legend bullshit?"

"Maybe, maybe not. But why did we find what we found? If they were art objects in someone's collection, wouldn't they be on display somewhere, not hidden away in some underground vault?"

"Could be a dozen reasons it got there, reasons far more likely than thinking that the Minoan civilization somehow continued and they all moved to Los Angeles some three thousand years ago."

"Yeah, maybe." Wants to sound noncommittal, as if she's only exploring an idea.

As they walk, Oz sees that the walls and ceiling are changing. Going from smooth to rough, rocks jutting out of the walls, timbers visible above. The path twists. Dr. Eisenfield must be fifty or sixty feet ahead with the others.

She feels a pressure in the air, as though it had become denser. She slows, scanning the walls. Mervin slows too, looking at her with a question on his lips but not yet asking it.

Up near the top of this tunnel she sees what appears to be a series of archways going forward, and she walks ahead looking up, until at the fifth one, she stops.

"What?" Mervin says.

Oz barely hears him. Her attention zeroed in on the arches, an anticipation, a keen edge of perception.

This fifth arch is different. Pattern recognition. She holds still. Five seconds later, she sees it. What looked like minor ridges at either end of the arch she now recognizes as carvings of snakes, then she deciphers the hands that grasp them, the arms leading back to the body and the head of the Minoan Snake Goddess, all carved expertly along the ceiling timber.

"Do you see it?" she whispers, knowing that since he was with her on Crete last summer, he'll get it.

Mervin turns, looks up, starts to say "See what?" but then stops and says, "Yes . . . snakes."

"That's Asasara."

"The snake goddess."

"Minoan, you see?"

"Well, I'll be . . ."

Oz looks down and to her left, on the wall, directly below the one snake she sees a tiny replica of the eye symbol she pressed to open up the original tunnel entrance.

She touches this one, and the wall slides away.

"Holy shit," Mervin says.

They are at the entrance to a large circular room. It must be thirty feet across Oz calculates.

"You'd better call him," she nods up the passageway.

"Yeah, he'd be pissed if he missed this." Mervin takes a step back and shouts, "Hey, over here, we've found something."

Oz and Mervin walk into the room.

In the center, she sees a raised circular platform. The platform itself appears to be made of rock and is about ten feet across. Upon it looks to be some kind of three-dimensional topographical map.

"Don't touch anything," Dr. Eisenfield says as he quickly enters the room and swerves to the right, Gina beside him.

Oz moves toward the platform to get a better look.

It's a section of the Mediterranean Sea. The island of Crete, the sixty miles of ocean between it and what is now called the island of Santorini, but what she's seeing isn't Santorini. This looks like the island of Thera, the way it was before the volcanic explosion blew it into several pieces. And look, it's an island within an island. Circles. Just like Plato wrote about Atlantis. This entire center section that got blown out by the volcano. Gone.

She taps two fingers on her lips. Some kind of map room. This is good. Very good. It's finally starting to unravel.

She glances over at Dr. Eisenfield to see if he's noticed what this is because once he does, he'll have to make the connection to the Minoans. He's telling one undergraduate to go back up and bring another five students down here.

Mervin points, "Wow, would you look at that."

She follows his gaze to the part of the wall banding the entire circular room up near the ceiling and sees a continuous mural, about seven or eight feet tall.

Even in the dim ambient light, she can see a mural crowded with a cascade of people and plants and animals and structures. She has the sense of some grand design, some pattern, some interconnectedness to it all.

But she feels a presence and glances toward Dr. Eisenfield, catching the tail end of him staring at her, flicking his head away, but not before she saw the anger in his eyes.

She found this room, not him, and he doesn't like that.

Dr. Eisenfield goes back to looking up at a part of the mural showing a series of images. The first is of an old man. A man bent and stooped by age. But then there are the images of four more men to his right, each one successively younger and more full of life than the last, until the man on the far right of this group appears to be in the prime of life.

Despite the noise of the other students and the distance between them, Oz clearly hears Dr. Eisenfield as he tilts his head toward Gina. "What does that suggest to you?"

SEARCHING FOR A WAY OUT

Gina has her mouth open. Probably gauging what to say, trying to figure out what he wants to hear. "Going from old to young, I don't know."

"Exactly. Someone who has already reached old age then reverses the process. Could be a clue. Could be there is something to these tales about an immortality drug?"

Oz flashes to the Snake Goddess, often associated with primal energy and creation, a creature who can shed its skin and so renew life. In other words, be immortal.

Could it be that Dr. Eisenfield is buying into the myth? This might work out.

The mural is huge and complex. So many layers. Oz sees the artist has depicted not just static images of the natural world but shows the animals and insects hunting, eating, building nests, foraging and the plants photosynthesizing sunshine, all picturing a highly connected world where everything interacts with every other thing and all the people up there on the mural—and she can see a town full of them—fitting right in, humans as a part of the whole design, a design that appears to her to be so integrated that it is nearly alive. A depiction of life she has never seen so vividly outside of actually being there. In fact, more so because the artist has emphasized those connections.

Animism. That's what this is. Where everything is alive, even inanimate objects, but more than alive, having a living spirit, a consciousness. Is this what the Minoans were up to? Some far-reaching concept of life where everything is alive? Maybe more than that. Maybe they've found a way to inhabit such a world. Where it is an everyday reality.

Maybe it's the same feeling she had in the cave on Crete.

She brings her eyes back up. Walks along the wall, scanning the mural. She stops. Recognizes something but . . . what is it? The drawing of an oddly twisted tree. Looks like a California oak. One that started life out mostly growing horizontally. Looks like it did this for a few years before shooting up, but even then, it did not go straight up but angled somewhat backward. Right next to it are a couple of rocks that seem to form the familiar Minoan symbol of the bull's horns.

Oz has seen this somewhere. Somewhere in the real world, she thinks, not just in some other drawing. This weird tree, this rock formation. Where has she seen it?

Her thoughts race, examining memories. And then she turns the image around in her mind. See it from another angle. Yes, that's it. She has driven right by this on the road in Topanga, on the way to one of the many trailheads.

This drawing, she guesses, is how it looks from the land angled toward the road.

Too much of a coincidence. She has to go out there. Now might be a good time. With the influx of the rest of the students from above now filtering in, she could leave without being noticed. And she's been down here a pretty long while.

Got to get back and take care of Circuit. Nickell is likely about to blow a gasket up there.

She slips back out into the corridor and races toward the entrance and, having thought of Nickell, remembers the bot he handed to her. She pulls it out of her pocket and releases it into the air where the bot powers-up and flies away.

46

Oz clenches her teeth against the visual onslaught above ground, the huge horde of jabbering people outside the fence pressing to get in, the line of security forces holding them back, the whizzing news and security bots overhead. The dozen or so students still above ground simply stare at this madness.

She just wants to find Circuit and get out of here. Chase down that image she knows is real.

Scanning, scanning, scanning. Where is Nickell? Don't see him in that little parking area, but she can't see that too well from here anyway. Got to move closer.

She walks through the gate, past the security agents, and into the street, dodging around news vans, the excited crowd hoping to get a glimpse of the treasures they've heard are being found here and even more security forces.

Two reporters, aiming their commDs at her, run up and begin firing questions at her, such as "Did you find Atlantis?" which she ignores, looking past them to see if she can spot Circuit or Nickell.

Another thirty feet into the crowd, she spots them. Along the edge of a weedy ravine, a little behind the mob, Nickell is bent over with a water bottle, dribbling it out so that Circuit can drink.

Points for him, Oz thinks. Maybe her blossoming trust is not a mistake.

She arrives eight seconds later and right away says, "Who told you about the device I found? Was it Sid Juvelics?"

"Well, hello to you too." Nickell straightens up.

Circuit comes over and leans into her leg. She reaches down and runs her hand across the dog's back.

Oz worries about others knowing she has the stone, but even more angry than worried. Feeling betrayed. "I need to know."

Nickell shrugs assent. "I overheard Gina telling Whitehead about you and she said that another graduate student told her, one who had been with you."

"Gina told Whitehead? That's not good. It's spreading and Sid must have told her." Oz practically spits out his name. "That weasel."

"You told this guy?"

"Not exactly. I somehow dropped it, he picked it up, and I had to tell him what it was." She looks up at the sky for a second and then decides. "Okay, stay here for a minute. I'll be right back."

"You don't have the time."

She ignores this and marches back over to the gate, shows the security agent her badge, and storms straight across the field to where Sid Juvelics is standing and laughing with a couple of the undergraduate women.

Without even shortening her stride, she grabs his arm and commands, "Come with me."

Stumbling backward and still laughing, Juvelics puts a mock-helpless look on his face for the benefit of the two undergraduate women that says he's just too adorable and all the women want to take him away for their own.

But after being half-dragged another fifty feet, he's not laughing.

"You drooling blabbermouth," Oz says, her face just inches from his, her voice sharp and unyielding. "Why on earth did you tell Gina what I told you down there? Huh? Why?"

"You didn't say it was a secret . . . I didn't think any harm . . . what's the problem?"

"The problem is that you're an untrustworthy, unreliable son-of-a-bitch." With each of these last four words, she is jabbing three fingers into his chest and he's going, "ow, ow, ow."

He's tries to grab her hand to stop the jabbing, but she slaps him hard on the face and he only has a moment to register the surprise when she slaps him again even harder and he collapses straight down to the ground.

He moans, rolling in the dust, holding his head in his hands.

Oz turns and stomps back across the field.

She's steaming. But anger is an emotional luxury right now, one she can't afford, because as soon as the news that she has this stone gets out, Eisenfield will probably toss her out of the department right then and there.

She just wants to get out of here now. Grab Circuit and go.

But when she crosses back over the street, Nickell says, "We have to talk."

"Not now." She grabs Circuit's collar.

"Yes, now. That was our deal."

She closes her eyes, knowing she has to endure even more. "What?"

"I see you released the bot. Thank you. But I need you to tell me what's going on down there. What the context is. What the bot can't give me."

"All right." Her shoulders slump and she lets out a big breath.

"Not here. It's too dangerous here. I don't know why Whitehead is interested in this stone thing, but I know him. He's going to come after you or the stone or both. You'd be better off not being alone. And you need to make a plan."

Oz looks at him for a long moment. "Okay, get your car and follow me."

47

Bug and Mr. Whitehead stand in the smaller of the two One Faith kitchens.

Whitehead drinks from a bottle of refrigerated distilled water.

"You should eat something," Bug says, concern in his voice.

"Now is not the time. A lack of food provides a certain mental clarity." He walks along the counter, one hand, trembling slightly, riding over the surface. "Where is Jerry?" Impatience.

"Said he was on his way down."

Bug stands in a kind of paralysis. He wants to stop Mr. Whitehead. He can't do to Tammy what he did. And to that Oz woman, what he did to her on stage. And what he appears to be doing to this Gina Woolander. Abusing them, hurting them, manipulating them. It sickens him.

Yet, he believes in Mr. Whitehead, the work he is doing, One Faith, the outreach to thousands of people who now have a direct relationship to God.

He wants to believe that Mr. Whitehead's behavior is entirely due to his dangerous overuse of the DTG machine and especially those South American herbs. He has done something to himself that is just not healthy. It has changed him, made him a kind of monster.

If only Bug could get him to stop, to rest for a while, then possibly all this gets better, and then he wouldn't have to act, wouldn't have to do something that would be disloyal.

But more than disloyal. If he has to act to stop Mr. Whitehead and that results in the collapse of One Faith, what happens to him?

Before One Faith, his life was going nowhere. Now, he is an important person. He has status. He gets to make meaningful decisions. With One Faith gone, all that disappears.

The hulking Jerry enters the room.

SEARCHING FOR A WAY OUT

Whitehead says, "Jerry, I need you to get something for me. This archeologist woman, Jane Ozzimo, has a small device, a black stone, that I need to have." Whitehead bores right into Jerry's eyes. "Bring someone you trust, someone who will keep their mouth shut, and go over to her place tonight, when she is home from the archeology site."

"Yes, Mr. Whitehead."

Bug was afraid of this, but hoped Mr. Whitehead wouldn't go this far. He's going to have to decide. He rests a hand on the kitchen counter to steady himself.

What is he going to do?

48

Oz drives her Electron less than twenty blocks to the tiny San Julian Park on East 5th. She wants to have Circuit with her and this little patch of open space is the closest place she could think of.

She and Nickell sit on a bench in the shade. Circuit rests on her haunches next to Oz, gazing at the shimmering skyline.

Electric cars whiz by on 5th Street, an old man with a crooked nose and a red baseball cap scatters bird seed in the other end of the park a few feet away and only one small sparrow is there darting back and forth picking up the seed.

After she tells Nickell everything she knows about what's underground, he says, "Look, I believe you're in great danger. When Gina reported to Whitehead and told him about this black stone thing, she said it had something to do with Atlantis and how this stone was almost magical, that you could make happen whatever you wanted to make happen. When he heard this, Whitehead got extremely interested. He's coming after it. No question."

"What are you suggesting? I can't stop living my life."

"For starters, you probably don't want to go home."

"Because of her," Oz nods down at Circuit, "I wasn't going home anyway. Going to a friend's. Out in Malibu."

"You know," Nickell says, "instead of you waiting for him to catch you at the time of his choosing, why don't you take the offensive? Help me set a trap for him."

"What do you mean? What kind of trap?" Oz doesn't like the word trapped. Being trapped is about the worst thing she can imagine. Of course, she doesn't need to imagine it at all. She was trapped in that canyon under that water and almost died.

"We lead him to you, but in a time and place of our choosing, where we can expose the real Whitehead."

SEARCHING FOR A WAY OUT

"And how would this not be really, really, dangerous?"

She feels the fear, but it's at a little distance. The odd thing is that she has some belief in him. A kind of calm about it, even though she knows he wants to use her as a kind of bait to lure in Whitehead.

"Sure, there is an element of danger, but we can control it. Since we're leading him to us, we won't be surprised, and although he won't know it at first, witnesses will surround him."

"I just don't see it. How does this work?" Oz says.

"We lead him to a secluded spot but one that is close to a public place and when he makes his move, you go out into that public—"

"Hold on. Just where is this place?"

"I was thinking down by the beach. Venice boardwalk. Someplace like that."

"Wait." Oz puts her hand up, fingers together. "What about the HOPE event tomorrow night?"

"But there's supposed to be eighty or ninety thousand people there, maybe more. He'd never try—"

"He's already supposed to be there, right?" Oz says.

"Yeah," Nickell says, drawing out the word to an extra syllable while he thinks about this. "He could use all those people as a cover, corner you somewhere out of sight, and then he'd have you, or so he would think. But since you know he's coming, you are never really cornered. When he makes his move, you dive straight into the crowd, and I'm there to record the whole thing and we expose him."

"Still sounds kinda weak. We're depending on him being so public relations conscious that he'll be too embarrassed to continue—"

"But here's the thing. We know he will come after you. Isn't it better to do it this way and not wait for him to take you by surprise at home, at the grocery store, in your car, just about anywhere? At least this way you have a chance. And, I think, a good chance."

"I don't... how will he know that I'm going to be at the HOPE event?"

"Tomorrow morning at the dig, you strike up a casual conversation with Gina and work that little piece of info into it."

"And I'm just supposed to ignore that's she told Whitehead about the stone?"

She just can't see Gina turning on her like this. Not that they were friends, but they sure weren't enemies. Has Whitehead so poisoned her?

"If you want to make this work, you will." He shrugs. "And I think you should tell me about this black stone. What it is and what it does?"

Oz had been hoping he wouldn't ask this. The less others know, the better. But...

"It has writing on it. Ancient Minoan writing called Linear A, well, a hieroglyphic version of it. And Linear A has never been translated, so even if Whitehead got his hands on it, he wouldn't know what it says."

"You don't either, do you? But you got it to work somehow."

"Yeah, sort of, but it was by accident, an accident I don't think he'll have."

"But which won't stop him from trying to take it."

She looks at him for a moment and wonders if she can trust him. Danger is ahead.

"Hey, I've got to go," Oz says.

"I should go with you. Just in case Whitehead—"

"No, I'll be fine. I have something important I need to check out. We'll talk tomorrow."

She stands and walks to her car, Circuit close by.

The man in the red cap still feeding that one lone sparrow.

49

They turn left at Old Topanga Road in densely wooded Topanga Canyon. Vegetation carpets the steep, jagged inclines, deep gullies, and mountain peaks. Yet, the lack of water distresses many trees. Some already down.

Oz's Electron doesn't much like having to chug up the long hill from Pacific Coast Highway, especially with the three of them loading down the car.

"What do you expect to find out here?" Midori says.

"That tree and rock formation I saw on the underground mural. I remember seeing it out this way. I'm hoping it means there is something out here, that it wasn't just a drawing on a wall that someone put there because they thought it was pretty or anything like that."

"Yeah, but like what? More of those tunnels?"

"No, not that. But maybe people. If the Minoans—the people that I am thinking of as Minoans anyway abandoned that building, where did they go? They must live somewhere. Maybe out here."

"Let me picture this. You knock on their door and when they answer, you ask them if they are the direct descendants of a civilization that everyone thought died out. What? About four thousand years ago?"

"More like thirty-five hundred."

"Excuse me." Midori laughs. "This ought to be interesting."

Oz doesn't expect to find anyone here. If they emptied the Signal building, they probably left wherever else they were too. But they could have left some equipment behind or documents or something that would explain more of the legend and what the technology was that those Minoans sent on ahead all those thousands of years ago.

As they turn, on their right is the old Inn of the Seventh Ray, closed for many years then burned to the ground along with about twenty acres just a couple of months ago. Oz thinks they're lucky that more hasn't burned around here.

Just as they pass Hondo Canyon Road, Circuit sits up in the back seat and barks once.

"What's gotten into her?" Midori says.

"I . . . " Oz says when sees it up ahead on the left. The California oak that began life growing mostly horizontally and the rocks that seem to form the familiar Minoan bull's horns.

Oz has slowed the car to about two miles per hour as she looks up.

Midori says, "Over there. An old mailbox and what might be a driveway, but it's . . . it's a little overgrown."

Oz feels excitement and apprehension and fatigue. But what she feels is anticipation. She's going to find something.

Oz stops the car, looks at the corroded, rusty chain drawn across the barely visible dirt driveway—if it is a driveway—and then looks at Midori.

"Here?" Midori says.

"Looks like it."

As soon as she opens the door, Circuit bounds out of the car, runs ahead ten feet, spins around and barks three times.

"I guess we are here," Midori says, standing up. "Wherever here is."

Oz walks over to the sagging chain stretched between the two posts. A very large gray metal lock hooks through the end of the chain and into a thick, iron eye-end bolted into the post.

When she touches the lock, it comes apart, and the chain falls to the ground. Is it just so old that it fell apart? Or was it designed that way?

SEARCHING FOR A WAY OUT

They all return to the car and begin driving slowly up the dirt driveway, Oz noticing faint tire tracks marking the soil.

She smells honey and jasmine and eucalyptus drifting in from the woods.

Must be an actual destination up ahead, she thinks, tracking the odometer. She knows from hiking in this area there is a steep ridge line up ahead and wonders just how far in this path will take them.

In the thick foliage, she hears many birds squawking and chirping.

Midori practically has her face pressed against the windshield, trying to see everything on either side of the road.

"This is like going back to the forest primeval," she says.

Oz glances in the rearview mirror and sees Circuit sitting up looking into the mirror at her. Almost like she wants to tell me something, Oz thinks.

At about a hundred yards in, the path widens and they see the first structures.

On the right appears to be the main house, but instead of a normal roof, there are a series of platforms all at different heights. On the left side are two buildings, one warehouse size and the other pretty much a shack.

"Do you think somebody is living here now?" Midori says.

"Awfully quiet."

Oz slows the Electron down to crawling speed, looking intently left to right and back again. No greeting party, no sign of anybody being around, but someone could easily be out there unseen.

They pull into the wide courtyard that circles around a fountain in the center, more like a rock formation that reaches toward the sky with water furiously gushing out from the top and running down the sides of the rocks into a ten-foot basin below where it churns relentlessly.

She steps out of the car. Scans three hundred and sixty degrees. Nothing. No humans.

Circuit walks over and sits right next to her leg.

A slight breeze wiggles the leaves on the grove of towering bamboo trees lined up a little behind the main house.

The fountain abruptly stops. A deep silence surrounds them.

Midori says, "That was no coincidence."

"Must be a sensor we tripped." Still looking out to the surrounding woods as if expecting someone to walk out of them.

"They know we're here." Midori scans around now too. "Oz. Tell me. What are you really looking for?"

Oz speaks carefully. "I've seen evidence of the lives of people who lived thousands of years ago on the archeological digs I've been a part of. From those experiences, I have a powerful sense there is some layer underneath all that I've seen. This layer has something to do with community. But more than that, how to live in harmony with each other, with this planet. I believe that somewhere in the ancient world, some tribe or civilization knew how to live together on the earth without screwing everything up and somehow that knowledge was lost. But I really couldn't put my finger on what any of these civilizations had done that would lead me to believe this. Until the legend."

"This is how you found out about the Minoans."

"Yeah, someone discovered the legend about a dozen years ago on Crete. Way before I got into archeology. And, although a good part of the source material unfortunately had been destroyed, enough was revealed to show a civilization so advanced for its time that I remember thinking then that these ancient Minoans must have found the key to living on this planet."

"The Atlantis thing. I remember."

"Kinda, but that was just a word, a concept," Oz says. "I didn't really know what any of all this meant until I had that experience

SEARCHING FOR A WAY OUT

in the cave three months ago. Then I knew what the Minoans had discovered or invented or created or whatever they did. I knew because I felt it."

Oz grasps at the memory of that moment. But over time, that memory has continued to fade, becoming more of a fact or an image of a fact and not so much anymore the feeling. But the feeling was important, the feeling that transported her back to the days when her mother read her stories about the lives of others and how she immersed herself in that, loved imagining herself as one of those people. As a little girl, she was so outgoing and curious and exploding with energy and for that one brief moment in the cave she had it all back. For one brief moment, she was free of all the emotional garbage that had littered her mind, trapping her.

Yes, that feeling is what she's searching for.

That's when Oz sees one of those robot insects she saw at the Signal building whiz by her head flying out deeper into the woods.

50

Oz smells chlorophyll, frogs, wet earth, jacaranda trees. Each distinct. Each a sign of water. Water in this drought?

Circuit puts her nose into the back of Oz's knee for an instant.

"Let's find out if anybody's home," Midori says.

But knocking on the house door brings no response, so they walk across the courtyard to the large, windowless, one-story, warehouse-like building, go down a ramp and open the door.

They are practically assaulted with the woody, earthy smell of highly concentrated fungi. Little daylight seeps in and no electric lights are on, but the same blue atmospheric glow Oz saw in the tunnels is here as well, but with a higher intensity.

Mushrooms everywhere, growing on logs, on wood chips, and on mounds of earth, the space nearly bursting with its fecundity, orange ones, blue ones, tall ones. All clustered on either side of a narrow path curving to the rear.

"I wonder if you can eat any of these," Midori says, turning her head across a wide arc to see all the room.

They arrive at what appears to be a mountain of metal. Old scraps of electrical boxes, rebar, car frames, light poles and many other shapes too distorted or torn apart to identify stacked up nearly to the ceiling. And from just about every crevice or edge or exposed surface, all of this metal sprouting thousands, maybe tens of thousands of mushrooms.

"Unbelievable," Midori says, a sense of wonder flushing her voice.

Oz bends closer. "The mushrooms are eating the metal. Absorbing it."

Midori spins around. "Then this entire building must be some kind of laboratory."

SEARCHING FOR A WAY OUT

"And they've found a way to break material objects down into basic molecular structure and—"

"—reabsorb it back into the natural cycle," Midori says, practically vibrating with excitement.

Oz, too, feels excited. Another clue as to what the Minoans have been doing. Not just exploring the mind, but sharpening it to be more creative. Already well-known for their art, their paintings and murals, they must have turned to technology like this.

Midori has run ahead, to the end of the building and shouts, "Oz, come here, you've got to see this."

Oz and Circuit hurry back. Midori points.

A large rectangular pit maybe twenty feet long by ten feet wide and about thirty feet deep.

Suspended over this opening is a large membrane glistening with the sheen of fungi. And just above it is a cauldron of sorts, an immense vessel that slowly pours out what Oz—judging from the smell—thinks is thick oil sludge and human waste.

It drips in large globs onto the membrane, spreads out, and then she can see what almost looks like an electrical charge streaming across the membrane as the fungi converges on the sludge, absorbs it, eats it, digests it, and excretes what appears to be clear and clean water down into the pit below. Not slow, but metabolically sped up fungi.

White rocks line the bottom of the pit, allowing her and Midori to see all the way to the bottom.

Midori bends so far over the edge of the pit she looks as though she might fall in. "This is amazing." She looks up. "You know what this means?"

"That all of those vats the city has been building to contain all the human waste might not be necessary."

"Holy shit." Midori laughs. "Pardon the pun."

If the Minoans did this, Oz thinks, what else have they done?

"Midori, let's check out the rest of the property."

"But..."

"We'll come back."

Next door is more like a shack than a building. A wooden structure built in the shape of an L.

Opening the door produces a cloud of dust. Nobody's been in here for a while. Narrow opening with little open space inside so only Oz can go in.

What she sees is shelf after shelf of what appears to be electronic equipment. Metal boxes of all sizes and shapes, some with dials and knobs, others with gauges, some with screens, but all of them covered in thick dust.

She steps in a couple of feet, rakes her hand through the air to push aside the cobwebs and brings her face up close to one of the metal boxes on a shelf pretty much at eye level. She blows a hard burst of air to see if she can dislodge the dust and read something that might tell her what it is. But that doesn't work, so she uses her thumb to wipe away some of the grime.

But there are no words to see. She taps her finger on the glass gauge, but nothing happens. She didn't really expect that anything would. It's just a pathetic mess in here. Just junk. Seems unlike the Minoans to have that fungi next door cleaning everything up and then dump all this crap in here.

On the right-hand side of this metal box is a dial. It's set to zero. It goes up to twelve. She turns it to eight. Hears nothing, sees nothing. She turns it up to eleven. Still nothing. So she leaves it there, backs out of the doorway and shuts the door.

Maybe all these are their failed projects.

"A lot of old junk," she says to Midori.

If she had stayed in that room a few seconds more, she would have seen the gauge needle jump and then rise. She would have seen

SEARCHING FOR A WAY OUT

the embedded diode lights flicker on at the front of the box. She would have heard the pulsating hum.

But she saw or heard none of those things.

And she didn't pull the box off the shelf and look at the plate on the back that had stamped on it the words "Weather Control."

51

Oz, Midori and Circuit return to the main house.

Oz knocks on the door. Again no response. She tries the handle and the door clicks open an inch.

"Do you think we should just walk in there?" Midori says, putting a hand on Oz's arm.

"At this point, yes."

Oz believes she is running out of time. Maybe not so much running out of time as running out of opportunity. She has to find something here on this land. Has to convince Dr. Eisenfield or go around him. Has to avoid Whitehead who, at the very least, will try to take the black stone from her and might even harm her. If she comes up empty here and the only piece of Minoan technology that she has is taken from her, then what is she left with?

What could she hope to find? Another black stone? A key to Linear A translation? An answer to why the Minoans came to California and what they've been working on all these centuries?

And she thinks about the labyrinth. Or what she thinks that map she found in the white room is showing her. A map that was way too conveniently placed in that room for her to find. And that old woman, the holographic image, her just happening to walk by.

Obviously, showing Oz some of their technology. Leading her on. But all for what? Why not show her more? Point her in the right direction? But then maybe this is the right direction. Then there must be something in this house. Even some tiny clue would be helpful.

They enter the house, move cautiously. Brilliant white walls all around. Oz touches one. Incredibly smooth. It must be some kind of plaster or even clay that's been worked repeatedly.

SEARCHING FOR A WAY OUT

The long and narrow room has a wood floor. No furniture. The end of the room is completely open to the forest, no wall, no glass.

They turn around and walk to the beginning of a hallway, where they encounter a California pepper tree. The floor has been built around the tree to allow it to exist right where it is. Oz looks straight up. The tree has got to be at least thirty feet tall, branches shooting off in abundance with its characteristic rain of leaves.

Whoever lived here was bringing the outdoors right in. Nature integrated. Oz glances at Midori, who seems even more awed than she is.

She can see several sections of the roof that are open to the sky. And see other trees growing in other parts of the house.

Wouldn't birds, insects, and dust overrun the house? Lots of dust. But when she ran her hand across the wall, her fingers were clean, and she hasn't seen one bird or insect.

And another thing, Oz thinks, it must be close to one hundred degrees outside, but in here it is very comfortable even with these openings. Air conditioning? Can't hear it. And not likely to be any since it would cost a fortune to run it all day and even then it wouldn't be able to make the house this temperate.

What invisible technology is doing this? The Minoans have a lot to show her here, apparently. Good. But where are they keeping it?

They walk down a long hallway. Oz smells eucalyptus, and she hears the creaking of the wood in the house as if it's singing. Everything is so still and so clear. It's as though the space itself is altered so that everything in it becomes more distinct.

How would you even begin to produce an effect like this? But it reminds her of what she experienced in the cave. Not the same, but similar. She just might be on to something here.

Oz opens the door to what must have been a bedroom. Again, no furniture.

A hard platform sits at the far end of the room. The eucalyptus tree she smelled passes through here on its way to the sky.

"What happens when it rains?" Midori says. "Does everything just get wet?"

"Well," Oz says, "since it doesn't rain anymore that doesn't matter."

"Yeah, but it used to rain."

"Good point."

She walks around the perimeter of the room. The far wall is missing, completely open to the outdoors, a large patio beyond that with two chairs.

The rooms hold just the platform and a built-in closet with a series of drawers. Oz pulls them out one by one. The drawers are empty except for a small metal object attached to a thin leather strap. When Oz picks it up, she stares at it.

Midori looks at it and says, "Isn't that a Minotaur?"

"That's exactly what it is." She turns it over in her hand. On the back, she sees the word Asterion.

"Who's Asterion?"

"The creature's proper name. The one used on Crete." Oz slips the strap around her neck.

They left this for her, didn't they? The Minotaur. The eater of humans. Are they telling her something about the journey she's on?

Circuit paces around the room.

Oz looks out into the trees and sees another one of those robot insects. Just hovering there as if it tracking them.

Well then, Oz thinks, they've got to be mechanical unless the Minoans have learned how to train insects. But if this thing is really watching us, who is it reporting to?

"Let's check out the next room."

She pops open the door, but once she sees what's inside, she stops dead. "Unreal."

SEARCHING FOR A WAY OUT

Midori peers around her and Circuit trots right inside, looks left, looks right, wags her tail.

Every other part of the house they've been in has had little or no furniture. The walls have been white. No color. Minimalism throughout.

But here the room isn't even a room. Not in the usual sense of it being square or rectangular. This is all curves and angles. She can't even use terms like trapezoid or octagon because, with walls slanting every which way, this isn't those either.

But forget the shape. She can hardly even see the shape of the room what with the fantastic profusion of plants and trees filling the space, the trees mostly just passing through, holes in the floor where they come up out of the ground from down below and holes up above where they travel through with some leafy branches appearing here in this room like giant bushes.

Two large tree trunks stand about seven feet apart. Both sawed down to around two feet high. Smoothed and sanded platforms now. Like seats.

On the walls, of those parts she can see, is a mural, much like the one under the Signal building, but this one covers every square inch of the wall, and it is animated. Figures in motion.

"This is fantastic," Midori says. "And I mean that in the most ethereal way possible."

"It fits though. Being way out here in Topanga, where nature is most abundant, and they have cultivated it, brought it right into their lives."

She moves quicker as her eagerness grows.

Slightly to her right, she sees a representation of the long-time archeological dig at Akrotiri on the island of Santorini. But it's a little odd. Instead of focusing on what has been uncovered at this site for the last sixty plus years, most of that work is angled to the side and the view looks off to the distance, toward a more western part of the island and the bay beyond that. The bay that didn't exist until the volcano blew that section of Thera out into space.

Oz doesn't think that whoever lived here and worked in this room had these animations running on this wall all day long, distracting them. More likely, what she's seeing is what she's meant to see. That robot insect outside. Feeding info to someone. Someone who's running these images.

And since they are showing her this, maybe they are telling her that this should be checked out.

Feeling manipulated. An actor in someone else's movie. But she has to see it to the end.

"Hey," Midori says, "take a look at this."

Down near the base of the wall Oz sees the image of the Signal building and just below it is one of the underground tunnels, a jagged, zigzag of a tunnel, and dead center in it is the half-human, half-bull, Minotaur. Bent back on its legs, it is swallowing a human whole. Half in, half out. Looks like a woman.

Oz shudders. So real. So horrible. One of the Minotaur's eyes is swung outward as if looking straight at her. She can almost feel the cold death, the being eaten alive. She turns her head.

Maybe then there is a labyrinth under the building. And maybe there is something very dangerous. Not a half-man, half-bull, of course, but something just as fatal. Something the Minoans put there to do. What? Not protect the building. Nobody even knew about the underground. So it must be something they used for themselves. Testing themselves. Confronting the Minotaur, whatever it is. And maybe they have it there for her.

Oz looks up. "Do you feel something?"

She senses a subtle change in air quality. Feels like the atmosphere before a thunderstorm. A tingling creeps up the back of her neck.

"What?"

SEARCHING FOR A WAY OUT

Circuit barks. One of the tree stumps glows.

A brilliant flash of pure white light blinds them and then recedes rapidly. But as their eyes recover, the form of the old woman begins appearing on that glowing tree stump like liquid being poured into a glass.

52

Two seconds later, the complete holographic image of the woman stands before them in such crystal clarity that Oz believes for a few moments that this old woman actually exists right here, right now.

Circuit calmly faces the woman as if waiting for her next biscuit, but both Oz and Midori are backing up as if to escape destruction.

And even as she's stumbling backwards, Oz sees that it's the same woman she saw inside the Signal building.

Then it clicks in her brain that this might be a good thing. That now might come some answers.

But the illusion of this old woman being present snaps when she speaks. Instead of words, her voice comes out as high-pitched tones interspersed with many hisses and pops.

Oz thinks it sounds like regular speech but just speeded up so much that it is completely incomprehensible. A person couldn't speak that fast, could they?

"Who is she?" Midori says, her voice higher and a little unsteady.

"Saw her in the . . . no, saw her holographic image at the Signal building."

Oz can't take her eyes off the woman. So strange, yet so alluring.

The figure moves, but the movement is like micro-sprints in space, changing positions without fluidity, the body transporting inch by inch too quickly to actually see the movement.

Oz blurts out, "Who are you?"

The old woman stops. Has the look on her face that she now realizes she can't be understood.

She points to the other sawed-off tree stump near where Oz stands. It's almost as if Oz can see an arc of tiny information packets streaming through the air.

SEARCHING FOR A WAY OUT

When Oz sits on the stump, the flat disc overhead—just like the one over the stump the old woman stands on—lights up.

The instant after that, the world seems to slow down around her. Midori and Circuit appear to be moving as though in a tank of water.

Her senses are more alive. Each plant in the room has its own separate odor. Each object has its own sound. She feels a unique molecular vibration of the space, of the trees coming up through the floor, of Midori, of Circuit, and even of the woman who is only a holograph.

The old woman gestures, then speaks. "Welcome to <hiss>".

The old woman has the kindest, most alert eyes she's ever seen. Just standing there waiting for her to . . . what? To assimilate? But then she notices that jerking motion of the old woman's body has stopped. She does not appear to be jumping from frame to frame, but to exist in a more fluid state.

"What . . . I . . . why are we here?"

"Hello Jane Ozzimo, my name is Aurora Pointe and . . ."

But the rest of what she says unravels in hisses and pops, the distortion too great to make out the words.

"I didn't get all of that."

"The technology <hiss> there yet <hiss> at a different <pop, pop>.

"Where are you?" Oz says. "I mean, I'm really only looking at an image of you, right? You are actually somewhere else."

"I am <hiss> . . ." Aurora turns partially around as if looking at something behind her or speaking to someone in her world.

Oz strains to see but cannot.

When Aurora turns back around, she says, "I know this will seem incomprehensible to you but <hiss> in the same world, just in a different dimension. A much <hiss> is the word frequency. You could say that we are in a higher frequency than you in this world.

Aurora turns around again. Oz can just see a corner of bright light coming through. The light beam strikes her.

She glimpses this other world, other frequency. Or more accurately, she feels it. The world in which this Aurora Pointe inhabits. The beam is an information flow. Oz feels it as variations of heat and cold like her body is a piano keyboard and the temperature plays a song.

Oz perceives a dense purity, a world where everything is both absolutely distinct and yet highly interconnected at the same time. And it's moving at such an incredible speed. No wonder the woman can't be understood here. Her words are traveling at the speed of light, and she is listening at the speed of sound.

But even more than all this, something peeks out from behind. Some color, some warm color, a feeling that Oz can barely touch but that magnetizes her, draws her in, awakening a deep hunger.

Aurora turns back, blocking the light.

"Can I call you Oz?"

"Yes." Oz feels transfixed to the tree stump, the light, the molecular field. "And can I call you Aurora?"

Laughter. "<pop> go ahead. Nice pendant you have on."

"I found it in an empty room. Why are the all the rooms empty except for this one?"

"Can't tell you <hiss> tell you later."

"Why are you here talking to us? What's going on over at the Signal building? What do you mean—*frequency*?" She has about a million questions, and at this rate, with this interference, she will get none of them answered.

"<hiss> a long time. Ever since you walked into that sanctuary cave on the island of Crete."

"You saw me there?"

"Most assuredly. And we have observed <pop> work."

SEARCHING FOR A WAY OUT

"I am having a very hard time understanding you. The words are not clear."

"Yes <hiss> different frequencies. But wait <hiss> our work. Important that you know."

"I'm missing so much of what you're saying." Oz leans forward as if to make the words clearer. She tells herself to focus even more. If she can just pay more attention, maybe she will understand it. She is on the edge of finding out, just another tiny bit more. Oh please!

"Yes," Aurora says. "Awful connection, then listen <hiss> the <hiss> do you understand?"

"No, no, I didn't get it."

"The Signal building. Go <hiss> down to the portal."

"Where?"

"The labyrinth <hiss> inside the metal tree."

"Where is the metal tree?"

"<hiss> east side of the river."

"How do I get in?"

"Simple <hiss>. But must arrive <pop>."

"What?"

"Before midnight. Tomorrow. Can't be late."

And then the image of Aurora blinks out.

The light from the disk above Oz shuts off. Sensory input dims and dissipates.

This world floods back in.

"What was that about?" Midori whispers.

"That's the woman I saw a few days ago in the Signal building. She's Minoan. Definitely Minoan. And they've been watching me. Did you hear? And she's leading me to the labyrinth, to the technology, to whatever they want me to find. This portal."

"You heard all that? It just sounded like a series of squeaks."

"Squeaks from a higher dimension."

Oz sees it now.

53

Mervin Chimney had been thinking about going to bed early. Long day at the dig and he feels wrung out. So when he hears a knock at the front door of the apartment, he's a little sloppy about the safety protocol and so doesn't take the normal precautions such as not opening the door without first looking at the security monitor or even asking who is there.

He'll never forget to do that again.

The instant he pulls the door open, a big guy with a full-face red mask with little horns jutting out of the top kicks in the door and nearly flattens Mervin.

Mervin jumps back but the guy jumps on him in a flash, knocks Mervin to the worn carpet, turns him on his belly, and clamps his arms behind his back where he slips a pair of plastic handcuffs onto Mervin's wrists before he can say what.

The guy's sidekick, a much smaller man wearing a rubber mask with a red, oversized nose, darts inside and disappears deeper into the apartment. Within seconds Mervin hears Melissa give a short, startled scream, then nothing.

A few seconds later, a handcuffed, gagged and struggling Melissa is pushed into the room by the little guy and dumped on the floor next to Mervin.

"Where is she?" The big guy says.

Mervin, confused because he thinks the guy must be referring to Melissa, who can be plainly seen right there in front of him, doesn't know how to answer the question.

He punches Mervin in the stomach, air whooshes out, and he can't breathe.

"Where is Jane Ozzimo?"

SEARCHING FOR A WAY OUT

Now he gets it. "Not here. I don't know. She didn't come home." Words he can barely squeeze out as his lungs desperately try to suck in more oxygen.

An answer that provokes another punch in the stomach. And gets him and Melissa securely tied up, at which point the pair of men stride back toward the bedrooms and Mervin can hear them in Oz's room tearing things apart. Obviously looking for something beyond just Oz herself.

He glances over at Melissa but she's looks to be locked into her own little world of terror, eyes glazed, struggling weakly against the rope.

Maybe ten minutes later he can hear them moving on to Mervin and Melissa's bedroom and the same trashing and ripping apart sounds start all over again until finally they both come out to rejoin Mervin and Melissa in the living room.

Mervin would like to be pissed but can't generate any anger being this afraid.

"Okay," the big guy says, "Jane has some kind of stone with writing on it. Do you know where in this apartment she's hiding it? And you really need to be truthful."

Mervin thinks furiously but doesn't know what the right answer is because he doesn't think that saying "I don't know" again is the answer this lug wants to hear, but he doesn't really have any other answers to give. What stone?

"Look, she's just our roommate. She comes and goes and doesn't tell us what she's doing. I don't know if she has a stone. I've never seen it."

The smaller one kicks Mervin in the ribs. "Tell us, motherfucker."

The big guy says, "Take a guess then. Where might this Jane be?"

Melissa tries to say something through the gag. The little guy lowers it so that she can be understood. "Tomorrow night. That

HOPE thing. At the coliseum. I heard her saying she was going." Melissa is practically crying as she says this, gasping and wheezing.

The big guy crouches down right next to Mervin. "If we don't find Jane and this stone, we'll be back, so anything you can do to help us would be greatly appreciated."

And he lightly taps Mervin on his chin just to let him know.

54

Oz had forgotten how dark it gets out here in Malibu. Not much city light interference. A sky full of stars. Thinks of stars as points of hope.

About an hour after a late dinner, she sits on the floor of Midori's spare room, Circuit beside her, right in front of the mirror attached to the back of the closet door, holding the Minoan stone in her hands.

Midori has gone to bed, but Oz is too excited for that. All that she's seen and experienced today has her juiced. Especially after speaking with Aurora and getting that tiny glimpse of that wondrous world behind her. Would die to explore that.

All this stimulation makes her want to try using the black stone again. Explore a little.

But wait. It might be good to first speak to Alexandros. Been a couple of days and she has so much to tell him.

Must be early morning in Greece. He'd likely be up.

She instructs her commD to signal him.

"You're lucky I've already had my coffee," Alexandros growls.

"Lucky I am."

"You've found something, haven't you?" The playfulness in his voice fades too serious.

She tells him about the tunnels, the map room, the house in Topanga and the encounter with Aurora.

"I don't know what to make of it all," she says, "but I think she's Minoan or certainly a descendant of Minoans."

"And she told you to go to this labyrinth, somewhere down in these tunnels, but which you have not yet seen, right?"

"Yeah. Fairly insistent about it too."

"They want you to know."

"But why?"

"Don't know why, but you wouldn't have even seen what you have so far seen unless they wanted you to. And they want you to see it because somehow you fit into their plans."

"You mean, I being manipulated." Oz's mouth turns down. Hadn't considered this in all the excitement. Another example of her misinterpreting what is right in front of her. Maybe.

"In a sense. But it's also an opportunity. However, if these are truly Minoans and they have been developing their technology of the mind for the last three thousand or so years and have advanced so far that they have transported to whatever this world is that you got a glimpse of, then it's possible she is leading you into this labyrinth because it's a test. And since it's a labyrinth, they probably have a Minotaur waiting for you."

"A Minotaur?"

"Something very powerful and very dangerous. This would be the real test."

"A test for what?"

"That's the question."

Oz shivers. Could get trapped down there. Never come out. "But it's a test I have to take, isn't it?" Small voice. What if passing the test is worse than failing?

"You have to make a choice."

"And if I do it, what am I looking for? What happens if I do pass the test?"

"You do have a hint," Alexandros says. "Think back to the myth. When Theseus entered the labyrinth, he had the thread that Adriane gave him. I think you have a modern version of that thread."

"Really?" Leaning forward, grasping at anything.

"The map. I've been studying the copy you sent to me and I think it's likely that this is a guide. Your thread, so to speak. And, if you remember, one of the prominent symbols on that map is the labrys, the double-axe, but on the map it is placed on the back of a woman, which makes the axe look more like a pair of wings, the wings of the Minoan butterfly goddess, which implies the cycle of life, death and rebirth."

"This is scaring me," Oz says.

"Which is likely part of the test."

"Then I'm already taking it, aren't I?"

"It would appear so."

Within a few more sentences, she has ended the communication and let her mouth hang open, her eyes go unfocused, looking into a much deeper abyss than anything that Dr. Eisenfield and King Zee Whitehead might have in store for her.

But she feels compelled to do it. No choice. Can't turn back because there is nothing to turn back to. Not anymore. Yet, rocketing forward like this is completely reckless. Even more reckless than she usually is. It's a trap. She knows it. But she can't do much about it.

So yes, use the black stone again. Maybe she can discover something useful before she goes back to the site tomorrow and locates the labyrinth.

And that thing Alexandros said about the labrys and the butterfly goddess, well that symbol is on the stone too. The stone she did not tell him about. Don't want him to know. Want to keep it to herself until she knows more.

The butterfly goddess is where she will begin.

Glancing over at Circuit, she sees the dog sits looking out the window into Midori's nearly pitch-black backyard, at the rows of vegetables, the wind turbine, and maybe even a few critters.

She touches the symbol on the stone and raises her eyes to the mirror.

The world vibrates around her. Or maybe it's just her that's vibrating. Her nervous system feels like a taut net, catching every sight and sound and smell in a sensory flood. It's like every particle of her attention salutes in perfect alignment. Like a laser lining up all of those previously scattered, harmless photons to produce a light with burning intensity. Here her neurotransmitters all fire in perfect unison, bringing her focus to an extremely precise and penetrating level.

And that's when she falls apart. Different aspects of her personality separate like shards of glass and she sees them each individually. Sees her withdrawn shard, the socially inept shard, the inability-to-express-love-to-another-human shard, her fear-of-being-trapped shard, the it's-her-fault-that-her-parents-died shard. All the abundant dysfunctional pieces of her life float right in front of her.

In the first instant, she is so overwhelmed she wants to stop, but then it all changes. She finds herself in a medium-sized room with tables of food and waiters carrying trays of champagne glasses filled to their brims. And in this room is a crowd of people where she can see all of their personalities in pieces floating just above their heads as well. She can almost reach out and touch them.

But wait, isn't that Alexandros over there by the punch bowl talking to Gina Woolander?

Strange to see them here, especially Gina, but she has come to think that the stone shows her exactly what she needs to see. So there must be a reason.

They are drinking and talking but Oz sees maybe fourteen or fifteen personality—should she call them packets?—floating just above each of their heads.

She has always admired Alexandros's levelheaded good sense, and so she grabs that personality packet and mingles it in with hers.

She feels it right away. A calm enshrouds her. Her thinking is less turbulent. Her mind zooms to the possibilities. What if she could find all the excellent traits she wanted and installed them in herself? Wouldn't she become a whole new person? A person not trapped by

SEARCHING FOR A WAY OUT

all the crap from her past that makes her operate in this world the way she does, the way that just doesn't work.

She looks at Gina. Unlike Oz, Gina is a friendly, outgoing person. Isn't that just what Oz would like to be? That ease of comfort and familiarity with others. Be socially adept.

She latches on to that packet of Gina's. Now, everyone in this room—and there must be almost fifty others—just looks friendly and approachable. She could strike up a conversation with anyone and feel just fine about it.

Then she realizes she knows these people, not well, but to some degree, and all of them have some trait that she might want, might grasp. As if they have been placed in this room just for this purpose.

But no, she feels stuck. Can't make that happen. A certain hesitancy blocks her. One of her own existing personality traits stubbornly gets in the way. She can see the ruinous result of living with this trait, but she can't dislodge it.

Oz walks closer to Gina, thinking maybe this will help. Neither Alexandros nor Gina seem to know Oz is right there. In fact, no one in the room notices her.

But as she gets within inches of Gina, the different personality packets or shards floating just above them both begin to swim between each other, and instead of Oz adopting a single personality trait, she feels as if she is merging into Gina and seeing what she sees, feeling what she feels, and this is totally different, so much more than just one aspect, and she frees herself and to understand.

Her commD signals and yanks her out. The urgent signal. Reluctantly, she lets go of the stone, breaking the spell.

Looking at the device, she sees that it's Mervin. What could he possibly want?

"Yes."

"Oz, the security forces are here. Two guys busted in and tied us up. They pretty much wrecked the place, and they were looking for you. Said you had an object, a stone they wanted."

"What? Who were they?"

"They didn't leave a calling card," Mervin says with obvious sarcasm, "but I think you'd better watch out."

The walls are closing in. Can't move, can't breathe. Trapped.

But a small corner of her mind remembers now that part of what she felt in Gina was darkness.

But that thought evaporates. She has to hide. To get away.

55

Eighteen minutes after the private Surrender Ceremony with only nine participants and no audience, King Zee Whitehead pulls the wobbly Gina Woolander into a smaller room just a few feet down the hall from the room in which the ceremony took place.

He sits her down on a folding chair as she recovers from her first experience with the DTG machine.

Standing over her, he says, "I need you to help me, to help One Faith. Do you think you could do that?"

She swivels her head up to see his face. She's smiling as if stoned, which, of course, she is. The South American herb that is part of the Surrender Ceremony and whose effects carry on for hours after the ceremony itself ends, gives exactly that quality.

She nods, her large liquid eyes swimming in her head.

"This black stone that we know Jane Ozzimo has could be vital for One Faith. We need you to get it from her."

"Oz?" Gina says this slowly, as if connecting the image of the person with the word that is the name. And making this connection focuses her a little more. "Take it from Oz? I couldn't do that."

"But you would really be . . ." He stops because Jason Buggleman sticks his head in the doorway and Whitehead says, "Jason, come in. Help me explain to Gina how important it is for us to get this stone device from Jane Ozzimo."

Bug sees Mr. Whitehead standing over an obviously dazed Gina. He knows she has just come out of the ceremony and he suspects—because she is far too disoriented—that Mr. Whitehead gave her a more potent dose of the herb than he gave the others.

"But I don't want," Gina stops for a moment, "I can't steal—"

"No, no, no, you are not stealing, my dear. You are helping thousands and thousands of people who will benefit from whatever this technology is. Isn't that right, Jason?"

Bug sees in Mr. Whitehead's eyes the command that he obey, that he support him in asking Gina to steal.

He's asking her now because Jerry could not find this thing earlier when he invaded Oz's apartment.

Bug says, "Gina, it's important that you listen to Mr. Whitehead. He has all of our best interests at heart and I am sure if you help us, then you will be doing a good thing."

He has a bitter taste at the back of his throat.

As Whitehead turns to Gina, Bug thinks about what God told him.

Earlier today, he had done his own private ceremony. Hooked himself up to the DTG machine in a small room by himself, ingested a small amount of the herb, and asked God what he should do.

It seems all God could think about was Tammy. More or less told Bug to find her. God with a one-track mind. Not being very helpful.

But how does he find her? He doesn't know how to find anybody. But he thinks he knows who would. Aren't journalists good at that kind of thing? And that journalist he met the other night, Nickell. The one who has already done a couple of stories critical of One Faith. Could he help?

If Jason helped him somehow, perhaps he would find Tammy. And if this journalist could bring to light some of Mr. Whitehead's mistakes, possibly that would stop him from doing all these things that bother Bug. Set him right. Get him back on track and then One Faith would be sailing again.

Gina bends forward, putting her face in her hands as if she's extremely tired and behind her fingers she says, "But it would be wrong... Oz is my friend. I couldn't—"

SEARCHING FOR A WAY OUT

"Listen Gina," Whitehead says. "This device that she has could open up a whole new way to communicate with God. And that's something that you know is extremely important. Don't you think Oz is being selfish keeping this device to herself, not telling anyone, not letting anyone use it?"

Gina looks through her fingers at Whitehead for five seconds, then says with reluctance, "I suppose so."

Bug doesn't know how Mr. Whitehead could know any such thing.

He sees Mr. Whitehead's face twitch as though feeling a mild electrical shock. He knows that Mr. Whitehead hasn't eaten for two days or slept much either. On purpose. Denying the flesh. Or, as Mr. Whitehead puts it, clearing the static off the comm line to God.

Bug didn't know there was any static on Mr. Whitehead's comm line with God, so he doesn't know why he needs to starve himself.

But now he's pushing Gina.

Like what he did to Tammy? Where does it end? Maybe he should contact Nickell. Give him something. Something that will wake Mr. Whitehead up.

Whitehead says, "Gina, will you help us?"

She pulls her fingers away from her face, the corners of her now down-sloped mouth pressed tight, her shoulders hunched forward, and in a voice that might belong to a nine-year-old says, "Okay Mr. Whitehead. Whatever you think is best."

56

Nickell sits on the way-too-comfortable couch in his narrow living room, sinking deeper and deeper into the cushions, while listening to Ramesh drone on over his commD about the video Nickell's bot has captured while flying all around the underground tunnels beneath the Signal building, Ramesh's voice lulling him to sleep, which he so desperately needs since last night he hardly got a wink, but here, right now, late at night, so late it could even be past midnight, trying to stay awake and talk to Ramesh about what the bot has recorded in dim detail because of the low light: the stunning discovery of the wild, raging river, the vast network of tunnels, the large room with the huge mural running all the way around it, the many smaller empty rooms, and that strange tree on the east bank of the river, a tree that looks more like a sculpture.

And while Ramesh is both praising him—good job getting that bot down there—and criticizing him. But what is all this? What do we see? What does it mean?—his mind drifts off to the story he's been building about Whitehead for so very long, which he's been hoping to make strong enough so that he can finally expose Whitehead for the fraud he is and using it to kill One Faith but realizing in his near-dreamlike, unfiltered state, that he doesn't have the smoking gun.

All he has is just another cult leader who just happened to destroy Nickell's sister. Happens to people all the time. Nothing special here.

But he takes an inventory of his evidence anyway, since he lacks the energy to focus on whatever Ramesh is saying.

He's got interviews with traditional religious leaders railing against Whitehead, but that just looks like a bunch of sore losers.

SEARCHING FOR A WAY OUT

A little better are the interviews with dissatisfied One Faith members but unfortunately most of them are not ones who have been damaged by the Surrender Ceremony but more like disgruntled consumers who just didn't connect up to God like they thought they were promised and are unhappy about it. More whiners.

But sure he has a video of his sister, Bonnie, and how loopy she is now and probably forever, has her on video talking about hanging out on the surface of the planet Venus, but he just can't bring himself to use it, just can't stand having that out there for everyone to see again and again.

And, of course, he's got Yellowjacket's story about Whitehead and his phony vision out in the desert and how that might be connected to the disappearance of Jasmine Too, the former girlfriend, but without a shred of evidence about any of that so if he put it out on the Internet he would get sued back to the stone age. And it doesn't help any that Yellowjacket comes across as pretty much a lunatic.

Then he's depending on the HOPE event and capturing Whitehead on video doing something stupid like attacking Oz and now that seems even weaker than when he first thought of it—well, when Oz first thought of it—but still it seems better than just waiting around until Whitehead moves first.

What then could make their plan stronger? One thing is if the video captured Whitehead or one of his people hurting Oz, or even killing her. Shit. Why does he think of things like this? Man, this is so perverse. Is he really this shallow, so wrapped up in his pathetic career that he would even consider this?

"Do you understand where we're going with this?" Ramesh says.

"Huh?"

"The bot. The bot! You must be doing better, finding something much more exciting, something we can actually report on and who cares if the security people find the bot. We get what we need first."

"Okay, okay, I'll see what I can do." Agreeing to do something for Ramesh that he has no idea what it is because he was more or less unconscious when Ramesh said it.

"Good night then."

Ramesh gone.

Nickell lets his chin drop just an inch or two while allowing his eyelids to slide down over his eyes. Just for a minute.

So when he hears—in a spacey, distant kind-of-way—his commD signaling him again he dreams it as part of some landscape that's normal and does not require an action on his part, but as the signal continues, he rises unwillingly to the surface and realizes that it must be Ramesh with one last thing.

But it's not.

The face of Jason Buggleman appears on his screen. Not a happy face. A face lined with stress. With lips scrunching and sliding over each other, pressing tight, wrinkles popping up on his forehead, eyes jerking back and forth.

"Good, you're there."

Nickell wakes up in a hurry. "Jason, didn't expect to be hearing from you."

"I have a problem. This woman I know, Tammy Box . . . works at One Faith . . . well, used to anyway. She's," he pauses for a second as if to find the right way to express what he wants, "I need to find her. Not at home, not answering her messages or isn't getting them and I was hoping you could help me."

"Sure. What do you need?" Nickell dances around carefully here because he doesn't know why Buggleman would contact him. If this woman is a One Faith staff member, does it mean she's in some kind of trouble with the organization, something to do with Whitehead, or is it just something between the two of them?

"She's hurt." The words come from Buggleman almost with a choking sound.

SEARCHING FOR A WAY OUT

"You—"

"No, not me. Mr. Whitehead. He's having problems with the . . . he's experimenting too much, and it's affected him and he took it out on her and she left. But I really need to find her. Help her."

Whitehead beating up female staff members? Now Nickell is fully alert. "Why ask me?"

"Journalists can find people, can't they? And, well, look, it's like this. Mr. Whitehead—"

"Would he do this to Gina, what he's done to Tammy?"

"He might."

Nickell feels responsible. Flashes back to high school. Dana. What he didn't do. How he didn't act in time. "Tell me more about what's going on there."

"Look I believe in One Faith. What Mr. Whitehead has created here is good, but he's . . . he just needs to realize he's pushed things too far, treated people badly and if he could just be brought back, you know, put some pressure on him to see the damage and to come back to what he originally created, then One Faith could continue and do a lot of good."

"What are you saying? That you want me to do more than just find Tammy for you?"

"Uh," And here Buggleman looks away from the screen, his sharp features angled off as if he needs to force himself to go on. "You probably know the DTG technology is not perfect. A number of people have been hurt and most of them have been videotaped. We've kept it hidden, but I could give you some of those videos and maybe you could use them to put some kind of pressure on him to realize he's gone too far. To bring him back. To get him right."

Less than a minute after he signs off, the videos arrive on his commD. Less than twenty minutes later he realizes he's hit the jackpot. Scene after scene of people hooked up to the DTG machine then passing out, or vomiting, or having some kind of seizure, their

259

twisting bodies on the floor, their tongues twitching out of their mouths, blood pouring from nostrils, people becoming frenzied and yanking themselves free from the machine and running away screaming with various One Faith staff members chasing after them.

Where are these people now, Nickell wonders? It must have cost One Faith a fortune to pay these people off and keep them quiet.

Finally. He'll have something he can use.

He sits back and thinks now he can get a good night's sleep. Until his commD beeps and he reads a message from Oz—no voice, no visuals—telling him about the break-in at her apartment and how the two thugs were looking for her and for the black stone.

Nickell jumps up and paces. He sees right away this has to be Whitehead. Sending these two to take the stone. He's already after her, so Nickell knows they have to act.

Then he has an idea.

These new videos. Use them right away. Use them when it will hurt the most. The HOPE event tomorrow night.

57

Friday morning. Halloween.

Oz and Dr. Eisenfield and about a dozen archeology students are down in the tunnels below the Signal building. Some continue studying the contents of the map room, others have fanned out to explore the rest of the tunnels, finding many smaller rooms, which Dr. Eisenfield insists that they all document with video. This takes a long time and is a good thing, Oz thinks, because with everyone being occupied, no one has gone across the river to explore there.

In one of the small rooms, Mervin found some crumbly organic matter that looks like old mushrooms. Maybe grown there. Only bits and pieces. Oz said nothing. Not telling anyone about her and Midori's trip out to Topanga and what they found. She believes at least some of the Minoans must have lived out at the Topanga house, and it makes sense that they would have either begun fungi experiments here and then brought them out to the house or the other way around. Fungi everywhere.

She stands below the mural in the map room looking up. And looking sideways. Keeping an eye on Dr. Eisenfield. Waiting for him to get out of the way so that she can cross the river and find the labyrinth.

But he keeps hanging around.

She can't wait all day. But before she slips out of here and runs down to the river, she needs to casually strike up a conversation with Gina and let her know she will just happen to be at the HOPE event tonight. Which then Gina will supposedly report to Whitehead and then her and Nickell's not-so-great plan to entrap Whitehead can begin.

The whole thing feels wrong, but she agrees with Nickell that it's better to be on the offense than waiting for Whitehead to find her.

Right now Gina is on the other side of the map room examining a part of the mural, which shows a man and a woman standing in the rain. They're both looking up to the sky, their hands outstretched and palms up. Behind them is what looks like some kind of electronic box.

Oz makes her way over while keeping her attention on the large stone map at the center of the room. Specifically looking at the island of Thera as it was before the volcano blew it into pieces.

She's trying to be casual, trying to appear she's not directly walking toward Gina on purpose, just going in this direction.

This feels awkward. Gina is going to know in a nanosecond that something's up. Oz has hardly ever started a conversation with Gina. Doesn't help either that she feels betrayed by Gina.

She tells herself to act nice. Act friendly. Be collegial.

But as Oz gets closer, Gina turns and smiles and walks right over to her as if she had been planning this all along.

"Hey, I was talking to Sid, and he says that you found some kind of object down here. Is that true?"

Oz considers sixteen different options on how to respond, none of them good.

"Sid, huh? Are you two together?" Oz says.

Gina seems nervous, but eager to engage her, which is very unlike Gina. Gina is far more interested in engaging with men.

"Not really. But I think he said something about some kind of stone, like the Phaistos disk. Had the same markings. Isn't that right?"

Oh, so this is what it's about. Since those two thugs from last night didn't find the stone at the apartment, Gina is nosing around to see if maybe she can get it.

SEARCHING FOR A WAY OUT

This pisses her off. She so wants to tell Gina to wake up, to get away from that maniac. And normally she would just let it fly. But she can't. So she feels this internal pressure, and it builds, but then it changes.

Like she has done a couple of times with the black stone, she practically pops outside of herself to watch her own mind. Observing what it is doing. How it is behaving. And this distance allows the pressure to seep out so that she can bite her tongue and not yell at Gina. To smile even.

Luckily, she's hidden the stone in her car. Didn't want to bring it down here and have it pop out of her pocket again, and if Whitehead and his so-called associates are waiting for her up there, she won't have it on her.

Oz sees that Gina's nervousness is increasing. She's not looking Oz in the eye. She's sort of dancing around in a tight little circle, although not really a circle more like a jagged triangle.

Gina's nervousness is making Oz nervous. She'd like to just tell Gina about her plan to be at the HOPE event and then split. But she's got to work it in.

"Sid might be exaggerating."

"But you found something, didn't you?"

Since Oz knows Gina knows she has something, it might be better not to deny it, not to have Gina hear her lying. "Yeah, I found something. But all of us here are finding things."

"Could I see it?"

Oz sees Gina's eyes scanning her body, probably to see if there is some telltale lump in one of her pockets that might be the stone. She's desperate. Whitehead must have some kind of hold on her.

"I don't have it with me. Maybe some other . . ." Then the idea hits her. "Hey, you know what I was thinking? I'm going to be at the HOPE event tonight. If you're there, I could show it to you then."

"Ah, sure. That might be okay." Gina's face gets all scrunchy, as if she's trying to work out some problem.

"Okay, then just message me." Oz turns and begins walking away thinking that went better than she could have hoped, but at the edge of her perception she hears Gina's faint voice saying "I'm sorry." Says this so softly Oz knows she was not really meant to hear it, but she can hear things now that she could never hear before.

Was Gina apologizing for what she's told Whitehead?

Oz looks around. Can't see Dr. Eisenfield. Now is the time to cross the river.

58

Nickell has worked furiously to assemble the video. To cut it down to size. To make it just minutes long from the many hours that Buggleman has given him.

Over the course of the night and this morning he's had to take three naps, none over an hour. But he stills feels like he could use a full eight hours.

He's so far watched fifty-five people struggling through a Surrender Ceremony or falling apart right afterwards.

Videos of people he's never heard of and who never made the news. Damage covered up—he supposes—by the One Faith legal firm, who must have doled out a lot of cash to keep this quiet.

There's Katlin Morray, formerly a vivacious 26-year-old department store retail manager, who is now pretty much catatonic. Lives—no, just exists—in her parent's home and only sits and stares. Responds to nothing. The One Faith staff members had to pull her out of the chair, their faces almost as panic-stricken as hers was blank.

Max Applebaum, 23, a software developer, who lurched out of his chair, still attached to the equipment, fell down, cut open his face, and then screamed for fifteen minutes.

Charlie Peenold, 41, insurance salesman, totally lost it, ripping the wires off his head, picking up the chair and bashing the equipment he had just been hooked up to, and when staff members tried to stop him, he began bashing them too. Three of them went to the hospital.

Margaret Tettlehouse, 28, an extremely overweight secretary, who had slumped forward and simply died right there in the chair. Somehow, Whitehead's lawyers got a judge to believe it was merely coincidental that she died right at this moment and had done so because of her weight. That she was a heart attack waiting to happen.

Each of these fifty-five videos made him angrier yet, more numb. Here comes another one and another and another.

But it was the fifty-sixth video that took Nickell apart. Bonnie, his own sister. They had videotaped his own sister. He saw her last flash of intelligence, her last contact with the world as she looked up and to the left, all hooked into the machine, a frightened concern on her face—she knew it was coming—and then something like a grand mal seizure grabbed her body like she was a paper doll and shook her hard.

He took no more naps after that.

59

What looked like an ordinary rowboat is not what it turns out to be.

The boat is tiny. Would be lucky to fit two people. Sitting on the plank, she looks for the oars. Missing. But then, just as she's about to climb back out of the boat and start looking around, a silent electric motor kicks in and begins ferrying her across the river.

Startled, she grabs both sides of the boat to steady herself. This is very handy, but the downside of not having to row is that now she has nothing to do except be surrounded by the choppy, swirling turbulence of the river, which is too similar to the waters in which she almost drowned. The skin on her head tingles in a kind of visceral fear.

But the land on the other side of the river materializes as if out of a mist, brilliantly illuminated by sunlight. Sunlight constricted to a tight cone, flooding over an enormous tree. A tree that stands like a jewel in the light.

Disembarking, Oz walks forward a few steps. Amazed by the beauty, she stops, flashes her eyes all around the tree, trying to encompass the entire form.

There is a spatial symmetry to the branches and leaves that pleases the brain, kind of like a Japanese Maple but stretched out even further to separate each branch so that it holds that space, yet still is part of the whole. An arrangement that projects a feeling of organized space, yet holds a certain natural wildness.

And the sunlight just makes the tree glow. Oz figures that the sunlight is being directed down here by a series of mirrors but somehow these mirrors, if that's what they are, have boosted the intensity of the light and drawn it in a tight circle around the tree so that its appearance is sharply defined. So that it marks the spot. So that no one can miss that this is where you need to be.

Inside the tree, Aurora said.

Closer to the tree, she sees it looks more like it is made of metal, yet she can see clearly that it has the suppleness and flexibility of a regular deciduous tree.

Oh yes. Now she sees it. This is a sculpture. A Minoan work of art. Beyond anything she has seen produced by them before.

And it has both a stimulating and calming effect on her. More than a sculpture, she thinks, this is a device of some kind. Designed to affect whoever is near it. Maybe prepare them for entrance into the labyrinth.

She runs her fingers across the surface of what on a regular tree would be the bark, but this surface feels like silk. Her fingers glide along the soft metal, and she thinks she feels a slight vibration, a pulse even.

Looking up, the cone of sunlight reveals a swarm of life clustering higher around the tree, maybe seventy-five feet up. All the way to the top of the cavern. Oz can't tell what they are. Insects? Birds? Bats?

These flying insects or robots or whatever they are, keep up a furious buzzing of activity flying out and back to the tree.

Are they messengers? Conveying information to the Minoans? To Aurora? So that they see her now and know what she's doing? Like that one out in Topanga. They're tracking her.

But that doesn't bother her so much here. She belongs.

As she walks around the metal tree, which must have a diameter of seven or eight feet, she sees, just above her, a sun symbol etched into the surface. The same symbol she has tattooed on the back of her hand. It's a common Minoan symbol, but this is not a common Minoan artifact.

SEARCHING FOR A WAY OUT

As she looks for an entrance into the tree, one insect flies down lower, just a few feet from her, and then up a steep path to her left.

She wants to stay and find the door to the labyrinth, but she wonders why just one of those little robots would act like that. A message to her?

She runs up a rocky, steep path that is more like a ramp, jagged walls to either side, travels a couple of hundred feet and is stopped at a wall.

Nowhere for that robot to have gone. But as her eyes adjust to the dim blue light, she can see a door in front of her. No handle.

But to the right she sees the same sun symbol she saw on the metal tree and below it an etched-in handprint, an invitation to put your own hand there, and when she does the door slides open.

When she feels the outside air rush in, she becomes much more cautious. This could be dangerous. No idea where she is or where this is leading.

She walks about six feet up a short tunnel and finds herself in what looks like an alley. An alley bordered on both sides by a low office building and the back end of various shops—a Chinese restaurant, a dry cleaner, a commD service center.

Two large bushes partially hide her and a very rusty fire escape that looks as though it hasn't been touched in about a hundred years.

No one out. Hot air stillness.

But she can hear the sounds of the Chinese restaurant floating out its open back door, the clatter of silverware, the spray of water, the crack of a dropped mug.

Plenty of trash strewn around. Garbage cans and dumpsters lining the way, black gunk underneath.

She walks down to the end of the alley and around the restaurant. Now she can see the Signal building three blocks away.

So there is more than one way to get in here. A much quicker way. A way for the Minoans to access the labyrinth without having to travel through all those tunnels and across the river.

Good to know.

Well, enough of this. Feeling urgency, she returns, descending the steep decline back to the metal tree below. Now to find a way in. See this labyrinth that Aurora says is there.

But as she approaches the tree, she looks out over the water and sees Dr. Eisenfield in one of the other small boats cruising across the river. Close now, a scowl on his face.

Suddenly, she feels exhausted.

60

In the small One Faith snack shop, King Zee Whitehead sits in a hard, plastic chair at a small round table flanked by the twins, Darsha and Twinkle.

They are making him eat. Bringing spoons full of decadence up to his mouth. Giggling as they do it.

He is pretending to resist. He is smiling. Smiling because he believes the technology from the ancient legend will soon be his now that he knows where Jane Ozzimo will be tonight. A technology that's rumored to be an immortality potion. A technology she either has or knows where to find.

Smiling because he's been good.

He's been simple. Not eating, not fucking. No giving in. Last night, he lay all night in bed with Gina but did not touch her once. Yes, there was temptation, but he resisted. God will look approvingly on that resistance.

And God will finally talk to him once he locates the ancient technology. He knows that's what God has been waiting for. He can feel it.

But also smiling because of the sugar rush.

Darsha and Twinkle have imported food, bypassing the thin offerings of the cramped, dreary snack shop. In a large bowl, they have dumped a brick of vanilla ice cream and have topped it with chocolate syrup, candied pears, caramel truffles, marzipan cherries and fried Oreo cookies.

On Whitehead's empty stomach, this load has had a severe effect. He's flying. Riding a giant wave of sugar rising higher and higher in his depleted bloodstream. His entire nervous system trembles. His skin tingles. Another spoonful please. He is so close to getting what he wants. The anticipation vibrates like a huge bell struck by the world's largest hammer. He is ringing out. And yes, another spoonful.

Couldn't he just run upstairs to his apartment and play his guitar for a little while?

Couldn't he just take these fine two young things upstairs and fuck the bejesus out of them? Sorry, Lord.

Couldn't he just hold on to this moment forever?

Apparently not.

The enormous Jerry Groot lumbers into the snack shop, and before he can utter a word, Whitehead says, "Pull up a chair, Jerry, and join us."

Instead, Jerry just stands in front of the table like a huge thunderhead blocking the sun. Darsha and Twinkle look at him with a disdainful disregard but continue to bring spoonfuls of ice cream up to Whitehead's mouth.

"Hey boss, we might have a little situation. Looks like someone's been tampering with the Surrender Ceremony videos. Like some got downloaded."

"Do you know which videos?" The smile on Whitehead's face has disappeared.

"No, not yet. It's a little hard to tell what even happened. We'll have to do a trace to get more details, but I thought I would tell you now. See what you thought."

"It's probably nothing, right?"

"Could be, but it looks like more than nothing. Looks like something."

"And just when I was in such a good mood," Whitehead growls.

He scoops up the bowl of ice cream and flings it against the wall. The bowl yanked to the earth by gravity, shattering into twenty-seven pieces, the two metal spoons clanging across the tile, but the chocolate syrup, fried Oreo cookie, candied pear, caramel truffles, and marzipan cherry topped vanilla ice cream plasters and smears

SEARCHING FOR A WAY OUT

against the wall, glacially sliding down to lump and puddle on the floor like an environmental toxic chemical spill.

61

The moment Dr. Eisenfield steps out of the boat, Oz knows her exploration of the metal tree and the land on the east side of the river has ended.

He looks determined, his lips all sealed up, his jaw muscles twitching as if he's grinding his teeth as he marches up the thin strip of land toward her.

He smiles, but Oz thinks there is not one ounce of friendliness in that expression. This is the smile of a human predator just before it strikes.

"Jane, what have we got here?" He gestures toward the tree.

"Might be a work of art. A sculpture." Oz keeps it simple.

"Built by Minoans, right?" The words come out of his mouth as a challenge.

Oz says nothing, just stands her ground and tries to construct a firewall around her emotions before they do something she might regret.

"You know Jane, I've been interested in the Minoan civilization for a long time. A lot longer than you've been around. And to tell you the truth, I've noticed some of the same things that you have. I've uncovered hints that the Minoans were more than a little ahead of their time. Hints that they might have developed some technologies or, a better word for it might be, some techniques of working with the mind that would be considered advanced even today."

"You noticed this on Crete, did you?"

From the day her Aunt Della put her into the sixth grade in California people have been talking down to her, talking around her, ignoring her or finding fault with her, and she lived with it because she was so damaged from the death of her parents and brother. She survived by crawling into a self-constructed shell. But while that shell

SEARCHING FOR A WAY OUT

might have worked for her when she was eleven, it sure as hell doesn't work now.

"Crete, yes, and other places as well," Eisenfield says, walking closer to the tree and looking at it as if he's interested.

"And you knew all this when I brought you up to that sanctuary cave and you pretended—"

"I did not pretend anything."

Oz whips up into a fury. "And all this time you've put down my thesis as some kind of fantasy and you knew it wasn't. Knew it all along. What's wrong with you?" She knows she's over the edge but doesn't care.

"Careful. You want to be very careful here. You see, I've heard a rumor that is very disturbing. That you have found something on this site, something important that you have not told me about." He pulls a piece of paper out of his pocket, unfolds it, and holds it up for Oz to see. "Something like this."

Oz gasps. In the photo is what looks like a replica of the black stone, except this one is broken. One end sheered off, its guts hanging out.

But he knows. She knew this would happen. But knowing doesn't help much now.

Oz points a finger at him. "Given your hostility to every idea I have, I thought it prudent that I work with it before I gave it to you." She feels defiant. How she gets when she feels trapped. Sometimes.

"A grave mistake, young lady." Dr. Eisenfield has that air about him of a man in triumph, one who is certain, one who believes he is in control. "But one we can happily rectify."

When he says the word *rectify*, he enunciates each of the three syllables distinctly, as though to imply how generous he is about to be.

Oz stands completely still, keeping her face from showing any emotions. Not giving anything away. "What?"

"I'm going to offer you a deal which you would be wise to accept. I will approve your thesis topic and your thesis—whatever that turns out to be. But, from now on, no matter what you find here at the Signal building, you give me full credit. The ideas you present in your thesis, you give me full credit. And you hand over the device that you found right now."

It's like he's ripping her heart out. She's being penalized because she's been successful digging into the Minoan civilization while he hasn't.

"What is that in the picture?"

"You tell me. This one obviously is broken. Inside are electronic parts way beyond anything we have. It was found in India about fourteen years ago. We don't know what it does. But the one you have works, doesn't it?"

An intense pressure in her head, squeezing, pounding. No good choice. A rapidly narrowing tunnel of freedom. Nothing going right. No way out.

"I don't have it with me."

"Then go get it. Bring it to me before we leave here today. If you don't, you're off the dig, your thesis is rejected, and you are out of the program."

Oz looks out over the choppy river water seeing the endless flow, bits of debris rushing along the constant stream. Like her life except that now she thinks her life might come to an end, at least the archeological part of it, the only part she's ever liked.

She turns back to Dr. Eisenfield and barely nods her head.

Far above them, near the top of the metal tree, hovering among the Minoan robot insects, is Nickell's news bot that he had Oz release here in the underground.

It had been hovering up there recharging its solar batteries with the sunlight being piped down into the chamber, but as soon as it saw humans down below it had descended twenty feet and had

SEARCHING FOR A WAY OUT

activated its camera and its directional microphone and had recorded everything in the crystal clear clarity that a professional news bot did.

62

Gina blinks six or seven times in the bright sunlight after having been down in those god-awful tunnels for the last couple of hours. Too much dust and dirt. Can't wait to take a shower. Got to go home and study for that test. But first she must help Mr. Whitehead. Do him this favor.

A favor she really wants to do for him. It's just that she doesn't want to do this particular favor.

If only his men could have found that disk thing in Oz's apartment last night, then she wouldn't have to do this. Oz must be keeping it with her. And she didn't look like she had it on her down in the map room, so it's possible she's keeping it in her car.

So that means she's going to have to break into Oz's car. How is she going to do that?

The entire business makes her nervous. But failing Mr. Whitehead makes her nervous too. He's so important. And his importance rubs off on her, doesn't it? Sure, he's too old for her, kinda yucky, but she can overlook that, can't she?

The car must be across the street in the dirt lot where everyone on the dig parks. At least she knows which car. Will have to sidestep that clump of the chronically unemployed who keep hanging around here, hoping that we'll find Atlantis somewhere in this mess and rescue them from their lives.

And she's got to look out for those two nosy news bots floating up in the air, but they're not doing much because not much is doing.

She only takes one step forward when she notices Sid Juvelics is rushing toward her all smiley and goofy-like, practically tripping over his own feet, and is going to want to talk to her, which she doesn't really have time for right now or maybe even want to make-out with her, which she really doesn't want at all.

SEARCHING FOR A WAY OUT

But when she turns her head and takes another few steps forward and sees all the city security forces, not only at the entrance, but walking around the perimeter of the fence, she changes her mind, thinking that having Sid nearby might be a good thing. A shielding thing. An attention-diverting thing.

And even though she pretty much knows all the guards by now and they all like her and everything and they shouldn't give her any trouble leaving and re-entering the site except to keep an eye on her that's more like a stare, the kind of staring that Gina well knows is just a sexual thing and which would inhibit her if she has to smash a window or two on Oz's car that might cause any of them to want to investigate and ask her some dumb questions like what is she doing?

But if Sid tags along with her, they might be more likely to curtail their own staring at her and actually perform their security duties, which are mostly just standing around.

And if she wasn't on this secret mission, she would likely somewhat enjoy their stares. But only if she looked right. Not fat or anything. Not like after every time she eats and believes herself to swell up like a balloon. She's thinking like this because she's hungry right now. Of course, she could always go somewhere and take a hit of syrup of ipecac and then throw up whatever she has for lunch. If only she didn't make so much noise when she vomited. Makes her have to find such out-of-the-way places.

When Sid finally reaches her, instead of her being annoyed with his presence, she can actually use it.

"Take a walk with me across the street."

To which he says, "Sure." Says this with enthusiasm.

She likes telling him what to do. And it's so easy.

She nods at the guard near the entrance as they pass through.

"You know that disk you told me about that Oz found?"

"Yeah, but I think it was more like a stone," Juvelics says.

"Whatever." Gina flicks her fingers in the air to show how unimportant the distinction is. "Well, I think that Dr. Eisenfield needs to know about it. Needs to see it."

She can't tell him who she's really stealing it for.

"Yeah, but—"

"It might be in her car and I need you to help me get it."

"Gina, are you kidding? You want to break into Oz's car?" Juvelics snaps his head around to see who might be watching them.

"Dr. Eisenfield needs to see it." Gina feels practically giddy using this commanding voice.

She finds Oz's old piece of junk-of-a-car, and now what? The windows are closed, the doors are locked, and she has no idea what the combination for the keypad is.

She looks at Sid. "Any ideas?"

He looks back at her like she could be mad or he's caught in something way over his head or perhaps seeing a slight opening to make his move on her, which would only happen if he helps her, and while Gina sees he's calculating this, sees it all over his face, she puts one hand on her hip, juts that hip out as far as she can, slides the foot opposite to that hip out so that whole leg is at an angle. Now she is practically all angles, elbow, leg, hip. All five foot, eleven inches of her.

She knows the effect this usually has.

Sid Juvelics appears to rapidly come to the end of his calculations. He swallows. Looks around. He whispers, "I have an app on my commD that opens car doors."

Now she feels nervous again. A block of fear sitting inside her. She hardly ever steals anything and going into someone else's car, well, she doesn't remember ever doing that. But she wants to please Mr. Whitehead. It's for a good cause and all, even if part of that good cause is the upgrading of her life. Isn't upgrading a funny word? But true, true, true. Doesn't she deserve a little more excitement? A little

SEARCHING FOR A WAY OUT

more fun? Everything is so gloomy around here. All her life, it's been like this. So tired of it. So hungry too. Want to eat something.

Sid has the door unlocked in forty-seven seconds and, despite his misgivings, seems to strut a bit in a moment of self-congratulation.

Gina rifles through the glove compartment, looks on the floor of both the front and back seats and then gets down on the floor in the front and uses her left hand to feel under the seats, coming up empty. Empty until she reaches up under the passenger's seat and finds a cloth bag where it had been taped up against the bottom side.

"Got it."

She backs out of the car, checks inside the bag and closes it right up.

Juvelics steps in a little closer to her and says, "We make a good team."

But before he can move any closer—his lips seem to be already puckering—Gina walks deeper into the parking lot.

"Thanks for the help," she says over her shoulder.

Sid Juvelics watches her as she drives her own car down the street. *Where's she going?* Sid thinks. *Dr. Eisenfield is down in the tunnels.*

63

Oz walks out of the end of the tunnel and into the large, empty basement room in the Signal building. The air feels cold as she ascends the metal stairs.

She doesn't want to give the Minoan stone to Dr. Eisenfield. But she has to. More than doesn't want to. It means defeat, giving away the likely key to the technology that she's been searching for ever since the experience in the cave. But if she doesn't give it to him, then she's out of the archeology department, out of school, out of a career.

Could she stall him? At least until tomorrow, after she's found and entered the labyrinth and has seen whatever Aurora wants her to see. That should make a difference, shouldn't it?

She hears someone thudding down the stairs from above and looks up. Sid Juvelics. Maybe she can just slip by him. But no, he stops.

"Hi, Oz."

"Sid."

He scratches his chin. "Hey, tell me something. About that stone you found. What was so important about it?"

"Never mind. It's nothing," Oz says, moving to slide around him, not wanting to talk about this with him, not now, not ever. She could kick herself for letting the stone fall out of her pocket so that he could find it.

"But there must be some value to it because I just saw Gina steal it out of your car." He grins.

The shock stuns her into taking a step back, bumping into the railing and then sinking against it.

"You're sure about this? You saw it?"

"Yep."

SEARCHING FOR A WAY OUT

Despite the shock, she's a little angry seeing him grinning like that. Guess this is his revenge for her knocking him down.

But the anger is small compared to the bolt of despair shuddering through her nervous system. Now what? If she's lost the stone, then...

"I tried to tell her to stop but she wouldn't listen," Juvelics says, shrugging his shoulders as if to show how courageous his efforts had been.

"You... then if..." Oz's jagged thoughts smash and collide into each other, the loss of the stone, a ripping of the flesh.

Oz blurts out, "Where did she go with it?"

"That's the funny thing. She said she wanted to take it to Dr. Eisenfield. But she just drove off. Just drove down the street. And he's right here." Sid shrugs even more and grimaces like a child, trying to ward off any potential blame that Oz might be about to lay on him.

Where would Gina have gone? Straight to Whitehead?

She feels as though gravity has doubled, weighing her down. Now she is even more pissed off. She pushes off the railing and runs up the remaining stairs.

Outside in the bright sunshine and the staggering heat, life goes on. Students still digging, security still roaming, people still clustering around the rim of the property. Except that her world has been turned upside down.

Got to think. Should she try to find Gina and take the stone back? But where would she be? If she took it right over to Whitehead at the One Faith building, then it would be next to impossible to get at it.

A deep sense of overwhelm submerges her. This is too impossible. One upside is that since Whitehead now has the stone, he will not be coming after her. But then her and Nickell's plan to entrap Whitehead won't work either.

She should tell Nickell what happened.

She dials him up, puts it on visual, wants to see his face, irrational, she knows, but can't help it. Not now.

As soon as he appears on the screen, she says, "Gina stole the stone out of my car. Whitehead probably has it by now. And I have been more or less kicked out of school. I know you don't . . . I . . ."

"Hold on. How are you kicked out of school?"

"Dr. Eisenfield will only let me stay if I hand over the stone to him. Now that's impossible."

"Wait a minute, wait a minute," Nickell says. "I've received data from that news bot I had you turn loose. Maybe . . . let me take a look."

Nickell retrieves the data block, fast forwards through a lot of landscapes and then zeroes in on the scene between Eisenfield and Oz, which he broadcasts to Oz so that she can see it too.

About a minute into it, Nickell breaks the silence. "He really said all this to you." More of a statement than a question.

"You see how screwed I am?"

"No, not at all, not since we have this video. Look, when are you supposed to meet with him?"

"By the end of the day. And you're thinking what? That I show him this video and threaten him?"

"No, let *me* threaten him. Threaten him with worldwide exposure."

"This will work?"

"You bet. Set up a meeting with him for later this afternoon, right before the HOPE event, which we're still going to, whether Whitehead is after you or not. I have another idea."

"Wait," Oz says. "I just thought of something. Even if Whitehead has the stone, he's not going to know how to activate it. I only figured that out by accident. He will still need me."

"That might be even better."

SEARCHING FOR A WAY OUT

When he's gone, she feels afraid. Not just because of Dr. Eisenfield or Whitehead, but because she's actually trusting him and that feels dangerous. Giving up control, but here she sees no other way. He can help her, but can she accept his help? She feels something. Some emotion. Some messy emotion that could sweep her away and leave her vulnerable. Does not feel safe.

Wait. She steps back and observes her own mind, thinking these thoughts, and tells herself that these are only thoughts, nothing else, and this creates a little space between her and her fears.

She'll run out to Malibu, feed and walk Circuit, and arrange the meeting with Dr. Eisenfield along the way.

"The Minotaur is already after me," she whispers.

64

King Zee Whitehead comes alone in a nondescript One Faith car.

Parks in the alley just behind the house on Logan Street, just a few doors down from Echo Park. Fucking trash heap now. Lake empty. No water. All the lotus plants long dead. Grass that turned brown, dried up, and blew away, leaving only bare earth. Bare except for all the garbage that has been dumped on it.

He wears one of those flexi-foam disguises. This one adds hair, a beard and alters the shape of his face so that it looks fuller, more fleshed out. He puts on sunglasses just to make sure no one will recognize him. But it's so bright out he needs them anyway.

He rips all this off the minute he steps inside Gina Woolander's apartment.

"Where is it?" He says.

She nods and gestures toward the kitchen table and he brushes past her.

Too much clutter everywhere. He hates clutter. It's distracting. The biodegradable pizza box on the counter has already begun its dissolution, still with a slice of pizza inside being eaten by three cockroaches who ignore the anti-cockroach robot, which is about the same size as they are and looks pretty much like a regular cockroach. But this robot limps and throws off the occasional spark and can't quite catch any of the real cockroaches who just step around it. What's it called? Robo Roach? Roach Hunter? He can't quite remember now.

He grabs up the cloth bag and yanks out the Minoan stone. It's surprisingly heavy. Black and covered with many symbols, some recognizable, some not. Turns it over. Same on the other side. Just different symbols.

SEARCHING FOR A WAY OUT

He carries it over to a thickly padded chair where he sits down. The broad, flat arms sprout pale red threads emanating from its interior through a tear in the fabric like a wheat field gone wild.

"Can I get you something to drink?" Gina says in a voice that lilts up with eagerness at almost every other word.

"No." He doesn't even look up, just turns the stone over and over again in his hands searching for the on switch.

Gina catches sight of the ipecac syrup bottle, visible because she hadn't closed the kitchen cabinet door. She quickly walks over and shuts that door now. And while in the kitchen, she shuts down her commD on the counter, which had been accessing a textbook for one of her classes. It had been displaying a section about myths and their intersection with the science of archeology, using the unicorn as an example of the trouble that myth causes researchers. A Maxwell Parrish-like illustration of a white horse with a horn.

Whitehead pushes two fingers across the surface of the stone, feeling for any bump or depression or anything that might be an operating switch. When nothing happens, he presses a finger on the symbol of the man, then on the woman, then the tree, the island, the sun and other symbols. He doesn't even know what they are. Nothing.

A white flash of irritation behind his eyes.

Whitehead then holds the stone very close and looks carefully along the edge of the stone, bringing his thumb and forefinger into the search by touching the edge all around the circumference. Still nothing.

He looks over to Gina, who stands in the middle of the room and asks, "Do you have any idea how to make this thing work?"

She shakes her head.

"Maybe the fucking thing is already on and we just don't know it." His lips compress, the cords in his neck bulge. He slams a fist down on the chair arm, causing several of the internal pale red threads to fly out. He jumps to his feet and yells, "Work you son of a bitch!"

Then he stares at Gina, who stands frozen about ten feet away. She appears not to know what to do. Not even moving a finger.

"This Jane person. How did she do it?"

"I . . . I don't know."

Whitehead roars. "I ought to smash this thing into a thousand pieces."

"Why is it so important?"

He needs to be in control. Tells himself to calm down. He glances at the floor, out the window, at the ceiling, then at her. Headache coming back.

"It might be a key. To Atlantis, to the immortality potion in the legend, who the fuck knows?"

He takes one step toward her as he says this. His voice glides smooth and wondrous. "For the longest time, I have made it possible for many, many people to speak to God. With the use of the DTG machine, I opened communication channels for those people. But for myself . . . for me, I've not had such an easy time . . ." And here he looks down as if seeing a vision. A vision of many attempts and many failures.

"I have so wanted to be in His Grace. There is so much I want to say but I can't yet reach . . ."

He slides the other foot forward. His face creases up as if he might burst into tears. "Could I get a hug?" He practically blubbers.

Gina shifts from frozen to melting, sympathy seeping into her brain. She wraps her long arm around him and they stand there, his torso heaving.

He lowers his voice to a near whisper.

"I so don't want to disappoint Him, but I've done some bad things Gina. I had to."

SEARCHING FOR A WAY OUT

She pats his back with one hand. "We've all done bad things, don't worry."

"But I want to do bad things to you."

Gina stops, then tries to squirm out of his tight embrace. An embrace that he makes even tighter.

"Mr. Whitehead. Please, please, I need to breathe, I need... oh please. I understand. I'm sorry that you... that things haven't... but please, I've got to get some air." Gina uses both hands to try pushing him back, but because he is so close, she cannot get any leverage. Her face blooms a flushed pinkish-red with the exertion.

"Gina, what about what I need? I need your understanding. You have no idea what I've been through." He nestles his head deeper against her neck.

I've been so terribly good, he thinks. I've restrained myself with her. But now, Lord, see how near I am to her smell, to her skin. Look, Lord, how I resist. You can speak to me now. I am worthy.

"Let me go, Mr. Whitehead and I'll find Oz and I'll get her to tell me how this stone thing works." The words rush out of Gina's mouth faster and faster as her desperation sinks its fingers deeper into her mind. "I know her. She'll tell me. I know how important this is to you. This is a key like you said."

"Think about it Gina. You're an archeologist. You know about the legend, about the technology brought over and hidden for thousands of years. And we're about to find this. We can serve God."

He has resisted his lust with her, showing God how strong he can be. He should have a reward.

Pushing her forward, he more or less carries her down the short hallway and into her bedroom. "Gina, you must help me?"

Gina coughs, face deep red.

He pushes her back on to the bed, hand still choking her. Brings his full weight on top of her. Looks directly into her wildly darting eyes.

That glorious feeling of power sweeps into him. He's where he wants to be. In control. What would God want? Does He want Whitehead's continued restraint or does He want him to demonstrate his earthly power?

God hasn't said. And Whitehead has been with this Gina several times and has faithfully restrained himself, so shouldn't God have said something by now?

That must mean that God would rather see him show his power. Yes!

With his free hand, he grabs the collar of her T-shirt and begins ripping it down.

Gina forcefully resists, her body thrashing, her arms trying to block him. He slaps her hard. She stops. He quickly takes both hands and yanks the shirt up over her head and then brings the one hand back to her throat so she just has time to cough and wheeze and get a little air before it is all constricted again.

She's crying. "Please, Mr. Whitehead. Please. I didn't mean it. I'll help you."

"Shut up." He slaps her again.

Big red welts on her face. Wet now.

Whitehead feels his blood rising down below.

He strips off the rest of her clothes and forces himself inside.

He bucks and sweats and groans and penetrates even deeper while holding her throat with both hands, driving down in a wild fury until he finally releases and triumph spreads across his face.

Looking down at Gina for her confirmation of his power, he realizes she is no longer in this world. For a moment he watches for her breath, but there is no breath to see.

No more Gina. Poor girl.

But this is a slippery thought that slides off easily to be replaced by the much more important thought that he now needs to find Jane Ozzimo and make her tell him the secret.

65

Nickell tried all the usual databases first: the gas company, the department of water and power, the mail distribution companies, the Department of Motor Vehicles, the voter registration rolls. But he came up empty. No Tammy Box.

They all list the same address, the one that is now abandoned. Of course, she was attacked by Whitehead only a few days ago, so she might not have had time to rent a new apartment. Or she might have moved far away. Which would put the kibosh on this whole thing.

And since she didn't report this to the police—must be scared shitless of what Whitehead might do if she did—she doesn't come up in that database either.

Well, she has to be some place.

Still groggy from having stayed up all night and then the short sleep this morning, Nickell wouldn't mind having coffee. He thinks he still has a couple of those Blast-Off packets around here. Just drop it in water and the packet does it all, heats the water, brews the coffee, has it ready in a minute. Loaded with caffeine.

He'll look for it after he does this one last search using the special face-recognition software. With the vast network of surveillance cameras throughout the city, anyone who ever goes outside is likely to be seen somewhere.

Nickell pulls up the surveillance footage of the area around the One Faith building from a few weeks ago when Tammy still worked there and has culled isolated snippets of video in which she appeared. Now he will use those images to make a more current match.

The software takes just under two minutes. Found three clips. All locations verified by GPS.

Clip number one. Wednesday. Two days ago. Culver City. Two views. She is seen head-on walking into a medical building. The camera must be on the building itself. She's looking beat up. Black eye. Limping a little.

Clip number two. Thursday. Van Nuys. She's entering Al's Security Gun Shoppe on Sherman Way. This is not good, Nickell thinks. She's in there a while so he fast forwards to when she comes out and she definitely has a package under her arm. She's looking straight down at the ground as she walks.

Clip number three. Thursday. Culver City. Maybe forty-five minutes or an hour after the previous clip. A dingy motel on Sepulveda, named the Zenith Inn, where the camera just catches her face as she walks into the motor courtyard and down to what must be her room, although he can't see that.

He hacks into the motel's database and finds her room number, links into the motel's commD system, and calls her, being sure to set the device to allow the video option. He wants her to see him, to see him with a friendly smile on his face. Or as friendly as he can get it right now.

"Hello." Said in a near whisper, as if she were almost afraid to speak.

"Hi Tammy, this is Nickell of The Data Transfer."

Dead silence.

He sees her on the screen.

"Tammy?"

"What do you want?"

"Actually, I want you to help me."

"I'm not interested in—"

"And to help your friend, Jason Buggleman." This is where he has to nail it. If she won't do it for herself, then maybe for another.

Even on the tiny screen, Nickell can see the fear in her eyes.

"You must have the wrong link. I don't know any Jason Buggleman."

SEARCHING FOR A WAY OUT

"Tammy, let's cut the pretending. Jason is helping me bring down King Zee Whitehead, something I am sure you would like to see happen, but he really would like to speak to you and I'm helping him out."

"Jason is part of One Faith. He... listen, I can't get involved with that again. No way."

"You do want to see Whitehead get what he deserves, don't you?"

"He almost killed me," Tammy Box says.

"I know, Jason told me. And Jason needs your help to stop him."

Nickell sees the creases in her forehead, the hesitancy, the lips tight against her teeth.

"I... I can't... it's too hard. Jason is..."

Nickell softens his voice, slows it down. "Listen, Tammy, I don't want to cause you more pain, more worry, but Jason has given me a lot of evidence that will be damning to Whitehead, but it would really help him to know that you're all right. He cares for you a lot. You know, he's really sticking his neck out here. If Whitehead finds out what he's given me then, that will be big trouble."

Tammy ponders this for twenty seconds. "How do I know that you're not lying?"

"Look at my past work on The Data Transfer website. You'll see two very unflattering stories about One Faith and Whitehead."

"I think I remember that."

Nickell can see her turning back and forth as if the pure indecision is physically twisting her.

"I'm scared," she says.

"I can understand that. He's a dangerous man who has hurt many people. Jason and I are trying to change that."

"Okay, okay. You can... I will talk to him."

"I'll tell him."

66

Almost nodding out at the wheel, Nickell thinks he now should have stayed at Zukor's and taken a nap there on his soft couch, but he wanted to come home and crawl into his own bed for a couple of hours before he meets Oz at USC.

He slaps himself to stay awake.

At the north end of Echo Park lake, he turns up Logan Street. Almost there. But the street is filled with city security forces, their cars blocking the street, their red and blue lights revolving, flashing a silent message of doom.

A sick feeling starts in his stomach. He doesn't know why, but he knows this is something close to him.

He finds a spot on Park Avenue and walks up, dreading each step. And yes, the activity is focused on his building. The security people going up and down the staircase, up to Gina and Belinda's apartment.

Out on the dirt patch in front, he sees Belinda slumped against her car, eyes pointed straight down, holding her head with one hand, looking more like a statue than a live human being.

As Nickell approaches, she raises her head, sees him, and staggers forward, wrapping her arms around him.

"She's dead."

And Nickell knows it's Gina. "How . . . you found her?"

"Horrible. I came home from an audition and there she was. They say she was strangled. Raped. Lying on her bed. Eyes closed, never . . ."

"Shit." Nickell can hardly see straight. A little piece of his journalistic self wants to ask questions, but that part of him is drowning.

He holds on to Belinda. "When's the last time you saw her?"

SEARCHING FOR A WAY OUT

"It's been days. Ever since she started hanging around with that phony Whitehead. I almost never saw her. I think she was only home today because she was studying for a test."

Hearing Belinda speak Whitehead's name makes him wonder. She's been spending 24/7 with Whitehead. She comes home finally because she has to study for a test, and then all of a sudden some random person off the street breaks in and kills her? No, that doesn't seem likely, but Whitehead killing her? Yeah, he's a bad guy, but why would he kill her? He's using her. He just met her.

And then he thinks he didn't really know Gina all that well, despite living next door. She's had lots of boyfriends. They come and go, so who knows? It could be any of them.

He feels a sadness that is only magnified by holding on to the weeping Belinda. What a shock that must have been, walking in and seeing the lifeless Gina just lying there. Hard to imagine. He's seen dead bodies before, but not someone he knew, not someone he could say was a friend.

His commD signals him and it's almost a relief because it gives him an excuse to break away from Belinda and her overwhelming grief.

He walks out about ten feet across the dirt patch, sees that it's Buggleman.

"Yes, Jason."

"I want to thank you. Thank you for finding Tammy, for convincing her . . . for all your help."

"That's all right." Nickell should feel good about this, but there are no warm spots inside. Just feels empty.

"You okay?" Bug says.

"I . . . no, not really. Gina—you know her—Gina is dead. Raped and strangled."

Jason says right away, "Mr. Whitehead."

Nickell alert, "What? You think he has something to do with this?"

"I don't . . . can't prove anything, but he's not been himself lately. Violent. He's messed up. Could be . . ."

"That son of a . . ."

His initial knee-jerk anger quickly turns inward, and he's faced with the realization that if Whitehead did this, then he's responsible. He led Gina to Whitehead. It's his fault.

He reaches out to one of the security cars to steady himself on the fender but misses and now—off balance—crashes to the ground, descending through layers of his own self-perceived failure, through his own circles of hell.

67

King Zee Whitehead leans over the tech's shoulder, hot breath on Pavel's neck. "What's taking so long?"

Pavel, the tech, tries to concentrate. "Give me just another second and we'll see which videos were downloaded and by who. It's taking this long because whoever took it used software to cover their tracks."

One Faith records as many Surrender Ceremonies as it can, which is almost all of them done here. Part of this is just to keep a historical record of the movement's progress, but Whitehead uses them as an analysis tool.

He wants to improve the technology. He wants this to work. So he'll watch a video, see how many of the participants say that they made a connection with God and how many had trouble.

And, of course, beforehand he's noted the setting on the hybrid MRI, the sound and light machine and, most importantly, the herbal dosage.

It's a balancing act. Both the electrical charge of the machines and the effect of the herbal mixture need to be strong enough to establish the connection to God, yet not so strong that it hurts people. So he constantly has to make adjustments. And because of this, there are plenty of videos with people who didn't do so well, and it's those videos that seem to have been targeted here. Videos that, if exposed to the wide public, could be misinterpreted and cast an extremely negative light on him and One Faith.

His anger and fear only increases the tremor in his hand. The left side of his face twitches. He sees ruin.

He feels violated. How could this happen to him? Who would dare cross him?

"You see," Pavel says, pointing at the instrument panel, "the incursion took place late last night. Luckily, we have our own software that can unravel what happened. Identify sources. They used their own regular access code but their software scrambled it so that we couldn't read it, but in just a few moments we should see something."

Whitehead paces, burning inside, burning more intensely with each step. Fucking traitor.

"Code coming up," Pavel says. "Belongs to one Jason Buggleman."

"Bug?" Whitehead is momentarily puzzled. Why him? But his anger burns through all that. He bets it has something to do with Tammy Box. They were friends. More than friends. He saw them in the hallways, down in the snack shop, out on the lawn.

He will teach that little traitor a lesson. But he's got to act fast. Got to get the videos before Buggleman does something stupid with them. Something stupid that might bring One Faith down and he can't allow that. He will not see the ruin of all his work just because this lovesick boy got his feathers ruffled over some meaningless girl.

He's got to move. Speed. He whips out his commD and connects with Jerry.

"Get the car right now. We have an appointment with Buggleman."

68

Oz stands out of the late afternoon sun in the shade cast by the Bovard Administration building on the USC campus. Standing not too far from where the original bronze statue of Tommy Trojan stood until nine years ago when a group of rival UCLA chemistry and engineering students melted it with their own portable furnace in the dead of night.

In its place, USC changed Tommy Trojan to a perpetual hologram. Really lights up this section of campus at night.

She waits for Nickell to show up for their meeting with Dr. Eisenfield, who doesn't know that Nickell will attend, or Circuit for that matter. Circuit who wasn't even supposed to be here.

Circuit sits and slowly wags her tail, mouth open, tongue lolling out, trying to dissipate the heat.

Whatever happens with Dr. Eisenfield today, she figures she will need to go back to Crete. Whatever answers lie here will surely point back there. That is the source. Maybe she can talk Alexandros into putting her on his team.

She looks off in the distance. That way and this. Where is Nickell? He should be here by now.

Almost unwillingly, she finds herself opening up to him. Not much though. It will take a lot to blast through her armor. But this ability to step outside of herself helps. Watch her mind. See its tricks.

And another thing, she now believes her inability to plan anything is tied to her layers of armor. If she could have done more long-term planning back then, she likely would have been much more aware of how her armor blocks that kind of thinking. With her focused on only short-term plans, the daily grind, that only keeps her armor in place because then she can't see it.

But now, when she thinks of her life in the terms of decades, it is even clearer to her now that if she keeps on doing what she has been doing and letting her screwed-up beliefs control her life, she will wither and she will die, a husk of emptiness.

Easy to say but difficult to do.

But part of her opening is because of Circuit. She loves this dog, and that love spills out, influencing her interactions with everyone else. Even Nickell, it seems. Although she's not about to call any feeling she has for Nickell love. Long, long way from that. If ever.

But Circuit. She had intended simply to drive out to Malibu, feed and walk Circuit and then return. Midori couldn't do it because she's already over on this side of town preparing the Zero Wasters for the HOPE event.

But Circuit wouldn't let her leave without taking her along. She barked, stood behind the car, forcibly resisted.

Oz didn't have the heart to say no. Anyway, what could it hurt to have her along? Feels better this way.

The odd thing—while she was out in Midori's yard trying to make Circuit stay—was that she smelled rain. When she looked up into the sky, she did not see one cloud, but still she smelled rain. Was it a hallucination? Some twist in her increased ability to smell?

Glances at her commD. Her meeting with Dr. Eisenfield is just minutes away. Where is Nickell?

She taps the screen to signal him.

When the visual comes through, she sees his eyes are flat, the skin of his cheeks and below his eyes seems to sag, and all he says is, "Oz."

Alarmed, she asks, "What's happened?"

"Gina's been . . . she's dead."

Oz feels the shock bolt down her body. Gina? "How did—"

"Someone got into her place and strangled her. I . . . I don't know what . . . listen, I'm not sure I can get over to you. I mean—"

SEARCHING FOR A WAY OUT

"What?" This is no time for him to fall apart. Oz puts a little steel in her voice.

"I can't just—"

"Are you helping with the investigation of her murder? If not, you need to focus. I need you here. If you are not doing any good there, then you need to be here."

"But if—"

"Unless you can magically bring her back to life, then move. Clear your mind."

"Jesus, don't you have any feelings?"

"If you only knew." Oz's brain races ahead. Got to hold all this together. "But decide. What is important now? Because while Gina no longer exists, you do."

"Okay, okay." She can hear the exasperation in his voice.

"I'll have to start without you, but you know where it is. I'll stall him. Just be here."

69

Outside the speeding car windows, the sky has a brown stilted haze. No birds fly. Too hot.

But Jason Buggleman does not perceive the scenery. His body trembles, fingers shake and twitch in spasms of fear.

Trapped in the back seat with King Zee Whitehead. Hands and feet bound by a thick, tight rope.

He never should have gotten into the car. Had an armful of clothes he was moving. Out on the sidewalk and they pulled up. And he just stood there frozen. They didn't even have to touch him. Just got in.

Jerry Groot drives faster now that they have left all the traffic behind on the freeway and are winding around up on Mulholland Highway at the western end of Los Angeles county in mostly uninhabited land.

"Did you think I wouldn't find out? And you gave them to that scummy journalist? Just fucking great."

Whitehead has a small gun in the palm of his hand. It has a pearl handle. The pattern on the handle looks like snowflakes.

"Why did you betray me?" Whitehead's voice carries no emotion. It's now just a cold piece of steel. It has a job to do.

"I . . . a greater purpose here. One Faith." Bug's raspy shaky voice. "I believe in One Faith. What you created. But lately . . . I know that you've been under a lot of strain but—"

"Shut up. You know nothing." A momentary flare up of anger then he calms himself and points a finger at Bug. "The greater purpose is what I say it is. Whatever I do is not for you to judge."

"But you were hurting those people. Tammy. And the others. How can that be right?" Bug's spine is rounded forward, huddling inside himself.

SEARCHING FOR A WAY OUT

"Right? What do you know about what's right? Especially for all the One Faith followers." Whitehead lets out a long breath. Looks out the window at the baked, brown hills streaming past. "They can't see past their own pathetic noses. They need me to keep their lives together in this fucked-up, empty culture. I guess you thought you were going to make this all right by giving that asshole those videos. Were you out of your mind?"

Bug cringes against the door. Short, shallow breaths hardly move his chest.

"But it's wrong the way you treat those women," Bug chokes out as he sobs.

Whitehead shakes his head and smiles. "You were always so simple. Took everything at face value. Treat women? You need to put things in perspective. I treat women far better than they're treated in our present world. And I am teaching them a lesson about the consequences of deviating from purpose. A demonstration of sorts. Yes, that's it." Whitehead snaps his fingers as if congratulating himself on his new insight. "But how could I expect you to understand that?"

"I'm sorry. I didn't mean—"

"Listen," He points his thumb at his chest. "It's me that carries this whole glorious enterprise forward. Don't you see?" Whitehead leans forward. "God gave me his vision and I know what to do."

Bug involuntarily moans, closes his eyes. "You hurt her, you scared Tammy half to death."

"You don't know how it feels when you have someone else's life in your hands. It's an intoxicating feeling. Tammy Box is an insect. She's nothing. Just one little person. But every day I have the lives of millions of people in my hands. They wait for me to speak, and they listen to what I have to say. They obey. There is no feeling like that. You can't even imagine. Sniveling little you."

Bug knew about Mr. Whitehead all along, but didn't want to know. When he was working with the geologic team out near the Cleghorn Wilderness Area and that one blistering hot day found Mr. Whitehead dehydrated and raving, carrying around a shovel for some reason, he wanted to believe that Mr. Whitehead had a vision of God.

That this was something he could latch on to and get his own life on track. But he knew better then and just didn't want to believe it.

Mr. Whitehead's car had broken down on the 29 Palms Highway. He had wandered off into the desert. He was lost. If Bug hadn't happened to have come along, he would have died.

If . . .

The ride bumpier now. Jerry has turned off Mulholland and on to a narrow dirt road that descends into a barren valley. A valley containing two large open-air vats filled with the overflow human waste that the city's sewage treatment plants cannot process.

As soon as Jerry stops the car, he flings open the back door and drags Bug out, yanking on the rope. He dumps him on the dry, flaking, pale earth.

Whitehead crouches down next to him, his face only inches away from Bug's.

"I'm sorry, Jason, old boy, but you know too much and you are a liability to me. May God have mercy on your soul."

Bug looks wild-eyed up into the sky.

Jerry picks up Bug like a sack of potatoes and walks over to the edge of the nearest vat, seemingly unaffected by the powerful stench in the air.

Bug screams, "God won't let you get away with this."

Whitehead just nods his head and Jerry drops Bug into the vat.

Bug struggles and squirms, trying to keep his head above the surface of sludge, but with his arms and legs tied, this is futile, and

SEARCHING FOR A WAY OUT

he soon sinks, his last scream obliterated by the human waste sewage filling his mouth.

70

As Oz and Circuit walk the short distance to the Von KleinSmid Center and Dr. Eisenfield's office, she wonders again where the Minoan black stone is. Could it still be in Gina's apartment? Or did she already deliver it to Whitehead?

Anger pushes this thought out of her mind. The closer she comes to Dr. Eisenfield's office, the angrier she gets. He's toyed with her. Intentionally made her life miserable, just to serve his own selfish ends.

She knows she should be cool when they meet. That would be the most beneficial. But . . .

The last few days have unleashed a deeper anger. Realizes more than ever how she has trapped herself and it burns.

Hold on. Got to see this through.

She knocks on his office door.

A muffled "Come in," can be heard.

The instant she opens the door and they step in, she can see Dr. Eisenfield looking down his nose at Circuit, a disapproving formation on his lips.

"You can't bring—"

"I've got nowhere else to put her."

"That doesn't concern me."

"It will." Oz sits on the hard wooden chair.

"What? You're giving me attitude?"

"In the cave on Crete, you knew all along that I had found something important, but you pretended you had no idea what I was talking about when I tried to show you. So you lied to me. And grabbing me was real professional, doctor." She stares straight at him, her face slightly flushed red, gripping one hand with the other in a tight ball.

SEARCHING FOR A WAY OUT

Eisenfield looks at her, looks away, looks back. "You're in no position to criticize me. You're hanging on here by the barest of threads, and all I have to do is make one little snip and you're gone."

"Why didn't you say anything back then?"

"Why should I have? By the way, you've brought the device, haven't you?"

"The device has been stolen."

Eisenfield lowers his chin, looks down, then roars to his feet, points his finger at Oz and appears to be about to say something hostile to Oz except that before any of his words can leave his mouth, Circuit stands as well, the fur on her back rises and she emits a low growl. A menacingly low growl that causes Eisenfield to drop his arm and say to Oz, "The dog has to leave."

"The dog stays. Especially if you're thinking of attacking me."

"Don't be ridiculous, I wasn't going to attack you." But he sits back down.

"Look," he says, "no device, no deal. If it really was stolen, then you need to get it back. Otherwise, the department is not—"

The door bursts open and Nickell barges in. Oz lets out a small breath.

"What are you doing here?" Eisenfield's forehead creases up and his hands fly into the air.

"Bringing you something to think about."

"You two need to leave." Eisenfield is about to stand again but catches himself and stays seated.

Nickell sets his commD on the edge of Eisenfield's desk and instructs it to play the video.

"Watch carefully," Oz says, "your future depends on it."

She makes a point of observing Dr. Eisenfield's face as he views himself in the video threatening her just hours before in the cavern underneath the Signal building.

He glances up at her once and she can see the mixture of worry, desperation, and defiance in his eyes. Oz experiences no pleasure from this, although she thought she would.

"What do you want?" Eisenfield says as if each word causes him pain.

"Stay out of my way." Oz leans forward in the chair, vehemence in her voice. "Stop badgering me, stop lying to me, just back off."

"Listen, you can't talk to me like—"

"I can talk to you—"

Nickell puts a hand on her arm, "Let me." He turns to Dr. Eisenfield. "As you know, I'm with The Data Transfer. I can have this video uploaded in seconds and then it will be immediately disseminated all across the world and—"

Oz stands up and interrupts, "Which means you will never get the chairmanship of the department. In fact, you'll be lucky to hold on to your job."

"Oz," Nickell says.

She sits back in the chair with ferocity. Glares at Eisenfield. Feels like leaping across the desk and breaking his neck. Years of anger erupting.

"You see the point," Nickell says.

Dr. Eisenfield bends forward, putting his head in his hands. "Yes, I see." He raises his head, looks at Oz. "I wanted the same thing you want. I have suspected for a long time that the Minoans were doing something beyond what is commonly thought. Way beyond. I just want to be a part of that."

"Maybe." Oz stands, the anger seeping out of her, gestures to Nickell. "Let's go."

Outside, the sun has nearly descended to the horizon.

As they walk, Oz is of two minds. Two warring minds. The dominant part of herself, the part that has ridden her for the last twenty-two years, tells her to keep her distance from Nickell. Don't

SEARCHING FOR A WAY OUT

get too close. Do not let in any soft emotions toward him. It will only hurt. But another part of her, the part that has just emerged in the last few days, has tasted the slight glimmer of freedom from her past and it wants more.

Is Nickell a part of that freedom, or is he just a distraction? She doesn't know, and it makes her nervous. In fact, it has less to do with trusting Nickell now than trusting herself.

But most important right now is that she finds the labyrinth and reaches the center where she will discover the technology. Aurora's promise. A promise that Oz believes holds the key to her freedom.

"Let's take two cars to the coliseum."

"We could almost walk there from here." Nickell looks south toward the Science Center right across the street from USC and knows that the coliseum is just on the other side of that.

"Takes too much time. I'm going to have to leave and get over to the Signal building fairly soon. I can't stick around. But you said something about an idea you had."

"Buggleman's videos of people suffering during and after the Surrender Ceremony give me plenty of ammunition. I spliced them together and intend to release it just as Whitehead begins to speak. It should spread quickly."

"You know, he still might come after me. If Gina got him the stone before, well, before what happened to her happened, he wouldn't know how to get it to work. But, you know, if she didn't get it to him then..."

"Then it might still be in her apartment. No, Buggleman thinks Whitehead is probably the one who killed her. So he's got your device."

"I'm sorry Nickell, about Gina, I know you... well, it's terrible. But you're doing something positive. Doing good."

"I sure as hell hope so."

"See you over there."

71

Oz, Circuit, and Nickell stand on the Coliseum floor, near the edge of a series of vendor tents set up for the HOPE event, not far from the stage, but angled off to the side.

More than one hundred thousand people jam the Coliseum like back in the day when there used to be games that fans could attend.

Oz feels a little claustrophobic, but she is also excited by all the energy in the air. People pumped up. Fired up that they might get a little piece of some hope. And since it's Halloween, maybe three-quarters of them have dressed up in some kind of costume.

She sees magicians, fairies, warlocks, witches. Lots of people wearing wings. Hoping to fly away? And even a fair amount of unicorns. Part of the reason for these magical costumes is the rumors of Atlantis fueled by the archeological dig at the Signal building.

Right behind them, in an empty booth, are Midori and twenty-seven of the Zero Wasters, costumed as human turds, getting ready to spring their surprise on the mayor.

When Oz first arrived, she felt hesitant as she was not costuming up with them, but Midori came right over to hug her.

Oz itches to leave and go down into the tunnels, but she promised Midori that she would be here at least for a while. And now is her commitment to Nickell to be here for their play against Whitehead.

The crowd surges all around her. The smell is dense, sweaty bodies, the heat of so many packed together, clouds of marijuana and other herbal mixtures filling the air.

Oz sees a man on the stage banging a gong, a sound amplified through the garage-door-sized speakers corralling everyone's attention. After fifteen seconds of that, he briefly welcomes everyone and introduces the mayor.

SEARCHING FOR A WAY OUT

The mayor of Los Angeles, Herman Finkelstein, is about sixty, slightly stooped, bushy mustache, and she knows he has tattoos on both arms although he's covered them up tonight by wearing a long-sleeve shirt.

He looks up into the lights. Tries not to squint. "Hello, Los Angeles."

People roar. They've been waiting. They want hope. They want the despair of the last twenty years to lift.

Mayor Finkelstein smiles and waves. "We have a bright future ahead of us. And we have found water! Right here underground." He points in the general direction of the Signal building.

Oz crouches and runs her hand down Circuit's back. Circuit wags her tail and tilts her head toward Oz. Circuit makes her feel steady or as steady as she can feel right now.

Midori signals to all the Zero Wasters, and they march out from their side booth and like insistent one-celled organisms persistently and inexorably glob toward the stage. A couple of them pull out spray bottles, hold them high in the air, and pulse out the sulfurous mixture, which brings audible groans from those nearby. Other Zero Wasters unfold signs and hold them over their heads. Signs that read "The city stinks, Mister Mayor," or "No more waste."

The mayor talks for ten minutes as the Zero Wasters filter in closer, causing their stink to extrude nearer and nearer to the stage.

The mayor says, "We have a solution to the infrastructure problem currently afflicting the city. We have always had the know-how to fix this, but we have not had the funds. But now," And here he looks up into the dark sky to make a significant rhetorical pause, "the city will build a glorious casino. A casino that will attract millions of dollars from tourists to generate the needed funds."

He looks out at the audience, expecting massive approval. A few people applaud, but a few also boo.

JOHN MOON FORKER

He gets a whiff of the sulfur and turns his head toward the source of the smell. Calculating this might be a good time to end, he says, "And now let me introduce to you our next speaker, King Zee Whitehead."

Oz's nerves flinch and she's glad she's out in this crowd where she can't be easily seen.

She looks up at the sky. Are those thunderheads?

72

Lightning rips across the sky, followed by a roaring thunder. This causes a momentary silence from the thousands of people here. Then some start clapping and whooping, a cause for celebration. It might rain. Actually rain.

When she sees Whitehead walk onto the stage, a creepy sense of fear seeps into her body. She just knows he will come after her once he can't figure out how to make the stone work.

Whitehead speaks in that commanding voice of his, which booms out of those enormous speakers. The voice floats and circles and entwines itself into a person's skull. Just like it did to her during the Surrender Ceremony.

Oz sees many heads turn up and lock on to Whitehead, listening with their entire bodies as though in a hypnotic trance. But for her it's like an echo of that time just a few days ago when she felt trapped and she wants his voice out of her head right now.

"We've all come a long way together," Whitehead begins. "We have suffered much to live in this degraded culture with its endless diversions from the truth. But for those of us who have connected directly to God, we know differently. We know the truth because God has told it to us. There are many of us who have not made this connection. But soon you will and then you will join us.

"Tonight, I am announcing a crusade. Spiritual warfare against the corruption, the phony religions, the hedonistic culture. And I am announcing a gift from God. A paradise for the deserving." He holds both hands up in the air, fingers spread. "You know what I'm talking about, you've heard it all over the news nodes, yes, the recent discoveries on my land." Whitehead pretty much points in the same direction as the mayor did before him. "The technology of the legend, the technology of lost Atlantis."

Oz hears the words and wonders if he has found a way to make the stone work. In one way, that would be a relief because then he wouldn't be coming after her, but it would also be worse. She needs the stone. She needs to explore what it can do, and he is exactly the wrong person to have access to that technology.

A flash of lightning and thunder occur almost simultaneously.

"Okay, here goes," Nickell says, keying in a command on his commD. "Uploading it to a dozen nodes. It should be all over the network any second now." He has his finger up in the air, almost pointing, but not at anything, more like digitizing the environment around him as if casting a spell.

She's never seen him smile before and it gives her a little warmth.

The commD, which Nickell holds out in front of him, starts running a video and Oz sees images of King Zee Whitehead at various Surrender Ceremonies, people having extreme bodily reactions to the machine and the liquid, the vomiting, the collapsing, the screaming, and the sections of video where Whitehead is doing to other women what he did to Oz, his hands running all over their bodies.

Nickell flips it out to 3D, so it sits in the air over his device. People nearby notice and they plug into the network on their own commDs.

Oz can't hear the audio because of all the noise here in the Coliseum, but the visuals tell the story. There is a savagery to Whitehead that makes her very alert. The danger more real.

If enough people tune into this, then Whitehead will be stopped and she won't be in danger.

One second later, lighting strikes a few hundred feet away. The power in the coliseum blinks out and even the commD network crashes.

73

A tremendous bolt of lightning rents the sky, accompanied by the boom of thunder. Now the rain begins. Sheets of water cascade down like slabs of iron finally set loose from years of imprisonment, roaring in their newfound freedom.

The sound and light crew controlling all the stage equipment scrambles feverishly to cover it.

Within a minute, the hard-packed soil of the Coliseum floor has become a raging river up to Oz's ankles.

People shout and cheer. For them, this is the real hope and they wallow in it. Splashing and stomping, giddy with delight.

Scowling, Whitehead leads his people down the stairs and off the stage where they weave through the crowd.

Oz has grabbed a roll of Circuit's neck skin to make sure she stays close. The lightning flashes cast a ghostly pale upon the crowd, some struggling, some joyously playing in the rain.

"I have to get over to the Signal building," Oz says to Nickell. "Come with."

Nickell has stuffed the commD in his pocket to keep it dry. "Where are you parked?"

They have to shout to hear each other over the blasting rain.

The stadium lights try to flicker and stay on, but the flashes of lightning allow Nickell to see Tammy Box working her way across the field in front of the stage. She holds something at her side. A gun.

Nickell points. "Look."

"Who..."

"She's got a gun. I've got to stop her." Nickell lunges forward and Oz with Circuit follow right behind.

Tammy stops twenty feet in front of Whitehead's slow-moving entourage, raises the gun and screams, "Where's Jason? What have you done with him?"

Whitehead stops, stares at the woman, rain scooting down his face, looking like a rat.

Nickell steps forward and calls out, "Tammy, don't."

But the rain drowns out his words.

Whitehead's man Jerry Groote circles around to get behind Box.

Nickell knows she doesn't see him so he runs forward shouting, "Tammy, watch out!"

She hears this and turns her head for a second. Groote rushes forward and Box catches the movement in her peripheral vision.

She swings her arm around and fires the gun just as Groote tackles her. The sound penetrates even this rain and the orange flash from the muzzle looks like an angry candle twisting in frustration. The bullet sails into the sky.

Those still close by instinctively dive to the ground. Whitehead flinches.

Groote brings his full weight on top of Box and grabs her hands. Half a second later Nickell barrels into Groote, nearly snapping his head off, which lets Box prop herself up on her elbows for a second before another One Faith staff member piles on top of her. The gun springs from her hand and into the mud.

People scream. Oz stands in this swirl of chaos and thinks death is near.

Groote has about fifty pounds on Nickell and shakes him off.

Oz and Circuit move off diagonally. As they walk quickly away, she looks back and sees Whitehead. Their eyes lock. And like some kind of volcanic eruption, he raises his arm, points at Oz and shouts, "Get her."

Oz and Circuit break into a full sprint.

74

Oz and Circuit run out into the parking lot into an ever-widening sea of cars, each rooftop a drum for the fat and profuse raindrops to beat upon. Thousands and thousands of them thunder in the downpour as they run.

She's soaked. Her clothes heavy, rubbing her skin.

With the water hitting her face and running down into her eyes, she can barely see, yet she keeps looking back and thinks she can spot Whitehead and his big thug chasing her.

She needs to keep going full tilt until she can find her car, which has got to be around here somewhere. She remembers the angle that she slanted in from when she arrived and tries to do it in reverse, but with this blinding rain, it's not so easy. Somewhere off the front of the Coliseum, by a small cluster of trees on a grassy area. That's where she remembers parking.

Only a few people have come out of the Coliseum so far to escape the downpour—too late for that—while most everyone else has stayed inside to celebrate this first rain in years.

She sloshes through one large puddle. An instant lake. Water accumulates on the asphalt with nowhere to go.

She sees several trees. Which one? To the left. Yes, must be. She angles off and now she can see her little Electron.

Unlocking and opening the door, they both pile in and Circuit immediately shakes her entire body, sending another million drops of water all over Oz and the interior of the car.

She slaps her wet thumb onto the identification pad, but nothing happens. She wipes the rain off her hand onto the seat, thinking that the wetness is the reason, but again, the car won't start.

Not now, she pleads.

She pounds on the dashboard three times. Sometimes that works.

Not this time.

A pool of panic spreads across her brain. She turns to look back, but she can see nothing through the rapidly steaming windows.

She locks the doors. Thumb on the pad again. Not even a spark, a tremor, nothing.

She is about to pound on the dashboard once again when her door window shatters, the force of the blow destroying the protective interlayer of polyvinyl butyral built in to prevent just this sort of thing.

Oz flinches to the right and the big hand coming in through the open space just misses her.

Circuit barks furiously, then growls and lunges for the hand, which snaps back.

Oz jams her thumb hard against the identification pad, and this time the car starts. She sits bolt-upright and throws the car into gear.

It lurches forward, clipping the car on the left. She grabs the wheel, and once out of the space, yanks it hard to the right, accelerating, looking out in the far distance to find the exit, heading for it and picking up speed. She glances in the mirror and dimly sees two figures running in the other direction. It must be them, and they are running for their car. They'll be on the road soon, so she has to lose them now.

But it's so hard to see with all this rain. She mistakenly drives past the lane that would have taken her to the exit and has to double back, losing precious time. Finally, she springs out onto South Figueroa Street, whips over to 39th Street, which is thankfully devoid of most traffic. The few other cars on the road move extremely slowly in the face of this onslaught of rain.

When she takes the corner at Broadway Place, the Electron slides sideways all the way across the street, and she worries that she'll have to slow down, which would let Whitehead catch up. She can't see him. But because of the rain, he could be fifty feet behind her and she still wouldn't see him, so she's got to go as fast as she can.

The rain beating down sounds like a machine gun on her car, on the road, on every single thing in the world. It's deafening. No other sound. It pours in her missing window, making her feel cold. Bone cold. Goosebumps on her arms. Fear arcs through her body.

Keep it under control, she tells herself.

Once she crosses under the Santa Monica tollway, she's on the southern edge of downtown.

She passes people who had been out walking but are now trying to stay dry, huddling in doorways of closed businesses, dark office buildings, under jutting marquees of movie houses.

Finally, on Santa Fe Avenue, she sees the dark Signal building up ahead but zooms right past it as she drives to the alley three blocks away and the secret entrance down into the underground.

All of this sudden water in the alley has dislodged years of garbage, gobs of sodden newspaper from back when newspapers were still being printed, rusty tin cans, age-gray two-by-fours, plastic of all shapes and sizes, and, of course, the rats. Dozens of rats flooded out of their homes and are now swimming in the oily water.

She drives all the way to the back end, and she and Circuit get out of the car. They run on black pavement past the dumpsters and the old barrels and to the wide, scarred, metal door.

Under the overhang, she gains a partial respite from the rain. Circuit shakes herself again and again, attempting to shed the water.

Looks closely at the door. All around the door. No obvious way to open it.

Back when she had come out this door from the inside, she had found a button. But no button is visible here on the outside.

It's so dark she can barely see anything, much less some button that might or might not be here, so she runs her hands all over the door and the surrounding frame to feel for it. No button, but she finds some raised lines.

This is taking too long. Got to get down there.

Maybe she should call Nickell. No, she told him to meet her here. Oh yeah, then she's got to send him the directions. The commD network works here. She transmits the information.

This is when she sees the headlights appear at the far end of the alley.

It's them.

Oz stands frozen. Unbelieving. How could they? But every instant is a capsule of time too long. Their car sends waves of water away like a ship at sea, drawing closer and closer.

She gets a fleeting thought—not going to make it.

Flipping on the light in her commD, she scans these lines. They are symbols. Symbols she's seen before. On the stone, down in the map room and out at the house in Topanga.

Quick now. She presses different symbols, but nothing happens.

Headlights coming closer.

Think. The sun, mushrooms, bull's horns, a dog, a tree, a woman no, not just any woman, it's the woman priestess. She presses that. Still nothing.

The car has stopped just on the other side of the dumpsters, and she can hear the sloshing footfalls approach.

What is the combination?

She presses the sun symbol and then the woman priestess symbol.

The door snaps open an inch. She jerks it open and she and Circuit dart inside, but as she tries to slam it close, a large foot blocks the way.

She whips back around, and they scamper down the tunnel.

75

Oz and Circuit fly down the rocky decline into the expansive cavern. She's got to get away from them. Lose them. But there's not that much room on this side of the river, as she well knows. No real tunnel system.

It's the metal tree that's important. She has to get inside that.

She rushes down to the metal tree just feet from the water's edge. The river roars. It's rising with the rain. Picking up speed. Chunks of what might be fungi whip by.

She desperately searches for a door handle to turn or a button to push but sees nothing, just like she saw nothing the last time she was here. But there must be a way in.

Circuit circles and barks.

She glances up the incline and can just see Whitehead at the top making his way down the rocky path. He'll be here in thirty seconds. She can't get caught out here in the open. Her eyes skim over everything without seeing anything. She's got to calm down enough to find a way in.

Oz touches the tree with her hands, hoping to feel what she can't see, feeling nothing at first until her fingers slip into grooves that seem to be specifically made for fingers. Her palms slide in next. Hand plates. Yes. Both hands fully in now. A panel slides open in the tree and she and Circuit both scurry in.

The panel slides closed behind them, and they are in near darkness. There seems to be a path, but it's so hard to see. Just as she takes a tentative step forward, three intensely bright and focused lights click on. Light of the same quality that Oz saw in that room on the third floor of the Signal building. Creates a precise visual clarity. And now it seems to have a purpose, almost an intelligence, as the cones of light circle overhead, scanning their bodies. They are being examined.

The labyrinth is preparing itself for me, Oz thinks. She touches the wall to steady herself.

The lights blink out simultaneously. Now things really look black. Her pupils have constricted. But in a few seconds the ambient light comes up and she can see down the path.

She walks more slowly than she'd like, but it's just too dim to move any faster. Circuit sniffs the walls as if there is something of interest to her.

Oz is not thirty feet down this narrow tunnel when she hears the metal tree panel sliding open behind her. She quickens her pace. But another fifty feet in, she stops to listen and she can plainly hear their feet slapping against the floor as they run toward her. She realizes they will be here in seconds. If only she had a weapon.

Just as she decides to run ahead, the entire wall moves, sweeping in a half circle, cutting off the tunnel behind her. Cutting off Whitehead. Can't reach her now.

She lets out a big breath she didn't even know she was holding in.

Circuit looks up at her as if to say what next?

She looks around. The walls here are not like the tunnel walls across the river. Not all soil and rock. These are pure white, smooth and solid. So solid they might be made of stone, but how would anyone work stone this smooth way down here?

This is so carefully constructed that it has got to be the labyrinth. How long has this been here? Since 1951 when Nickell told her the building went up?

Well, Aurora wanted her to come here to the portal. Maybe this portal leads to the world she got a glimpse of out in Topanga. And this being a Minoan labyrinth, you must go to the center and face the Minotaur. But, of course, it wouldn't be the Minotaur because the Minotaur doesn't exist.

SEARCHING FOR A WAY OUT

A tiny sense of adventure sprouts in the weeds of fear. She moves ahead on the newly created opening down the path to who knows where. Then abruptly she comes to a dead end. The path just stops. What is this supposed to mean?

It means the labyrinth wants her to stop.

And right then the walls shift again and Circuit has to step quickly to avoid being separated from Oz, but the walls move and shift again and again and this last time Circuit doesn't make it. Cut off. Separated.

She reaches for Circuit but too late. She's gone.

No, this can't be happening. Can't even hear her, but she must be right on the other side of one of these walls.

The space Oz now finds herself in is tiny, with no apparent way out.

Oz looks up but sees no ceiling. Just darkness.

So tight in here. An old and familiar feeling arises in her mind. Too close. No way out. Trapped.

Then the white walls fade into darkness and at first she only hears the water. But she knows instantly where she is. Then comes the visuals and she is inside it. That canyon, that flood, her parents, her brother and all of them standing against the canyon wall trying to stay dry in the pouring rain and the water in the canyon rising rapidly, but this experience of it is happening in super slow motion. So slow that it's as if she could step in between the moments of time.

She can read every nuance of expression on all of their faces and can practically feel what they feel. Her brother bored but slightly excited by all the water. Her father, annoyed that they are even here, not wanting to have walked all this way, somewhat tired, and beginning to worry about how to get out, while her mother, who is feeling an indifference to the weather and a distance from her husband, emanates an undercurrent of protectiveness and a love for both Oz and her brother. Amused by Oz coupled with an admiration for her curiosity and her adventurous spirit, even if it has brought them down here in the rain.

Oz perceives all of this in an instant, and it is all extremely clear because of the infinite slowness of time that is being forced on her in this tiny enclosed space.

But what strikes Oz the most is how she saw none of this back then. That she was just so wrapped up in her own 11-year-old mind that it was like they weren't even there.

She feels a sadness that just keeps intensifying as she has to relive that moment over and over, each time becoming more brutal until just on the verge of pain, the images stop.

The light glows, and she can see again.

The walls shift and the open passageway looms ahead. But still no Circuit. She pulls the map out of her pocket, hoping to find her way, to find her path.

The map is soaking wet too. Unfolding it, she sees it is entirely blank.

She's lost.

76

Whitehead races down the hill to catch that bitch, but it's so rocky he has to watch his footing. Slowing him down even more is Jerry, who just lumbers along like some fucking overfed cow. At this rate, they'll never catch her. Got to speed things up.

There must be even more of this tunnel crap inside that tree, but no matter how many tunnels are in there, he will track her down and make her talk.

He pats the gun in his pants pocket. Prepared just like a good boy scout.

He glances back. Jerry is so slow. Well, the big guy just isn't cut out for this sort of thing. Once he gets everything all squared away, it might be time to get a replacement for Jerry. Someone more suited for the job.

He had observed how the woman had gotten inside the tree, and he too put his hands in the carved slots. The door slides open.

"Come on, we haven't got all day," Whitehead says.

Groote tramps down the end of the decline, breathing hard, small beads of perspiration lining the top of his forehead. "Yeah, okay, okay."

Once inside the metal tree, and after the examination by the three lights, Whitehead scoots down the initial long hallway. Twenty-five feet in, he turns and says, "Hurry up."

Jerry murmurs something and Whitehead says, "What did you say?" Anger rising in his throat right from the reptilian brain.

"I said, what's the rush? There is only this one passageway."

"You buffoon. There's no time to waste. We've got to catch her." This is when he needs Bug but, well, he's sort of eliminated Bug from the picture, hasn't he, so that won't be happening.

"I don't appreciate being called names."

"Look, Jerry," Whitehead says practically shaking with impatience, the world moving much too slow and him seeing that Jerry is only making it all the worse. "We've got to get to her and make her tell me about this... about... shit, about the future of my business."

He might just run on ahead and leave Jerry behind, but he'd feel a little safer with Jerry's muscle right behind him.

Whitehead knows well that this stupid stone in his pocket is useless unless he can get it to work, and so he'll just have to force her to tell him. Otherwise, it's just a piece of junk. But this piece of junk could be the key to finding the potion or whatever it is. Jesus Christ, he doesn't even know what he's looking for. Is it a liquid? A food? A document with the right mumbo-jumbo on it that once spoken gives eternal life? Or is it some object of technology that he has no idea what it might look like? It might even be this stupid stone itself. Which is all the more reason to catch that bitch. After that, he'll deal with that nosy journalist.

But man, he has to hurry, and he's never going to catch this woman if he's going to be slowed down by this oaf.

"Hurry up," he calls back.

Groote mutters to himself. Breathes hard. Seems to Whitehead to slow down even more. Maybe on purpose.

"Now what?" Whitehead has half-turned back toward Groote, becoming more irritated by the second, feeling more like he shouldn't have even brought this big lug down here with him. He can take care of this woman all by himself.

But as anger infuses his mind and controls him, he decides to make it clear to Jerry Groote that he absolutely knows who he's talking to and knows his place. He takes one step back toward Groote. That's when he feels the vibration. Two seconds later, the wall in front of him rotates.

The open-mouthed Jerry disappears on the other side.

77

With Oz's directions, Nickell has found his dripping-wet way down to the metal tree, having just retrieved his flying bot and tucked it inside of his commD.

Using the water drops on the ground and the wet handprints on the tree as a guide, he finds the carved slots and has the door open.

Once inside, he's blocked. Overhead, three lights circle, running their beams all over him.

Some kind of security system he figures. But then who is checking him out? Where are they? Where is Oz?

Feels a little on edge here. Not sure what to do next. Makes him uncomfortable. Leaks into a tingly fear. Of what? Of the unknown? He can't see.

Blink. The intense lights shut off, his eyes adjust, and a pathway becomes visible before him.

The door behind him remains closed. Nowhere to go but forward. The walls are so close together he can touch them.

Then the path ends at a wall. When he turns, he now finds himself in a room with no exit. It's small. The light, already dim, dims even more.

• • • •

ONE CLEAR, COLD NIGHT, he and Dana Mostolinni were at the high school working late on a story for the school newspaper. They were just inches apart.

The adult Nickell is freaked because he is in two places at once. He sees the memory as a three-dimensional real event, yet he is inside his teenage body feeling what he felt, thinking what he thought.

Dana was a good deal shorter than him, so he had a complete view of her bleached blond hair and her ever-present black roots. She had a small nose that was ever so slightly upturned and seemed to give her face an impish quality that her energy only supported.

He was so close to her he could smell her scent. Something like peppermint and cloves, although probably neither, but something so fresh he was drawn to it. They had been working for hours and had talked and laughed and told each other secrets. He felt so connected to her at that moment.

The Nickell watching all this in the walled-off tiny room in the folds of the labyrinth trembles as he knows what's coming next.

And sure enough the teenage Nickell raises his hand to put on her shoulder and opens his mouth to tell her how much he likes her, how much he cares about her, but his hand stops, his mouth shuts, and he lowers the hand without her ever knowing that he had done that.

He was afraid. Afraid he'd somehow screw it up.

Nickell feels the regret, a sharp blade of pain.

This triggers an avalanche in his head of other regrets—his sister Bonnie, Gina, and all the other moments in his life when he didn't act, held back, not making a decision that became a decision by his not acting. These regrets stack up higher and higher. He can feel their weight, and he feels himself sinking under this weight, growing heavier and heavier until his own accumulated indecisions paralyze him.

78

She doesn't walk forty feet before the wall shifts again, raising her hopes to see Circuit on the other side of it. But no, just another path with the wall sliding closed behind her, forcing her to go just the one way. A good thing, as she is so disoriented that if she had a choice, she wouldn't know how to make it.

The fungi light stays dim to the point of shadowy darkness. It feels as though something might lurk around any bend in the path.

Oz hesitates, stops then starts again, doing this over and over, trying not to be surprised, to not have something jump out at her from the darkness. She hardly dares to breathe.

As she walks along the passageway, she hears what sounds like someone pounding on the other side of the wall. Which wall? Off to the left? It's got to be Whitehead. One of these times when the wall shifts she's going to run right into him, then what?

But she must be heading toward the center of the labyrinth. The path could go nowhere else. And that's exactly where she needs to be.

But the walls close in again, holding her in a small space.

Oz is transported back twenty-two years to the canyon.

Again, everything moves in slow motion so that every detail can be examined, every emotion registered, every motivation plain to see.

When her brother is hooked by that branch and dragged into the raging river, she sees her father's face just before he jumps in the water. It is turned toward her mother, his eyes finding hers and Oz sees they held a fatalism and a self-blame for all that was happening, the same self-blame that Oz has carried all these years, and it strikes her now that they both can't carry that blame. That just doesn't work. One or both of them misperceived the situation. Maybe there is no blame. At least not the kind that you have to carry for the rest of eternity. The kind that allows no redemption.

All these years her mind has been a prison, the bars of which are these thoughts of self-blame. And she has allowed these thoughts to trap her. And seeing that look in her father's eyes hints that maybe it doesn't have to be that way.

But there is more to this.

As she stands under the ledge in the pouring rain, she feels her mother's aloneness. Like a curtain surrounding her or a layer of personality that she wears. A sleeve of separateness.

A perception of her mother that Oz is stunned to be having now. Had not seen this. Or had no words for it as an eleven-year-old.

It almost feels as if this was one of her mother's habits. The habit of being lonely.

Such an odd thing to realize. As if a personality trait is just something you can put on or take off like you would a pair of pants.

Then her point of view shifts. Instead of being inside her eleven-year-old self looking at her mother, she is outside herself. But not eleven anymore. The full-grown, present-day Oz.

And she can see the same curtain of aloneness drawn around her. She knows it was that same curtain that lifted from her in the cave on Crete. Can see how her mother's aloneness and her own aloneness connect. It's like she inherited it. Or picked up the habit of being lonely from her mother.

This is what the labyrinth is teaching, what the Minoans were on to. Part of it anyway. A key to unlocking the workings of the mind so that you do not have to be at its mercy. This is what the black stone was showing her as well.

Then the labyrinth leads her in a sequence to the end, to when her parents disappeared into the water and when she was trapped beneath its surface.

SEARCHING FOR A WAY OUT

She stops breathing altogether, and the panic fills her mind. No, she's not ready for that. Can't go through that again.

She stops and whirls around looking for any way out, for an end to this. No, no, no, she can't have that feeling again. That desperate clawing to free herself from the bottom of the river and reach up for air. That consuming terror. One more second down there, she's sure she would have died.

Then the images of her mother and the water are gone. She's fully back in the dim, unending passageway.

Get a grip, she tells herself. Slow down. There's nowhere to run to. She's trapped here too.

She takes a deep breath. Listens intently all around her and hears nothing. No walls shifting, no pounding on them.

Okay, let's figure this out.

What could the Minoans have been up to with this labyrinth? If they created this in the image of the labyrinth on Crete, then they would have supplied this one with the modern equivalent of a Minotaur. Which is what all these images from the past are all about, right? You get to face the worst things in your life. But to what end?

Is this a way to overcome them? Is that what the slow-motion experience of them is all about? That if you go slow enough and become aware of all the data you missed the first time, then you can deal with it?

But she doesn't feel like she's dealing with it very well.

She now remembers the cave in Crete. The drawing on the floor. The mind within the mind.

But maybe she interpreted it the wrong way. Maybe it was being the observer who exits the mind. Who watches the mind from a distance. Maybe that's the real you.

The mind takes on the habits like loneliness and fear and they govern the person throughout their lives. But those habits do not burden the observer if it doesn't want to be, and the Minoans figured out how to make that choice available, how to free the being inside.

And this freedom from the control of the mind is the freedom she's always looked for but just didn't know what it was, what to call it.

Must get to the center of the labyrinth.

But the wall doesn't shift, and she is thrust back in her own private little auditorium and she's already underwater and it's all very slow. She notices each bubble of air escaping from her mouth, all the swirling branches, moss, leaves, she sees in the wild cacophony all around her. A few fish whip by as if they are on an amusement ride and she notices the sandy streak of color at the bottom of the river and then she feels within her own body the exact center of the fear, the terror of being trapped underwater, her clothes tangled in the tree branches and her pulling desperately at them trying to free herself but doing it in such a panic as to be totally ineffective.

But before she can re-experience the freeing of herself from that branch that did come, the images stop. She's back in the passageway.

She's on all fours and breathing hard.

The images weren't supposed to stop like this.

Then she hears the water. This is not part of the labyrinth's theater. This is real.

79

King Zee Whitehead doesn't know at first whether he is having a vision or an actual experience.

At the dead end in the passageway, where he is forced to stop, where the space narrows and the light diminishes, an abrupt transition thrusts him into a vast space. Into the most magnificent chamber in a royal castle where the ceiling rises to infinity like some sort of heavenly crystal cathedral.

Just ahead of him, in the very center of this immense room, is a golden throne. A chair set high above the floor that looks like it must weigh over a ton.

The chair itself appears to be made of thick gold strands woven in an intricate pattern of startling complexity.

Black obsidian, luminescent steps ascend to this throne. It drew Whitehead toward it as though magnetized.

And then he sees him. Sitting on His throne. The Supreme Being.

But strangely for Whitehead, he can only get glimpses. For some reason, he cannot raise his head or his eyes high enough to see God's face.

But it is Him. He knows that with certainty. And with that certainty he feels a soaring exultation. Finally. Here he is on the verge of his greatest triumph and now he has the chance, no, the honor, to speak with God.

On his knees, he ascends partway up the black obsidian steps to be closer to God. He can feel God's eyes on him. Bathing in the warm glow. What a glorious feeling.

Then God speaks in a deep, resonant voice that sounds like ancient oak. "Speak. Be concise. Do not waste time, my son."

"I have searched for you for so long, my Lord. I am in your service. I am bringing your message to the world."

"Yes, you have done well. But your work is not done."

"I know. I know. There is so much yet to do." Whitehead feels the love of God course through his veins. Veins no longer filled with his blood, but with pure liquid joy.

"My son, are you ready to obey me in all things? To trust what I tell you to do?"

"Of course, my Lord. I will follow you to the ends of the earth."

On the very last syllable of this last word, he feels as if he is floating. Rising ever higher. But the strange thing is he can see himself down there on those steps kneeling before God, but here he is up so high, and still he cannot see the ceiling, although somehow he knows there is one.

Ornately carved sculptures decorate the walls. Sculptures of cherubs and angels blowing trumpets, heralding the glory.

The walls are more like golden tubes rather than flat surfaces, half-circles of gleaming metal lined up one after another in the shape of luxury.

He looks down at himself there on the obsidian steps. His image does not please him. This is worse than looking into a mirror, which he already hates.

Something odd about this space. His memory jogs him.

This room . . . this castle. He's seen it before. Where was . . . and then it comes to him. This seems very similar to a castle he read about as a child in one of those interactive books. That's an odd coincidence.

He looks down at the throne, at himself and at God and realizes that now he can see God's face. Pretty far away, but he does see it.

And doesn't that face look familiar too? Isn't that the face of, oh, what's his name, that actor who played God in that stupid movie? But . . . how can this be?

SEARCHING FOR A WAY OUT

This all now looks more like a stage. Some kind of production, set up for some purpose that cheapens this experience for him. Not what he wants. Block it out. Stop it.

He forces himself to dive down, to re-inhabit his body and to see God through his own eyes, not that fake stagey view from above.

"Here me now," God says, as if Whitehead's interlude in the sky had never happened.

Whitehead says, "Yes." Again, he cannot raise his head and eyes high enough to see God's face.

"You need to be even more pure. Let no distractions take you away from your purpose. Be single-minded."

"I understand," Whitehead says. Yes, he has been slack. Has lost sight of his true purpose. He needs to be in control.

"Find and use the immortality technology because I want you to be my agent on earth for eternity."

"Yes, my Lord." He knew there was an immortality technology. He didn't want to admit his doubts before, but now there are none. It must be true.

"So I say to you, do not let anyone or anything stand in your way. Do what must be done."

"Of course, I will obey."

And he waits a moment for God's final words. Instead, the lights flicker, the castle disappears, the throne vanishes, God is gone, and Whitehead is back in the narrow passageway.

He shakes his head in a muddy flash of disorientation. To have spent that time with God. To have been that close. His devotion now is completely pure. He is totally dedicated. God has given him the power here on earth, and he will wield it in His name.

But he must find his way here through this maze. That technology is in here somewhere. Find the girl, make her talk, and then grab the immortality technology. All that he deserves to have.

JOHN MOON FORKER

Then he hears the surging water somewhere behind one of the walls.

80

On all fours, Oz gasps for air and grips the earthen floor. Wet skin and sodden clothes from the rain, but it might as well have been from this memory, the imagery so real, so consuming, so invasive that her body and mind believe it.

And the sound of the water is close, but she's not sure just where it's coming from.

She raises her head. Alert and listening.

It's more what she's not hearing now. Missing that background sound, a kind of humming before. Not now.

She stands and hears a popping noise. The wall shifts again but this time it stutters and then stops, open maybe a foot. The wall behind remains open too.

Maybe there is some kind of malfunction and all the doors have opened up.

She moves forward, wary of what she might meet. Her body braces in the anticipation of some unplanned encounter. Like Whitehead and his bodyguard.

Twenty feet ahead, she sees a crossroads. A crossroads only made possible by the partially opened walls. This is much less like a labyrinth and more like a maze to her. A maze you can never get out of.

But her thoughts about the accident of twenty-two years ago continue despite the abrupt termination, or was it a malfunction of what she now sees as the Minotaur?

Underwater and panicked, on the verge of drowning, she had stopped her struggle, stopped moving, even stopped thinking and just observed. It was as if she had all the time in the world. All of her attention focused on one thing. Her survival. But in a solidly deliberate way.

One by one, she found exactly the points where and how her clothing had entangled with the tree branch, untangled them, and then swam to the surface.

Something took over from her flailing, panicked mind. Something much greater and much more powerful. Something she believes connects to the work of the Minoans, to what she experienced in the cave, to what she has witnessed these past few days and what she hopes will be discovered when she reaches the center.

She's got to move. Got to find Circuit and get to the center of the labyrinth before midnight.

She runs down the passageway, slowing only to squeeze through the slender openings left by the malfunctioning walls.

Three minutes later Circuit trots into the space vacated by Oz. Noses over the knee and handprints in the earth, smells the scent, wheels around and gallops down the corridor.

81

King Zee Whitehead steps through the narrow opening where the wall has popped open.

Excellent. He'll find the woman in no time if all the walls are busted open like this.

As he approaches a bend in the labyrinth, he hears the slapping footsteps of someone running toward him.

He stops, pulls the gun out of his pocket, points it upward. In this delicious moment of anticipation, he hears that churning water again.

Jerry Groote barges into view and, seeing Whitehead, tries to stop suddenly, but his momentum causes him to stumble forward a few steps so that he has to steady himself with his hand on the wall.

"Mr. Whitehead, Mr. Whitehead, I am so glad that I've found you," Groote sputters out the words while trying to catch his breath. "I've had the most amazing experience. I was in—"

"Jerry, we don't have time for that right now. We've got to find the woman. What's back that way?" He nods down the passageway out of which Groote had just come.

"But Mr. Whitehead, this is important."

"Don't bother me with this drivel. Let's go."

Jerry Groote's unnaturally eager face now droops back into its normal, hardened mask. He shakes his head. "I'm tired of listening to you. You listen to me for a change."

Whitehead feels a tidal wave of exasperation. Someone getting in his way again. Not just in his way, but in God's way. He is on a mission from God, is God's agent on earth. No time to put up with fools.

He shoots Jerry Groote in the head.

82

Oz doesn't run far, skirting through narrow openings where the malfunctioning walls have not shifted completely before she comes to the end. The center of the labyrinth.

She walks into a perfectly circular room that's maybe sixty feet across.

Same fungi blue illumination only a few degrees brighter. The space appears empty except for a brilliant white stone bench built into the wall running all the way around the circle.

But it's the floor that draws her attention. Like in the cave on Crete, Oz sees that the entire floor is one large, complex and highly detailed representation.

Representation is the best word she can come up with at first. It's not a drawing, not a painting, not an illustration. Far more than any of those. Far more realistic.

As she steps out onto the floor, it's more like she's stepping down into this representation, as if she's gone into a separate reality. Some other land.

On a dirt footpath, a creek just to her left, maybe seven feet wide, meandering along, willows and birch and ash trees wrapping around both banks, but it is the sounds that grab her. Crickets and frogs and birds. Abundant life. She sees two large, yellow, tiger swallowtail butterflies swooping around each other, bees everywhere, their buzz vibrating the air.

Like out in Topanga, more plants, more animals, more life. A message from the Minoans?

Then she sees a young woman in a meadow of tall grasses and purple flowers on the slope of a hill.

SEARCHING FOR A WAY OUT

She sits five feet away from the one tree, a craggy, gnarled, blackthorn tree. No berries. A single raven stands on a branch, calm and silent.

The woman watches Oz. She wears a soft, off-white linen shirt and coal-black pants that fit tightly around her ankles. Barefoot. Legs crossed. A breeze catches the edge of her clothes and Oz sees them move.

Hair similar to Oz's. Same length, same style, same color.

Oz wonders who the woman is.

This question ignites a sensation within. Oz feels the border between her and the other woman disintegrating. Her consciousness and that of the woman's merge.

Oz is right there in the meadow under the sun. It's warm. The air feels fresh against her skin.

Sharp light, like in the white room on the third floor of the Signal building. Everything in acute relief, everything extremely distinct, everything clear, clear like she's seen nothing before. Like this is a new world.

She is seeing out of this woman's eyes, but she is still herself. Somehow she knows the woman's name is Kitane, but most people call her Kit.

A voice—not her own—in her head laughs. "Wondering where the Minotaur is?"

"You're speaking to me?"

"You're quick. That's what I like about you?"

"This isn't a..."

"A drawing? An illustration? Maybe not."

Oz touches the blackthorn tree to see if it's real. Feels that way. "Am I supposed to guess?"

"You're supposed to do what you came here for." Kit sounds serious, no sarcastic banter.

"Aurora wanted me to come here. To the center of the labyrinth. To find the portal." Oz can't tell if she's talking to a real person, a robot, or a Minoan from another world.

"Ah, Aurora. I believe I saw her here a little while ago."

Oz glances around, but it's freakish doing it with another's eyes. "Wait, you're not her are you?"

"No, I am not."

"But you could tell me where to find her or the portal, couldn't you?"

"Observe closely. What you saw in the cave on Crete was a drawing made about four thousand years ago. We've made a little progress since then. Go ahead and look around you. Feel it. Especially feel it."

When Oz looks out at the meadow and the sun through the consciousness of this woman, she sees everything as alive. Each insect, blade of grass, each flower, each rock in the ground, all pulsing, vibrating, communicating. Kitane is bathed in a vast web of life, a flow of information. And this woman's senses—hearing, smelling, seeing—shower Oz in a sensory flood.

Oz recalls her speculations about the cave on Crete. "You've been exploring and investigating the mind. You know how to use it."

"That and a few other things."

Yes, Oz says to herself. And not just the more acute senses, so much greater clarity, no distracting thoughts, tremendous sharpening of attention and concentration.

"This is the labyrinth, right?" Oz asks.

"One of the labyrinths."

"What is it here for?"

"To face the Minotaur, of course."

Oz knows Kit is smiling, but she just can't see it. "What is the Minotaur?"

SEARCHING FOR A WAY OUT

All that terror she felt out there in those enclosed spaces. Reliving that time now seems to belong to someone else. The Oz that was alone, cut off, always seeking the dead. But here now with Kitane she feels connected.

"The Minotaur is a teacher."

"To show me the way to the portal and the world beyond. Where Aurora spoke to me from. Are you in this other world? If so, how do you get there? Why did you go?"

Oz has spent years communing with the dead. Digging up artifacts all over the world and seeing into the lives of those long gone. Sensing them beyond their material artifacts. Finding and putting together clues from those long-dead civilizations to reveal how they lived, how they believed they fit into their world. Because, if she could do that, she might learn how she fit into hers.

But now a new feeling. Her connection to this Kitane is wide open. Cannot hide, cannot shut down, cannot say no.

The feeling at first is a mystery. She doesn't know. It's a little scary. But then she feels that maybe her heart, that stone, cold, hard organ, is coming to life.

"What is beyond the portal is not important right now," Kitane says. "This is about you. About you and the Minotaur."

"You mean I haven't yet—"

Kit's voice changes, deeper, sharper. "Did you think it was going to be this easy? Focus. Who do you think I am? And think on this, you're to blame for … "

But Kitane just blinks out. Oz is back in the circular room. The floor is a blank white, but her mind is a roaring cacophony of poisonous thoughts. She puts her hand to her throat and staggers backward a few steps, her other hand outstretched to brace herself because she thinks she's about to fall.

But what is that foul smell?

The smell of malevolent sweat.

JOHN MOON FORKER

King Zee Whitehead stands by the doorway, heaving, breathing through his mouth but grinning a grin of malice, pointing a small, pearl-handled gun at her.

"Okay sweetie pie, now you're going to tell me how to work this thing."

There, in his other hand, is the black stone.

She hates him. She hates him like she's never hated anything in this life.

83

Whitehead holds the black stone up in the air as if Oz couldn't already see it. "Now you're going to explain to me how this thing works. Your little piece of magic here where you can see the future and find your way to ancient treasures because right now it doesn't do shit."

When she came out of her encounter with Kitane, Oz found herself sitting on the floor and now comes up to a squat like maybe she's getting ready to spring forward and jump God's representative here on earth.

But she hates Whitehead and uses that to focus a rising anger.

"And if I don't, you'll kill me like you did Gina?"

"Ah yes, poor Gina. Too bad about that girl. But no, not like her, I'll just shoot you."

Oz can't help but look at the gun barrel pointed at her. If she sprang forward, he'd put a bullet in her before she got halfway to him. "But then you'd never figure out how to make that thing work."

"Aren't you the sassy one."

He chuckles, and Oz thinks this chuckle is exactly like the one she's heard him utter on the commD nodes, when he's on stage and being all supportive of someone who has just gone through the Surrender Ceremony, but here this chuckle is because he's killed Gina, which only ratchets up her fury.

"And I'll bet you're going to say that God told you to kill Gina."

He sputters as if he's talking in tongues, trying to force out three different sentences at once until he roars, "Don't you even bring God into this! You are not worthy. You have no idea."

"Right, your own private little world where only you know God and everyone else gets the message secondhand from you and only you."

Oz wants to provoke him just enough so that he might come closer but not become so pissed off that he shoots her. But she's got to work some opening, distract him just long enough so that she can take him down, get that gun away from him.

She figures even if she tells him what he wants to know, he'll still shoot her.

Well, now he's worked up all right.

Clenching his jaw, he says, "Not ten minutes ago, I spoke with God."

"In here?" Oz says her voice rising with incredulity. "You spoke with God in the labyrinth?"

"Of course, it was in here, you fool."

"What did he tell you?" While she is fascinated to know how the Minotaur would deal with someone like Whitehead, what it would show him, her legs are cramping. Even if she had an opening to leap at him, her ability to do so is evaporating. She has to lower one knee to the ground.

"You fucking bitch. You can't even begin to understand. I am serving Him. I have a purpose." He swings the gun out in an arc, as if to encompass the entire world.

In the distance, Oz can hear the roar of water, or at least she thinks it's water. But whatever it is, it's getting louder, coming closer. And she also hears machinery that she assumes is what moves the walls, hears it starting and stopping as if it's having a difficult time operating, like some broken elevator caught between floors.

The fear she felt when she first saw the gun has been replaced by a focus on survival. The anger has zeroed her in. Every move she makes, everything she says, has to be calculated. An exquisite balance on the razor-sharp edge.

She has to bring him closer.

"Remember when we were on stage together?" Oz says. "When you were touching me."

SEARCHING FOR A WAY OUT

His eyes flick for a second.

"Running your hands up my thighs. Higher and higher. Deeper."

"What are you doing?" he says. "Some kind of trick." But even though he's saying this, he takes one step forward.

"You kind of freaked me out. I wasn't expecting it. But now..."

"Oh, you're so obvious." Whitehead smiles but takes another step forward. "You need to tell me how to make this stone thing work."

"And just what is it you think the stone does?"

"Don't be coy, little girl. I know this thing doesn't belong here. That you dug it up and that it's part of the legend that leads right to Atlantis and the immortality technology. So your goddamn stone here is some kind of map or something and you need to tell me how to turn this thing on right now."

"Atlantis is a myth." She says this with a certainty that she doesn't really believe. But she needs to feel certain. Her mind is leaking. What Kitane said to her, blaming her for the deaths. But how would Kitane know that? Focus on the trouble you're in right now, she pretty much yells at herself. But how *did* she know?

"Shut up and just tell me." Whitehead straightens his arm and points the gun directly at her heart.

She might have pushed him about as far as he's going to be pushed. "You need a mirror. You have to be looking at a reflection of yourself when you are holding the disk."

"Fuck." He gestures his stone-holding hand up in the air. "Where the hell am I going to ... hey, wait a minute. What about water? Seeing yourself in water."

"Yeah."

He waves the gun. "Then we go find water. He pauses a moment, thinking. "Okay, you and I are going to take a little walk. Get up."

The roar of water is even louder. She wonders if he's hearing this.

"What about that?"

"About what?"

"That sound."

Before he can even open his mouth, Oz perceives a motion out of the corner of her eye.

A blur.

Circuit.

Streaking like a bullet, she leaps jaws first onto Whitehead, clamping down on his upper leg, and Oz jumps forward, grabbing his gun hand, all three of them falling to the earth.

84

As their bodies slam to the floor, a loud expulsion of breath screams out of both their lungs.

Water pours into the room.

Her left hand grips his right wrist, keeping him from pointing the gun at her, and she drives her forearm into his neck while he has his left hand on her throat, his fingers arrayed on her jaw. Her arm blocks his hand from choking her, so instead he inches his fingers up her face toward her eye.

She presses harder.

He fires the gun and the loud shattering noise causes Circuit to let go of his leg and back up a short way, allowing him to use his now-free leg to kick her and she flies backwards yelping in pain.

Oz explodes into a fury. With the surge of adrenaline boosted by this rage, she forces her arm down like a pile driver on his neck. She'd like to kill him.

He's gasping and choking, but still his fingers inch upwards on her face.

He tries to swing his gun hand back and forth violently, hoping to shake her grip, but she hangs on.

Oz realizes she's not in the best position to stop him. He will reach her eye soon. She can't hold him off, and she can't let go of his gun hand.

She is in far better shape than him, but he's at least fifty pounds heavier than her and will grind her down, given enough time.

Out of one eye, she sees the black stone lying on the floor.

She snaps her right arm off his neck and grabs his little finger and bends it back into a position it's probably never been in.

Whitehead screams.

More water floods the room. Several inches deep now.

She's got to get that gun.

The more she bends that finger, the less attention he can give to the gun hand and so Oz tries to slap his hand against the ground so that he will let go of the gun, but she can't quite get it there.

"Get the fuck off me," he shouts.

Oz shifts her head forward and sinks her teeth into his ear, provoking fresh screams. Tastes blood.

But now a wall of water rushes in and both she and Whitehead float off the floor, their bodies twisting and swirling underwater.

She feels fear. A lot. This is how it felt twenty-two years ago when she was dragged into that flood. At the mercy of the powerful water. Can't breathe.

Must hold on.

An even more powerful wall of water surges in, causing her to let go of Whitehead and he wraps both hands around her neck. She opens her mouth in surprise and water gushes in.

Whatever air she had left is gone.

More water streams in and she can feel him being swept away, but it is too late.

She sinks. No air, no energy, and she is down at the bottom. The last bubbles of air rise around her.

Beyond fear.

Blackness.

85

The subzero, arctic, intense cold of loneliness freezes her heart. Trapped and no way out.

Is she dead? If not, what is she? Where is she?

Oz looks around at a barren landscape where the predominant color is a light dirt brown. No life. All the same desolate, flat, parched earth except for one thing. Off in the distance, she can just make out a path. A thin little trail that almost doesn't seem to be there. But the longer she stares at it, the more visible it becomes. The strange thing is if she turns a little and looks in a slightly different direction, she gets the same result. At first, she sees a barely visible path, but if she holds her gaze steady, that path becomes more and more real.

She turns and turns again. Same thin trail.

Oz feels a pounding in her head as though her blood is in a panic and gushes through her veins. Fear at its most powerful, set loose by her complete breach from everything she has ever known. Unanchored. Nowhere to go. No way out. Stranded.

Here's where she should tell herself to get a grip, but Oz sees nothing to get a grip on.

Then, a voice right behind her. She whips around. Aurora.

"Oh, am I glad to see you," Oz says. "Where am I? What has happened to me? Am I dead?"

"That has a low priority right now," Aurora says this in a deliberately slow voice, as if to calm Oz.

"But—"

"Ssh."

Oz closes her mouth. But so many questions. She looks at the older woman.

Aurora is dressed as though she's going to a formal celebration, with white silk pants, ruby slippers, and a scarlet cotton shirt buttoned right up to the top. Just slightly taller than Oz, she stands straight as a steel beam.

"It is good to see you Jane Ozzimo, because we need your help."

I'm the one who needs help, Oz thinks. "We?"

"The few of us remaining from a long line of ancestors going back to Crete." Aurora's words are distinct and soft. "We have been watching you for years."

"Why would you do that? I mean, when I spoke with you at the house in Topanga, you said you were in some other dimension, some other world. You're not even really here, are you? What is that world?" Oz distinctly remembers the quality of the light and the feeling that seeped through to touch her and she wants it to touch her again. "Please tell me."

"Like I told you then, the best way I can describe it to you is it exists at a higher frequency, but it's the next step in our evolution. You see Oz, we have been unrelenting in our search for knowledge, for the essence of life, for how it arises, for how the mind works, and that's why we need you. Because you have those same qualities. You persist, you see the value of what has been created in the past. You have a talent for that. And we have left much behind. In one sense, we are asking you to be a caretaker. In another sense, we want you to keep on exploring."

"Me? You've made a mistake. I'm so screwed up that—"

"Stop." Aurora holds up her hand. "Tell me what you learned from your experience in the cave?"

"On Crete?"

"Where else?"

"I thought, or I suspected anyway, because of what I saw in that drawing on the floor, that the Minoan civilization had been exploring the mind, had come up with some insights but what those were wasn't all that clear right then—I had so little time—and I've been trying to track that down ever since."

SEARCHING FOR A WAY OUT

Thinking of her thesis, had forgotten all about it. Surprises her how insignificant that part of her life seems now.

"Yes, the mind. That was our biggest challenge for a long time."

"But one you overcame?"

"You've used the black stone. What do you think?"

What she thinks is that they seem to be aware of everything she does, which makes her believe she knows only a tiny slice of their technology and what it can do.

"You figured something out, obviously. A way to use the mind. A system of mind control. Something like that."

"Look, it might be helpful if you were to think of the mind as a tool. Something you pick up and use when you need it, then put it down when you're done. A magnificent tool, but just that. And once you can use it that way—instead of it using you—this opens the universe up to infinite explorations. Things move much quicker."

"Why are you telling me all this now?" Oz's voice rims the edge of exasperation.

"You were in a labyrinth and presented with memories. Memories that your mind has used against you. You were supposed to resolve them out there in the labyrinth—which is what we built it for—but all the water cut that short. Water unleashed when you switched on the rainmaker, which caused the flooding, which damaged the electrical circuits and disabled the labyrinth. So you are not done."

"The rainmaker?"

"Topanga."

"You mean that dusty shack? That old electronic whatever it was?"

"That would be the one." Aurora touches Oz's arm. "We still have a little work to do. When you were with Kitane, what did you experience?"

Seems so long ago. Like a different life. But then it was, wasn't it?

"I felt as though I had merged with her somehow. Became part of her. Inside her consciousness."

"Saw things from her point of view?"

"Yes, but more than that, like her point of view was my point of view."

"Who is Kitane?"

"I don't . . . I think she was trying to tell me she was the Minotaur." Oz remembers now those last words were cut off . . . blaming . . . that whatever guilt Oz had rummaging around in her head when spoken out, they became solid. They became real. Her guilt is undeniable. If only she had not . . . if only she had not done so many things.

"Do you feel trapped in your beliefs and memories?"

She feels trapped right now. "Maybe sometimes but I don't—"

"Were you trapped in Kitane's beliefs and memories?" Aurora says.

"No."

"But you were a part of her?"

"Ah . . . sure."

Oz feels as if a drill is boring into her head. Why so many questions?

"Just a part of her, or you were her?"

"I . . . well, for a short time I felt as if we were the same person." This is how she remembers it now, but did she think that then? She'd have to trust her mind to know that and she's not so sure that would be a good decision.

"So if you think Kitane is the Minotaur, who are you?"

They've stopped walking. Aurora's face is just inches away, her intense dark eyes giving no ground.

Oz recalls that the old myth of the Minoan labyrinth and the human-eating Minotaur at its center was about an external force, an external danger that Theseus had to defeat with a sword.

SEARCHING FOR A WAY OUT

But the Minotaur is not an external danger, is it? All the danger comes from within and if Kitane is the Minotaur and she is Kitane, then she is her own Minotaur. She has been eating herself all these years. Yes, she's always known that—in theory anyway—she is to some degree responsible for her bad feelings, inept decisions, and wrong behaviors, but it is clear now she is completely responsible for everything and for every choice she has made and will make.

But Aurora told her that the flood of water stopped the labyrinth, broke it, and that she had not completed the journey.

What difference does it make now? She can no longer make any choices, can she? She turns her head toward Aurora. "I . . . I see all this now, but it's . . . I'm dead."

Aurora smiles. "Let's not get overly dramatic."

"But I drown."

"Well, you're here and you still have to make a choice."

Oz looks down and lets out a breath. "What choices are left?"

"Take another look around."

Oz scans the horizon in all directions. "It looks endless."

"Endless means what?"

"That I could go in any which way," Oz answers in a rote way as though she is in grade school and this is a lesson to be learned, but she feels empty, disconnected.

"Yes, and that means what?"

"That I just have to choose."

"So choose."

"Choose what? Based on what?" Her nervous system—or whatever she has instead in this place—has agitated into a frenzy. Nerve sparks fly. Her body shakes.

"What do you want?" Aurora puts a hand on Oz's back as if to steady her. "Suppose you are eleven years old and something terrible happens. Do you have to live with it for the rest of your life?"

"I see what you're getting at but now... now there's nothing. I'm finished."

"Come on, Oz. Pay attention. Focus. That's what you are good at."

Oz does what Aurora asks, gathering the flailing strands of her attention, holding herself still, directing her awareness outward.

This is when Oz sees a small figure in the distance walking toward them.

"Who is that?"

"Someone you need."

As the figure draws closer, Oz feels a primal disorientation, a world-upside-down feeling, an anticipation of the profound yet mysterious.

Then she sees it is a young girl. It is her 11-year-old self.

Looks so real. Can barely bring herself to look at this girl because she has not yet gone through the life Oz has. There is still so much promise, so many choices to make. Yet, she can't look away.

The girl walks right up to the adult Oz and puts her hand into Oz's.

Oz slips into her younger self's consciousness. Sees things the way she saw them then. Sees the limits, sees the options, the decisions made and realizes in a concrete way that she did what she had to at the time. She was protecting herself the only way she knew how. She didn't have the tools then to do it any differently, and as she grew up, she was stuck in the habit of those decisions and a prisoner of the armor that she created to protect herself with.

For the first time ever, she feels love for that little girl.

"Oz," Aurora says. "Now it is time to decide. To choose."

"But I don't even know what the choices are."

"Yes, you do." The corners of Aurora's mouth twist with impatience. "What do you want?"

SEARCHING FOR A WAY OUT

"I want to live, to be free of all of my bad choices, to start over. To have a chance."

"What would that mean to you?"

Oz puts her hand on her forehead. "I've been so alone. So lonely. But I don't want to be. I want to be with people, with live human beings. I love my parents, my brother, my friend, my dog."

With these words, Oz bends forward, furiously wiping away the tears rolling down her face, and her 11-year-old self reaches over, slides her small arms around Oz's neck and hugs her. Oz's tears increase and she's sobbing but feels the good warmth of the girl. She closes her eyes, feeling sad but deeply connected to this girl and that feels so wonderful. She's a thunderstorm in a sunny sky.

But, when she opens her eyes and stands back up, the girl is gone as if she were a mist burned off by the sun.

Aurora says. "I must go."

"No, please don't. I can't be alone here."

"You are not alone. You know that now and you won't be here long."

"What? What's going to happen?"

"The dog. That very special dog."

86

An insistent humming begins, followed by a deep vibration behind the walls, and within moments a complex machinery kicks into gear. The electricity in the labyrinth comes back online and a powerful suction drains the water out faster than it had come in.

The dog-paddling Circuit finally finds footing on the floor and scampers over to Oz.

Circuit smells Oz's sodden body, nudges it with her nose, licks her face, whines once.

She lifts her head and pricks up her ears, yelps once, then breaks into a full sprint, out the entrance and down the passageway. Still some water on the ground, which causes her to sometimes slip and crash into the wall, but she recovers immediately and keeps up her breakneck pace.

Doesn't have to go that far at all before she sees him. Then she barks as loud as she can.

• • • •

NICKELL STANDS ON A large rock, shivering. Soaking wet. Even though the water is almost gone, he hasn't descended to the passageway floor.

He's not at all sure what's real and what isn't.

He wants out of here right now.

That dog! Barking, barking, barking. Why doesn't she shut up? Nickell puts his hands over his ears, but that doesn't do any good.

He gets down off the rock—all that water is gone—but he's still dripping.

SEARCHING FOR A WAY OUT

He tries to shoo Circuit away but she just barks more, lunges at him and runs back a few steps. She does this over and over again, becoming more frantic with each passing moment.

Nickell takes two steps toward her and she moves ahead as if leading him, but then runs back when she sees he's not following and practically screams at him.

"Shit," he says. "Okay, okay." And he starts walking, but she doubles back to sink her teeth into his pant leg, trying to drag him forward. She only lets go in order so that she can bark in a continuous and deafening stream.

He tries to latch his mind on something. Anything. He's a journalist, right? Look for the story. You came down here wanting to get the inside scoop on all the legend and Atlantis business. Well, now here you are. Start recording. Focus on that.

But this damned dog won't leave him alone. Must have a reason for this behavior.

Giving in to the dog's urging, he runs behind Circuit, who keeps turning her head to make sure he's following, barking at him to go faster.

He runs and runs and it feels good to do just this, to not think, to not see all the garbage in his head, so he just turns it on and almost catches up to Circuit but with four legs she just zooms ahead even faster.

Circuit turns into a room. Nickell follows, and he sees Oz's body on the floor.

He stops. Frozen in place. What should he do?

Puddles here and there. All white room.

But him just standing there sends Circuit into a paroxysm of barking.

He walks over, bends down and touches Oz's neck. No, no, no. This can't be. She can't be dead.

He thinks of his CPR training. Should he try it? What if it doesn't work? But if he doesn't try it, then . . . no, he's got to try. Got to bring her back. Can't lose her now.

He pulls Oz over onto her back, pries her mouth open with his fingers and checks to see that her tongue is not blocking her windpipe. It's not good.

He pinches close her nose with his fingers, covers her mouth with his and blows. Yeah, what is it he does now? Isn't he supposed to be looking to see if her chest rises? Didn't see that.

Try again. He blows harder and the chest rises.

Now he does the chest compressions. He puts one hand on top of the other and presses down. Supposed to go down how far? Wasn't it an inch or two?

He does about five quick compressions and stops. Feels like he's going to break her rib cage. But he can't stop. She's not responding.

Wait, there's supposed to be a rhythm here. Press and breathe. Need to go faster, too. Then he remembers. Thirty compressions at a good pace.

After the thirty, he gives her two breaths, then back to doing thirty more compressions.

"Come on," he says. She's got to come around soon he thinks, or she won't be coming back.

Circuit has stopped barking but paces all around the body.

He covers her mouth again and really blows. He feels some kind of tremor underneath. Backs off and sees she's trying to get air. Guides her head to the side with one hand. A little water comes out then she vomits, much more water coming out now.

Her face is so red.

She coughs again and again and moves her arms and legs so slowly, as if coming out of a winter-long hibernation. Her eyes and nose leak liquid, and it all runs down her face and drips off to join the pool beneath her.

SEARCHING FOR A WAY OUT

Nickell feels a tremendous sense of relief. Let's loose an enormous exhale.

She turns her head back up, looks at Nickell for five full seconds before saying, "What?" Then coughs about sixteen more times.

He puts a hand on her shoulder. "You going to be okay?"

"Don't know yet." She coughs up more water and then keeps coughing for more than a minute.

• • • •

CIRCUIT COMES OVER and licks her face. She grabs onto the dog with one hand. "Hi, girl."

"Circuit found me, brought me here. Saved you."

"A special dog." But then Oz remembers and comes up on her elbows. "Where's Whitehead?"

"He's here?" Nickell glances all around him. "Didn't see him."

Oz sits up and the room spins. Dizzy. Light-headed. Her chest hurts, her throat sore.

She remembers the girl, remembers that before she got the nickname Oz, her parents used to call her Janey. Likes that memory.

Was that all a dream?

But Aurora? Giving her the Minoan technology. How is that possible?

Then she feels the burning motivation inside, the single-pointed purpose of her life, now free of her distracting emotional garbage, her layers of armor. No longer seeing herself as the enemy, no longer looking for something to fix herself.

Her mind on the workbench. Pick it up and use it.

Explore and discover. That's what she does.

Find the portal room. Find it now.

She stands up, still dizzy, swaying a little. Then she sees it. The black stone on the floor. She stumbles forward ten steps and picks it up, glad to have the stone back.

JOHN MOON FORKER

Raising her eyes, she notices a door at the back of the room cracked open half an inch.

87

The instant she steps through the doorway, waves of deep vibrational sounds penetrate her body. She smells electricity, hears its snap and crackle, sees white bolts of energy twisting back and forth like a pissed-off snake in that same brilliant, burning-white illumination casting the room into razor-sharp clearness.

To her left sits a stone basin full of blue-tinged water, maybe five feet across. Nickell behind her, Circuit an inch away from her right leg.

She rapidly scans the room for any sign of Whitehead.

Nothing. He's not here, but they didn't see his body in the other room. Did the water wash him out into the passageway? Should have checked.

This room is not as large as the one they just came from, but the ceiling looks a few feet higher.

At the far end of the room stands an eight-foot-tall, horseshoe-shaped arch. Could be stone or metal. The obvious source of the energy. Alive with this pulsating dance of electrons.

A distorted visual field behind it. Waves of blue sky? Heat waves? Energy waves? Oz doesn't know what.

Her breathing still isn't right. It's as though she's fighting for air with every breath, and with every rise and fall of her diaphragm, she feels some pain behind her ribs.

Nickell pulls his commD out of his pocket and with a series of clicks has set loose his one tiny news bot, which zips up into the air and begins circling the room searching for anything its algorithm decides is worthy.

"He's not here," Oz says. "Do you think he's still alive?"

"Don't know. Didn't see him anywhere." Nickell points at the arch. "Is this what you're looking for?"

"Must be." She stops, very aware that she has gotten her hopes up to an almost feverish pitch, so much so that she knows she's set herself up for disappointment. So she goes slow. Concentrates her attention to sense every possible thing, to miss nothing and walks precisely toward the portal, looking through the opening and it's as if she can see the air. Air with a viscous quality, an atmosphere filled with tiny sparks. Air brings waves of stimulation to her senses so that her vision, hearing and sense of smell elevate.

At six feet from the opening, Oz sees a blank field, solid gray, not the back wall of the room as she would expect, but when she creeps in closer, to about a foot away, then she can see what's on the other side. Running right up to the edge of the portal is a dirt path. And this path slopes down sharply into a forested valley. Mountains flank the valley, trees covering all the land she can see.

But what's most striking to her is the motion. The place appears to be teeming with life. Thousands of buzzing insects, hundreds of birds flapping across the sky. A sense of motion in and among the trees, as if maybe even they are moving. And this motion is really moving. Zipping around at high speeds. Is this what Aurora meant by higher frequency?

Oz perceives the potent presence of life and she feels a part of it even though she's not physically in this other world. It's magnetic, drawing her ever closer. Inches away.

And one small figure walks up the path from very far away.

She feels so alive, tingling with this alertness. And it's all emanating from the other side of this portal. The thick, almost liquid-like, energy-dense air flowing over her and infusing her with these sensations.

This is even more powerful than what she felt in the cave on Crete. Way beyond that.

This must be what Aurora wants her to find, to know about. This must be what Oz has been searching for all these years.

SEARCHING FOR A WAY OUT

Just a few more inches and she could be over there, be in this other world.

But she hesitates. Would crossing over mean never coming back?

She looks back. How could she leave Circuit behind? Who would take care of her? And Nickell? What about him?

Maybe she could just step inside this other world, check it out, and then just step back. Should be easy. Look, she can see the path on the other side leading right up to here, so they must use it both ways. The Minoans had to be going both in and out. It couldn't all just be one way.

But even if she could come back, would she? After feeling this way, and maybe even better than this once over there, would she turn around and return to this world? This world where she's felt isolated and alone for so long. No, stop. That's just her mind talking, holding on to old and now unimportant wounds.

"Come here." She waves Nickell over. "Stand real close to the edge here. Do you feel it?"

When Nickell stands next to her, he looks up as though overwhelmed, spreads his arms out. "I feel something. Yes. Wow. This is incredible. I feel so energetic, like I could do anything."

"Exactly. I so want to go in there. See it. Feel it. It must be—"

"Don't," Nickell cuts in. "I . . . you . . . what if you can't come back? No, please. Don't risk it. You mean a lot to me." Nickell blushes but does not look away.

Oz touches his hand. "Yes, and you mean a lot to me too. You did save my life, after all." She gives an impish grin.

She turns to look down at Circuit. Tugging at her heart. Which way?

Then Aurora is there, right on the other side of the portal.

"You're real," Oz says with wonder.

"You might say that."

"Could I explore it?" Oz gestures toward the space behind Aurora. "Just for a little while."

Lines crease across Aurora's face. "No, you are not prepared. Each of us spent years getting our minds and bodies ready for the transition. Someone not prepared for this increase in frequency would suffer physiological and psychology damage."

"Just stepping through here?" Oz gestures to the ground on the other side only inches away.

"Were you to step through, the environment would transform to a frequency more of a match for your current vibration. What you see here matches our vibration." Aurora sweeps her arm out to encompass her world. "Yours would be different. And you might not like it."

"Okay, okay, I get it. But I have a different question," Oz says. "Back when . . . when . . ."

"When you thought you were dead?"

"Yes. You said about the technology. About how you wanted me to protect it, to use it. What am I supposed to do?"

"The technology—much of it—is powerful. You only saw a couple of things. And by the way, go easy with the rainmaker next time."

"Yeah, I guess I should."

"We did not want to use our technology on a large scale because we did not want to call attention to ourselves knowing we were coming here. And we did not think it wise to hand it over to a government or corporation. We needed a single person we could trust."

"How am I supposed to know what to do?"

"Don't underestimate yourself," Aurora says. "You have at least two people to help you. One of them is standing next to you."

Nickell says, "Aurora Pointe."

"Mr. Lamont Nickell. Glad to see you here, too."

SEARCHING FOR A WAY OUT

The news bot floats overhead, patiently recording.

"We have little time," Aurora says, "At midnight—well, a couple of minutes after—this portal seals off."

"Why seal it off?"

"It seals because of the way the planets are aligned—a property of magnetism and gravity—and they won't be aligned to open this portal back up for a long time. You will be an old woman when that happens. Maybe you'll be ready to join us then."

"But I still don't know what you want me to do?"

"The house and land in Topanga. Take it. That's where most of the technology is anyway. You'll figure it out."

"But how would I . . . the city . . ."

Aurora grins. "Already done. The deed has been altered. And keep practicing with the stone. It's a first step, not the end." Aurora and Oz both glance at the black stone in Oz's hand. "It is its own kind of portal. You have much to explore."

"But I still don't understand this." She points through the portal. "Why . . . where . . . I mean, what's over there? What are you doing there that you couldn't do here?" Her curiosity is sharp and Oz wants so badly to know.

"You know our work here, right?"

"That the mind is controllable, no, more than that, the mind is a tool, one you can use or not use." Oz has her hand flat out in the air as if measuring.

"Yes. Through constant questioning, we sought to find total freedom, to be fully alive every moment. And we succeeded up to a point. But then we found that there's more. Much more."

"You mean being in this other dimension?"

"Are you familiar with animism?"

"A belief that everything is alive, infused with spirit. The mural in the map room. That's what I thought when I saw it then," Oz says.

"And that's what this world is. Manifestly so. It's less a world that we discovered and more of one we created. It's where we want to live. Zero waste." Aurora points a finger at Oz. "I think you're familiar with the concept."

"Yup." Oz peers more closely through the portal. Longs to walk in this world just over the threshold. No waste. "Then the fungi in that building in Topanga are connected to that. To the waste."

"That's the seed. That's where you and your friend Midori start."

Oz sees a path ahead, a future where she can make a difference. Go beyond herself.

Nickell has been rocking from foot to foot but can restrain himself no longer, "Do you know where Atlantis is?"

Aurora says, "Oz can tell you all you need to know about Atlantis."

"What? What are you talking about?" Nickell turns toward Oz. "You know about Atlantis?"

"If I have this right, Atlantis is not a place, it's a state of mind."

"Yes, and another thing," Aurora says. "There is a person running around in here. One King Zee Whitehead. He'll be here soon."

"What?" Oz says sharply. "Where is he?"

"Don't worry, you'll do just fine. But remember to keep your mind from clogging up things. Lamont, please hold and restrain Circuit there. For her own safety."

As Nickell stoops and grabs Circuit's collar, Aurora winks at Oz and Oz, because her senses are so sharp standing so close to the portal that allows her to just about see thoughts in the air, knows. Aurora is having Nickell grab the collar not to restrain Circuit but so that *he* will be restrained because he's just too tied in emotionally to bringing down Whitehead and would likely do something foolish.

"Remember Kitane," Aurora says, and steps away from the portal.

SEARCHING FOR A WAY OUT

At that moment, Whitehead bursts through the doorway, coughs twice, dripping wet, a wild glare in his eyes and that gun back in his hand.

"Just who I'm looking for."

He smiles.

88

Circuit growls. Nickell grips her collar.

Oz observes Whitehead. He's in bad physical shape. Maybe he didn't die like she did, but he got plenty battered anyway. Not standing up straight. Kind of crooked. A rough, scraping cough. Thin, greased-back hair. Body shaking. Face splotchy and turning more red with each cough while his hand with the gun in it swings erratically out to the side.

Then he points the gun at her.

She watches his finger tremble on the trigger, smells his soggy clothes, and waits for him to falter.

"What's that?" He flicks his wrist at the portal.

"It's a gateway," Oz says. She can feel Nickell's tenseness beside her. But he's stuck holding Circuit unless he lets go. Which he might. She needs to move first.

The emotion of anger blooms inside. Whitehead had his hands all over her. He killed Gina. She wants to hurt him.

"Gateway to what? To Atlantis? Is that the way?" Whitehead swings his gaze around the room, taking in the sizzling, arcing electricity, and the hum of the machinery beating on his skull. He waves the gun. "What the hell is all this?"

Oz tries to push her anger away but her mind insists that it stays, so she gains only a little distance. But there is a gap.

"We just got here," Oz says. "We don't know what this is."

She coughs and a little more water leaks from her mouth and she spits more of it onto the floor. Her ribs ache. Can't afford to pay attention to that right now.

Whitehead almost turns a grimace into a smile. "Oh, come on. You lying, little slut. I'll bet you know where the immortality potion

SEARCHING FOR A WAY OUT

is, don't you? Probably right through that opening, and I'll bet that's just where you were headed."

"We haven't found it yet, but I think we're getting close. It doesn't appear to be in this room." Thinking to get him out of here.

"The shit just pours out of your mouth." Whitehead shakes his head. "Don't fuck with me. Where is it? This is my land, and everything here belongs to me."

"Is this where you buried Jasmine?" Nickell says, picking up on Oz's deception.

Whitehead's mouth twists left, twists right. "Shut the fuck up!"

"Or did you bury her out in the Cleghorn Lakes Wilderness area?"

"Shut up, shut up, shut up. You dumb fuck." Whitehead shakily raises the gun hand up toward the ceiling and fires a deafening round. "One more word out of you and the next bullet goes into your head."

Out of the corner of her eye, she sees Nickell glancing furtively up into the air. The news bot. It hovers near the ceiling, videoing continuously. Gunfire always engages the news algorithm.

"Now," Whitehead says to Oz, "why don't you just hand over that stone thing you got there."

"So that I can show you how it works?" Good. She wants to get close.

"Or not. Just give it to me."

Oz thinks this is an odd answer as he was so insistent earlier that she explain it to him. What's changed? Does he think he can figure it out on his own? Did something happen to him down here like what happened to her? Some incident from his past that he had to relive? Was it his version of God?

She walks toward him, looking directly into his eyes, focusing all of her attention on this one point. His body seems to shudder, almost as if it's taking all of his strength to remain standing.

When she is within six feet of him, he tries to straighten his shaking arm, then says "Time to die," and pulls the trigger.

The bullet zips three inches past the side of her head.

Oz leaps forward, grabs the gun out of his hand and tosses it behind her where Nickell picks it up.

She stands close to Whitehead. Eye to eye. She bores in. "Been there, done that."

He roars with anger and brings his arm around in an attempt to wrap it around her neck. But Oz anticipates his move as though he were making it in slow motion. Her anger flares up and this time she just shoves it down in a hole so deep that it's buried, shuts down her mind, then fluidly moves with stunning quickness around Whitehead, yanking his arm high behind his back. Him going down to his knees, the fight draining out of him.

She forces him to his feet. He struggles against her grip, but when she clamps down on his neck—with Circuit barking as though possessed by a demon—she pushes the stumbling Whitehead to the basin full of the blue water.

She extends her hand with the stone. "Hold on to the edge of this. Right. Now look into the water. Think of God."

Oz presses the symbol of the priestess.

His eyes drift to the water and he is instantly entranced.

Oz watches his face for a moment then looks into the water herself, expecting to find her version of God or whatever fragmentary beliefs about God she might have accumulated over the years, but what she sees is Whitehead's reflection. Not a mirror copy of the Whitehead standing next to her, but an image of a man whose face is twisted by strong, conflicting desires. Emotions swimming on his face as though in tangible liquid form, swirling and clashing and ripping apart.

SEARCHING FOR A WAY OUT

As she stares at the image, Oz realizes she is merging with him much like she did with Kitane, but far more intense, because here it is a living, breathing person.

Bits and pieces of what he's experiencing float into her consciousness. Shards of memory and powerful impulses. Oz feels his sexual lust, a hot primitive urge he cannot resist. Does not want to resist. But far stronger is his lust for power. He wants to rule.

Then she is absorbed into his devastating conflict. His need to be with and to speak to God. The innocence and longing of it. The plea for guidance.

And here she experiences the memory shard of him, maybe half an hour ago right here in the labyrinth, of doing just that or, at least, him thinking that he did that.

He believes he is back with God right here. God is shouting at him, belittling him, criticizing him, commanding him, which he both loves and hates.

She feels his mind torturing him. A fist of destructive emotion pounding him.

Yes, his mind. It has full control, not him. It paints this picture. It calls the shots. He cannot escape.

And experiencing this, she feels both a revulsion and a fascination but realizes that getting caught in either is a danger. Seeing him twisted inside makes her see how twisted she has been and how she always has to be vigilant to keep from getting sucked down that hole again.

He cries out, "No . . . but you told me."

Both Whitehead and Oz still hold the black stone between them.

He cringes and fumes and sputters and pleads to be told what to do.

And then there is the regret. The life he should have had, but never will.

This echoes within Oz. What about her life? The life she never had. The life with parents who were alive and had stayed that way. That life.

Thinking that way is the trap. The mind trying desperately to escape the present moment. To latch on to some identity, no matter how corrupt. Instead of once again being swamped by her old habitual patterns, she now watches her own mind, brings awareness to its wild and destructive impulses and this light of awareness stops the thinking.

She can breathe. The life she will have is the life she's making right at this moment. And the next and the next.

Whitehead lets go of the stone, staggers two steps, falls to one knee, then rises again. "I have to . . . have to . . ." He looks around the space as if he has no idea where he is and the terror and panic deforms his eyes.

He whispers, "Atlantis." Turning, he runs across the narrow room and right through the portal.

Oz still feels him, still connected to him, although the energy fades. She can see what he sees on the other side. And what she sees terrifies her. Bleak. Oppressive claustrophobic feeling. Utterly trapped.

Aurora was right. The frequencies change. Whitehead is not in the forested canyon bathing in that wonderful high energy. He's in some kind of metal landscape. Thick plates of it. Nothing alive in sight. And he is moving so slowly. When he takes a step, it's like trying to move through thick mud. His thinking is slow. His mind is dull. Everything is blurry.

So maddeningly slow. Oz can hardly stand to feel in small doses what he's feeling full on. Lower frequency. Less and less and less.

And there is a really primitive, foul smell like sulfur mixed with shit mixed with burning metal.

SEARCHING FOR A WAY OUT

Other beings on the periphery. Slow moving too, but moving toward him. Nothing friendly about them. Closer now.

Oz feels the connection weaken and just before it cuts off completely, she feels the one thing he wants now. To go back to his room at One Faith, just sit on the floor and play his guitar.

"Oz. Oz!"

Aurora at the portal.

The arcing energy all around the portal sparks higher, the vibrational sounds deepen, shuddering through every bone in her body.

"Don't have much time. Come closer."

Oz dashes over and is only an inch away from the opening. She can see the forest behind Aurora being swept by a strong wind, branches sway violently and dust swirls in funnels twenty feet high.

Aurora opens her mouth but no words come out. She closes and then opens her mouth again. "I am so glad for our time together."

Oz feels the intense chaos all around her. "You're leaving? Forever?"

"Leaving, yes. Forever, who knows?"

"Thank you for believing in me."

The energy vortex spirals counterclockwise, the room shakes, both Nickell and Circuit lose their footing. Oz holds on to the edge of the portal to steady herself, and the energy from the other side licks her fingers, bringing heat and nerve impulses shooting up her arms straight into her brain.

Oz can barely see her and just before the tunnel closes, Aurora calls out, "Go to Thera. That's where we began our journey thousands of years ago."

The portal snaps shut. The shaking stops. The vibration ceases. Absolute stillness in the room. No sound. The portal seals and disappears, the surface now looking like just an ordinary wall.

Nickell and Circuit stand up. Circuit comes over to Oz and nuzzles her hand.

"Are you all right?" Nickell says.

With Circuit right by her side, she walks over to the pool of water and looks down into it. What does the future hold for her? What does the past . . . wait, wrong question. Can't live in the past, can't live in the future. There is only the present. Exactly where she wants to be. Yes, right here, right now.

"Never better."

"We have a lot of work to do."

In the water's reflection, she sees herself as a little girl—that brave, curious, adventuresome girl that she thought was lost forever.

She is the creator of every thought, every action, every circumstance in her life. Whatever happens is her doing. Her story.

She reaches down and strokes Circuit's head.

Her heart is wide open. She walks back and puts her arms around Nickell.

"Let's go."

89

Oz stands in the shade of a four-thousand-year-old wall on the island of Santorini, or Thera, as the archeologists like to use the ancient name.

Thousands of miles from home.

She holds her commD. A full 3D image of Nickell gleams in front of her. She listens, watches his face. She longs to be with him. But she is on a mission here and it is exhilarating.

Early morning back home. He's outside the house. Can see the tall bamboo behind him.

Springtime in the Mediterranean and it's already hot. She has joined her friend Alexandros Papadakis' team here on the island. A project she proposed and pushed to make happen, planning out how to bring it to reality with the use of the black stone and giving Alexandros a chance to persuade the Greek government to fund it.

She reaches down to scratch the panting Circuit behind the ear. Thinks how close she has become to this dog. How they are hardly ever separated.

She had never figured out where this dog came from or how she seemed so familiar with the land in Topanga and how she and Aurora seemed to know each other. But once here on the island, this dog, who she once thought of as a mutt, turns out to be a Cretan Hound. Almost never see this breed of dog anywhere else, especially not in a kennel in Los Angeles.

It couldn't possibly be that Aurora planted Circuit in the kennel for Oz to become attached to?

Could it?

Could they have planned this far ahead? Impossible.

"So how is Midori doing?"

Nickell laughs, "She's a great big ball of fire running all over the city doing who knows what, preparing something. She's been over here working in that building or laboratory, or whatever you want to call it, with all those mushrooms every day for weeks. She trying to get the city to allow her to test the fungi on the waste vats. Without any luck so far."

"I'd like to see that."

"When are you coming home?"

"About a week or two, maybe," Oz says. "Even though we've found their school, we haven't found the training room, and that's what I'm really aiming for."

"Well, when you get back, we could have one of Midori's home-brewed beers. She's turned it into an art form."

"I can practically taste it." Oz smiles.

"I miss you."

"I miss you too, and I can't wait to get back. It'll be soon. Listen, I'll talk to you tomorrow."

Oz cuts the connection and the last wisps of the 3D image evaporate.

She walks and Circuit rouses herself and tags along.

Since that transformative night on Halloween, many things have happened.

She right away moved out to the house in Topanga.

Because of the video, Nickell became famous for about a day. Then the video was suppressed. But he quit The Data Transfer and was immediately hired by L.A. Beacon. A step up in his world.

Soon after, he moved in with Oz. This happened after one afternoon when they were out in the woods near the house. They had stopped by that little creek and had sat together on a log. Neither felt the need to talk, and they just became absorbed in their surroundings. He touched her arm, she put her hand on his face and then they kissed. Oz felt as though it was the first true kiss she had ever had.

Oz smiles at the memory of it now. She had changed so much, like the floodgates of old emotions that had been practically buried, rushed out. She is open and alive and in love.

Still, something nags at the back of her mind. Something that isn't quite clear. But something that lurks back.

The armor she's surrounded herself with since her parents and brother died has not disappeared. She can feel it. Doesn't know what she can do about it.

She's not done. Didn't confront the Minotaur.

And then there's that portal where she last saw Aurora. It has been examined about a million times by all kinds of government agencies and their experts, and no one can figure it out. It's now just a blank wall. Which has made most everyone disbelieve the video.

Of course, the video couldn't capture the feeling of that energy. Even so, almost everyone in the public believes it is the entrance to Atlantis. The ones who still believe anyway. If only they knew.

But when the federal government took over the property, that was the final blow to One Faith. With the disappearance of Whitehead gone, and Nickell's video of him walking into the portal being disbelieved–because there is no portal–they had pretty much collapsed anyway.

But she held tight on to Aurora's last words, about going to Thera because that's where she said they started.

She, Alexandros Papadakis, and the team dig a little west of the town of Akrotiri. Back in the 1960s, the Minoan city of Akrotiri became famous for an excavation that uncovered an ancient settlement, one that had hot and cold running water, had multi-storied buildings and a profusion of beautiful wall paintings. Much of which was preserved for all time by the volcano's eruption. Preserved anyway until archeologists starting digging things up.

And Alexandros and Oz thought they would dig there too. Until one evening when Oz took Circuit for a long walk.

She came upon a large mound, not so high, but spread out, the mound covered by large rocks that at first glance appeared randomly strewn about.

But she stopped and looked and stood there and looked closer and waited and heard the sounds of banging way back at the dig behind her, the chirps of many birds, the wind touching the earth, and she smelled the soil and the faint metals and the large rocks themselves and her concentration narrowed and narrowed on to that mound until she realized these rocks had not randomly been located there by nature.

She and Circuit walked on to the mound and she looked at every rock as she circled the base until she finally came to one that had a Linear A inscription and she could read it right away: "Entrance."

And this is where she had the team begin digging.

As she walks now, she sees Alexandros up ahead, crouching down, holding a small chisel, tilting it forward and back as if to test its weight. Although it looks more as though he's simply lost in his thoughts.

"What have you got there?"

Alexandros turns his watery, sleep-deprived eyes toward her, "I think I'm in a classroom here, but what did they do? What took place in this room?"

"Yeah, but I don't think we're looking for an ordinary classroom. Not for what they were doing."

"Remind me how you talked me into doing this?"

"Okay, it's not another Plato's academy, but it is a school. We know that. A special school where the best and brightest students on Crete were sent."

SEARCHING FOR A WAY OUT

"Yes, I know, and they appear to have been developing their next generation of leaders who were being groomed to run their civilization."

"But more than that," Oz says. "Somewhere in here is where the mind exploration and training took place. The development of their most advanced technologies which weren't, of course, much in comparison with what they later developed but for then—"

"Except for—"

"The mind technology, right? With that, they are even ahead of what exists today other than what they did."

"Then boom. Here comes the volcano," Alexandros says.

"Which they seem to have known about far in advance and maybe, just maybe, they used as a cover for their getaway before the barbarians invaded. Those nasty Greeks." Oz smiles.

"Hey, quit picking on the Greeks. This was probably Attila or someone like him that was threatening them."

One worker runs up to Alexandros and says something in Greek and runs off.

"Looks like they found something. I've got to check it out. Coming?"

"Right behind you."

Oz, Circuit and Alexandros arrive at what they had all previously thought was a buried wall, but now one of the student archeologists has uncovered a small corner of a door.

Oz smooths her hand across the surface of the tiny exposed part of the door. Her concentration zeroes in. Her senses are fully alive. She studies the surface, then closes her eyes. She's that little girl who walked the neighborhood, who investigated every backyard, every crevice, every living thing she came across. Who wanted to know all the natural world and all the ancient people who lived in it.

She and Alexandros spend over an hour carefully removing thousands of years of caked-on dirt and debris. Oz finds the edge of the door and works around it to expose all of that edge until finally they see the entire door.

Oz then takes a thin knife and works it into the tiny gap of the door's edge until she can pry it open a fraction of an inch.

If she pulls on it now, the door will open. She looks at Alexandros and he nods.

Through the years of struggle and loss, the brief shining moments of light, the times when she did not want to live, all seem like a murky sediment that has been washed away when she is doing what she feels is right and as she pries open this ancient door, she knows more than ever that her purpose is to explore.

Don't miss out!

Visit the website below and you can sign up to receive emails whenever John Moon Forker publishes a new book. There's no charge and no obligation.

https://books2read.com/r/B-A-FVXPC-QVUDF

BOOKS 2 READ

Connecting independent readers to independent writers.

Milton Keynes UK
Ingram Content Group UK Ltd.
UKHW030856151124
451262UK00001B/117